LITTLE
DO
WE
KNOW

LITTLE
DO
WE
KNOW

Tamara Ireland Stone

HYPERION

Los Angeles | New York

First Edition, June 2018
10 9 8 7 6 5 4 3 2 1
FAC-020093-18110
Printed in the United States of America

This book is set in New Caledonia LT Std, Avenir Next, Century Gothic Pro,
Neutra Text, Officina Serif ITC Pro/Monotype
Designed by Marci Senders

ISBN 978-1-4847-6821-1

Reinforced binding
Visit www.hyperionteens.com

SUSTAINABLE Certified Sourcing
FORESTRY
INITIATIVE www.sfiprogram.org
SFI-00993

THIS LABEL APPLIES TO TEXT STOCK

For my best friend.
I miss you more than you know.

You have come here to find what you already have.

Hannah

There were thirty-six steps between Emory's bedroom window and mine.

The first time we counted, we were six years old (forty-two steps). The second time, we were twelve (thirty-nine). The last time, we were fifteen. We pressed our backs against the side of her house, interlocked our arms, and heel-toe-heel-toed to mine, laughing and stumbling, starting over until we got it right.

That patch of grass knew everything about us. That was where we learned to walk, where we ran through the sprinklers on hot summer days, and where we held tea parties for our stuffed animals.

When we got older, a single text with the word *GRASS!* would send the two of us darting out our back doors, bound for our spot smack in the middle. We'd stay out there for hours—staring up at the stars, talking about music and books and boys, practicing our kissing skills on our own upper arms—until we couldn't keep our eyes open or until our moms made us come inside, whichever happened first. Once we started high school, when we had bigger news and even more delicious secrets, we'd say things like, "You know you can tell me *anything*, right?" and we meant it deep in our souls.

But no matter how long two people have known each other, or how many times they've said those words, there are still some things you *think* but should never say to your best friend.

I know, because one day, I said those things.

And then Emory said those things.

And that was the last time either one of us crossed those thirty-six steps.

Emory
Day 273, 164 to go

Mom was alone. I could tell by her shoulder. When David stayed over, it was bare, with a thin strip of pink or black silk peeking out from between the covers. When he wasn't there, she slept in one of Dad's old concert tees like she always used to.

I tiptoed across the room and sat on the edge of her bed, but she didn't move until I rested my hand on her back and gave her a little shake. "Hey, Mom," I whispered, "I'm home."

She let out a groan and strained to open one eye. "Hi, sweetie. How was the party?"

"Fun."

A chunk of my dark hair fell over my shoulder, and she reached up and pushed it back. "Did Luke drive home?"

"Yeah." I felt a pang of guilt, but I ignored it.

"I like him," she mumbled. "He's a good guy."

Her head sank back into the pillow, and her eyes fell shut.

3

"Yeah, he is." I pulled the covers up to her chin and kissed her forehead.

She was snoring again by the time I shut her door behind me. As I walked back down the hallway, I pulled my phone from the back pocket of my jeans and texted Luke:

Goodnight.

We came up with the code word when we started dating eight months earlier, and we both thought it was kind of brilliant. If Mom happened to read my texts—which she did at random, ever since David convinced her that's what "good parents" did—I imagined she'd let out a happy sigh and tell me she thought it was adorable that Luke and I texted each other before we fell asleep at night.

I closed my bedroom door, turned the lock, flicked the light switch on and off, and then walked to my closet and dug deep in the back, feeling for the metal stepladder. I carried it to the window.

Luke was already in position, pressed against the side of Hannah's house, right between her mother's perfectly manicured rosebush and some giant flowering shrub. When I had the ladder in place, he poked his head out and checked to be sure the coast was clear, and then he stepped into a sliver of light coming from the streetlamp.

He took off running across the lawn, his green-and-white scarf trailing behind him and his matching Foothill Falcons jacket catching the wind like a pair of wings. He played it up, throwing his arms to each side, flapping them like a bird. Or a bat. Or an insane person.

I covered my mouth to stifle my laugh as he climbed up the stepladder. "God, you're a dork."

He swung his leg over the sill and landed on the floor with a soft thud. Then he hooked his thumb toward Hannah's house. "She doesn't think I'm a dork. She thinks I'm dead sexy."

The smile slipped from my lips. Across the lawn, I could see Hannah's face, low in the bottom corner of her window between her curtain and the white-painted frame.

I started to say, "Ignore her," like I always did, but then I changed my mind. If she insisted on watching us, we might as well give her something to see.

I unwrapped his scarf and slid his jacket off, letting it drop to the floor. I pulled his T-shirt over his head. "What are you doing?" he asked. I brushed my fingertips down his bare arms and over his chest, and then I pressed my body against his, kissing him as I eased him backward toward the window. I pressed his shoulders against the glass and kissed him even harder. He made a show of running his fingers through my hair.

Hannah was dying. I could feel her scorn and disgust all the way across the grass. I imagined her grasping that cross pendant of hers so tightly it left four little indentations in her fingers, as she prayed for my soul and prayed even harder for God to strike down my evil boyfriend, sneaking in my bedroom after curfew. But to be fair, the image was over-the-top.

I started giggling. I couldn't help it.

Luke flipped me around, pressed my back against the glass,

and lifted my hands above my head. I laughed even harder. "You're going full soap opera," I said.

"Hey, you started it."

I hitched one leg over his hip and pulled him closer.

"She's totally watching," he said. "Keep going."

But I didn't want to keep going. I wanted to kiss Luke for real, not for show, and certainly not for Hannah.

"I think she's seen enough." I looked over my shoulder, blew a kiss in her direction, and pulled down hard on the shade.

"Are you ever going to tell me what happened with you two?" Luke asked.

"Nope." I didn't see the point. Hannah and I hadn't said a word to each other in over three months. She didn't go to school with us, and between my play rehearsals and her church choir practices, our paths rarely crossed.

It wasn't the way I wanted it, but it was the way it was.

I led him over to my bed, and when he sat on the edge and parted his legs, I stepped in between them. I let my fingers get lost in his dark brown curls and tried not to think about Hannah.

"Well, when you two start talking again, remind me to thank her."

"For what?"

"I'm going to fall asleep tonight thinking about that kiss."

That made me smile. Two seventy-three, I thought to myself. Only I didn't think it to myself. I said it out loud. Luke pulled back and looked at me.

"What did you just say?"

"Nothing."

6

I felt the flush heat my cheeks. I hoped it was dark enough in the room to keep Luke from noticing.

"Why did you say 'two seventy-three'?"

"I didn't, I said . . ." I tried to think of something that rhymed with *seventy-three*, but I was coming up blank.

Luke wasn't about to let it drop. He brought his hands to my hips and pulled me toward him. "Come on. Tell me."

"I can't. It's embarrassing."

"It's me," he said as he undid the first button on my blouse. "What is it? You have two hundred and seventy-three freckles?" He kissed my chest.

"Maybe." I giggled. "You want to count them?"

"I can't." He kissed another spot. "It's too dark in here. Tell me."

"I can't tell you. You'll think it's weird."

"Of course I will. You're weird. In a good way." And then, without taking his eyes off mine, he popped another button open.

"Ooh, I like that one even better." I reached into the back pocket of my jeans for my phone, opened my Notes app, scrolled down to Day 273, and typed:

"You're weird. In a good way."

"Okay, fine. Here." I handed him my phone.

Luke ran his fingertip over the glass, scrolling down slowly, scanning the entries. "Wait, who said the stuff in the quotes?"

"You did."

"Seriously?"

"Yeah. I started on the night we met. You said this thing that made me laugh."

"What did I say?"

I reached over his shoulder and scrolled to the top so he could read the first entry.

Day 1: "I think I'm in big trouble, Emory Kern."

He laughed quietly. "I was right. I knew you were fun."

"Sure." I grinned. "But after all those boring girls you'd been dating, it wasn't like it was a high bar or anything."

Luke pointed at the last entry, Day 437. "Why does it end here?"

I shrugged like it was no big deal. "That's August twentieth." The day Luke was leaving for University of Denver, moving into the dorms, and I was hopefully doing the same at UCLA.

"Oh," he said. And then it got quiet. And awkward.

I cracked a joke to lighten the mood. "So, no pressure, but that last one better be damn good. You should probably start thinking about what you're going to say right now."

Luke returned his attention to my collection of quotes.

"What? No way!" Luke started laughing so hard, I had to cover his mouth to muffle the sound.

"Shh . . . You're going to wake my mom up."

He pulled my hand away. "How did you not laugh in my face when I said, and I quote, 'These songs make me feel like you're in my arms.' I did *not* say that."

"You did. You made me a playlist, remember? Because you're adorable." I kissed his nose.

"I thought you meant this was embarrassing for you, not for me." He looked up at me from under his long eyelashes, a mischievous smile playing on his lips. And then he swiped left. The little red delete button appeared on the side of the screen next to 273 days of carefully collected Luke-isms.

"Luke!" I panicked and tried to grab my phone from his hands, but he was too quick. He held it in the air, out of my reach, threatening to wipe the whole thing out with a single tap.

"Kidding. I wouldn't do that." He swiped right and the red button disappeared. Then he dropped the phone on my comforter and kissed me.

It was the kind of kiss I'd wanted when we were back at the window: long and slow, patient and teasing, soft and eager, all at the same time. God, I loved kissing him. I loved doing everything with him, but I might have loved kissing him most.

He flipped me onto the bed, straddled my hips, and pinned my shoulders to the mattress. "You're the coolest girl I've ever known."

I smacked his arm. "I already have my line for today. I don't want more choices."

"You surprise me. I've never dated anyone who surprised me." He undid another button.

"See, now you're just showing off."

"Also, you have this insanely amazing body and I want you, like, all the time." He popped the last button.

I rolled my eyes. "You're going the wrong way with this.

Now you just sound like every other guy." Luke-isms were never basic.

"Hey." He came down on his elbows so we were face-to-face. "Seriously. I love you. And you're my best friend. You know that, right?"

I sucked in a breath. Not because of the love part—we'd said that practically every day now—but because of the best friend part. An unexpected and overwhelming wave of sadness rippled through my whole body. Without thinking, I turned my head toward Hannah's house.

Even though she broke my heart, and pissed me off, and I wasn't sure we'd ever find our way back to each other, Hannah had been my best friend for seventeen years. I wasn't about to give her title to anyone else, not even Luke.

"You okay?" he asked.

I looked back at him. "Yeah."

"You sure? You look sad."

"I'm fine." I took a long breath and smiled. "I love you, too." That one was easy to say.

Hannah

I stripped off my church clothes as fast as I could and changed into my running gear. I could feel angry tears building up behind my eyes, but I pushed them down when I heard a knock on my door.

Mom opened it and poked her head inside. She took one look at my feet and said, "You're going for a run? Now?"

"Yep."

"But we're in the middle of a conversation."

"No, we're not. You and Dad can talk all you want. I'm done."

I jammed my foot into my running shoe and sat on the edge of my bed. I still couldn't get my head around what they'd told me. Graduation was only three months away. Of all the things I'd had to worry about, I hadn't thought college was one of them. Suddenly, everything was up in the air. I tried to tie my laces, but my fingers were shaking too much.

"I know you're upset, Hannah. You have every right to be." Mom sat next to me. She started to put her hand on my leg but thought better of it, so it kind of lingered awkwardly in the air before she rested it on the comforter between us. "Your dad was doing what he thought was best for—"

I cut her off. "You'd better not say for *me*. You'd better say for the school. He was doing what he thought was best for the school, like always."

"That's not fair, Hannah. And it's not true. Your dad has made a lot of sacrifices for the school, but he's made a lot for you, too. More than you'll ever know."

I grabbed my other shoe off the floor, slid it on my foot, and laced it as fast as I could. I couldn't wait to get out of there. All I wanted to do was feel my feet slapping hard on the pavement and fill my lungs with air until they burned.

I didn't say anything else, so Mom kept talking. "It was an investment. Dad thought it would have paid off by now. It will, soon, and when it does, it will benefit *everyone*. The school. Our family. Your future. It might not look like it on the surface, but he did do this for you, Hannah."

It was all I could do not to laugh in her face. "He spent all my college savings, Mom. I might not be able to go to Boston University. How is that for *me*?"

"That's not what we said. You're going to BU, no question. All we're saying is that you might have to defer for a year and go to one of the community colleges first. Lots of kids do that."

"I worked hard in every class for four years to get into my top school. I've spent every second of my free time on extracurriculars and volunteering, not to mention all those hours practicing and touring with SonRise, all because you told me that a cappella choir would look good on my college applications."

"Oh, come on . . . That's not fair, Hannah. You love performing with SonRise. And I encouraged you to do it because you have a beautiful voice, not to get you into college."

She continued. "You got into a great school. Defer for a year, give us a chance to let the investment do what we know it will do, and then transfer. Your diploma will still come from BU."

Mom must have noticed that her words were making this sound like a done deal, when they hadn't pitched it to me like that in the living room ten minutes earlier.

"Listen," she said with a new, more positive lilt in her voice. "We're not saying it's definite. Not at all. We just thought we'd better give you a heads-up."

A heads-up?

I couldn't even look at her. And I knew that wasn't entirely fair. She wasn't in this alone. And the whole thing had to have been his idea, not hers.

"Now I'm wishing we hadn't told you." She punctuated the thought with an exaggerated sigh. That set me off again.

"No, you should have told me months ago! You should have told me back in December, when I got my early admissions letter. We went out to dinner to celebrate. And you and Dad knew we couldn't afford it the entire time. How could you have done that?"

Mom had a strange look on her face. She bit down hard on her lip and looked out my window. Something was off.

I thought back to that night. Mom and Dad looked like they were about to burst with pride the entire time. They couldn't have been faking it.

I started mentally piecing together the timeline, trying to figure out what had changed since then, if the money hadn't been a problem back in December. It hit me like a slap. "It's Aaron, isn't it?"

The music director spot had been open for more than a year. In January, when Dad finally lured Aaron Donohue away from a huge mega-church in Houston, he'd said his prayers had been answered. His "dream team" was complete.

"Aaron has been a huge asset to the school, but he was an expensive hire."

Aaron. The irony wasn't lost on me. It would have been hilarious if it wasn't so horrible. I moved for the door, more eager to get out of this room and this house and this town than I'd ever been before.

"Hannah." I stopped. I looked over my shoulder, biting my tongue. "Everything will be okay. All we need is faith."

Yeah, I thought, that's all we need. Maybe I could just show up at the BU admissions office on the first day of school and say, "Hi, my name is Hannah Jacquard. I have no money, but here, take this. It's a ton of faith."

"God will provide, Hannah. You know that. He always does."

I wished I believed that as much as I used to. My eyes narrowed on her. "Does He, Mom?"

She stared back at me, her expression a strange mix of

14

shock and disappointment, and for a split second, a part of me wished I hadn't said it. But a bigger part of me felt relieved that I finally had.

"Yes, I believe He does."

"Well, He'd better get a move on," I said. "Tuition is due in June."

I stormed out of my room, down the hallway, and past Dad, who was still sitting in the living room, where we'd had our "family chat." I heard him call my name.

I stepped back so I could see him through the archway. His face was blotchy and his eyes were red, and seeing him like that made me want to throw my arms around his shoulders and steal Mom's words. That it would all be okay. That we just needed to pray about it. But I rooted my feet in place and didn't speak.

"I'm so sorry." Dad's whisper cut through the silence. "I made a mistake. I'm going to fix this for you, I promise." His voice cracked on the last word, and I couldn't help it, I stepped toward him. He was my dad. I'd never been that angry with him, and I didn't have the slightest clue how to do it.

The words *It's okay* stuck in my throat, but I swallowed them back down. It wasn't okay.

I opened the door and stepped out onto the front porch, my heart beating so hard I could feel it pounding against my rib cage. I took the front steps in a daze, and when I reached the walkway, I took a hard left, stepping over Mom's flower bed, heading straight for Emory's house. I was halfway across the grass when I stopped cold.

I stared at her house, feeling heavy and empty at the same time. I wanted to run inside and tell her she was right, not just about Dad, but about me, too.

Until three months ago, I would have.

But I couldn't do that.

I turned and took off running in the opposite direction, bound for the foothills. I reached the intersection two blocks later, and I punched the crosswalk button so hard it made my knuckles throb. When the light turned green, I bolted across the street and through the parking lot, only slowing down when I reached the three metal barriers designed to keep bikes off the trail. My feet hit the dirt path, and I veered left and disappeared into the trees.

The money was gone. I knew Dad had been investing in Covenant Christian School's performing arts program from his own savings, after he'd spent everything in the church budget and then everything the larger local churches had invested, but it never occurred to me that he'd dip into my college fund, too.

The path began to twist and climb steeply. I locked my gaze on the little wooden trail marker at the top of the hill, widened my stride, pumped my arms harder, and picked up the pace. I didn't take my eyes off that sign, and when I finally reached it, I gave it a victory slap. Then I took a hard right and kept going, following the bends and curves of the narrow trail.

My parents had always talked about college like that was the natural next step after high school. A no-brainer. They always said they'd pay for it and never seemed to care about tuition costs or out-of-state fees. If only I'd seen it coming, I could have been prepared. I could have applied for scholarships or grants or something.

I needed BU. From the moment I opened that acceptance letter, it symbolized a whole lot more than a four-year college plan. It was my chance to live in a city where nobody knew me, and no one was watching or judging or analyzing my every move. For the first time in my life, I wouldn't be Pastor J's daughter. And that meant I could be anyone I wanted to be.

The path wound up and up, twisting past my neighborhood again before the trees obscured the view. Three miles later, I reached the series of boulders that marked the peak, and I climbed to my favorite rock—I'd always called it my praying rock, and more recently, my thinking rock.

I took a deep breath. And then I screamed as loud as I could.

The sound sent birds from their nests and squirrels from their homes, and it felt so good to let it all out that way. Tears streamed down my cheeks, mixing with the sweat dripping off my forehead, and I wiped the mess away with the hem of my T-shirt.

I sat on the cold stone with my legs folded and let my head fall into my hands. I rocked back and forth, sobbing and shaking and gasping for breath, not even trying to control myself.

I was furious at my dad, but I was even more furious with myself.

Because Emory was right.

She was right about everything.

Emory
Day 275, 162 to go

I rubbed my eyes as I padded down the hall.

"Morning, sleepyhead." Mom was standing at the stove wearing black yoga pants and a bright orange tank top. Her hair was piled on top of her head in a messy bun, and a few dark strands had come loose, framing her face. She was quietly humming like she always did when she cooked.

The coffee in the pot was cold, left over from the day before, so I dumped it out in the sink and made a fresh one. While I waited, I rested my head on the counter and closed my eyes. "Why are you so chipper this morning?"

"I've been up for hours." She pointed toward the dining room using her spatula. "I've been productive."

I looked up. The table was covered with pages ripped from bridal magazines. "That's one word for it," I said as I walked over to get a closer look.

She'd carefully organized all the bridal gowns into neat

piles: Strapless dresses in one stack. Full-length ball gowns in another. Short, more playful dresses next to sleek, elegant sheaths. There was a smaller pile of colorful gowns.

She came up behind me and rested her chin on my shoulder, studying her work. "Am I going overboard? Because you can tell me if I'm going overboard."

"You're going overboard."

"I know," she said, sighing as she reached out and picked up a photo of a much younger woman in a sequined gown that made her look like she'd just stepped straight out of an animated movie. "I want to do it right this time, but . . . maybe I'm too old for this princess stuff?"

Over the last few months, I'd learned more about bridal gowns than I'd ever wanted to. I could identify raw silk from organza, a mermaid silhouette from a ball gown, and a sweetheart neckline from a bateau. I could tell the difference between a chapel- and a cathedral-length train, and a dropped waist from an empire.

I reached into the pile of straight-lined sheaths and chose a simple-looking one with a scoop neckline and none of the bling.

"I like this one," I said.

"Something older."

"Something elegant." I handed it to Mom. "You'll still look like a princess."

She slid her arm around me as she studied the picture. "I'm not sure I can pull off strapless." She pointed at her chest. "I don't have the boobs to hold up a dress like that now that I've lost all the weight."

Mom used to own a catering company, but when Dad

left three years ago, she stopped cooking, then she practically stopped eating, and eventually, she stopped getting out of bed almost entirely. Within six months, she'd lost forty pounds and all her clients. Then one day she cleaned out her catering van, found a therapist, and joined a gym. And that's where she met David the Douchebag.

"Maybe this?" She reached out and picked up a similar-looking dress with thin straps. "It looks comfortable. I could actually dance in this one."

"I like it." I took it from her hand and set it in the *yes* pile as she popped a forkful of omelet into her mouth.

When we were done rummaging through the stacks we had six styles we agreed would look best on her. She fanned the pages in front of her and drummed her hands on the table. "God, this is so fun! I feel like a teenager."

"Teenagers don't usually get married, Mom."

"Fine. I feel like a late-twentysomething who's young and in love, with her whole life ahead of her."

"Which makes me?"

She thought about it for a second. "My younger but much wiser sister."

The younger sister part was true enough. I wasn't so sure about the wiser part, especially in light of recent events.

Then she jumped up and kissed my forehead. "I'm going to take a quick shower. You've got dishes," she said as she skipped off down the hall. "Our first bridal salon appointment is in an hour, so make it snappy."

I took a sip of my coffee and sat there a little longer,

studying the dresses again. Careful not to ruin our new piles, I pulled out one that had caught my eye a few times from the stack of rejects. I lifted it in the air and gave it a closer look.

It was a simple A-line with a low scoop neck and tight cap sleeves. The model's hair looked like mine: long, straight, and dark brown. Her eyes were bright blue, too, and we both had high cheekbones. She seemed taller than me, but that might have just been the three-inch strappy sandals on her feet. She was prettier than me for sure, but I could kind of see myself in her. I could definitely see myself in that dress. No time soon or anything—at least not until college was over and my acting career was well established—but someday.

As I ran my fingertip over the curves and seams, my phone buzzed.

Luke: Hey what are you doing?
Emory: Wedding planning with my mom
Luke: Fun.

I typed the word *hardly*, but then I deleted it and instead typed a simple, *Yep*.

I had to do everything I could to make Mom's wedding perfect. Nothing else mattered.

Besides, it was all almost over. Graduation was three months away. The wedding would be over in five. In six months, she'd be moving into D-bag's loft in the city and I'd be living in the dorms.

Luke: I'm going to practice. Want to see a movie later?

I typed *Sure*, and hit SEND.

And then I picked up the picture of that dress again. A little part of me wished Luke and I were building toward that kind of a future. But we weren't. In six months—in 162 days to be exact—we'd be over, too.

Hannah

When I walked into the kitchen on Monday morning, I found Dad standing at the sink, filling up two travel mugs—steaming hot coffee for him and tea with a splash of milk for me, operating like he did every morning, as if nothing had changed.

"You ready?" Dad asked as he twisted tops on the travel mugs. He was wearing a multicolored hoodie and a pair of skinny jeans with black slip-on Vans, looking more like an aging punk headed for the skate park than a pastor-turned-principal heading to his day job.

"Yep."

He handed me my tea. "Here, sweetie."

"Thanks."

It was the most we'd said to each other since I stormed out of the house the day before.

That was the problem with attending a school ten miles

away. None of my friends lived anywhere near me, so if I wanted to avoid riding to school with Dad, I would have had to get up a full hour earlier, catch the public bus, and transfer twice.

By the time Dad and I reached the intersection, I was wishing I'd done that. We always listened to music or talked about the news, and the silence was killing both of us. I could hear him slurp his coffee and thump his fingers nervously on the steering wheel. I stared out the window, watching the neighborhood blur by. The post office. The car wash. Foothill High School. The diner next door.

"I'm glad you know," Dad finally said as we merged onto the freeway. "I hated not telling you. We don't keep secrets in our family."

I didn't think we did either. Not until the day before.

"I have a plan," he continued. "I made a few calls last night, and I'm meeting with a bunch of the churches in our network this week. They're bigger than us, with deeper pockets and a lot more resources. I know they realize this school is a huge asset to the community. It's in their best interest for us to succeed."

"Mm-hmm," I mumbled. I'd heard it all before.

"We just need enough for your first year. After that, everything will be fine again." He tightened his grip on the steering wheel.

Dad signaled and turned onto the private street marked with a metal sign that read COVENANT CHRISTIAN SCHOOL in neat block letters. He followed the narrow road, lined with roses and lavender bushes, until it opened onto the parking lot in front of the sanctuary.

The church looked quintessentially Southern Californian:

mission style, with white stucco walls, arched windows, and red roof tiles. Right after I was born, the church decided to build the adjacent school and the church leaders tapped my dad, who had been the associate pastor, to be the new principal and oversee the construction.

He had a say in every aspect of the new campus, from the height of the cafeteria ceilings to the pattern of the stained-glass windows in the library. He'd designed a series of pathways that connected every building and led to a sprawling green lawn where we ate lunch on warm days. And he made sure the whole campus was surrounded by trees that sheltered it from the neighboring office buildings and gave us a bunch of smaller, almost secret places to sit and study, or just be alone and pray.

Dad loved everything about that school. Mom used to joke that I'd been an only child until the day Covenant was born.

He drove around the back, into the faculty lot, and pulled into the spot marked RESERVED FOR PRINCIPAL. He cut the engine, and then turned toward me. "I've got this, okay?"

When I didn't answer, he leaned on the console and came in closer, until I had no choice but to look at him. "I'm not asking you to forgive me. What I did was wrong. I'm asking for you to stick with me a little longer. I'm going to do whatever it takes to make this right, okay? Do you trust me?"

And suddenly, there was Emory's voice in my head.

You have a blind spot when it comes to your dad, Hannah. You'll believe anything he says. Believe anything he believes. When was the last time you had an opinion that was entirely your own?

"Hannah. Please."

25

I could tell how much Dad needed to know I was on his side. And at that point, what good would it do me not to be? "I trust you," I said.

He pulled me into a hug. "That's my girl." Then he released me from his grip. "Let's get going. We don't want to be late."

He climbed out of the car and shut the door, and I watched him cross the parking lot, doling out greetings and the occasional fist bump to the kids he passed. I stayed in the car until I heard the first bell ring, and then I got out and walked toward the sanctuary doors. I didn't rush. I didn't feel like it.

As I got closer, I could hear an upbeat Top 40 song playing inside. Dad liked to keep Monday Chapel "chill and fun," not all "heavy and churchy." I walked down the center aisle to the first row and fell into my usual seat next to Alyssa.

Her feet were kicked out in front of her and her head was reclined against the back of the pew. "Morning," she mumbled as she peeled one eye open. Then she closed it again and went back to dozing.

It was all I could do not to tell her what happened, but I'd promised my mom I wouldn't. "Let's keep this to ourselves," she'd said when I returned from my run the day before. "You know how fast information spreads around the church."

I leaned forward, waving at Jack and Logan in the seats next to Alyssa. They were sharing a pair of earbuds and watching a YouTube video of another competitive a cappella choir on Jack's phone. "Morning," Logan said.

I reached into my backpack for the flash cards I made for my chemistry test and began thumbing through them. I was only on the second card when Alyssa sat up taller and pointed

26

at the stage. "Ooh, look. My future husband got a sexy new haircut over the weekend."

Aaron stepped onto the stage wearing a light blue Covenant Christian T-shirt with jeans and a pair of black Toms. He took his guitar out of the stand and brought it with him to the bench next to the pulpit. He didn't have his usual baseball cap on; I assumed that was because he wanted to show off his new haircut.

I hadn't thought much about Aaron, but that was probably because Alyssa thought enough about him for herself, and me, and, like, six other people. Not that I had any problem seeing Aaron the way Alyssa did. He was definitely cute. And confident, but not cocky or anything. Which made him even more adorable. But when I saw him onstage, all I could think about were those words Mom had said the day before. "Aaron's been a huge asset to the church and the school, but he was an expensive hire."

Translation: I would be going to BU next year if it weren't for him.

"I have to study," I said to Alyssa, tapping my fingernail against my flash cards.

She plucked them from my hand. "What could possibly be more important than my future husband's sexy new hair?"

"World hunger. The roles of women in developing countries." I grabbed my flash cards back. "Me not failing Chem."

Alyssa looked back at the stage, and I followed her gaze. Aaron shuffled through a stack of sheet music on the bench next to him. Then his eyes flicked toward the front row. He tipped his chin toward us and grinned.

I glared at him.

When he looked away again, Alyssa slapped my arm. "Did you see the way he just smiled at me? That boy's mine."

I laughed under my breath. "Boy?" I asked.

She rolled her eyes. "Stop saying that. He's not *that* much older than me."

"He's *five* years older than you!"

"Four," she corrected. "I'll be eighteen next month."

"Whatever. He's still practically our teacher."

"He won't be in June," she said with a wink.

The sanctuary lights dimmed and the stage lights came on. I used to cringe at what came next, but after three and a half years, I'd gotten used to it.

My dad ran in from the side of the stage wearing a lavalier mic and waving his hands wildly in the air. He stopped in the middle, bouncing on his toes and looking out at us. And then he lifted his arms into the air and yelled into the sanctuary, "This is the day that the Lord has made!"

We all yelled back, "Let us rejoice and be glad in it!"

"Nice!" He lowered his arms. "Wow, you sound unusually spirited for a Monday morning. Amen!"

"Amen!" everyone yelled back.

He insisted that everyone call him Pastor J because Pastor Jacquard sounded overly formal and no one could ever pronounce it anyway. My friends always told me how lucky I was to have him as my dad. They said he was more like a friend than a pastor, and that they told him secrets they'd never tell their own parents. That always used to make me proud. Lately, it made me wish he wasn't my dad so I had someone like him to confide in.

"Before we get to official business, a few quick announcements." Dad paced back and forth across the stage as he spoke. "As everyone in this room knows, this is a unique school. We gather together for Monday Chapel. Throughout the week, we meet in smaller groups and share what's going on in our lives. We come back to this room with our families every Sunday. We connect," he said, interlacing his fingers. "We *get* each other, don't we?"

Out of the corner of my eye, I could see heads bobbing in agreement, Alyssa's included. "Amen," she whispered.

Dad's heart was in the right place, but it bugged me when he talked about Covenant like that, as if he'd singlehandedly created this perfect teenage utopia where everyone got along, talked openly about feelings, and never said or did anything to hurt anyone. Nice visual, but it wasn't true. We judged each other; we just did it more subtly and about different things, like who was the better Christian.

"Our annual Admissions Night is in three weeks, and I'm going to need all of us to come together as a team."

I glanced around, taking in all the empty rows in the back of the sanctuary. When I was in elementary school, Dad used to turn away hundreds of kids every year, but by the time I was in middle school, things had started to change. Applications were on a steep decline and Dad had started letting teachers go, cutting back programs, and taking out loans from bigger local churches.

Over dinner one night, he told Mom and me all about his new plan.

"We're going to focus on the performing arts program. We

already have an incredible dance troupe and drama department, a competitive show choir, and of course, an award-winning a cappella group," he'd said as he patted my hand. "And we're in LA, after all!"

Mom snickered. "We're in Orange County. LA is an hour away from here."

"Close enough," he'd said.

Dad spent the next six months getting investments, beefing up our drama and dance departments, hiring new directors and upping their budgets.

Admissions Night had always been a big deal, but lately, he seemed to be pulling out all the stops, more determined than ever to fill that room. And now I knew why.

Aaron.

Me.

"I want each one of you to think about the reason you're here at Covenant." Dad slowly paced the stage, stopping to smile at specific students. It was his way of connecting, of drawing them in. He told me once that he tries to find the people in the crowd who don't seem to be hearing the message, or the ones he knows need to hear it most, and he makes a point to look directly at them. "Maybe you were someone who never quite found the right group in middle school. Maybe you felt a bit lost. Maybe you felt pressured to do things you knew weren't right."

I heard a few scattered *amens* around the room as Dad made his way to the other side of the stage. "Or maybe you came here to make the most of your God-given talents in music and dance. No matter what brought you here to this family, you're in a place where you belong."

Dad kept pacing, looking out into the sanctuary, pausing to let his words sink in.

"I bet every one of you knows someone who needs this place as much as you did."

I thought of Emory. She used to come to church with me all the time when we were little, and she never missed any of my choir performances, but over the years, I could tell she'd become more uncomfortable in this room. When I asked her to come to candlelight service last Christmas Eve, she scrunched up her nose and said, "I'm gonna pass this year. That's your thing, not mine. You understand, right?"

I told her I did, and I'd meant it, but it still hurt.

"Right now, I want each one of you to close your eyes and picture that person." Dad was still pacing the stage. "I'm going to count to three and I want you to say that person's name out loud. Ready? One. Two. Three."

The auditorium filled with sound. I couldn't think of anyone else, and I wasn't about to say Emory's name, so I mumbled something unintelligible, knowing the names would all blend together anyway.

"I know I'm your principal and not a teacher, but I'm giving out a little bit of homework today. I want to see the person you just named sitting right next to you on Admissions Night. Amen?"

"Amen!" everyone yelled.

Dad pointed at Aaron. "Aaron has been working so hard

on a new promotional video, and he's finishing it up this week. When he comes around, be yourselves. Ham it up. Have some fun! Show our community what this school is all about. Amen?"

"Amen!"

"Okay, let's get to today's sermon." I heard the whir of the projection screen as it lowered from the ceiling.

I knew from all the time I'd spent singing on that stage that the first row was hard to see from the glare of the spotlights, so I pulled out my Chem flash cards and kept them on my lap. I figured if he happened to notice me with my head bent down, he'd think I was praying.

Emory

Day 276, 161 to go

"Why do I feel like people are looking at me?" I slid my tray down the lunch line.

"It's your imagination," Charlotte said as she reached for a basket of fries.

"Yeah, I thought so." I tossed my purple feather boa over my shoulder with dramatic flair, and it hit the guy standing behind me right in the face. I apologized even though he didn't seem to care.

I reached for a salad and changed the subject. "I like your hair, by the way."

Charlotte's long blond hair was twisted into a soft braid that started at one temple and continued over the top of her head, framing her face like a crown.

"Thanks. I think I've finally got this one down. I'm going to post the video tonight."

My hair looked the same every day; I liked sleeping too much to get up early and mess with it. But Charlotte's hair always looked different. She wore it in sophisticated-looking updos, braided it in fishtails, or let it hang in big, loopy curls. Once she mastered the new technique, she'd post a short tutorial video on Instagram. Last time I checked, she had over twelve thousand followers.

I looked over my shoulder at Luke's table. His back was to me, but I could see him at the far end, talking with his friends. He broke from his story long enough to take a sip of soda.

I was just about to turn away when Lara noticed me. Once she did, that was it. It was like I'd flicked my fingertip against the first domino. Lara elbowed Tess, who leaned into Ava, who nudged Kathryn, and one by one their heads turned to look at me. Eyes widened. Jaws dropped. And then it was the guys' turn. None of them even tried to hide their surprise. They laughed and pointed until it snaked around to Luke, the final domino to fall.

When he saw me, I tilted my head to one side and gave him a flirty wave, feeling all Marilyn Monroe and hoping I looked the part. He covered his mouth, but I could tell from the crinkles next to his eyes he was smiling.

When I stepped up to the counter to pay for my lunch, the cashier looked at me sideways. "What?" I asked, and she shook her head and said, "Nothing," as she handed me my card.

Charlotte was business as usual. "Are you skipping the theater today?"

"No. Why would I?" I stuffed my card back into the pocket of my denim skirt.

She gestured over at Luke. "Look, you don't have to keep doing this. How many days left?"

I didn't skip a beat. "One hundred sixty-one."

"Have lunch with your boyfriend. It's okay. I know you made a big deal out of it, swearing you'd never ditch Tyler and me like I ditched the two of you when I started dating Simon, but seriously, it's okay. We get it. And we like Luke. You don't have to hang out with us at lunch."

"Sure, I do."

"No, you don't. Seriously. Even if that would make you a ginormous hypocrite, I'd never say so."

"Not to my face."

"Never to your face."

I laughed. "Well, it's not about you two anyway. *Our Town* is four weeks away and if I don't get my Emily Webb lines down, Ms. Martin's going to strangle me. Or replace me, which would be much worse."

I pointed at the double doors that opened onto the path that led to the theater.

"Go. If I don't show up, it's because Mr. Elliot sent me home, not because I don't love the hell out of you."

I tossed the purple boa over my shoulder, spun on my toes, and moved across the cafeteria like a runway model. I could feel every eye fixed on me. I ate it up.

When I reached Luke, I set my tray on the table, threw my boa around his shoulders, and sat on his lap. He squeezed my thigh. And then he kissed me.

It was a little kiss. A school kiss. Not a get-a-room kiss, but it might as well have been. I could feel everyone watching us.

I licked my lips. "You taste like peppermint."

He reached into his sweatshirt pocket and held up a roll of Mentos. "Freshmaker?"

Luke dropped a mint into my palm, and I popped it into my mouth.

"So . . . I assume there's a story behind this," he said as he played with my feathers.

"There is an excellent story behind this."

I said it loud enough for Tess and Kathryn to look up from their food, and for Ava and Dominic to stop talking. Luke's twin sister, Addison, waved her hand toward her chest and yelled, "I've gotta hear this," reminding me why I liked her most.

"Okay, so . . ." I sat up a little taller, twisting toward them. "I'm at my locker between third and fourth. I'm just about to leave for class when I turn and find Mr. Elliot standing there with his arms crossed, looking all stern." I mimicked his posture and expression. "In this real quiet voice, he asks me if I'm aware that I'm in violation of the school dress code."

Using Luke's shoulder for balance, I stood so everyone at the table could see my outfit in its entirety.

"I think he's referring to my skirt, right? So, I give it the fingertip test." I stretched one arm to my side, demonstrating. "And it barely passes, but it does, so I figure I'm in the clear. But then he waggles his finger at me and says, 'Bare shoulders are not allowed, Miss Kern. You know that.'"

I scanned the cafeteria to be sure there weren't any teachers in sight, and then I pulled the boa down, exposing my shoulders.

Even Tess looked surprised. "Um. It's a tank top. The

dress code says they aren't allowed, but everyone wears them anyway."

"Right?" I slapped my hand down hard on the table. "That's what I thought! But apparently, this is not a tank top, Tess, this is a 'dress code infraction.'" I curled my fingers around the words as I said them.

I had everyone's undivided attention. I liked that.

"Anyway, Mr. Elliot keeps going, telling me I have to go home and change because what I'm wearing is 'distracting to the boys,' which is nuts, right?" I looked at each of the girls. Ava nodded. Kathryn said, "Duh." Tess rolled her eyes. Then I looked right at Luke. "Are you distracted?"

He shrugged. "Sure, but I'm pretty much always distracted by you."

"Of course you are." I kissed the tip of his nose. "And that is completely your problem and not at all mine. Anyway," I said, addressing the group again. "I tell Mr. Elliot that I have something that will cover my shoulders, and he thinks about that for a minute and tells me to go get it. Then he walks away."

I took a sip of Luke's soda and got right back to my story.

"I go straight to the theater, figuring I'll find one of my sweatshirts backstage or in the greenroom or something, but there's nothing. So, I go to the prop room and rifle through the costume racks, and voilà. I found this hot little number." I modeled it again. "It covers my shoulders just perfectly, don't you think? And I've always looked good in purple."

Everyone laughed and I curtsied. Then I hopped off Luke's lap, took the spot next to him, and reached for my sandwich. I was starving.

Addison stood and came down to our end of the table. "Scooch," she said to Brian and Jake, and they both slid over so she could sit between them. "So, Emory. You're going to Luke's game on Wednesday, right?"

"This Wednesday?" Charlotte, Tyler, and the rest of our drama group friends always met at the diner after Wednesday rehearsals, drinking coffee, eating chocolate chip cheesecake, and running lines together. I couldn't imagine missing it. And I needed to practice my lines.

"It's the first game of the regular season," Luke said. "You've never even seen me play, not in a real game, at least."

"But I don't know a thing about lacrosse." I could tell by the looks on their faces that it wasn't a very good excuse.

"That's okay," Addison said. "I'll talk you through it."

I'd never been to a school sporting event. I always assumed I'd graduate from Foothill High School without ever seeing one. But what could I say? It was Luke.

He wrapped his hand around my waist. "You can wear one of my jerseys."

I giggled. I couldn't help it. "Your *jersey*?" Luke was broad-shouldered and at least five inches taller than me. I'd swim in one of his jerseys. Plus, wearing my boyfriend's jersey sounded so . . . mainstream. So . . . girlfriend-y.

"Does it say *Calletti* in big letters across the back and everything?" I asked.

"Well, it doesn't say *Jones*."

I started to make another joke, but I could tell this whole jersey thing was important to him, so I changed course. "Can I make a few alterations?"

"Sure," he said. "I've got dozens of jerseys. Do what you want with it."

"Uh-oh," I heard Jake say. "Elliot's heading this way."

I looked up. Mr. Elliot was over by the cash registers with his eyes locked on me.

"That's my cue." I wrapped up my sandwich and adjusted the boa to be sure my shoulders had the appropriate amount of coverage.

I gave Luke a kiss. "See ya," I said as I headed for the double doors that led to the theater.

Hannah

"Testing. Testing, one, two, three." Alyssa pulled her hair into a ponytail while she waited for Jack to connect the next microphone. When he was done, he gave her a nod and she stepped in front of it. "Testing. Testing, one, two, three. This one's not working," she yelled up toward the balcony, tapping her fingernail on the mic.

I could see Aaron up in the sound booth, behind the glass, bent over the mixing board, sliding levers up and down. His voice came over the sound system, Godlike and omnipresent. "Try again."

"Testing. Testing," she said. "Nope. Nothing."

Alyssa slapped my arm with the back of her hand. "Hey, I have something to show you after rehearsal." She tipped her head toward the sound booth again.

"Aaron?" I spat his name out like it was toxic on my tongue. I wasn't in the mood to hear it, but I knew I didn't have a choice. Ever since he came to Covenant, Alyssa had been on a personal mission to find everything she could on him. The last time she'd spent the night at my house, she made me watch all these videos she'd found of him performing at his old church.

"I found high school stuff." She grinned. "Get this. He was in a band."

I lowered my mic stand and twisted the knob, tightening it in place.

"And guess who else I found?"

"Who?" I tried to sound like I cared.

"His girlfriend, Beth. Well, I think it's Beth. She kinda looked like that picture he showed us on his phone a couple weeks ago."

"You do realize you sound like a stalker right now?"

"Me?" She looked at me wide-eyed. "No. I'm just a girl who happens to be intensely curious and infinitely resourceful."

"Who is also kind of stalker-y," I joked.

She ignored me. "You'll never guess what he played."

Guitar seemed like the obvious answer, so it was probably wrong. I tried to picture a young, high school Aaron on a stage. I couldn't really see him as a front man, but it wasn't like he was bassist material either. Before I could say anything, Alyssa answered her own question.

"Dude, my boy was a *drummer.*" She raised an eyebrow. "I mean, that acoustic guitar thing he does now is adorable and all, but a drummer? That's just hot."

41

"I'm pretty sure you're not supposed to refer to our choir director as *hot*."

Logan looked over at us and raised an eyebrow. "You know what else is hot?"

Alyssa put her hands on her hips. "What?"

"Your mic."

Alyssa blushed and took two giant steps back while the rest of us tried to stifle our laughs.

Aaron's voice filled the room again. "Well, everything seems to be working. I'll be right down."

The three of us totally lost it.

A minute later, Aaron reappeared at the back of the sanctuary carrying the video camera in one hand and a tripod in the other. When he reached the front of the room, he set everything up, ignoring our laughter and Alyssa's bright red cheeks.

Over the last few weeks he'd been running around campus with that camera in his hands, jumping onto tables during lunch to get shots of people eating together, buzzing around the library getting footage of everyone studying, and popping in on classes to show our teachers in action. At first, I thought it was pretty cool how hard he was working to capture the spirit of our school. Now, I couldn't help but wonder how much my dad had spent on that brand-new video camera.

"Okay. I'm almost done with the two promo videos, but I don't have enough SonRise footage, so I'm going to keep this rolling." He pressed a button on the recorder and stood in front of us in his usual spot. "Pretend the camera's not there. Let's start with 'Brighter.'"

"Brighter Than Sunshine" wasn't a new song or anything, but it was a fan favorite. We'd been singing it in local competitions for the last four years, so the whole thing came naturally for us, and we hardly had to think about the words and the harmonies anymore, which made it especially fun to perform. It was an easy pick for Admissions Night, one we knew we'd nail.

Aaron took his place in front of the stage. It was impossible not to look at him, so I sucked in a deep breath and pushed down my anger, telling myself to focus on the music and forget about him.

He gestured to Alyssa and she whispered, "Four, three, two, one."

Then he pointed right at Jack and me, and we sang.

"Mm . . . bop-bop. Mm . . . bop-bop."

All four of us had our eyes fixed on Aaron's hands, watching them cut through the air, moving back and forth in time with the music. Then he pointed at Logan, who sang in his rich, clear voice, "I never understood before. I never knew what love was for. My heart was broke, my head was sore, what a feeling."

Aaron's left hand moved with the tempo, keeping the three of us on the beat while he directed Logan through the verses. And then he pointed at me for the chorus.

"What a feeling in my soul, love burns brighter than sunshine."

By the middle of the song, we all relaxed into it, looking at each other, turning our palms toward the ceiling or closing our eyes when we felt a special connection to the lyric. We were having fun with it. We sang the last two lines in four-part harmony.

"I'm yours and suddenly you're mine, and it's brighter than sunshine."

Aaron closed his left hand into a fist and brought his right finger to his lips. It was quiet again. The little red light on the camera was still on.

"That was good," Aaron said. "Logan, you were a bit early on that second verse. You have to watch me. I'll tell you when to come in, okay? And Hannah, I'd like you to hit those first few words in the chorus a little harder. *'What a feeling in my soul . . .'*" he sang. "Really deliver that line, okay?"

Normally, I would have thanked him for the feedback. Instead, I grabbed my water bottle off the pulpit and took a huge gulp.

"Awesome. Let's do it again."

Alyssa spoke quietly into her mic, "Four, three, two, one."

Two hours later, after four more takes of "Brighter" and three rounds of "Dare You," the other song we were planning to perform for Admissions Night, Aaron called it. The four of us let out a collective sigh and practically sprinted to the first pew, reaching for our backpacks before he had a chance to change his mind.

"Hey, Alyssa, can I catch a ride home with you?" I asked. "Dad's working late again." It was true, but mostly, I didn't want to have to sit in the car with him again.

She checked the time on her phone. "I would, but I can't today. It's twenty minutes out of the way, and my mom will kill me if I don't let the dog out."

I looked over my other shoulder. "Logan?" I asked.

He stuffed his water bottle into the pocket of his backpack. "Can't. I'm taking Jack home, and he's clear on the other side of town."

"Guess I'll run the track." But I didn't want to run the track. The track bored me. I wanted my path. I wanted my rock.

"Sorry," Alyssa called over her shoulder as she headed for the door. "I'll text you later."

I had nothing else to do and I wasn't in a hurry to run, so once my friends were gone and Aaron had returned to the sound booth, I walked back to the stage and started disconnecting the microphones.

Aaron had demanded a ton of new equipment as a condition of employment, saying he couldn't build the kind of music program Dad wanted without it. In addition to the velvet-lined microphone box sitting next to me, there was that camera, perched on a professional-quality tripod. And then there was all the stuff in the sound booth, like the 64-channel mixing board and a superfast computer he could use to edit our music and videos.

Aaron had to have known our school was in financial trouble when he'd accepted the job; he'd been hired to help fix it. Staring at all that fancy equipment made me wonder if he had any idea how much my dad sacrificed to hire him. Did he know Dad had picked him over me?

I was still lost in thought when I heard Aaron's voice behind me. "You know they pay me to do this, right?" he joked, grabbing a cord and winding it around his arm.

"Yeah, straight from my college fund," I mumbled.

"What?"

"Nothing."

I snapped the buckles on the case and carried it backstage to the music room. I slid it onto the shelf next to all the boom mics and lav mics and other equipment. When I got back to the stage, Aaron was turning a dial on the tripod, disconnecting the video camera.

"Hey, do you have a minute?"

I tried to think of an excuse, but I was drawing a total blank, so I mumbled "I guess."

"Great!" He sounded a little too excited. "I was hoping you'd be around tonight. I could really use your opinion on something."

He picked the tripod up in one hand and the camera in the other, and headed for the back of the sanctuary. I followed him through the double doors, and then we took a sharp right and started climbing the narrow staircase that led to the balcony.

I couldn't remember the last time I'd been up there, but it looked the same as it always had. There were eight rows of dark mahogany pews, exactly like the ones down in the sanctuary, and along the back wall, a long table draped with a blue silk runner held all the brass offering plates. It was quiet. It always was. No one ever went up there except on Christmas Eve and Easter Sunday, when all the *Chreasters* took over and there was nowhere else to sit.

The sound booth looked like a room trapped in time. The walls were lined with brown metal shelving units and stocked with old microphones, reel-to-reel tape recorders, and other equipment that looked like it hadn't been used in decades. I walked toward the soundproof window and looked down into the sanctuary. I stared at the enormous wooden cross that hung on the wall behind the pulpit.

When I was little, my mom used to work in the office a few days a week. She'd bring me with her, and I'd sneak up to the sound booth to watch my dad preach during Monday Chapel. I remember thinking my dad looked different from that vantage point. More important.

I'd hung on his every word, even back then. Everyone had. If he'd stood on that stage and told us the sky was purple, not blue, we all would have walked outside and seen the sky through entirely new lenses. But over the last few years, that changed, and not only for me. I wasn't sure if it was because of the drop in enrollment or the novelty of Dad's contemporary approach had worn off, but there had been a shift that rippled throughout the community. He'd disappointed them. I'd felt it. Dad had felt it, too.

"Here." Aaron patted the stool next to him. "Have a seat. I want to show you something."

He angled the computer monitor so I could see it better, and I immediately recognized the SonRise website. Aaron redesigned it right after he arrived. The whole thing was heavy on images, light on words, and looked more like the website of an indie rock band than a Christian a cappella group. Our most recent YouTube videos were embedded in slick-looking frames, along with black-and-white photo stills from our past performances and links to download our music.

"I've been working on the promo videos."

He clicked the mouse and an image filled the screen. In it, the sanctuary was completely packed with kids, all holding hands, lifting them up to the sky. I'd never seen that picture, but it couldn't have been new; the sanctuary hadn't been that full in years. The caption read: *We will tell the next generation about the glorious deeds of the Lord. —Psalm 78:4.*

"This is a lot like the ads Covenant has run in the past," Aaron said. "It's designed to attract the typical Christian kid in the Orange County area who's looking for a great college-prep, Jesus-centered high school."

Then he opened another window, and a familiar black-and-white photo of SonRise filled his monitor. Logan was looking at the camera, expressionless; Alyssa was half smiling at something outside the frame; and Jack and I were looking at each other. We took these professional shots right after we won the Northern Lights competition my freshman year. I kind of thought we looked like a cheesy early-eighties band, but everyone seemed to love this shot. Unlike the other ad, everything about it looked hipper and less churchy. The text read: *Find your voice. Sing your song.* There wasn't a cross to be found.

"This new one is designed to target kids interested in the arts." He clicked the mouse and a video opened. "I was up all night working on this, so if you don't like it, lie to me, would you?"

He smiled.

I didn't want to smile back, but I didn't know how not to. It was one thing to glare at him from a distance, avoid eye contact while he was directing us, and speak to him in clipped sentences, but it would have been rude to do any of those things when he was sitting right next to me.

"Just kidding. I genuinely want to know what you think."

The video started with a slow camera pan across the campus. Then it zoomed in on a bunch of kids in classrooms, hanging out in the quad during lunch, and working together in the library. Aaron did the voice-over instead of Dad, and rather than describing the idyllic campus tucked into a hillside where you could hear God's voice in the trees, he called it a place for quiet reflection and soul-searching.

And then the video moved into new territory I'd never seen before: SonRise performing in competitions, and to a packed house during the Christmas musical. There were still images of the four of us goofing around on the tour bus, and the four of us practicing, and the four of us teaching kids to sing during our summer mission trips. Aaron's voice faded away and SonRise took over, singing the mainstream songs we always sang. It moved on to footage from the dance and drama department performances, and ended with the date and time of Admissions Night, sprawled in big letters across the screen.

"Wow," I said. "It's good. It's really good."

"Are you just saying that because I told you to lie? Because you know I was kidding about that, right?"

"No, it's really good. I mean it."

He was watching me like he was trying to figure me out. "You look . . . kinda puzzled."

I was. I remembered him running around campus shooting that video over the last two weeks, before I'd known the story about how he'd been hired, and thinking how lucky we were to have him. He worked hard for my dad and for our school. As mad as I was about losing my tuition, that part was hard to ignore.

"I'm just wondering how you made this so quickly?"

"Well, for one, it's my job." He started listing the reasons using his fingers. "Two, your dad, my boss, wants all the videos done by Friday so we can send them around to the local churches and ask them to play them during Sunday services. And three." He stopped. "Never mind. Three's not important."

I gave him a look. "What's three?"

"You don't want to know."

"Well, I didn't really care much before, but I do now," I joked.

His mouth turned up at the corners.

"Fine. Three. I have no life. After you guys leave for the day I come up to this pathetic man-cave and spend hours alone up here. If it wasn't for that mini fridge over there, I might starve or die of thirst. I work until midnight, go home and sleep, and come back and start into it again. How do you think I redesigned the entire SonRise site in, like, four days?"

"Well, I like it. And I'm not just saying that because you don't have a life and I feel sorry for you." I looked at him. "It's good."

"You think?"

"Yeah," I said. But he must have heard the inflection in my voice, because his eyebrows pinched together as he looked at me.

"But?" Aaron asked.

"No," I said. "No *but*."

"I thought I heard a *but*."

"It's nothing." I hesitated to say anything. I knew he was following Dad's direction, going after the theater and dance kids exactly the way he was supposed to. "Both videos are inspiring and all, but I guess I'm wondering how you're going to reach everyone else."

"What do you mean?"

"Well, you've got your churchy people and you've got your Hollywood wannabes, but that's a pretty small portion of the students here. Think about what my dad said during chapel today. Most of the kids that came here as freshmen felt . . . lost in some way. Something was missing from their lives, and the people at Covenant filled the gap. We became the friend group they couldn't find or the family that splintered apart. Lots of the kids here are the ones who didn't feel like they had anywhere else to go."

"And neither one of these videos is reaching out to them."

"Not really."

Aaron crossed his arms and studied the screen.

"Sorry," I said. "I don't want to be critical. I know how hard you've worked."

He shook his head. "Not at all. This is good." He grabbed the can of Coke sitting next to his keyboard and took a big sip. "So how do we get to the others?"

"I don't know." I rolled my eyes. "That's why they pay you the big bucks."

I felt the anger rise into my chest again, and I wanted to

kick myself for forgetting I was mad at him. For a minute there, I'd been acting the way I'd always acted around Aaron. But everything with him was different now that I knew what Dad had done. I stood and reached for my backpack.

Aaron set his Coke down and adjusted his cap on his head, his gaze still fixed on the monitor. "I'll make a third one," he blurted.

"How? I thought everything had to be done by Friday."

"No life, remember?" He raised an eyebrow. "The filming and editing aren't the problem. I just need an idea and script."

The room got quiet again. Was he was waiting for me to come up with something? Because if that was the case, he was sadly mistaken. In a roundabout way, I'd paid his salary. I wasn't about to do his job for him, too.

But then one of the photos on the monitor caught my eye. It was a picture of Kaitlyn Caziarti, standing at the pulpit, sharing her testimony.

Kaitlyn had transferred a few months into her junior year after she was the subject of a vicious rumor that spread around her old high school. She didn't share the details, but she talked about how hard those months had been, when no one believed her side of the story, not even the friends she'd known since elementary school. Her parents kept telling her it would die down, but when it only got worse, they finally agreed to let her change schools.

She talked about how everyone at Covenant had been so kind and inclusive, welcoming her right away, treating her like she belonged there. I remembered cynically thinking that I'd seen plenty of vicious rumors spread across our campus, too, and that she probably shouldn't let her guard down so completely. But then I'd glanced over at Dad, beaming as if he was proud of the world he'd built for her.

In the car on the way home that day, he'd told me that Kaitlyn, and all the kids like her, were the reason he accepted the job of running Covenant all those years ago. "They need us," he'd said matter-of-factly. "I'll do whatever it takes to make sure this school is always around for them." I'd admired him for that.

Now I felt a pang of guilt for being so angry at him. He was still that same person. Even if I disagreed with his methods, his heart was in the right place. His heart was *always* in the right place.

"Have you seen a testimonial since you came to Covenant?" I asked Aaron.

"Not yet. Why?"

"People give them during Monday Chapel sometimes. They talk about their lives before they came here. The mistakes they made. The bad things that happened to them. They talk about how Covenant helped them turn their lives around. They always remind me what I love about this place. Maybe you could get a few of them to let you interview them on camera. You could piece the stories together, add in some music. I bet it would be really powerful."

Aaron took his cap off and combed his fingers through his hair. "I like it. That could have real viral reach, too. People love personal stories."

"Exactly."

"Would you help me?" Aaron asked.

"Me?" No, I thought, wishing I'd left the room when I had a chance and wondering why I'd brought up the testimonial thing in the first place.

"Sure. Maybe you could ask them. You could even do the interviews, if you wanted to. Everyone knows you. They'd do anything for you."

"Hardly," I huffed. "They'd do anything for my dad."

"Same thing."

I narrowed my eyes at him. "We're not the same person."

His expression changed. "I'm sorry. I meant it as a compliment." He rested his hands on his knees and leaned toward me. "What do you think? Do you want to work on it together?"

I stared at him, reminding myself that none of this was his fault. Aaron probably had no idea where Dad found the money to hire him. But that didn't make me want to help him.

Still, the money was gone. What was done was done. Now I needed to get away from this place more than ever, and the only way I could get to BU was to make sure that sanctuary was standing-room-only on Admissions Night.

Anything I could do to help him would help me, too.

"Okay." It came out more like a reluctant sigh than a two-syllable word, but Aaron's face lit up anyway.

"Awesome." He bumped my shoulder with his. "This will be fun, I promise."

Emory

Day 277, 160 to go

"Now, remember, this is the first time we see George and Emily interact," Ms. Martin said from her spot in the first row of the theater.

I tightened my grip on the script rolled up in my hand.

"This scene is important because it sets up their friendship. We, the audience, need to feel the two of you connect on that stage in the same way you do in real life, right?" She gave each of us an encouraging nod. "Emory, tell Tyler something you think he and his character, George, have in common in this scene."

I didn't hesitate. "They both suck at math."

"Fact," Tyler said. The rest of the cast chuckled from their spots offstage.

"How about you, Tyler?" Ms. Martin said. "Name a trait of Emily Webb's that you also see in Emory in this scene."

I couldn't imagine what he'd say. Aside from the fact that

55

our names were almost identical, I didn't feel like I had any-thing in common with the character I was portraying.

Tyler locked his eyes on mine. "Emily Webb is sweet and pure and everything—"

"Yep, that's me," I interjected. Everyone laughed.

"But she's also a straight shooter," Tyler continued. "She says what she thinks. You know where you stand with her. She's not just being nice to George in this scene because he compliments her. She genuinely likes him. He makes her laugh. And she probably also finds him ridiculously good-looking." Tyler waggled his eyebrows and I laughed.

"Man, that was deep. Now I feel bad that I only said you sucked at math."

Ms. Martin took her seat and leaned forward with her elbows on her knees. "Okay, good. Let's go."

Tyler shook out his hands and cleared his throat, and I tipped my head to my chest, feeling the stretch all the way down my back.

We looked at each other.

"Hello, Emily," Tyler said.

"Hello, George." I rocked back on my heels.

"You made a fine speech in class."

I cocked my head to one side as I delivered my next line. And then Tyler gestured toward one of the two tall wooden platforms behind us and told me he could see me from his bedroom window, doing homework at my desk each night.

"Do you think we could set up some kind of . . . telegraph thing, from your window to mine?" he asked. "And whenever I get stuck on an algebra problem or something I could look over to you for, like, hints."

I furrowed my brow, like I was about to object, so he jumped back in. "I don't mean the answers, Emily, of course not . . . just some little hints."

Suddenly, I heard my phone chirp. I ignored it and kept going.

"Oh, I think *hints* are allowed," I said.

Chirp.

"So, yeah . . . um . . . if you get stuck, George, you whistle to me. And I'll give you some hints."

Chirp.

"Shit," I said under my breath as I slapped my script against my leg.

"Okay, this is ridiculous. Whose phone is that?" Ms. Martin was on her feet with her hands on her hips.

"Mine," I mumbled. "Sorry. I forgot to turn it off."

Chirp.

"Well, go do that, please. We'll wait."

I dropped my script on my chair and hurried over to my backpack. I dug around inside, pushing wrappers and pens and scraps of paper out of the way, searching for the phone before it chirped again. When I finally found it, I silenced the ringer and read the screen:

Mom: CHECK YOUR EMAIL!!!

I tapped the envelope icon. The message was right on top:

FROM: UCLA Drama Department
SUBJECT: Invitation to Audition

I read the message quickly, trying not to burst, and then read it again, taking in the information that time. I was typing out a quick text to my mom when Ms. Martin yelled, "Whatever's happening over there isn't as important as this scene, Ms. Kern!"

I stood and waved my phone in the air. "I got an audition from UCLA!"

Within seconds, I was surrounded. Ms. Martin even left her seat and climbed the stairs to join the cast in congratulating me. Charlotte tackle-hugged me from behind and screamed, "I told you!" right into my ear. Tyler wrapped his arm around my neck, pulled me in close, and gave me a noogie. "Badass," he said.

"Not until I get in," I said, wiggling out of his grasp.

"You'll get in," Charlotte said.

After a few minutes, everyone returned to their spots, but Tyler and Charlotte stuck around to read the whole email.

"You have two choices of audition times," Charlotte said. "This Friday or next Wednesday."

"This Friday," Tyler said. "Get it over with."

"I can't," I said. "My mom can't take me. She has a big catering job in the city."

"Can Luke go with you?" Charlotte asked.

"No, he has an away game."

Tyler looked at Charlotte. "We'll take you."

"Yes!" she said. "I love a good road trip."

I laughed. "It's hardly a road trip. UCLA is forty-five minutes away."

"Not with traffic," she said. "It will take over an hour to get there and at least another hour just to get off the freeway in Westwood. Trust me. It's a road trip. I'll bring snacks."

"Go on Friday," Tyler added. "There's plenty of time to rehearse on the way."

"Hey, you three!" Ms. Martin called. We all looked up. Everyone was standing there, staring at us. "Do not get senioritis on me. You all still belong to me until the curtain falls on *Our Town*. Back to work."

We scrambled back to our stage marks.

"Okay," Ms. Martin yelled. "Let's take it from the top. No scripts this time."

I was beaming. I couldn't wait until rehearsal ended so I could tell Luke.

Tyler shook out his hands. I rocked my head from side to side. And then we looked up at each other.

"Hi, Emily."

"Hi, George."

Tyler pulled up to the red light and stopped. As we sat there waiting for it to change, he slammed his hand on the steering wheel and yelled, "Question!" Charlotte and I both jumped. "If you could trade places with anyone for one month, who would you choose?"

It was Tyler's thing: the Question Game. We'd been playing it forever, usually late at the diner over coffee and cheesecake. Tyler asked the questions, and Charlotte and I had to answer as fast as we could. We couldn't provide any explanation or ask for details, and if we took too long to answer, duplicated each other, or said something Tyler thought was lame, we had to sing a song from a popular musical. Neither of us could even remotely carry a tune, so we tried hard not to blow it. Tyler was the only one who really understood the rules, and they were subject to change without notice.

"You actually abhor silence, don't you?" I asked.

"I do. Can't stand it. Trading places. Go."

"Michelle Obama," I said.

"Ellen DeGeneres," Charlotte said.

"Michael Jackson," Tyler said. "When he was alive."

Charlotte shot him a questioning look. I knew she was dying to say something, but she didn't want to sing.

"Next question. Money is no object. You can live anywhere in the world for one month. Where do you go?"

"India," Charlotte said.

"More specific," Tyler told her.

"Mumbai."

"New York City," I said.

"Durham, Indiana," he said.

Charlotte looked over her shoulder at me, and I rolled my eyes.

Tyler turned onto the road that led to Charlotte and Luke's street. Their neighborhood looked nothing like mine. Lots of mature trees and huge houses with long driveways and little lights evenly spaced in the landscaping. Mine was a lot flatter, with less greenery, more sidewalks, and busier intersections.

Two blocks later, he turned right and gunned it up Luke's steep, narrow driveway. He came to a stop behind Mrs. Calletti's silver BMW and put the car in park. "Hey, can we come to Calletti Spaghetti tonight?"

On Tuesday nights, I went to Luke's house for their weekly family dinner. Attendance was never optional for Luke and Addison, so at the beginning of the school year, when his mom asked if I wanted to join them, I made it a priority, too. It made me feel like part of the family.

"No."

"Why not? I'm a great conversationalist. I'm especially good with parents."

"Goodnight. Thanks for the ride." I got out, closed the door behind me, and waved them off.

Luke's house looked as welcoming on the outside as it did on the inside, with lots of windows and white painted shutters framing each one. I stepped onto the walkway, tiny pebbles crunching under my feet as I followed the path that led to the front door.

"Hello!" I yelled as I stepped inside. I didn't have to knock anymore. The Callettis' house was practically my second home. Kind of like Hannah's house used to be.

I dropped my backpack in the entryway and followed the smell of tomato sauce. I walked through the living room, past the walls lined with Calletti family photos taken over the years. Luke and Addison as babies in matching outfits. Luke and Addison as little kids, standing in front of a waterfall during some family camping trip. Mr. and Mrs. Calletti on their wedding day. The whole family on the beach in jeans, starched white shirts, and bare feet.

"There you are!" Mrs. Calletti was standing at the stove holding a wooden spoon and stirring something in a big orange stockpot. She wiped her hands on a black apron with white bubble letters that read SHIITAKE HAPPENS.

Addison was sitting on a barstool at the kitchen island typing on her phone, and Luke was slicing through a loaf of French bread.

"You can help Luke slice," she said, using her spoon to point at him. "And, Addison, help your dad set the table please, and don't say 'one sec' again. How was rehearsal?"

It took me a moment to realize she was talking to me. "Good," I said. "Actually, really good. I have news."

Mrs. Calletti stopped stirring. Addison stopped typing. Luke stopped slicing. And Mr. Calletti, who was reaching into the silverware drawer, stopped cold.

"I've got an audition at UCLA."

"Told you!" Luke's dad crossed the kitchen and high-fived me. His mom yelled, "I knew you would!"

Luke dropped the knife on the counter and hugged me. "See. You've been all worried for nothing."

"What do you have to do for your audition piece?" Addison asked as she opened the cupboard and removed five water glasses.

"Heather from *The Blair Witch Project* and Phoebe from Shakespeare's *As You Like It*."

"Okay, I've gotta see you do Heather," Addison said. "Just give us a few lines."

I hadn't thought about Heather in over a month, but I suddenly had a crystal-clear vision of her in my mind, with her gray wool cap and those big brown eyes. I stepped away from Luke and got into character, speeding up my breathing and feeling my limbs begin to tremble.

"It's all because of me that we're here now . . . hungry, and cold, and hunted." I let each of the words linger in the air for a moment before I said the next one. "I love you, Mom. And Dad. I am so sorry." I paused, panting and shaking. I squeezed my eyes shut, and then I opened them wider. "What was that?" I whispered. I waited for a long time, listening. And then I continued. "I'm scared to close my eyes and I'm scared to open them. I'm going to die out here."

I bowed while all four of them cheered. Mr. Calletti even let out a "Woot-woot," and that made me laugh.

"Seriously, that's the most I've thought about that scene in over a month!" I said. "I've spent all my time trying to get my lines for Emily Webb down—she has this long monologue in Act Three, and I can't seem to get it to stick." I sliced the last piece of bread and tossed the pieces into a bright orange bowl. "I'm supposed to be off book by the end of this week, but I'm far from it."

"Well, I think you're going to kill it," Mrs. Calletti said as she picked up the pot of sauce, dumped it over the spaghetti

63

noodles, and stirred it all together. "Grab the bread, would you, Luke?" she asked over her shoulder as she headed for the dining room.

As soon as we were alone, Luke wrapped his arms around my waist and kissed me behind my ear. "Damn, that was hot."

"How is being lost in the woods and chased by a witch *hot*?"

"I don't know, but it definitely is. Need me to run lines with you in my room after dinner?"

I wrapped my arms around his neck. "I'd love that."

"I'll get you off book," he said suggestively, and I buried my face in his neck and kissed him.

"Oh, will you now?"

I was still laughing as I pulled my phone from my pocket and wrote it down next to Day 277.

Hannah

"I'm going for a run," I called as I flew past the kitchen.

"Dinner's almost ready," Mom called out.

"I'll make it a quick one."

"Wait a sec," Mom said.

I didn't want to wait a sec, I wanted to get outside. I'd been thinking about my run all afternoon. A crisp breeze had blown all the thick smog away, and the air smelled clean and new. I was itching to feel my feet against the pavement, to fill my lungs with air that hadn't been trapped between walls all day.

I stopped anyway.

"Will you do me a quick favor when you get back?" She wiped her hands on the towel draped over her shoulder. "I'm putting my youth-group mission-trip presentation together for Admissions Night, and I want to include some pictures from your trip to Guatemala last year. Would you send me a few of your favorites?"

"Sure."

I waited for Mom to return to the kitchen, and when she didn't, I knew she hadn't stopped me to ask for pictures. I shifted in place, feeling antsy.

"Have you given any more thought to going?" she asked.

Ah. There it was.

"That trip is for high school students, Mom. This summer, I will no longer be a high school student. Remember?"

"You'd go as a junior counselor. Since we don't have a full-time coordinator this year, we need as many older volunteers as possible."

"I've done that trip four years in a row."

She leaned against the wall and folded her arms across her chest. "I know, but . . . this trip is kind of our thing. And, it's just . . . I guess I didn't realize the last time was the *last* time."

Mom had been doing this off and on since my early acceptance letter to BU arrived. "This is the last time we'll make valentines for the Sunday school kids together" and "This is the last time I'll turn the milk green for Saint Patrick's Day." Every *This is the last time* statement seemed to be followed by Mom leaving the room to find a tissue.

I wondered if part of her was secretly hoping they couldn't afford to send me to BU so there wouldn't be any more last times.

"I'll go again, Mom, just not this summer." I was hoping she wouldn't get all emotional. I really wanted to go for a run.

"Actually, I was also thinking about Emory."

"Emory?" That got my attention. "Why?"

Mom got this dreamy look on her face. "Remember how the two of you got up early every morning and played soccer with the local kids? She seemed to love being there. She really seemed to connect with the Lord on those trips."

She didn't "connect with the Lord." She loved those trips because they were the least churchy things my family had ever forced her to do.

"Besides, it seems like she really needs it." Mom added it like it was an afterthought, but I knew it wasn't.

"What makes you say that?"

"I had a long talk with Jennifer yesterday," she said.

My heart started pounding hard. Had Emory finally told her mom what happened?

"What did she say?" I asked.

"Nothing specific. We're both just worried about you two. You've fought before, plenty of times, but not like this. Never for this long."

I reached for my cross pendant and twisted it in my fingers.

"Please tell me why you two are in a fight."

She knew what Dad had said. She didn't know that Emory had overheard him, but that wasn't what our fight was about, not really. I wanted to tell her everything else. For the six millionth time in the last three months, I wanted to tell her, but I couldn't. I swore I wouldn't.

"Please, talk to me."

Mom was pressing this subject more than usual, and I wasn't sure why, but I knew what came next. She had this way of creeping inside my mind, breaking down the wall I'd so strategically built around it, and making me say things I promised myself I'd never say.

I bit down hard on my lip and shook my head. "I don't want to talk about it."

"But you always tell me everything, Hannah. Please. You can trust me."

I held my breath and told myself to keep the words inside, locked away where they belonged. I couldn't tell Mom. She'd go straight to Emory's mom. And Emory would hate me forever for betraying her.

I needed to get out of there, fast.

"This is between Emory and me." In hopes of killing the conversation, I added, "And Jesus." Mom didn't say anything else, but I could feel her eyes on me as I opened the front door.

As soon as I reached the bottom of the steps, I took off running. I hung a right and rounded the corner, heading in the opposite direction of Foothill High School. It was after six thirty. I couldn't risk crossing paths with Emory on her way home from rehearsal.

Later that night, I opened my laptop and started making a list of some of my favorite testimonials.

There was Kevin Anderson, whose parents were semi-famous and had split up in an ugly and very public divorce, and Bailee Parnell, who had to change schools after she was caught doing drugs in the girls' bathroom during her sophomore year. Skylar Bagatti had been struggling with anxiety and depression since she was eight. And then there was Kaitlyn and the mysterious rumor.

I remembered each one of them standing at the podium on the stage, telling their stories, and thinking they weren't immune to gossip, just because they were here. But I also remembered how my eyes drifted over to my dad as they spoke. He looked proud. And I was reminded that, for all Covenant's imperfections, he had created something unique.

There were plenty of stories like theirs, but four seemed like a solid number to start with. I sent individual texts to each one, explaining the video project and asking them to meet us the next day at lunch at the Grove, a small area at the edge of campus that was surrounded by trees. Within twenty minutes, they had all replied yes.

I looked at the string of responses, feeling a little better. I had no idea if any of it would help, but it least it felt like I was doing *something*. Which seemed like a lot more than Dad was doing.

Emory
Day 278, 159 to go

"Ow!" I shot Charlotte a look in the full-length mirror as I twisted out of her grasp.

"Hold still. You're going to mess me up." Charlotte pulled another chunk of my hair into her hands, wrapped it around another piece, and pinned it into place.

"Don't make it look too fancy," I said. "I'm going to a lacrosse game, not the prom."

"Trust me. This one's complicated, but it will look totally casual when I'm done." She pulled at one section and started braiding it. "Ooh . . . wait." She stopped. "Want me to weave some green-and-white ribbon in as I go?"

"God, no."

"Why not?"

"Um, maybe because I'm not six years old."

She stared at me with wide, exaggerated eyes. "Well, someone is certainly lacking school spirit."

"Seriously?" I pointed at the gigantic white number thirty-four on my chest. That alone seemed like more than enough school spirit for one person.

Charlotte went back to braiding, and when she reached the end, she handed me her compact. "Take a look."

I spun in place, turning my back to the full-length mirror. "Wow. Sorry I ever doubted you."

Charlotte was messing with another loose piece when there was a knock at the door.

"Come in." I expected it to be Mom. I turned around and started to ask what she was doing home so early, but I saw David standing there instead. "Oh . . . Hi."

"Hey." He folded his arms across his chest in that buff-dude way, like he was trying to impress us with his bulk. "I just got home from New York."

I squeezed the compact as hard as I could.

"I'm looking for your mom. I heard voices and thought she was in here with you. Hey, Charlotte," he said.

"Hey, David." She said it way too cheerfully.

"Gig in the city. Home at eight." I always answered D-bag with the fewest possible words. He didn't deserve full sentences.

"Oh, okay . . . I didn't realize it was going that late or I would have stopped at my loft on the way home from the airport."

His loft? Pompous dickhead. I squeezed the compact even harder.

"When is her big fund-raiser?" he asked casually. "Is that this Friday?"

He knew the answer. Aside from the wedding, that fund-raiser was practically all Mom had talked about for the last month. Was he actually trying to make polite conversation?

"Mm-hmm," I mumbled.

"Good. I wanted to be sure I was going to be in town. She's planning to stay at my place afterward." He leaned against the doorframe. "Are you heading out?"

"Big lacrosse game at school," Charlotte told him.

"Cool. Well, have fun." He closed the door. I didn't let my breath go until I heard it latch.

"David's so nice," Charlotte said. "I don't understand why you don't like him."

I felt sick to my stomach.

"He's not David to you."

She narrowed her eyes. "You seriously want me to say, 'D-bag is so nice.'"

"Yes, I do, but without the inaccurate 'nice' part."

"You know, he's going to be your stepdad in a few months. You should probably stop calling him D-bag."

"Never." I stared at her in the mirror.

Charlotte stared back at me. "You did catch that, didn't you?" She rested her chin on my shoulder. "Someone's got the whole house to herself on Friday night."

When I arrived at the stadium, all Luke's friends were clustered together in the bleachers, decked out in green-and-white Falcons gear and impossible to miss. I spotted Mr. and Mrs. Calletti right away, and they waved. Aside from their group and a few other parents scattered around, the bleachers were fairly empty.

"Where is everyone?" I asked Addison.

"It's California lacrosse, not Texas football."

As soon as I sat down, Lara leaned forward. "Oh my God! Your hair looks amazing. Did you do that by yourself?"

"Nope, all Charlotte." I pulled my phone from my back pocket and clicked on her Instagram account. "You should check out her stuff. Her tutorials are really easy to follow." I handed my phone to Lara. She watched, and then passed it around so everyone could see.

And then I unzipped my sweater, showing off what I'd done to Luke's jersey.

A professional seamstress had been at the theater earlier that day, altering the costumes for *Our Town*. I showed her Luke's jersey and asked her if she could do anything to fix it, and her eyes lit up. "Give me fifteen minutes," she'd said. I watched her cut the whole thing along each side and sew it back together, transforming it into a cute, form-fitting dress.

"I want to do that to Dominic's!" Ava said. She'd tied the bottom of his jersey on one side, at her hip.

"Come by the theater during lunch or after school. The sewing machine is all set up. I'll do it for you."

The horn blew and the announcer's voice came over the loudspeaker.

"I don't think I'll ever understand this game," I admitted as the two teams ran onto the field.

"It's like ice hockey," Addison said.

"Yeah, I don't have a clue about ice hockey." She looked at me like I just told her I had eleven toes. "What? I don't have a sporty family like you do."

My parents never watched sports when I was growing up. I couldn't remember a single time my dad threw me a ball or even tossed me a Frisbee. But apparently, things had changed, because when I went to visit him and his replacement family last summer, he took us all to a Chicago Cubs game. They had season tickets and everyone was totally into it. I didn't know when to cheer, so I just sat there nursing a Coke and working on my tan.

Addison pointed straight down at the white line that cut the field in half. "Okay, stay with me. There's Luke. He's a midfielder, so he and two other guys on the line can run the whole length of the field."

She pointed to the three players on the far right. "Those are the attackmen. They stay close to the cage and try to score."

And then she pointed to the left, and I followed her finger. "The three defenders stay down there with the goalie and try to stop the other team. All the players use those sticks to pass that little white ball around and beat the crap out of whichever guy has it." She looked back at me to be sure I was keeping up. "That's pretty much all there is to it. Next week I'll make Luke take you to one of my games and explain how women's lacrosse is played. It's totally different."

"Why?"

"There's no contact. I used to play men's lacrosse so I could smack people, too, but then the guys got a lot bigger and my parents decided it was too dangerous."

The horn blew again, and her head whipped back to the center of the field. Dominic Murphy and some other guy were crouched low on the ground, staring at each other.

"That's called the face-off," she said. Then she cupped her hands to her mouth and screamed, "That's yours, Murph!"

I stayed quiet, watching the game, taking it in. At first, I mostly watched Luke, but after a while I tried to follow the ball instead. When Luke finally got it, and started sprinting toward the Falcons' goal, I found myself leaning forward just like Addison did, craning my neck to see what was happening, unable to take my eyes off the action. He pulled his stick back and swung it toward the goal, and the ball slammed hard into the upper right corner of the net. Everyone in our section jumped up, clapping and screaming as the announcer called out, "First goal for the Falcons by senior Luke Calletti, number thirty-four!"

As Luke was running back to the white line, he looked up at the stands and when he saw me, he gave me a little wave. I waved back. And then I yelled, "Go Luke!" louder than anyone else.

By halftime, I was completely into it, yelling along, jumping to my feet every time we scored, and covering my mouth when any of the guys took a hard hit. Luke got another goal in the third quarter. And he had three assists, which sounded like a big deal when Addison explained it to me.

When the game ended, we gathered our stuff and I put my sweater on. Addison started to say something, but then she looked past me, over my shoulder, and said, "Oh, hey!"

I turned around and saw Luke's parents. Mrs. Calletti gave

me a fist bump and said, "Well, it looks like you survived your first lacrosse game. What did you think?" Her dark hair was peeking out from under her Falcons cap, and she was wearing one of Luke's jerseys, too.

"I loved it," I said. "But I had no idea how hard they hit each other!"

"Just wait until next year," Mr. Calletti said. "That was nothing."

His comment didn't register right away. Not until I took in his outfit. He was decked out in Denver gear. Denver cap. Denver jersey.

I was at a loss for words, so I made a joke instead. "Is there anything you didn't buy?"

"Nope." He lifted his pant leg to show off his Denver socks.

Luke's dad was beaming at me, eyes full of pride, and I tried to match his expression, but out of nowhere, it had hit me. I'd never wear Luke's Denver jersey. At some point in the not-too-distant future, some other girl probably would, but it wouldn't be me. My throat tightened. I bit the inside of my cheek, pushing the emotions back down where they belonged.

Addison must have been able to tell I was upset because she took one look at my face and changed the subject. "We'd better go. Everyone's heading to the diner."

But I didn't want to go to the diner. Not yet. I gestured in the opposite direction. "I'll meet you there in a few minutes. I need to grab something from the theater."

I hugged Mrs. Calletti, and then Mr. Calletti, and waved good-bye before any of them could question me or offer to come along. I followed the walkway that led from the stadium to the theater in a daze, and I when I arrived at the backstage door, I was relieved to find that the janitor hadn't locked it yet.

I slipped inside, walked straight to the stage, and sat down on the edge with my feet dangling over the side. I looked around, taking in the room. The aisle lights were still on, casting a glow on the dark red velvet seats, and I inhaled the scent of old wood and damp towels. They say our sense of smell is most closely linked with memory, and I believed it. I already knew that any remotely similar scent would forever bring me right back to this room.

It was almost over. All of it, and all at once. High school. Performing on that stage. My relationship with Luke. Mom and me, and our family of two. It was bad enough that I'd already lost Hannah. Soon, the rest of it would be gone along with her.

I looked down at Luke's jersey-dress, staring at the number thirty-four, thinking about the end of us, and feeling this uncomfortable tightness in my chest. But I couldn't remember the last time I'd cried, and I wasn't about to do it now. Not yet. There were still 159 days until we were officially broken up. Still, I wasn't sure how I was going to keep it down that long.

As I sat there in the silence, I realized what I had to do.

I stood and left the theater, stepping into the cold night air, walking to the diner with a determined stride and rehearsing what I was going to say to Luke when I saw him. But when I got to the parking lot, I couldn't go in.

I could see everyone through the window. Luke and his teammates must have just arrived, because they were still standing in clusters, taking off their jackets, trying to figure out where everyone was going to sit. By contrast, on the opposite side of the restaurant, I saw Charlotte, Tyler, and the rest of my drama friends, looking like they'd been there for hours. They were smashed into one booth, even though they probably would have been more comfortable divided up into two. The table was littered with empty plates, dirty forks, crumpled-up napkins, and half-empty glasses.

There was a little flower garden overlooking the parking lot, complete with flamingos and garden gnomes, and it cheered me up a little bit. I sat on the curb and took a few deep breaths, clearing my head. I was about to make my move when my phone buzzed.

I checked the screen.

Luke: Where are you?!?

I typed back.

Emory: Outside

I stood and watched him spin a slow three-sixty, trying to figure out where I was. When he finally spotted me, he furrowed his brow and held up a hand.

I held mine up, too.

"You okay?" he mouthed.

I shrugged.

And then he held up a finger, as if to say, "Wait there," and I watched him pocket his phone and leave. I returned to my spot on the curb and waited for him to round the corner.

"Hey." He sat next to me.

"Hi." I scooted closer to him until our hips were touching and rested my arm on his leg. I looked up at him. "You were amazing tonight. I can't believe how fast you were out there. Seriously, I had no idea that would be so fun."

"Addison said she explained the game to you."

I smiled. "She's an excellent teacher. I've got it down now, so if you need me to explain it to you or anything . . ."

He smiled back. "I'll keep that in mind." Then he bumped his shoulder against mine. "Stop making small talk. What's up?"

"With me?" I asked.

"No, with that garden gnome behind you," he said. "Yes, with you."

"Nothing." The word caught in my throat. I didn't want to talk about it. We *couldn't* talk about it. We'd promised each other that we wouldn't even *think* about it until we were packing our respective bedrooms into boxes and taking trips with our moms to buy new sheets and storage cubbies for our dorm rooms. August was five months away. We were supposed to be making the most of our time together, and that meant ignoring the inevitable end.

Luke looked at me.

"I guess it's just all hitting me, you know?" I finally said.

I could practically hear the clock ticking in my head and see the second hand speeding up. I bit the inside of my lower lip until it hurt. And finally, I said what I'd been thinking ever since I saw that wedding dress on my table a few days earlier. "I've just been wondering if, maybe . . . we're making this whole thing harder on ourselves than it needs to be, you know?"

Luke made a face. "No. I don't know."

"Do you think we should break up?" I spat the words out as fast as I could before I changed my mind.

Luke started laughing, but when he realized I hadn't even cracked a smile, he stopped cold. "No. Why would we break up?"

"You're going to Denver. If I'm lucky, I'll be at UCLA, and if I'm not, I'll be at some other California school. But I'll be here. And you won't be. You'll be living a thousand miles away from me."

"In five months."

"But it's inevitable." I massaged the back of my neck.

"So, you're saying you want to break up *now*, because it's only going to get harder to break up later? You know that's ridiculous, right?"

The way he said it, the expression on his face, everything about that moment made my heart feel like it was being squeezed in a vise.

"We could try long distance," he said, as if he'd been thinking about it, and I smiled at him, because it was a sweet thing for him to say, and even sweeter because I could tell he meant it. But we'd already talked about that.

"No, we can't." My parents started dating in high school, and they stayed together, even when they went to colleges on opposite sides of the country. Mom never said she regretted it, but I'd always wondered if she had. Either way, it didn't work out so well for the two of them, and I wasn't about to go down the same path. "That's too much pressure. You're going to meet new people and I'm going to meet new people. . . . It isn't fair to do that to each other."

"And spending the next five months apart is?"

I reached down for a pebble and played with it. "Maybe."

"Well, I disagree." He shook his head dismissively. "I think this—*us*—is all worth it, and I'm not giving up a single day because if I do, I know I'll regret it when it's over."

When. I felt that squeeze on my heart again, tight and painful, like someone gave the vise another crank or two.

"Think about it this way," he continued. "Years from now, when you look back, will you regret this?"

I pictured a future me, thinking back to my senior year at Foothill High School. I'd remember my friends, and the diner, and all the time I spent in the theater, but I had a feeling that the first image that popped into my head would be of Luke. I'd remember Calletti Spaghetti with his family, and the two of us going to the movies, and doing homework in his room, and him sneaking in my window. I'd remember this night, going to his first lacrosse game, and I'd remember the parties I always dreaded but, in the end, never really minded that much. And all I could think was, I'm so in love with this guy. Crazy, giddy, stupid, silly in love with this guy.

"Never," I said.

"See? Neither will I."

His words were perfect. *He* was perfect. Aside from Hannah, I couldn't think of anyone else in my life who got me the way he did.

"Say that again. I need an entry for today." Day 278 was still blank.

"I will never regret this." He gave me a small kiss. And then he said, "I know your problem."

"I don't have a problem."

"Sure you do. There are all these events coming up, but each one marks the end of something, right? Prom. Graduation. Your mom's wedding. We need something to look forward to. Something that's just for us."

"Like what?"

He got this weird look in his eyes. "You've never been camping."

I crinkled my nose. "God, no."

"See, that's a problem. You know how much I love camping. I'm going to make that my parting gift to you: I'll turn you into a camper."

"Parting gift? Dude, you're not helping."

"We'll pack up the Jetta and take off. We can drive along the coast—take the slow route." He traced his fingertip in the air like he was visualizing the map. "We'll camp on the beach and hike in the woods. We can sleep under the stars."

Those summer trips to Guatemala with Hannah's church youth group had been my only experience with "roughing it," but at least we had clean floors and bunk beds with actual mattresses. Camping was totally different.

"No, you'll love this. Wait." He reached into his jeans pocket and pulled out a nearly empty roll of Mentos. He handed one to me and popped the last one into his mouth, and then he peeled open the empty wrapper. He used the side of his hand to flatten it against his jeans. "Do you have a pen?"

"Um. No. Maybe ask the garden gnome."

"I'll be right back."

He went into the diner and returned with a pen. He drew a jagged line down the long end of the wrapper and then made a little dot. "We're here in Orange County. All we have to do is drive straight west and pick up PCH." He drew a line from the dot to the Pacific Coast Highway. He drew little waves to indicate the ocean, and then drew another dot on the coast.

"We'll stop here first. There's this great beach in Santa Barbara and you can camp right on the sand. And then from there, we'll head to Big Sur." He made another dot. "It's about a ten-mile hike in, but there are these great hot springs back in the woods."

That actually sounded pretty cool. Maybe even cool enough to make me forget about bugs crawling over us at night and snakes slithering outside the tent.

"And then we'll go to Santa Cruz. We can stop at the boardwalk and ride the roller coasters and play Skee-Ball, and then we'll camp a few miles down the coast in this town called Capitola. I haven't been there since I was a kid, but I've been dying to see it again. My mom has pictures. I'll show you when you come over for dinner next week. There are these little cabins on the beach painted blue and orange and yellow. You'll love it."

"When are we doing this?" I laughed like this was all a big joke, a fun dream, but he looked at me in all seriousness and said, "I don't know. How about the week after your mom's wedding?"

"You're not kidding?"

His eyebrows pinched together. "I don't kid about camping, Em." And then he went right back to his sketch.

I watched him, realizing, maybe for the first time, just how much he loved me. He must, because he somehow *knew* how much I'd need him next summer, and that I was going to need to disappear after the wedding, without me even telling him why.

He kept going, creating little dots and lines, until he drew a star and wrote *SF* underneath. "And if we're not ready to head home once we hit San Francisco, we'll keep going all the way to the Oregon border. We can stretch our little road trip out for at least two weeks or more."

"You're insane."

"Yep." He looked at me. "Prom. Graduation. Road trip." I liked the way he looked at the whole thing: little moments adding up to something bigger, rather than a series of events counting down to the end. "And the best part? It'll just be us. No one else."

I saw the image so clearly in my mind: The two of us driving along the coast with the windows down and the music blaring, my hand resting on his leg and my feet on the dashboard, tapping along with the beat.

I turned my head, taking in the view on the other side of the window. His friends. My friends. We were always surrounded by people, except when Luke climbed a ladder and slipped into my room in the middle of the night.

It reminded me of what Charlotte heard D-bag say in my

room earlier. I'd forgotten all about it, but now I felt my whole face come to life.

"What's that look for?" Luke asked.

"My mom has that big catering gig in the city on Friday. It's going to go late. So late that D-bag happened to mention that she's planning to crash at his apartment afterward."

He smiled. "Really?"

"Really." I pictured Luke walking through the front door. "You won't have to sneak in through the window. And you don't have to leave until morning."

"Can we make pancakes?" he asked.

I started cracking up. "Yes, we can make pancakes."

He kissed me in that way that made the whole world disappear, and for a moment, all that sadness I'd been bottling up began melting away.

Luke pulled away and rested his forehead against mine. "Let me be sure I have this straight. We're going on a road trip, having a sleepover on Friday, and you don't want to break up with me anymore?"

"Not right this second. Ask me again next week."

I started to kiss him again, but he leaned back and shook his head. "Nope. I'm not asking you again. This is your last chance. After this, you're stuck with me until August twentieth." He held out his hand. "Deal?"

I shook it. "Deal."

Hannah

"Wait. You're doing what?" Alyssa asked.

I let out an irritated sigh. "I'm helping Aaron gather a few testimonials for one of the videos he's doing, that's all. It shouldn't take long." I shut my locker door. "I'll meet you in the quad when I'm done."

Apparently, Alyssa was still stuck on the first part of what I'd said. "You're spending lunch with Aaron?"

"Yeah, it's this video for Admissions—"

She cut me off. "I can help. Let me, like, hold the microphone or something."

It didn't seem right to bring anyone else. "These guys might be nervous as it is. I don't want to make it a bigger deal. I'll tell you everything he says, okay?"

"Promise?"

"Promise."

I shut my locker and took off for the Grove. When I arrived, Aaron was already setting up the video camera and Skylar, Kaitlyn, and Kevin were talking with one another at the picnic table. I slid in next to Skylar. Bailee arrived a minute later.

"Thanks for doing this," Aaron began. He explained the video and what he was hoping to get from each one of them. "We're only going to use a small piece of your story, but just talk. Say as much as you want and we'll edit as needed. We don't want you to sound scripted."

The way Aaron said "we" wasn't lost on me. It made me feel good to be part of something that might help the school. And it made me temporarily forget how angry I was about the fact that he was here in the first place.

"I'm going to start rolling," he said, taking his place behind the camera. "This is perfect. Just stay where you are and talk. Hannah will ask the questions."

The five of us spoke while Aaron filmed, and before I knew it, the lunch bell rang. After the others gathered up their stuff and took off for class, I stayed behind and helped Aaron put all the equipment back in his bag.

"You're good at this," Aaron said as he threaded his head through the camera strap and adjusted it across his chest. "You have a way of drawing people out. You let them speak without talking over them, and when they're done, you're right there with the next question, encouraging them to keep going."

"I didn't really think much about it."

"Exactly." He nodded. "You're a natural."

The bell rang.

He tapped the video camera. "Want to help me edit this after school? I'll show you how it's done. Then when you're at BU next year you can start your own investigative journalism show on YouTube. You'll be famous."

"I don't want to be famous." I grinned. That BU part still made me feel like I wanted to punch something. But unlike the day before, I no longer wanted to punch him. "But yeah, I can help," I said. "Why not?"

After school, the sound booth door was locked and Aaron was nowhere in sight, so I waited on the first pew in the balcony, leaning on the railing overlooking the sanctuary and checking my Instagram feed.

I scrolled past a selfie of Alyssa in her bedroom, another of Logan and his dog at the park, and a bunch of posts from all my old friends from middle school, who were now all at Foothill High. And then Emory's face blurred by and my heart started racing. I backed up.

She was standing on the stage in the theater with her arms outstretched at her sides, like she was mid-monologue, delivering important words to a rapt audience. Her hair was piled up on the top of her head and her cheekbones looked even more pronounced than they usually did. She looked beautiful. Then again, it was kind of impossible for her not to.

I was careful not to like the photo. Even though she

probably knew I never stopped following her—just like I knew she hadn't stopped following me—I didn't want to make things more awkward than they already were.

"Hey, sorry I'm late!" I looked up. Aaron was jiggling the key in the bolt. "Staff meeting went long. Come in."

I dropped my backpack next to the shelving unit and followed him.

"Grab a soda from the mini fridge," he said. "I'll get everything set up." Aaron sat on the stool and kept talking. "I imported all the raw footage after lunch and started working on it a bit, cutting out the obvious stuff. Now we need to figure out what to keep." He tapped on an icon and our little lunch in the Grove came to life on the screen. "We're looking for sound bites. We don't need long stories, just short, punchy, grabby sentences." He slid a notebook and a pen over to my side of the desk. "When you hear something you like, mark the time."

Then he pressed PLAY and we sat there, watching and listening, pausing when we heard something interesting and taking note of the time stamp. When we got to Skylar's story, I found myself listening even closer than I had during the others'. It wasn't her story about her struggle with her mental health, it was the other things she'd said in the interview, about how the people at Covenant made her feel welcome, even though she wasn't religious.

When she'd said it in the Grove that day, Bailee had turned to her in disbelief. "You're not a Christian?"

"Nope," Skylar said matter-of-factly. "Never have been."

"What are you?" Kevin had asked.

"Nothing, I guess. Why? Does it matter?"

Everyone looked away from her, shifting positions, and I could tell it was getting uncomfortable. Faith, or rather, lack thereof, was one of the things people at Covenant were especially judgmental about. If Skylar hadn't noticed, it was because people had kept their opinions to themselves, not because they didn't have any.

Now, Aaron laughed under his breath as he paused the tape. "Maybe we cut that part."

I smiled. "Yeah, I doubt Dad would consider that a key recruiting message."

Aaron highlighted that section of the video and pressed the delete button, and Skylar's words were gone, as if they never existed.

"I wonder what that's like." I hadn't meant to say it. I was thinking aloud. I wasn't really looking for an answer, but since Aaron was the only person in the room, he obviously took it that way.

"What, to not be a Christian?"

"No, not just that. Everything. How can you listen to Dad in Monday Chapel, and hear all the things our teachers tell us in class, and not *believe* in any of it?"

"Skylar seems comfortable with the whole thing." Aaron opened a new file and started pulling all the segments we'd flagged into an empty video screen. "I've always been kind of fascinated by what other people believe. Or the fact that they don't believe anything at all. Haven't you?"

I never would have used the word *fascinated*. Curious, maybe, and if I was being totally honest with myself, not even that until recently, when Emory and I got in our fight and she accused me of never having an original thought of my own.

As soon as I let Emory's words in, the rest of them flooded in, too, swirling around in my mind, growing louder and louder. *It's easy to just agree with your dad, isn't it? Why think for yourself when you don't have to?*

My heart started pounding faster.

You have a blind spot when it comes to your dad, Hannah. You'll believe anything he says. Believe anything he believes. When was the last time you had an opinion that was entirely your own?

My stomach knotted into a fist, and I twisted in my seat, trying to loosen it.

You're a fucking sheep.

"You okay?" Aaron asked.

My eyes snapped open, and I realized my hands were pressed into the sides of my head. "Yeah," I said, slowly lowering them.

"Hey. It's okay. Whatever it is."

I nodded, even though it wasn't okay. Nothing she'd said to me that morning was okay.

"Do you want to talk about it?" he asked.

I could feel the blood rising into my chest, past my cheeks, and settling into the tips of my ears. I shook my head, but deep down, I wanted to tell him. I hadn't talked to anyone about what happened between Emory and me that day. Not Mom. Not Alyssa. And even though I couldn't tell him the big reason we'd fought, I was dying to release the words she'd said, because they'd been trapped in my mind for months and sometimes they felt like they were multiplying and preparing to take over.

Aaron twisted on the stool, facing me, and leaned in closer. I stared at him, realizing I wasn't quite as angry with him as I had been earlier that week. After all, I'd known him for months but I'd only been mad at him for a week. And in all fairness, I didn't have much reason to be. He might have been the reason I lost my tuition, but he was still Aaron. I liked him. I trusted him. And I really needed someone to talk to.

"It's about my neighbor, Emory. You don't know her." I glanced around the sound booth to be sure we were alone, even though I already knew we were. "We've lived next door to each other all our lives. We've been best friends since, well, forever. But we got in a fight a couple months ago. It was horrible. And I said something I shouldn't have said, and she said something she shouldn't have said. . . ."

I played with my fingernails nervously. Aaron was watching me, waiting patiently, silently giving me permission to keep going.

"Anyway." I took a deep breath. "What she said to me that day made me start questioning things. My faith mostly. I started seeing my life a little differently. I started hearing my dad differently. And I stopped praying, because . . . well, I don't really know why. It just didn't seem to be doing any good anyway."

The room got silent. I glanced up at him, wishing I hadn't said anything. What was the point? I knew what Aaron was going to say before he opened his mouth. He was going to tell me that prayer works. That I needed it now more than ever.

92

That my faith was my foundation, and all I had to do was believe that God was working on it. I just had to be patient.

Aaron leaned in closer, resting his elbows on his knees. "You know it's okay to question this stuff, right?"

He took me by surprise. "It is?"

"Sure."

Dad wouldn't think any of this was okay. Mom wouldn't think it was okay either.

For we walk by faith, not by sight. —2 *Corinthians 5:7.*

"I don't even know what I'm looking for," I said.

"But I bet you will when you find it."

He smiled at me.

I smiled back.

"Thanks," I said.

"Anytime." He reached for the mouse, returning to our project. "I think the world would be a better place if people stopped every once in a while and questioned everything they thought they knew."

After dinner that night, I was in my room, trying to finish an essay for English class, but I couldn't concentrate. I couldn't stop thinking about what Aaron had said in the sound booth.

I stood and walked over to the window, peeling the curtain to one side, and looked out.

Across the grass, I could see Emory in her bedroom, standing in front of her full-length mirror, talking and pacing and gesturing with her hands, and I could tell she was rehearsing. If things had been different—the way they used to be—I would have been sitting on her bed with my legs folded underneath me, script in hand, reading other characters' lines.

I watched her, thinking back to all the time we'd spent in her room, talking and listening to music, or in my room, curled up on my comforter, binge-watching shows on my laptop. I missed her. I missed her so much it hurt.

I thought back to what she'd said to me the day we fought. *When was the last time you had an opinion that was entirely your own?* And I thought back to what Aaron had said to me in the sound booth earlier. *It's okay to question this stuff.*

"I'm not a sheep," I whispered. The words ricocheted off the glass and hit me like a slap me in the face.

It wasn't true.

I *was* a sheep.

But I didn't want to be one anymore.

I stepped away from the window and stood a little taller, feeling a new sense of purpose as I let the curtain fall and returned to my desk. I hid my essay in the background, opened the browser, and navigated over to the search box. My hands were trembling as I typed, *Religions of the world.*

The screen filled with links. Christianity. Islam. Hinduism. Sikhism. Buddhism. Judaism.

I clicked on one and scanned it. And then I went back to the search screen and clicked on another one. I scanned that, too. I did it over and over again, until I found one that caught my attention, and then I read it top to bottom. When I was finished, I returned to the page full of links and clicked on another. I scanned. I read. I clicked again. I read until the sun went down and the streetlight clicked on. I was still reading at 2:00 a.m., even though my eyes were heavy and burning, and my neck was stiff.

I expected to feel content at some point, but every answer I found led to another question I'd never even thought to ask.

Emory
Day 280, 157 to go

"I just want to apologize to Mike's mom. And Josh's mom. And my mom. And I'm sorry to everyone."

I paced back and forth in front of Tyler's Prius as I waited for him and Charlotte to get there. I could see the school bus on the other side of the parking lot, waiting to take Luke and the rest of the lacrosse team to their away game in San Bernardino.

Suddenly, I heard the locks click open, and I turned around to find Tyler walking toward me, arm extended, key fob in hand. "Who are you talking to, crazy lady?"

I looked right into his eyes, gripped his chin in my fingers, and said my next line. "I was very naive."

"Were you now?" he asked.

"Yes. I'm so, so sorry for everything that has happened."

Charlotte climbed in back and gave me shotgun.

"Because in spite of what Mike says now, it *is* my fault—"

Tyler was starting to back out when I heard a loud slap against the passenger window. I jumped. I turned to find Luke with one hand flat on the window and the other pointing at the lock, a smile on his face.

"Hey, easy on the Prius!" Tyler yelled.

Luke and I had already said our *good-bye*s and *good-luck*s, and told each other how excited we were for our *goodnight*. But I was full of nervous energy, and I was so happy to see him again, I got out of the car and threw my arms around his shoulders. He picked me up so we were face-to-face, and I wrapped my legs around his waist.

"Hey, you," I said.

"Hey." He kissed me. "You're going to kill this thing. Okay? Everyone at UCLA will wonder how there was ever another Heather or a . . . what's her name?"

"Phoebe."

"Right. Phoebe." He kissed me again. He tasted like a candy cane. "Go get yourself into UCLA Drama."

I unwrapped my legs and jumped to the ground. "Go remind Denver why they're lucky to have you."

I stood on my tiptoes and kissed him again. And then I got back in the car and leaned back against the headrest, grinning to myself.

"You guys are gross," Tyler said.

My head fell to one side. "I know, right?"

Tyler took a left out of the parking lot, following the signs to the freeway, and I picked up where I'd left off. "I'm so, *so* sorry for everything that has happened, because in spite of what Mike says now, it *is* my fault. Because it was my project, and I insisted . . ."

We drove like that for the next hour, me reciting lines, Charlotte feeding me the ones I couldn't remember. When we were a little more than halfway there, Tyler pulled into a Starbucks drive-through, and we loaded ourselves with sugary caffeinated drinks, and then hit the road again. When Tyler finally made it to campus a little over two hours later, I was feeling better. I'd done both monologues countless times, and I could feel the caffeine and adrenaline coursing through my veins.

I pulled out the instructions I'd printed the night before, along with the parking permit, and directed Tyler to the right lot. The three of us got out and walked through campus, passing groups of people huddled around tables and kids flying by on skateboards. I pictured myself as a student, walking to class, meeting new friends in the library to study, running lines with my drama buddies in the theater.

Charlotte wrapped her arm around my shoulder and pulled me into her. "Promise me one thing?"

"Anything."

"Ten years from now, let me be your date to the Oscars. I'll do your hair and help pick out your dress and stuff, too, but bring me, okay?"

"Who says I'm not going to be *your* date at the Oscars?"

"Me," she said. "I enjoy acting, but not like you do. You *love* it. I'm going to make a great drama teacher, like Ms. Martin. You're going be in the movies."

I hugged her hard. "I love you, and I'm going to miss the hell out of you next year."

"I'm going to miss you more."

We continued down the path that led to the theater. The two of them weren't allowed inside, so they hovered around the sculpture garden while I walked up to a long table and introduced myself to a guy with dark hair poking out from under a purple beanie. I handed him two copies of my headshot and résumé, and he crossed my name off the list.

"How many people are auditioning today?" I asked.

The guy looked around, like he wasn't supposed to share the information. He set his elbows on the table and leaned in anyway. "A little over two hundred on the list. About thirty auditioning today and forty next week. The rest are via video submission. Ten spots to fill." He handed me my name tag. "Take a seat anywhere in the first three rows. Good luck."

"Thanks." I put on a brave face and tried to ignore how clammy my hands suddenly felt. Two hundred people. Ten spots. I'd planned on slightly better odds. I wondered if any of them had ever been on TV. I hoped I'd made that experience clear enough on my résumé.

As soon as I stepped through the doors, I recognized the theater from the drama school's online videos. It was smaller and less ornate than the main one, with rows of movie theater–style chairs and blank gray walls. There were props on the stage: a round table with two chairs set at an angle, and a living-room set with a brown couch and a glass-topped coffee table.

I took a seat in the second row and set my bag by my feet. I visualized myself climbing the steps and crossing the stage. I'd stand on my mark and root my feet in place.

While we waited, I looked around, sizing up the competition. Smack in the middle of the third row, I spotted a girl in a bright blue blouse with a round face and shoulder-length blond hair. She immediately reminded me of Hannah. Her hair was more curly than wavy, but the overall look was close enough. She caught me staring at her and grinned, and my heart sank deep in my chest, because she looked more like Hannah when she smiled. It made me think about all those performances on the Foothill stage, looking down into the audience at the beginning of every show and seeing my best friend sitting in the first row, rooting for me. It made me realize for the first time that Hannah wouldn't be in the audience for *Our Town*. She might not be in the audience for any of my performances ever again.

The room darkened and the spotlight clicked on, illuminating the stage. A man in brown corduroy pants and a white collared shirt walked to the center, cleared his throat, and introduced himself as Ben Waterman, the chair of the drama department.

I checked the time on my phone: 6:06. Luke was probably just getting to the field. I pictured Addison and the rest of their friends huddled together in the rival school's bleachers, dressed in their green-and-white Falcons gear, trying to look intimidating but probably failing at it.

"You'll be performing backstage in a private room," Mr. Waterman explained. "Stay here until you hear your name, and then follow Tess to the audition room." Next to him, a woman with dark hair and straight-cut bangs raised her hand. I assumed that was Tess. "First, you'll perform your contemporary piece, and then we'll call you back to perform your classic piece. Any questions?"

No one had any, so he wished us luck and left the stage. Everything was quiet while Tess consulted her clipboard. Then she called the first name, and we were off. Performer after performer disappeared backstage and then returned to the theater, but I was only half paying attention. I was running through my first monologue in my head, over and over again.

After an hour, my name still hadn't been called. I was tapping my foot nervously and biting my lower lip, when I felt my backpack vibrate. I looked around to be sure no one had heard it, and then shifted in my seat, reached down into my backpack, and slid it out of the pocket, shielding the screen to hide the glare.

It was from Addison. "Goooooaaaaaal!" it read. She'd included a picture of Luke with his stick raised high in the air and his mouth open wide. He looked happy.

"Emory Kern."

I dropped my phone in my backpack as quickly as I could and stepped into the aisle. I threw my shoulders back as I walked to the stage, hoping I looked confident and prepared, because I didn't entirely feel it. Before I left the theater, I stole a quick glance at Hannah's doppelgänger.

Inside the audition room, Mr. Waterman was seated in the center of a long table, with two women on either side of him. He thanked me for coming as I took my spot on the big black X directly in front of them.

"Thank you. My name is Emory Kern and my first piece is from *The Blair Witch Project*."

I took my gray wool cap from my back pocket and pulled it over my head, down low, until it brushed my eyebrows. I began breathing, fast and hard, making my hands tremble and my shoulders heave, so when I spoke the first words my voice would already be clipped and shaking.

I began speaking slowly and evenly, delivering each word exactly the way I'd practiced, but soon, I was no longer standing in a room on the UCLA campus. I was gone, completely absorbed into the world of the Blair Witch, where I'd spent days walking a path that led back to the exact same spot. My nose was running and tears were sliding down my cheeks as I delivered my final line: "I'm going to die out here."

I let the silence build in the room. And then I stood up straight and looked all three of them in the eyes, one at a time. "Thank you." And then I smiled much larger than I'd intended to. Because inhabiting Heather's body and mind like that had been nothing short of exhilarating. And because I knew I'd nailed it. I returned to the theater feeling pumped with adrenaline and slightly sick to my stomach.

"Meredith Pierce," a woman's voice said, and the next person walked past me.

Back at my seat, I reached into my backpack for my water bottle, my fingers still trembling as I worked the cap and brought it to my mouth. I took giant gulps, feeling the cold water slide down the back of my throat.

"What did you read?" the guy next to me asked, and I told him between sips of water. "Ah, great flick. I've seen it, like, twenty times."

"Me too."

I'd watched it twice in the last two days alone, first on Wednesday, in bed on my iPhone, and then on Thursday, when Mom mentioned at dinner that she'd never seen it before. I forced her to sit on the couch with me with a bag of microwave popcorn between us. She thought it was terrifying, but I'd seen it so many times, I barely flinched.

I was feeling good, but nervous, watching people continually leave the room and return a few minutes later. And once everyone was finished with their first pieces, Tess started calling everyone's name a second time.

"Megan Kuppur," she began. "Carin Lim," she said a few minutes later. And she went on while my heart pounded. I took deep, slow breaths, listening for my name to be called again. When I felt my phone vibrate, I jumped in my seat. I dug it out of my bag and read the screen.

Addison: Call me as soon as you can.
Addison: It's important.

I did a quick scan of the room, now that I knew the order, and tried to estimate how much time I had to sneak away and make a quick call. I decided I couldn't chance it. There were only six people in front of me.

A few minutes later, I heard, "Emory Kern." I wasn't ready, but I shook it off and walked toward Tess anyway, saying my first lines in my head, over and over again.

Think not I love him. Think not I love him. Think not I love him.

I scanned the theater for Hannah's double again, but she

must have already performed her second piece, because she was gone.

Inside the audition room, I threw my shoulders back and smiled wide. "I'm Emory Kern. For my second piece, I'll be reading from William Shakespeare's *As You Like It*."

The woman sitting next to Mr. Waterman had a kind smile. "We're ready whenever you are, Ms. Kern."

I shook out my hands. I rocked my neck to each side. I let out a slow, even breath. And then I stood there quietly, inhaled, and began. "Think not I love him, though I ask for him. 'Tis but a peevish boy; yet he talks well. But what care I for words?"

I kept going, my voice loud and clear and exactly the way I'd practiced. When I got to the last few lines, I turned it up, projecting my voice, feeling each word leave my body. I was almost done, and I was nailing it. I said the last line, "Wilt thou, Silvius?" and I let it linger in the air before I gave the admissions team a small smile, bowed, and said, "Thank you."

I fell into my seat and reached for my water bottle and my phone at the same time. I called Addison. She picked up on the first ring. "Hey. How did it go?" she asked.

"Good. Is everything okay there?"

"Sort of. Luke got hit and he went down hard. He didn't get up for a full minute. But he seems to be okay now. Dad thinks it's a broken rib from the way he was holding his side when the coach led him off the field."

"Are you with him? Can I talk to him?"

"The team doctor is checking him out. But don't worry, I'm sure it's nothing."

I checked the time. Charlotte, Tyler, and I had planned to

go shopping at a nearby mall and get dinner while we waited out the traffic. "I can come straight home, but it will still take me a couple hours to get there."

Addison didn't sound concerned. "Really, he told me to tell you not to rush back. He's planning to go home on the team bus, so he won't be home any earlier anyway."

"Okay," I said with a sigh. I wished I could make the miles between us disappear. "Text me if anything changes."

"Promise. Oh, and Luke told me to give you a message."

"What?"

"He said 'goodnight'?" She giggled. "I have no idea what that means, but it seemed important to him that I told you, so there you have it."

I smiled into the phone. "Tell him I'm glad he's okay. And that I said 'goodnight.'"

Hannah

"What are we doing tonight?" Alyssa asked after SonRise practice ended. "I want to do something fun. Jack and Logan don't have plans either. We could all go get pizza, or go bowling or something."

I hadn't told her I'd made plans to help Aaron finish up the video. I wasn't keeping it a secret from her or anything, I was just kind of hoping it wouldn't come up.

I glanced over at him on the stage, gathering up all the microphone stands to return them to the storage room.

Alyssa followed my gaze. "Ooh, I have an idea! Let's see if Aaron wants to come."

"He can't. He has plans."

"Sure," Jack said. "I bet he's got plans for a big Tinder-filled evening." Logan laughed hard. I hadn't realized the two of them were standing behind me.

Alyssa slapped him with the back of her hand. "He does not. He has a girlfriend." Then she laughed along. "He's going home to an empty house to FaceTime with her? Which is even more pathetic." She looked back at me. "You're the one who told me he didn't have any friends here. Let's take him out, show him the town and all that."

Before I could say anything else, she turned her back on me and strutted toward the stage. "Hey, Aaron," she said as she climbed the steps. She gestured toward Jack, Logan, and me. "The four of us are going out tonight, and we've decided that you should join us. What do you think? Wanna come?"

"Tonight?" Aaron asked. He looked right at me. "Oh. I thought you were going to stay and finish our video project?"

Our video project.

Alyssa flipped around and locked her eyes on mine.

"But it's okay," Aaron said with a dismissive wave. "Seriously. I shouldn't have asked you to stay and work on a Friday night."

A slow smile spread across Alyssa's lips and before she said a word, I knew exactly what she was thinking. She turned toward Aaron again. "No, it's cool," she said. "I'll stay and help you two. We'll get it done faster, and then we can meet up with Logan and Jack." She raised an eyebrow at me and then looked back at Aaron. "Sound good?"

The word *no* was right on my lips. There were only two stools in the sound booth, and Aaron and I could barely squeeze ourselves into that area in front of the monitor as it was. Besides, this was *our* project.

But none of that mattered, because Aaron answered right away. "Sure," he said. "Give me a minute to put all this stuff

107

away, and we'll get started." He left through the door, carrying the mic stands in both hands, and Alyssa skipped down the stairs.

Alyssa gripped my arm. "This is even better!" she whispered.

It wasn't better. It wasn't better at all.

"You ready?" he asked as he walked past us, down the aisle, and out the back doors that separated the sanctuary from the foyer.

As we followed him up the steps that led to the balcony, Alyssa asked, "So, what's Beth doing tonight?" She looked over her shoulder and shot me a grin.

"She's going out with her friends," Aaron said as he reached the landing and turned toward the sound booth. Alyssa and I followed him.

"So, you two are pretty serious?" Alyssa asked.

"I guess."

"What does that mean, you *guess*?"

Aaron worked the dead bolt, jiggling the key in the slot a few times and leaning into the door until everything lined up and it unlatched with a thunk. "Well, we've been together for six years and we're talking about getting engaged this summer."

Alyssa looked at me, and then back at him. "You're *talking* about getting engaged?"

He pushed the door open, stepped inside, and flipped the light on. "Sure. It's time. We've been together since our sophomore year of high school. Our families have been friends all our lives, so . . ." He trailed off as he gestured to the mini fridge. I knew what he meant.

Aaron kept walking, heading straight for the computer, but

I stopped and grabbed three sodas from the fridge. I handed Alyssa a Sprite and took one for myself, and then grabbed a Coke for Aaron. I moved quickly. I wanted to get to the open stool before Alyssa could claim it.

"Here." I handed him the can.

"Thanks." He smiled.

Alyssa didn't seem to mind that she didn't have a seat. All her attention was focused on the mixing board. She had her whole body bent over it, sliding controllers, and messing with dials. "What do these stickers mean?" she asked, pointing at four colored dots that seemed to correspond with a set of controls.

"Those are for SonRise." He pointed at the blue dot. "That's you, Alyssa."

"Aww, how did you know blue was my favorite color?" She popped her hip as she said it.

I could tell by the way Aaron looked away that she was making him uncomfortable, but Alyssa didn't seem to clue in. He ignored her and said, "Jack is green, Logan is orange, and Hannah's red."

"Why am I red?" I asked.

"I don't know. I didn't give it much thought." He looked away from the monitor. "But you're definitely red."

I laughed self-consciously. "What does that even mean?"

"I don't know," he said, laughing along as he propped his leg against one of the rungs. "When I'm mixing your music together, your voice is always the loudest. And I don't mean that in a bad way, it just the . . . most dominant. I turn it down and turn up the others up to blend in with you."

I had no idea what to say to that. If anyone was red, it was Alyssa. She was the hot one, the fiery one, the daring one, the fun one. Like Emory. *I* was the blue one. I'd always been the blue one. The calm, the ocean, the sky, the color of stillness. I was the even-keeled one, the voice of reason, the yin to their yang. The blue one, no question.

When Aaron turned back to the monitor, Alyssa raised her eyebrows and shot me a well-check-you-out look. I played it up, giving her a cocky smirk.

"Okay, back to work." He tapped his finger against the monitor. "We're close. All we need to do now is get the whole thing down to one minute—a minute thirty, tops—and it's just short of two minutes long. So, we're looking for about thirty seconds to cut."

He slid me my notebook and a pen, and then he stood and gave his stool to Alyssa. "Hannah, you navigate. Do what we did yesterday, only this time, instead of flagging the good stuff, flag the parts that seem unnecessary. Extra words. Guttural pauses, like *ums* and *likes*. Anything that slows things down. Got it?"

"Got it," I said as I pressed PLAY. I kept my finger on the mouse, ready to pause and rewind.

"I'm going to finish editing the background music." He put his headphones on and moved over to the mixing board.

Alyssa and I watched the screen. The video began with that same aerial view of the campus, panning slowly, then zooming in on the empty picnic table in the Grove.

She was with me for the first twenty minutes or so, and then I could tell she was getting bored. She kept letting out loud sighs, swiveling around on the stool, and stopping to check her phone. When I got to the end of the recording, I leaned in close to her and whispered, "I'm done. Want to tell Aaron?"

She looked at me, wide-eyed and nodding. She tapped him on his shoulder, and he took his headphones off and draped them around the back of his neck. "We're ready for you," she said. She stood up so he could take her stool.

Neither one of us spoke while Aaron methodically worked through the cuts I'd recommended. He showed us how to zoom in to the audio and clip it so it wouldn't sound choppy, and then how to smooth it back together. He played it from the beginning. Kevin sounded articulate and totally fluid; you couldn't even tell where Aaron had spliced the video.

When he was done, the whole video clocked in at one minute, thirty seconds exactly. Aaron pressed PLAY and the music swelled as the campus came into view.

I peered over my shoulder. Alyssa was standing behind us with her hands on her hips, eyes glued to the monitor. As we watched, I heard her suck in a breath.

The second it ended, she said. "Whoa. Okay, you guys. That. Was. Amazing." She shoved her arm between Aaron and me. "See. Legit goose bumps."

I had goose bumps up and down my arms, too.

"It's perfect." I smiled at Aaron.

He smiled back.

I must have been caught up in the moment, because suddenly, I reached over and rested my hand on Aaron's leg, like I'd known him for years.

As soon as I realized what I'd done, I jerked my hand away. My jaw fell open. I started to say, "I'm sorry," but nothing came out.

And then I panicked. I looked at Alyssa, but she had already turned away, reaching inside the mini fridge for another Sprite. As she walked back toward us, she popped the top and took a big sip. "Seriously. It's so good." She patted Aaron's shoulder. "Pastor J's gonna give you a fat raise for that one."

My heart was racing and my hands were trembling. I could feel sweat beading up on my forehead.

Aaron seemed completely unfazed. "It still needs a few adjustments. A couple of those transitions were clunky, but it's getting close."

Alyssa set her soda on the desk and brushed her hands together. "This calls for pizza, don't you think? Or a late movie?" She pulled her phone from her pocket and checked the time. "Come on, it's only nine thirty. Let's get out of here."

"You go ahead," he said to her. And then he looked at me and said, "It's okay. I promise." I had a feeling he wasn't talking about our early exit.

"Are you sure?" I asked. I wasn't talking about that, either.

"Positive." He pressed his palms together, like he was begging me to believe him. "I'm going to finish up here. I need to get this to your dad tonight." He pointed at the door with his chin. "I'll send you the final in a few hours."

"Okay," I said. I gathered my stuff and left the sound booth in a daze.

Alyssa and I walked through the balcony, past the pews.

Neither one of us said a word as we stepped down the narrow staircase, across the atrium, and through the double doors. Outside, it was dark and cold. The wind felt good on my cheeks.

"Okay, what was *that?*" Alyssa asked once we were a safe distance from the sanctuary.

My heart started racing again. She'd noticed.

I played dumb anyway. "What was what?"

She pressed the button on the key fob and her car doors unlocked. "You know what I mean! With Aaron!" We both climbed inside and buckled up, and then she shot me a look I couldn't read.

"What about him?"

She turned the key in the ignition and backed out of the parking space. "Oh, come on. Don't tell me you didn't catch that! Didn't you hear what he said about Beth?"

My breath left my body like air from a popped balloon, all at once.

"'We're *talking* about getting engaged'?" she said. "'Our parents are friends. I've known her all my life.' He made it sound like an arranged marriage or something."

"Yeah, that was weird." I tucked my hands under my legs, trying to get them to settle down.

"Weird, but good-weird!" She slapped her hand on the steering wheel. "He's not going back to Houston until June, so that gives me a little over two months." She shot me a cocky grin. "I'm pulling out all the stops now, and I have you to thank."

"What did I do?"

"You let me crash your date," she said. She patted my leg. "I swear, you've always been the best wingwoman."

That night, I sat in bed with my laptop open in front of me, toggling between ten different windows I'd opened after I'd typed the word *afterlife* into a Google search engine an hour earlier.

I'd read a few short pieces from familiar newspapers and scanned interviews with some of the world's leading scientists, doctors, and spiritual leaders. I'd opened a bunch of in-depth articles specific to religious beliefs, and I'd even found an at-a-glance chart that showed how each faith viewed the afterlife. I was about to click on another link, when I heard a noise outside.

I tossed my laptop onto my comforter and climbed out from under the covers. I pulled my curtain to one side.

Emory must have just shut her window, because she was still standing there, looking out, like she was waiting for someone.

It was Friday. It was almost midnight. That meant Luke would be hiding in the rosebushes next to my house any minute now.

My phone vibrated on my nightstand and I jumped. I picked it up and read the screen.

Aaron: Look what we did . . .

We. Again.

I clicked on the attachment and pressed PLAY. The adjustments he'd made were minor, but important. He'd moved some pictures in the montage around so they synched with the background music even better, and he'd shortened a few of the clips so the whole thing moved a little faster. I'd loved it back in the sound booth earlier, but I loved this one even more.

I texted him back. *It's more amazing! Dad's going to love it.*

Thanks, he replied. *I hope so.*

I didn't know what to say next. All I could think about was the way I put my hand on his leg. Part of me felt like I should explain, but I didn't know how to, so I tried to explain Alyssa's actions instead.

Sorry about the way Alyssa put you on the spot about Beth, I typed. *That was kind of uncool.*

There was a long pause. Then the three dots flashed on the screen, and I knew he was replying.

Aaron: It's okay.
Aaron: I didn't mean to shut her down.
Aaron: It's just that Beth and I are a complicated story.

I wanted to hear it. I wanted to keep texting with him. I thought about Alyssa and felt guilty. And then I thought about his girlfriend and felt even guiltier. But I texted him back anyway.

Hannah: I'm not at all sleepy . . . ☺
Aaron: ☺

Those three dots showed up on the screen again.

Aaron: She wants to get married.

Aaron: We were going to get engaged over Christmas,
          but then I took this job, so we decided to hold off

Hannah: What about you? Do you want to get married?

My whole body felt buzzy and caffeinated. I paced back
and forth as I typed. And then I went back to the window and
looked down, half expecting to see Luke there. But it was quiet
outside.

Aaron: Eventually. Sure. We've been together since tenth
          grade.

He'd said that in the sound booth, too, but I didn't understand why that was so important.

I decided to get some water. I opened my door as quietly
as I could. The house was dark and silent, so I tiptoed into the
hall, typing as I walked. I was feeling red.

Hannah: That doesn't answer my question.

In the kitchen, I took a glass out of the cabinet, filled it with
water from the sink, and downed it in two gulps. I rested the
phone on the counter and watched the screen. My heart started
racing as I waited for those three dots to appear again.

I was refilling my glass when his next text appeared.

Aaron: Truth?

Hannah: Yes, please.

I didn't move. I kept my gaze fixed on my phone. Aaron answered almost immediately.

Aaron: No.

Aaron: I'm nowhere near ready.

Aaron: I'm not sure why she thinks she is, or that we are.

I waited to see if he had more to say. After a few moments of silence on his end, I typed back.

Hannah: You should tell her that.

Aaron: I know . . . I've tried . . .

Hannah: But you love her?

He didn't reply for a long time.

Aaron: Yeah, I do.

Aaron: But . . .

Hannah: ???

Aaron: Things are changing, I guess.

I typed, *Like what?* but before I had a chance to hit SEND, he started replying again.

Aaron: I have no idea why I'm telling you all this, btw.

Aaron: Totally inappropriate

Hannah: No it's not.

Aaron: I shouldn't be telling my student/boss's daughter about my relationship problems.

Aaron: I'm blaming my hermit/friendless status.

Hannah: ☺

Hannah: You can talk to me.

Aaron: Thanks.

Aaron: Don't mention it to your dad though, okay?

Hannah: Why would I tell my dad?

Aaron: IDK . . . you two are close.

We used to be. We weren't so much anymore. It had been months since I confided in him, and given our current situation, I didn't see that changing anytime soon.

Hannah: I don't tell him everything.

I flipped around and looked at the clock on the microwave: 12:03. I was about to type a reply, when something outside the window caught my eye: a red car drove straight through the intersection without stopping at the sign. It rolled slowly toward my house, until it stopped with a jerk when it hit the curb.

I leaned over the kitchen sink, craning my neck, trying to get a better view.

Red Jetta. Late arrival, but it was Luke's car. No question.

I watched and waited, ready to duck down low as soon as he cut the engine and stepped out, but nothing happened. His headlights were still on, steam rising from the tailpipe. And I couldn't be sure, but it looked like his head was resting on the steering wheel.

My phone vibrated, but I didn't pick it up. I was too busy watching Luke, waiting for him to move. I checked the time on the microwave: 12:07.

Aaron: Meet in the sound booth after services?

I reached for my phone again and typed a reply to Aaron.

Hannah: Something's happening outside.
Aaron: You okay?
Hannah: Yeah . . . it's weird.
Hannah: My neighbor's boyfriend sneaks into her room at
          night and he always parks in front of my kitchen
          window.

It seemed odd to call Emory "my neighbor," but it was easier than going into the specifics.

Hannah: He pulled up and stopped the car, but he's not
          getting out.
Hannah: I can see him.
Hannah: His head is on the steering wheel.
Hannah: I think something's wrong with him.

I opened the window and listened for sound. There was nothing.

Hannah: Hold on.

Leaving the phone on the counter, I ran to my room and peeled the curtain to one side, expecting to see Emory standing in the open window, waiting for Luke like she always did. But her shade was lowered and that faint bit of light still illuminated the edges.

I grabbed my sweatshirt off the back of my desk chair, pulling it over my head as I returned to the kitchen window.

Luke's car was still there. The lights were still on. The engine was still running. And he still hadn't moved. The clock on the microwave read 12:13. Ten minutes had passed since his car rolled to a stop. My phone chirped.

Aaron: What's going on?
Hannah: BRB.

Without even thinking, I opened the front door and stepped outside. The late night air stung my throat.

I stuffed my hands in my pockets and quickened my steps, scanning the neighborhood to be sure I was alone. Then I stepped onto the grass. The blades tickled my feet and the dew seeped in between my toes as I cupped my hands to my face and peered into the passenger window.

Luke's eyes were closed, his head was resting against the driver's-side window, and his arms hung limp at his sides.

I knocked on the glass. "Luke!" I whisper-yelled.

He didn't open his eyes. He didn't even flinch.

"Luke!" I yelled louder. I knocked harder.

Nothing.

Emory.

I reached for my phone to text her, but then realized it was still sitting on the counter. I knocked on the window again, but he still didn't budge, so I opened the door as slowly as I could, reaching inside to balance his weight and push him back into the seat as I did.

"Luke. Wake up." I shook him. "Luke. You have to wake up."

I reached in front of him, cut the engine, and turned the headlights off. When I breathed in, I gagged. The car reeked with this horrible, sour smell, and I looked down on the passenger seat. There was puke. Everywhere. When I looked back at Luke, I realized it was all over one side of his jacket, too.

He didn't look hurt. No cuts. No bruises. I crouched down, and that's when I noticed something. His jacket had fallen open, and his T-shirt was raised up on his left side. I slowly lifted it higher.

His skin was swollen under his rib cage, and his whole side was dark purple, almost black. I touched it lightly, but he didn't react at all. And then I brought my fingertip to his neck and felt for a pulse. I couldn't find one.

I came in close to his ear. "Luke. It's Hannah. I need you to listen to me, okay?" I watched his eyes for movement, but saw nothing. "I'm going to get help. I'll be right back."

I sprinted across my front lawn, up the stairs, and into the house. I shouted for my parents while I ran to the house phone, and then I dialed 911. As I waited for someone to answer, Dad ran into the kitchen. "What's wrong? Are you okay?"

Mom was on his heels, tightening her robe around her waist. I pointed at Luke's car through the window.

"It's Luke. His whole left side is swollen and purple, and he's barely breathing."

Dad raced for the front door. I shoved the phone into Mom's hands and took off after him. We rounded the corner together, and when he reached Luke's car, he opened the driver's-side door and crouched down. I leaned over his shoulder.

Dad felt his wrist, like I had, looking for his pulse, and when he couldn't find it, he tried his neck instead. He lifted Luke's shirt and pressed his fingertips below the bruise and above it.

"What's wrong with him?" I asked.

"I'm not sure," Dad said.

"Is he going to be okay?"

Dad shook his head. "I don't know."

"Shouldn't we pull him out and give him CPR or mouth-to-mouth or something?"

"I don't know, Hannah!" Dad's voice shook. The sirens wailed in the distance. "That ambulance needs to be here now!" he screamed. Dad never screamed.

I didn't know what to do with my hands. I rubbed them on my sweats. I wrapped them around the door frame and unwrapped them again. I kept my eyes on Luke's face the entire time. I closed my eyes and prayed under my breath. "Please, Lord. Let him wake up. Please, let him wake up."

"Luke!" Dad grasped his shoulders. "Come on, son, I need you to try to talk to me. Stay with me, okay? Help is on the way, but I need you to stay with me."

The sirens grew louder.

Dad stood and wrapped his arms around Luke. I thought

he was going to try to move him, so I stood by, ready to help, but he kept his head bent low and his mouth right next to Luke's ear. I couldn't hear what he was saying, but I could see his lips moving. And then I realized he was talking to him.

I could see the blue-and-red lights spinning now. The ambulance flew through the stop sign without even slowing down, and I waved my arms in the air, signaling it. I kept waving, even after it pulled to a stop right next to me.

The EMTs jumped out and raced toward the car. As Dad and I stepped away to make room, I heard a phone chirp. I felt for it in my pocket, thinking it was mine, and then remembered it was still inside on the kitchen counter, where I'd left it, mid-text exchange with Aaron.

And then I saw Luke's phone on the floor in front of the passenger seat, screen bright, with a message waiting. I ran around to the other side, opened the door, and gagged again; the puke smell was even worse over there.

Emory: Where are you?!?

The phone was locked. I couldn't reply, so I took off running for her house. The sprinklers must have come on at some point, because by the time I got there, my bare feet were covered in mud.

"Emory!" I screamed. I couldn't quite reach the window, so I slapped my hand against the gray siding below it instead. "Emory!"

She pulled hard on the shade, and it snapped up. Then she slid the window open and leaned out. Her long hair dangled over her shoulders, barely covering the black lace lingerie thing she had on.

"What are you doing here?"

"It's Luke. Something's wrong."

She must have seen the glow from the ambulance lights around the corner, because her eyes grew wide and she left the window without saying another word.

I ran back to the car. By the time I got there, the whole neighborhood had gathered along the curb, dressed in sweats and bathrobes, watching the scene unfold. Dad was standing on the sidewalk with his arm around my mom.

Luke was already on the stretcher; they were wheeling him around to the back of the ambulance. Without thinking, I ran toward him.

"Wait!" I yelled as I slid in next to the gurney. I grabbed his shoulders and lowered my mouth to his ear.

And I said the first thing that came to mind.

Emory

Day 280, 157 to go

Luke was blue.

I couldn't see much from where I stood, but the skin on his left leg was blue and his whole body was rigid. His neck was twisted to one side at an uncomfortable-looking angle.

"Luke!" I screamed as I pushed my way through the crowd, fighting to get to him. But then one of the paramedics stepped in front of me and put her arm out, blocking my way.

"Please, let us do our jobs. Stay back so we can help him."

"That's my boyfriend!" I lunged forward, but she wrapped her arms around me and I couldn't move. The other EMTs loaded the stretcher into the ambulance while I desperately tried to twist out of her grasp. "Please. I want to go with him!"

"I'm sorry," she said as she loosened her hold on me. "Family only. You'll need to follow us." She let me go, climbed inside, and slammed the doors behind her.

The sirens blared, and the lights flashed, and the ambulance sped away, leaving me standing in the middle of the street. I wrapped my arms around myself, and that's when I realized I was wearing a thin layer of sheer black lace. And nothing else.

Hannah's mom was there in a matter of seconds, covering me with a bathrobe and leading me over to the curb.

"I have to go with him." My voice didn't sound like my own.

I didn't even get to see him.

I didn't get to talk to him.

"I already called your mom." Mrs. J's voice was clear and strong. "She's going to meet us at the hospital, okay?"

I looked up, trying to make sense of what she was saying. "My mom? When did you call my mom?"

"About ten minutes ago. Right after I called nine-one-one. I called her cell and she told me she was in the city." She led me to the curb. "She's on her way to the hospital now. She might even beat us there."

I only half heard her. I was still stuck on the first part. "Ten minutes ago?"

"Ten or so. Maybe a little longer. That's about when Hannah found him and called nine-one-one." Mrs. J handed me off to her daughter. "Take her back to her house and help her change. I'll go get the car."

Hannah rested her hand on my shoulder. For a heartbeat, I forgot everything that had happened over the last few months. I started to lean into her and let out the sobs that were building in my chest. "You okay?" She stepped closer, as if she was about to hug me. And it all came back to me.

"No." I stepped back and her hand fell to her side. "It's okay. I don't need your help." I walked away from her.

The neighborhood looked strange and fuzzy as I made my way to my house, like I was seeing it through dirty glasses. Inside my room, I was still in a daze. My hands were shaking as I pulled my yoga pants on, zipped up my sweatshirt, and stepped into my Uggs.

Music was playing softly in the background. When I first put it on, I wondered if Luke would recognize the playlist he'd made me; the one he said made him feel like I was in his arms. I'd been looking forward to teasing him about those words he said.

That was about thirty minutes ago.

Right after that, Mom had called to check in. I asked about her catering gig and she asked about my audition, and then we'd congratulated each other and decided we'd go out to celebrate on Saturday night, just the two of us. We exchanged *I love you*s.

As soon as we hung up, I'd texted Luke *Goodnight*.

That was about twenty minutes ago.

I looked around for my phone and found it on top of my dresser, right where I'd left it.

I'd been texting with Charlotte after I put on the black lace lingerie she dared me to buy in LA a few hours earlier. I'd been studying the way it clung to me in all the right places, feeling sexy and pretty, as I piled my hair on top of my head, then let it fall over my shoulders again.

Good call, I'd typed.

Told you! Charlotte replied.

See, this is why I never pass on a dare, I'd said, and she replied with laughing-face emojis.

That was about ten minutes ago.

Ten minutes ago.

Ten minutes ago, Luke was a hundred feet away.

Hannah and her dad were with him.

And I wasn't.

I heard a horn honk.

Everything was still hazy as I grabbed my stuff and made my way to Mrs. J's car. I collapsed in the passenger seat and buckled my seat belt, and then I turned to look at Hannah, expecting to find her sitting behind me. But she wasn't there.

Back in the street, I'd pushed her away and said I didn't need her, and she *listened* to me? The Hannah I'd known all my life never would have left me alone. Not like that. Not when I needed her. She would have forced her way into her mother's car whether I wanted her there or not, and if the situation had been reversed, I would have done the same. What had happened to us? Were we *that* far gone?

"Do you know how to reach Luke's parents?" Mrs. J asked.

My stomach dropped.

The Callettis.

I nodded, and as she backed out of the driveway, I dialed Addison's cell phone number. I counted the rings. One. Two. Three. Four.

"Pick up," I whispered as I tapped the side of my foot against the door.

"Hello?" Addison's voice was deep and gravelly, and I could tell I'd woken her up.

My heart started pounding and my mouth went dry. "Something's wrong with Luke."

Hannah's mom was kind, which was to be expected; I'd known her all my life and she'd never been anything else. As we sat side by side in the empty waiting room, she rubbed my back and handed me tissues from her purse (even though I wasn't crying). She asked me if I wanted to find a bathroom so I could splash some water on my face. I politely thanked her and gave her a simple no. But then she held out her hands and asked, "Will you pray with me?"

I didn't see the world the same way the Jacquard family did, but I'd always respected their beliefs. I held hands and bowed my head when we said grace at dinner, and gave Mrs. J a genuine *thank you* whenever she told me she'd been praying for me and my family—which seemed to happen a lot, especially over the last few years.

I didn't feel like praying, but Mrs. J had been like a second mom to me and I couldn't imagine saying no to her, so I let her take my hands. She squeezed them in hers. "I know it's not your thing, but give it a chance. It might help. It always helps me."

She bowed her head and I did the same. "Dear Heavenly Father," she said. "We don't always understand your will, but we know that you hold us in your strong, loving hands and comfort us when we are in pain. We need your comfort tonight, Lord. Bring peace to our heavy hearts. In Jesus's name we pray. Amen."

She opened her eyes. They were wet with tears. "I'm so sorry, Emory."

Something was off.

That prayer wasn't a prayer for Luke. She asked God to give *us* comfort, not him.

I pictured his body again—rigid, contorted, and blue—and the questions began swirling around in my mind. I opened my mouth, but then I heard someone yelling my name.

Addison and her dad were heading right for us. Luke's mom raced toward the information desk. Mr. Calletti and Mrs. J shook hands, and I overheard her say, "My daughter was the one who found him." She gestured toward the waiting-room seats. "Sit down. I'll tell you everything I know."

Hannah

After the sirens silenced and my neighbors padded back into their houses, I sat on the living-room floor, staring up at the cross that hung above our fireplace. Dad stayed outside for a long time. He said he needed the fresh air and a little alone time with God.

It was after 1:00 a.m. when I finally climbed in bed. I closed my eyes and tried to sleep, but I couldn't get the image of Luke out of my head. I pictured his lifeless body folded over the center console, his eyes half-open, and his skin colorless and cold to the touch. His full lips were parted, drool sliding down the side of his cheek.

My laptop was still open on my bed, and I stared at the screen, thinking about everything I'd been researching only an hour earlier. There was a knock on my door. I slammed the laptop closed.

Dad poked his head inside. "Can I come in?"

I nodded as I reached for the box of tissues.

He sat next to me, wrapped his arms around my shoulders, and squeezed me hard as I buried my face in his chest and let the tears fall. "There wasn't anything you could have done."

"Are you sure?" I asked.

I felt my dad nod into my shoulder. "Yeah, sweetie. He was almost gone when you found him. He passed by the time the paramedics arrived."

"How do you know?" The question came out in a squeak.

"I was the associate pastor for ten years. I spent a great deal of that time in hospitals, sitting next to bedsides, leading people through their final hours. I recognize death when I see it." He gripped my hand harder. "The color of his skin, and the way his limbs began to change . . ." He stopped short and the room got quiet again.

"Why?" I whispered.

I wanted to know why Luke was hurt, and why he got behind the wheel of a car, and why Emory wasn't with him—she was always with him when they pulled up to the house. I wanted to know why his phone was on the floor and why the passenger seat was soaked in vomit. I wanted to know why something so horrible had happened to him.

"I've been wondering the same thing." Dad nodded knowingly. "If he'd gone to Emory's house, you wouldn't have seen him. If he'd parked anywhere else, he'd still be there, all alone. But he came here. You found him, maybe not in time to save him, but at least he didn't die alone out there. He pulled up here. Under *our* kitchen window. And you happened to be getting a glass of water when he did. There's a miracle in that, sweetie."

I didn't know how to tell Dad he'd misunderstood me. That I already knew that answer. Luke pulled up in front of our house because he always pulled up in front of our house on Friday nights. It wasn't divine intervention; it was a booty call.

Dad kept talking. "I know it seems so unfair, doesn't it? Why would the Lord bring someone into our lives and not allow us to help him? But I've been outside for a long time, thinking and praying and listening, and I finally realized that Luke wasn't beyond help when he arrived—not in every sense. I believe he could hear me in those final minutes, Hannah, and if he could—if he listened to what I said and did what I told him to do, if he asked for forgiveness for his sins, and asked Jesus to come into his heart—he's with Him now. I want to believe that's why he showed up here. We couldn't save his life, but I'd like to think we saved his soul." Dad shook his head and said, "The Lord sure does work in mysterious ways, doesn't He?"

I wasn't in the mood. I didn't want to hear Dad's meant-to-bes or the everything-happens-for-a reason stories; I'd been hearing those my whole life. And I didn't believe that God magically steered Luke's car to my house, or made me thirsty at that exact moment, as if He had nothing better to do at the time.

I was tired of praying and crying and sitting there wondering what I could have done differently. I wanted answers—real, solid, tangible answers. I needed to move. I needed to act. And

I needed Dad to leave, because if he spat out one more lame bumper-sticker saying, I was afraid I might scream.

"I'm exhausted," I said. "Can we talk about this in the morning?"

He hugged me. "Of course. I'll wake you up if your mom calls back." He planted a kiss on my forehead. "You did a good thing tonight. But I'm so sorry you had to see that." He patted my leg. "Let's keep talking about this, okay?"

"Okay," I whispered.

He left my room. A few seconds later, I heard his bedroom door open and close. I waited for a long time, listening to be sure he wasn't coming back out. And then I tiptoed out of the living room and into the kitchen.

I looked out the window.

Luke's car was still there.

The house was quiet, so I went to the front door and peeled it open. I raced back to Luke's car, tiptoed over to the driver's side, ducking down low, and lifted the latch. I slid behind the steering wheel.

As soon as I closed the door, the pungent smell stung my nostrils again, but this time, it was different: Luke's car smelled like lemons and fresh-cut grass. The mess had been scrubbed from the passenger seat and the dashboard was spotless, too. And that's when I realized how my dad had spent his "alone time with God."

I felt a pang of guilt. Dad might have been flawed in some human ways, but deep down, he was such a genuinely good person. It was his way, to do something kind like that and never say a word about it. It made me second-guess how I'd been treating him lately.

I looked around. The rest of the car wasn't quite as clean. There was a half-finished bottle of Gatorade in the cupholder and an empty bag of Funyuns smashed in the passenger side door pocket.

Inside the center console, I saw the usual stuff, like charging cables and earbuds. A tube of lipstick caught my eye, so I picked it up and gave it a twist. Deep red. I could see a color like that on Emory. I counted three unopened Mentos rolls and one that was almost empty.

Then I spotted a blue piece of paper on the floor behind the passenger seat. I reached behind me and picked up an envelope with an *E* on the front. I turned it over. Luke hadn't sealed it. For a second, I wished he had.

I sat up taller in the driver's seat and gave the neighborhood another quick glance. And then I curled myself around the steering wheel, worked the flap, and removed the card.

There was a small white heart in the center, and inside, in boyish-looking handwriting, his words:

Em,

I love you. I love seeing you rehearse onstage. I love watching you with your friends. I love the way you play with your hair when you're nervous, and the way you look at me like I'm the most important person in the room. I love seeing you in my jersey. I love hearing you yell my name in the stands. I love our "goodnights" and I can't wait to tell you "good morning."

Prom. Graduation. Road trip.

Luke

P.S. Sorry. I know that's a bit long for Day 281. Feel free to paraphrase.

He was in love with her. That was clear. I could hear it in his voice. I could feel it in the bend and flow of the words, and even the spaces between them, and it surprised me.

And now he was dead, and my heart broke all over again, not for me and what I saw, but for Emory. Luke died in his car, in my front yard, under my streetlamp, in my dad's arms. And Emory was right around the corner the entire time.

I hated that I was the one who found him. I shouldn't have been the last one to hold his hand. It should have been her.

I opened the door and threw up all over the pavement.

Emory
Day 281, 156 to go

By 6:00 a.m., the doctor had come out to the waiting room three times with an update on what was happening with Luke. The first time, she told us they were working hard to repair a small tear in his spleen. She said it was too early to tell, but they were doing everything they could.

The second time, she told us that Luke was fighting hard but that he'd lost a lot of blood. She held out a clipboard authorizing a transfusion, and Mr. Calletti signed it and passed it back to her. She warned us that even if he survived the surgery, until he woke up, they had no way of knowing if he'd have any permanent brain damage. "He went some time without oxygen," she'd said carefully. "We don't know how long that was."

The third time, she told us he was awake. Groggy. Medicated. But alive. He was able to speak. He seemed to have full motion in his body. His brain function appeared to be normal.

Luke's dad looked like he was about to cry. His mom smiled with her whole face. Addison hugged me, but I must have been in shock, because I couldn't move or smile or feel a thing. That image of him, blue and lifeless, was still stuck in my head and I wasn't sure I was going to get rid of it until I had something to replace it with. When I could see his face and touch his skin and kiss his lips and hear his voice, maybe then I'd believe he was going to be okay.

Somewhere after 8:00 a.m., she returned. "You can take turns saying hello, but keep it short, okay?" Mr. and Mrs. Calletti stood.

Mr. Calletti gestured to me. "Emory can go in, too."

"Is she family?" the doctor asked, looking at him sideways.

"Yes, she is," he said, and I felt tears well up in my eyes.

But I didn't let them fall. I was too happy to cry.

"He's lucky you found him when you did," the nurse said as she checked Luke's IV drip. "He almost died last night."

"I did." Luke said it under his breath. The nurse didn't hear him.

I looked down at his bloodshot, sunken eyes and his face, bloated from all the medication he'd been given over the last seven hours. His dark curls were matted and stuck to the side of his head, and his lips were dry and cracked. A bag of yellow fluid hung on a rack behind his right shoulder, dripping down to a needle inserted into a vein on the back of his hand.

"This will kick in quickly," the nurse said to me. "I'll go

ahead and let you stay until he falls asleep, but keep it down. No one can know you're in here."

I waited until she left the room, and then I sat on the bed. I took his needle-free hand in both of mine and smiled down at him. "Damn. You look like shit."

He smiled back. "I feel about twenty times worse than I look." He tried to sit up, but then he winced, took a deep breath, and settled back into the pillows with his teeth still clenched.

"Wait. Let me help you." I leaned over him, carefully lifting his shoulders and adjusting his pillows until he said he was comfortable.

And then I twisted my mouth up on one side and looked around the room to be sure we were still alone. "You ruined my surprise, you know."

I unzipped my sweatshirt halfway so he could see the black, low-cut lace camisole I was wearing underneath. It looked like it took all the effort he had in him to lift his arm off the bed, but he slowly moved his hand toward the zipper and tugged on it until my sweatshirt opened all the way. He took a piece of the fabric in between his thumb and forefinger. "I ruined our sleepover."

I leaned down to kiss him. He smelled sour, like medicine instead of peppermint. Not that I cared. "You didn't ruin anything. There will be other nights."

"But no pancakes."

I let out a laugh. "I will make sure you have pancakes when you wake up."

"I like that you saved my life while wearing lingerie. That's, like, superhero hot."

I almost corrected him. I started to. But then, I didn't see the point. So Hannah found him first. I was there, too.

I zipped my sweatshirt up and sat next to him on the bed again. "Do you feel like talking about it?"

Right before his mom let me into his room, she warned me that he might still be in shock. That he probably wouldn't want to talk. He needed to sleep and heal first, she'd said, and I'd agreed. But Luke had been in surgery for almost three hours, isolated in the ICU for another two, and he had a row of staples holding his stomach together. So, if he wanted to talk, I wasn't about to stop him.

He let out a long, heavy sigh. "I don't know. I can't remember much. The doctor said it will all come back to me over the next few days, but right now, it's all just a bunch of random scenes and images that aren't in order and don't fit together.

"I remember being at Shawn's party. I talked with Ava. I remember telling Dominic that my side was killing me and that I thought I might need an X-ray; I figured maybe I had a hairline fracture on a rib or something. But even then, I didn't think anything was *wrong*-wrong. I remember getting your text saying you were home from LA, and by then I was feeling really dizzy."

"Then why did you get in the car?"

He gave me a sleepy smile. "You were waiting for me." I could tell the drugs were kicking in. His face was starting to relax and it took more effort for him to speak. "I wanted to . . . wake up with you."

I probably should have scolded him for not going home right away, and for not asking his friends for help, and for not

140

calling his mom. I should have looked him in the eye and told him he did the wrong thing—that he never should have gotten behind that wheel when he could barely stand—but I couldn't bring myself to do it.

"I don't remember anything after that." His eyelids fluttered a few times, and I could tell he was struggling to keep them open. "After that, I . . . I . . ." he stammered. "I don't know how to explain it. I was in so much pain, and then suddenly, I wasn't. It felt so . . . good." I felt his hand begin to relax in mine. "I didn't want . . . to leave the water." He wasn't making any sense. His words slurred together as his eyelids fell closed.

I leaned in closer and smoothed his hair off his face. His curls were coarse and stiff, not soft like they usually were. "You're okay now. You'll be out of here soon, I promise." I kissed his forehead. He tasted like salt. "And I'm afraid you're stuck with me because I'm not leaving until you do."

The bag of yellow fluid was almost gone, and his whole body seemed to be melting into the bed. His head fell to one side, and he stopped struggling to keep his eyes open.

I sat on the edge of the bed for a long time, watching him. He looked so sweet, so peaceful, and all I wanted to do was climb in next to him and tuck my legs between his, but I was afraid to get too close. Besides, I was trying not to get kicked out, and I was pretty sure the hospital staff frowned upon co-sleeping with patients.

There was an oversize chair upholstered in scratchy-looking green-and-yellow plaid fabric in the corner, and I walked over to it and flopped down hard. I curled myself up into a ball, tucked my legs inside my sweatshirt, and closed my eyes, hoping the nurse would take pity on me and let me stay for the rest of the day.

I felt the fatigue everywhere—in my shaking hands, shallow breaths, and heavy limbs. I couldn't wait to close my eyes, but I couldn't put off the inevitable any longer.

I typed out a text to Hannah. *Thank you for finding Luke. He's going to be okay now.*

Unlike all the other texts I'd started and deleted over the last two-plus months, that time, I pressed SEND. I waited, watching the screen for a response, but none came, so I let my head drop back into the chair, closed my eyes. I pictured Luke and me driving along the coast, windows down, music blaring, fingers intertwined. My mouth turned up at the corners as I drifted off.

Hannah

Everything felt warm. And bright. I reached around for the covers so I could pull them over my face and block out the sun, but I couldn't find them. I closed my eyelids tighter and shifted position, away from the light. I took a long, deep inhale, and winced when the smell registered in my brain. Lemon. Ammonia. Something that smelled like BO and nasty socks. I peeled one eye open and realized I was still in Luke's car.

My neck was stiff and my back was tight, and I let out a groan as I twisted in place, looking around, trying to piece the night together. And then I remembered why my eyes felt red and puffy and my throat was sore and dry.

I reached for my phone on the passenger seat. There were four messages from Mom, all sent in the middle of the night, but it was the one on top that caught my eye. It had arrived about a half hour earlier, at 6:43 a.m.:

Emory: Thank you for finding Luke. He's going to be okay now.

I tucked my hair behind my ears and sat a little straighter. I stared at the phone. "No," I whispered, not because I didn't want it to be true, but because I didn't think there was any way it could be. I read it again. And again. And again.

He's going to be okay now.

I was about to type a reply to Emory, when my phone rang, and Mom's picture appeared on the screen. I answered it right away.

"Is it true?" I asked.

"Yeah. Looks like it." She laughed as she said it, as if she couldn't believe her own words, and then she went straight into the details, talking fast, using words like *blood transfusions* and *surgeries* and *staples*, but as hard as I tried I couldn't grasp it. All those details slipped through my mind like sand through my fingers.

Luke wasn't dead.

He was alive.

"I would have called you a few hours earlier, but it was so touch-and-go, and I didn't want to get your hopes up," she said. "But once they'd changed his status from critical to stable, I had to tell you."

"He's okay?" I still didn't believe her.

"Emory's with him now," she said.

As soon as I heard her name, I remembered reading that card Luke had written to her, and how my heart had shattered into a million pieces for her. "Tell her I'm on my way."

Mom said, "Hannah, wait—" but I hung up before I let her finish her sentence.

I raced inside to give my dad the news, and I'd barely had time to change into jeans and a clean T-shirt before he was calling to me from the kitchen with two travel mugs, one filled with fresh coffee and the other with steaming hot tea.

The hospital was only six blocks away, but we drove in silence while I rehearsed what I was going to say to Emory in my head.

I'm so sorry. I'm sorry for what you overheard. For not defending you. For what I said. It didn't come out right. Please. I can't stand fighting with you anymore.

Ten minutes later, Dad pulled into the hospital parking lot. He found an empty space near the front, and as soon as he killed the engine, I bolted from the car. Dad was right behind me.

Inside, we found Mom sitting alone in the waiting room. She told us that Emory's mom had gone home to get Emory some clean clothes, and Luke's family just left, too, to get his things and pick up his car. Emory was still with Luke, but he was heavily medicated and probably wouldn't be awake for a few more hours.

"Can I see him?" I asked.

"Family only," Mom said. "They wouldn't let me in, either."

"But they let Emory in?"

Mom hesitated for a moment. "Luke's parents said she was family."

"But I need to see him." I didn't need hours, I didn't even need minutes, I needed one second—two, tops—to prove to myself that he was alive, and to replace the horrible image in my head with a new one that wouldn't haunt me for the rest of my life. I had to see his chest rise and fall, and the color back in his cheeks, and his fingers relaxed instead of curled and cramped.

And I needed to see Emory.

"I have to talk to her."

"This isn't the right time, Hannah."

My throat tightened. "Did Emory say that?"

She didn't seem to know how to reply. "No, but she's focused on Luke right now. Please, just trust me. You and Emory have a lot to work out, and you will, but not here, not now." She squeezed my hands a little harder. "She'll come to you when she's ready. Give her space."

"I've been giving her space. I don't want to give her any more space. Emory needs me. Especially right now."

"She'll come around," Mom said.

I wasn't so sure about that, not anymore. I thought back to that day I came home from church and found Emory in my room, shaking and pacing the floor. She told me what happened, and I went straight to the living room to get my mom, even though Emory had begged me not to. My mom wasn't there, but my dad was, so I brought him back to my room instead. When we got there, Emory was gone.

"What was she upset about?" Dad had asked.

I had no idea how to tell him. I started with, "This guy—" And that's when he cut me off. "Again?" Dad rolled his eyes and said, "Look, I know she's your BFF and all, but she's changed.

146

I'm not sure this friendship is in your best interest, you know?"

And I said, "I know."

I didn't defend her. I agreed with him.

And Emory had heard the whole thing.

And then I made it worse. She called me a fucking sheep. And I told her maybe my dad was right; maybe we shouldn't be friends anymore.

"Did you hear me, Hannah?"

My head snapped up, forcing me back to reality.

"No. Sorry."

"I said, there's a cute little chapel right around the corner." She pointed toward a sterile-looking hallway. "Walk all the way to the end, then take a left and follow the signs. If you pass the courtyard, you've gone too far."

I didn't move.

"Go, sweetie." She wrapped her arm around me and squeezed. "It will help."

Actually, it sounded nice. Familiar. I stood and walked away in a daze, following Mom's instructions until I saw a sign that read INTERFAITH CHAPEL mounted to a white wooden door. I pulled the handle and stepped inside.

It felt like leaving one world and entering a whole new one. The room was quiet and peaceful, a far cry from the high-pitched noise of screaming babies and the low drone of the newscast I'd left back in the waiting room. The walls were painted in light green, with framed photographs of nature scenes hanging on each one. The carpet was earth-toned, too, and soft under my feet, unlike that stark-white institutional flooring in the hallway. It smelled like lavender and vanilla.

Three rows of dark wooden benches lined each side of a narrow aisle, and I followed the path to the front of the room, where there was a wide wooden ledge lined with tiny white candles.

Between each candle, there were individual religious texts. A Holy Bible. The I Ching. The Quran. The Hebrew Bible. The Book of Mormon. The Tao Te Ching. The Guru Granth Sahib. The Kojiki. The Book of Rites. There was even a book of Zen meditations and another book of quotes from famous people. Each one had been placed on a piece of light blue silk, protecting and showcasing it, as if it were special and important.

One by one, I lifted each book in my hands and took my time admiring it. I ran my fingertip over the covers, enjoying how the raised lettering felt against my skin before I opened it and thumbed through the thin pages. I studied the gold-tipped edges and the mystical-looking scripts, and even though I couldn't read the words, I thought the writing was beautiful.

The last one I picked up was a book of Zen meditations. It was smaller than all the others, with a simple red cover. I turned the pages, skimming over them like I'd done with all the others. Right at the beginning, I spotted a page with the words *The Beginner's Mind*. It described the benefits of daily meditation and included a bulleted list of instructions. *Sit comfortably*, it began.

I looked around. I was completely alone. I walked to the first bench and sat. I wasn't necessarily comfortable, but at least I felt safe. I figured if Mom or Dad happened to come in, I could mutter a quick *amen* and they wouldn't think anything of it. I tried shifting into a different position, folding my legs underneath me like the illustration showed, but the bench was too narrow.

I glanced around the room again. There was a spot on the floor right next to one of the candles that looked perfect, so I took the meditation book with me and sat with my legs folded. I opened the book in front of me and read.

Notice the breath, it said. *Don't force it. Breathe normally. Notice each inhale. Notice each exhale.*

I began breathing, in and out, slowly, evenly.

Thoughts will drift in, the text said. *That's okay. Notice each thought, and then let it go.*

My eyes fell shut. I breathed in and out. And I tried to let the thoughts drift in and out of my mind, but they were relentless. The harder I tried to notice them and let them go, the more seemed to come at me, multiplying before my eyes. And then there was one I couldn't ignore: What if my mom comes in and sees me like this?

I peeled one eye open and checked the door. It was closed, and I was still alone in the room. I skimmed the page, looking for advice.

Get rid of any distractions. Silence your phone. Close your door. Set a timer and be sure nothing comes in between you and these ten minutes.

I grabbed my phone and texted my mom:

Hannah: You were right, this room is nice.
Hannah: I'll be back in fifteen. Need to be alone.

She replied almost immediately.

Mom: Take your time. We'll be in the waiting room.

I turned the ringer off and got back into position. Legs folded. Spine straight. Hands resting comfortably on thighs. Chin tucked. Eyes closed. Breathing in. Breathing out. Breathing in. Breathing out. Watching thoughts drift in. Feeling frustrated when I couldn't get them to drift back out.

I felt a lump in my throat when I thought about Luke, out cold, cheek pressed into his steering wheel. My stomach knotted up when I pictured the panic on my dad's face the night before. I wanted to cry every time I thought about how Emory told me she didn't need me and walked away.

I must have been doing something wrong, because my whole body was shaking and my mind was about as quiet as an LAX runway.

But I stayed with it. And after a while, I realized the thoughts were coming a tiny bit slower, and my body wasn't reacting quite the same way.

"Inhale," I told myself. "Exhale. Focus on your breath."

I felt a tiny, relieved smile begin to form on my face. The next breath I took was a little deeper, a little slower. I watched it. I pretended I could see it flow in a circle through my nose and out through my mouth.

Thoughts came and went, and I noticed them. They were still there, but they seemed smaller and less significant now, more like thin clouds than one big interconnected, ominous storm.

And then the timer went off.

I opened my eyes and glanced around the room. I didn't feel like a changed person or anything, but I did feel a tiny bit calmer. It was nice. I took a picture of those two pages before I returned the book to its spot on the mantel, just in case I wanted to try meditating again.

As I walked back to the waiting room, I thought about what Mom had said earlier; that I should give Emory space and let her come to me when she was ready to talk. It still seemed impossible to do, but deep down, I knew she was right.

Emory
Day 283, 154 to go

As soon as I stepped into the hallway, I felt every head turn in my direction. Under normal circumstances, I would have enjoyed the attention, but I'd spent the last two nights sleeping in a scratchy armchair in a hospital room, and even though I'd taken a shower that morning, my hair still felt stringy, my eyes looked like someone had punched me, and I didn't completely trust my legs to carry me from class to class.

"Everyone's looking at me," I said as I dialed the combination on my locker door.

"Yeah, you're right. They are," Charlotte said, looking around. "And . . . Tess and Kathryn are heading straight for you."

I didn't want to talk to Luke's friends about what happened on Friday night. I was tired of thinking about it. And I was just plain tired. I needed to get through three periods so I could get to lunch, because the only place I wanted to be was in the quiet theater, pretending to be Emily Webb, escaping into her world and blocking out mine.

"Emory, are you okay?" Tess threw her arms around me, then backed up so Kathryn could do the same.

"I'm fine. Thanks for all your texts. Addison and I have been reading them to Luke all weekend. They made him laugh."

Suddenly, Dominic was there, wrapping his arms around my neck from behind. "I'm so sorry, Emory." And then he let me go and launched straight into what happened during the game and the bus ride home. "Luke kept saying his side hurt and he was feeling nauseated, but the doctors checked him back on the field and didn't find anything wrong. He said he wanted to get an X-ray over the weekend. He was convinced he had a cracked rib."

"He seemed fine," Tess said. "I talked to him at the party, and I guess he seemed kind of . . . buzzed. . . ." She trailed off, and I could tell from the look on her face that she was realizing she might have misinterpreted the events of that night.

"He was sitting on the couch for a long time," Kathryn added. "He looked kind of . . . pale. I asked him if he was okay, and he told me he was waiting for you to get home. He seemed sort of out of it, I guess, but . . ."

I remembered that. Tyler, Charlotte, and I were driving home when he texted me and said he felt horrible. His stomach hurt. He was light-headed. I told him it was okay if he wanted to go home, but he said he wanted to see me.

"I would have driven him home if I'd known," Dominic said.

"We all would have done something, I swear . . ." Kathryn added, looking at Dominic and Tess for support.

"You had no way of knowing how bad it was," I said. "Luke didn't even know."

Parroting the doctor's words, I explained what had happened. I told them how that hit Luke took during the game had left a tiny, almost microscopic puncture in his spleen that no one could have caught without an MRI. How his abdomen had slowly filled up with blood the entire time he was on the bus and throughout the party. How, the more he moved, the more that puncture turned into a tear and his blood pressure dropped.

"The lacrosse team has a bunch of cards and stuff for him," Dominic said. "Coach is organizing a visit to the hospital after school."

"He'd love that."

Luke's hospital room already looked like a flower shop that blew up inside a balloon factory, but I wasn't about to tell Dominic that. "He's out of the ICU and in a regular room now, so he can have visitors. They plan to release him tomorrow morning, and hopefully, he'll be back at school next Monday."

"I heard you never left his room all weekend," Tess said, changing the subject.

I rolled my eyes. "One nurse had it in for me. She tried to kick me out about ten times."

The bell rang.

"We'd better get going," Charlotte said as she tipped her head toward our math class.

"See you at lunch?" Kathryn asked.

"Can't," I said. "I've got *Our Town* rehearsal."

Tess hugged me again. "Thank you for finding him," she said.

I hadn't corrected Luke in the hospital a few days earlier, and I didn't correct Tess, either.

When the lunch bell rang, I practically sprinted for the theater. I didn't stop at the cafeteria for a sandwich. I couldn't even imagine eating anything.

Melanie and Tyler were already on the stage, running through their first scene, and when they saw me, they both stopped mid-sentence. As soon as I hit the top step, half the cast was there, taking turns hugging me, surrounding me with so many questions, I couldn't even tell who was asking them.

"How's Luke?"

"What happened?"

"Are you okay?"

I let out a yawn. "Luke will be okay. And I'm exhausted, but fine."

"You should go crash in the flop room," Melanie suggested. "We can wake you up when it's time to go to class."

My whole body felt weak, and my eyes were heavy. It sounded so nice to crash into that squishy couch and sink deep into its green velvet cushions, but it sounded even better to be with my friends in Grover's Corners, New Hampshire, in 1901.

The stage was already set up for Act Two—a large platform

representing George's bedroom and another one a short distance away, representing mine. There were two tall ladders in between them. "Homework scene?" I suggested, and the cast moved to action.

I tossed my backpack on top of the pile with the others and climbed to my spot on the high platform. I'd been practicing this scene all week, but the dialogue was bouncy, with lots of back-and-forth, and I knew I'd never get it down until Tyler and I could work on it together.

I reached the top and sat, legs folded in front of me. Tyler sat on the other platform, facing me. I could see his script in his hands, but I knew he didn't need it. He was keeping it handy in case he had to feed me a line.

Charlotte, who was playing the part of the stage manager, stood at her mark and set up the scene for the audience. She paced the stage as she delivered her lines, and I tried not to be jealous of the solid performance she was giving during a totally voluntary, completely casual lunch rehearsal.

Charlotte looked up at Tyler and me and shifted into her non-acting voice. "Okay, now the choir sings, and Simon Stimson says his lines, and then . . . go."

Tyler and I sat hunched over, pretending to do our homework. I flipped imaginary pages and wrote with an invisible pencil. And then Tyler whistled.

"Emily," Tyler said with a wave.

"Oh, hello, George." I let out a heavy sigh. "I can't work at all. The moonlight's so terrible."

We went back and forth, him telling me the math problem he was struggling with and me giving him hints until he figured it out. The lines came easily to me, until there was a pause in the conversation and it was my turn to kick us off again. I searched my brain, but my line was nowhere to be found.

I looked up at Tyler and motioned for him to feed it to me.

"Choir practice," he said.

"Right. Got it. Thanks." That line always made me think of Hannah, and I made a mental note to connect it to her, so I wouldn't forget it.

Moonlight. Choir.

Grass. Hannah.

I shook out my shoulders and rocked back and forth, settling myself back into place.

"My, isn't the moonlight *terrible*? And choir practice going on. You know, I think if you hold your breath, you can hear the train all the way to . . ."

It happened again. I had no idea what to say next. I fell back onto the platform and stared up at the stage lights hanging on the batten above me. "I'm never going to get this down." I draped my arm over my eyes.

My brain didn't feel big enough to handle it all—Mom's wedding, Hannah, UCLA auditions, *Our Town* lines, and now Luke. I had no idea how I'd pull it all off.

"Hey." Tyler was suddenly right next to me with a supportive hand on my back. He must have climbed up there, but I hadn't even felt the platform jiggle. "You okay?"

"No."

"You've got this."

"What exactly have I 'got'?" I asked. "I don't know my lines, I don't know my blocking. I just keep screwing everyone up. And for what? The rehearsal? The stage time? At this point, it's not going to get me into UCLA or anywhere else for that matter."

"You do realize the message of this play, right?" Tyler asked.

"Sure." My arm was still over my eyes. "It's about life on a farm and falling in love and watching the people you love die. So, you know, that's awesome."

He ignored the sarcasm. "It's about being alive. About noticing all the little things, because no one ever knows if it's the last time they'll see them."

It reminded me of our summer plans. Our road trip. Our pact to not think about the end so we wouldn't miss out on the present.

"Stop thinking about what happened to Luke. And what *could* have happened, and what *almost* happened. He's okay. He's here. Life goes on."

I hadn't let myself cry. Not once. Not during all those hours in the waiting room with Mrs. J when I thought he was dead. Not when Luke's mom came in to tell us he was going to be okay. Not when I finally saw him, bruised and broken and shaken and weak. I don't know if it was his words, or the fatigue, or a combination of everything, but when Tyler pulled me into him and hugged me hard, fat, hot tears started spilling down my cheeks all on their own.

"I don't cry," I said into his shoulder.

"Oh, you're such a badass."

That made me cry even harder.

But he was right. I pulled up that mental image of Luke and me driving along the coast, warm wind streaming through the windows, fingers interlaced and resting on the center console.

We sat like that for a minute, and then I dried my face and took a deep breath. I looked down and saw Charlotte standing below, staring up at me with a worried expression on her face, like she didn't know if she should climb up the ladder and join us or leave it all for Tyler to handle.

I waved to her. "I'm okay," I said. And then I looked at Tyler. "I'm done now." I kissed his cheek. "Thank you, George."

"You're welcome, Emily."

And then I stood up, brushed imaginary dust off my jeans, and rooted my feet in place. "Let's do it again," I called down to the cast.

Hannah

"I'd planned a completely different sermon for this morning's Monday Chapel, but I'm going to save it for next week. Because over the weekend, something horrible happened to our family. And then something incredible happened."

Dad paced the stage, stopped right in front of me, and looked down. The stage lights were dimmed so he could see me clearly.

Alyssa wrapped a supportive arm around my shoulder without taking her eyes off my dad. Jack and Logan were staring at him, too, waiting for him to continue. They'd already heard the story—it was all Dad could talk about at church the day before—but none of them seemed to mind hearing about the boy who died in front of our kitchen window again.

"It started with a glass of water." Dad stopped in the center of the stage. "That's it. One glass of water." He let his words hang in the air. "Hannah had no reason to leave her bedroom that night, except for the small fact that she was thirsty."

Dad went on. He told everyone how I'd bravely opened the car door, helped Luke sit up, checked his pulse, and lifted his shirt to see his injury. He told them how I'd run to get help and called 911, making me sound like a levelheaded heroine when I'd been racing around, panicked and shaking and freaking out the entire time. He went on to explain what happened when he got outside and saw Luke for himself, rapidly losing blood and oxygen, no pulse to be found.

I felt sick reliving the details. It was bad enough that I couldn't get the image of Luke's face that night out of my mind. How his skin turned blue, and his hands began to clench and stiffen. Because I had no newer image to replace it with, that was the one that stuck. The one I kept seeing when I closed my eyes. The one that woke me up several times a night.

"That boy died in my arms, with my daughter holding his hand. I know this beyond a shadow of a doubt. He was gone, well before the ambulance arrived.

"But then a miracle took place. In that ambulance, he took a breath, and his heart began to thump, and the color returned to his cheeks. And from what I understand, that was the easy part, because for the rest of the night, he fought with everything he had, through a blood transfusion and a three-hour surgery. The Lord decided not to take him. He decided to give him a second chance.

"He wouldn't have had that second chance if Hannah

161

hadn't found him when she did." Dad locked his eyes on me and smiled. "Luke is resting in the hospital, and they tell us he's going to be fine."

Scattered *amens* came from all around the sanctuary.

"That experience last Friday night has me thinking a lot about death, and what lies beyond this life right here," he said, finger pointed sharply at the ground. "When our time here is over, we'll each be face-to-face with God and we'll have to decide what we believe. You in this room . . . you're the lucky ones. Because you *know* this isn't the end.

"I'm going to heaven someday." Dad sat on the step, nodding slowly, meeting eyes with the kids in the audience. "Raise your hand if you are, too."

I didn't turn around to look, but I was pretty sure every hand in the room was up. But mine was right where it had been the whole time, flat on my leg, my palm pressed into my thigh, trying to stay quiet and still. I thought about everything I'd been told growing up, and everything I'd read the other night. The world's leading scientists didn't believe heaven existed. The major religions of the world couldn't even agree that it did. Some believed in reincarnation, others believed in an opulent afterlife, and some never even addressed heaven because their focus was entirely on life, not death.

I wanted to raise my hand like I would have so readily done just a week earlier, clinging to the easiest answer, the one I'd believed all my life, but I couldn't do it. I didn't know what I believed anymore.

Dad was so certain that everything that happened that night was meant to be. He was so certain that Luke had pulled up to the front of my house and God had led me to the kitchen sink at that exact moment. He was so certain that if Luke hadn't drawn those breaths in the ambulance, he'd be in heaven right now, looking down at us, and thanking us for saving his soul.

Where did all Dad's certainty come from? Where had all mine gone? I didn't want to doubt anymore—not after what happened to Luke—it was simply too much to take on. More than my brain could process. I wanted to *know* again. I wanted the questions to disappear so I could throw my arm in the air and believe again. But it was as if my hand was glued to my leg.

I couldn't sit there a second longer. I reached for my back-pack and stepped into the aisle, walking fast for the double doors. When I was out in the empty foyer, I spun a slow three-sixty, trying to figure out how I'd gotten there and where I could go. All the classrooms were off-limits during Monday Chapel. The library wouldn't be open yet. The car was locked. And then I looked over my shoulder and saw the stairs that led to the balcony, and I went straight for them, taking them two at a time.

When I reached the top, I collapsed into the back pew. I could still hear Dad talking, so I grabbed my earbuds from the side pocket on my backpack, jammed the connector into my phone, and turned it on.

It was still open to the meditation session I'd been listen-ing to as I fell asleep the night before. "Focus on the breath," it said. And so I did. I placed my hands to my sides, palms up, and let my head fall forward. I followed the instructions, breathing in through my nose and out through my mouth, noticing each inhale and exhale.

The sermon must have ended. Through the meditative chimes in my ears I could hear Aaron playing his guitar and people singing along. And then I heard the bell ring. But I didn't move. I wanted to hide in the balcony all day, ignoring my classes and my friends and everything else. I wanted to forget about everything that happened over the last three days and clear my mind.

Ten minutes might have passed. Maybe even more. I'd stopped thinking about time and death and doubts and everything else. And for a moment, I felt it. I wasn't fighting the thoughts anymore. My mind was completely quiet. I was still. It felt incredible, like my bones were gone and my whole body was filled with helium instead. I pictured myself lifting off the pew, floating past the edge of the balcony, and traveling over the whole sanctuary like a stray balloon.

"You okay?" I opened my eyes to find Aaron sitting next to me.

It was a simple question, but I didn't know how to respond. I was okay, and I wasn't. I pulled my earbuds out and let them drop to my lap.

He hooked his thumb toward the sound booth. "Want to talk?"

I nodded. At least it would be quiet in there.

I waited while he jiggled the key in the lock and carefully opened the door, and then we both slipped inside and walked straight to our stools in front of the computer monitor, like it was our spot.

Aaron didn't say a word. He sat facing me with his hands on his knees, leaning in, waiting for me to begin.

"My neighbor Emory is an actress," I said. "Back in sixth grade, she got this part on a TV show. They only shot the pilot and two episodes before it was canceled. But after that, every time we'd watch TV together, she'd narrate what was going on behind the scenes, you know, telling me all the stuff you couldn't see. She'd point out flaws in the set that no one would have noticed, and tell me how all the actors were probably sitting off to the side, playing on their phones or catching a nap until it was their turn to step into a scene. She said she couldn't watch TV the same way again. The magic was gone."

Aaron nodded, but he didn't say anything.

I looked out the sound booth window. The stage below was empty.

"My dad stood up there, talking about what happened the other day like it was some big miracle, but he never mentioned anything about the paramedics, or the intubation tube, or the medicine they shot into Luke's arm, or the paddles they brought to his chest after they drove away from us. He only talks about the magic. Like those TV shows, it's all about the story onstage, and never about what's going on behind the scenes. He's in charge of what people see and hear. And they see and hear what he wants them to see and hear.

"I feel like Dorothy in *The Wizard of Oz*," I continued. "Like I'm peeling back the curtain to find that everything I thought was big and bright and real is really just one guy with a bunch of levers and sound machines, orchestrating the whole thing."

I was talking fast, like I was afraid if I stopped I wouldn't be able to finish.

"It's not that I think my dad's lying up there. He's not. He believes everything he's saying. And if it were a few months ago, I would have believed it, too. I would have loved that story he told today. I would have been in the front row, feeling blessed and honored, like a saint, because God had chosen *me* to be part of a miracle. But I don't see it that way anymore."

Aaron hadn't taken his eyes off me once.

I combed my fingers through my hair as I gathered my thoughts.

"I don't want to feel this way. I liked the magic. I liked the show."

"I'm sorry," Aaron said.

"No, that's the thing. I'm not sorry. It feels good to be curious. I like questioning everything. I feel awake. But I'm scared, too. I'm afraid that every doubt I have is pulling me away from my dad, and from my mom, and from the people in this church—like Alyssa, and Logan, and Jack, and *you*—who believe with their whole hearts, because I'm not sure I'm one hundred percent *in* anymore, you know? And that's terrifying."

But it was exhilarating at the same time. I pictured myself as that balloon again, floating around the sanctuary, weightless and free.

"I feel awake. I'm scared to keep opening doors, but I'm so curious to learn what's behind them. And now I know too much. I can't go back. I don't want to."

When I finally stopped for breath, I realized that Aaron had a huge smile on his face.

"I sound insane, don't I?"

"No. You sound happy."

"Do I?" I let out a nervous laugh. "I thought I sounded as confused as I feel."

"You don't sound confused at all."

He was right. I wasn't confused. I felt strong. Brave. Alive. Red.

Aaron took his cap off and set it on the desk, and I found myself following his movements. My gaze settled on his chest, and then his shoulders, and then his lips. I thought about our text exchange on Friday night, and all the others we'd had over the weekend. I remembered the easy way I'd touched his leg a few days earlier.

And then I must have channeled Alyssa or Emory—the truly daring, truly red ones—I let my hand slide onto his knee. And that time, I didn't pull it away.

I looked up at him from under my eyelashes.

I waited for him to move.

I waited for him to lift my hand away.

I waited for him to do something or say something—*anything*—but he was still just looking at me wearing that expression I couldn't read.

And then his mouth turned up at the corners. It was slight, but I caught it.

I slid off my stool and he parted his legs, like he wanted me to step in between them. And so I did.

I moved closer, letting my hand trail across his thigh and over his hip. I heard him suck in a breath. And then I felt his hand on the small of my back. He was tentative at first, but then his fingers tightened and he urged me closer.

I thought about Alyssa and how she'd hate me forever if

she knew what was happening. But I didn't stop. And then I thought about Beth, and how horrible I was to let this happen. But I still didn't stop. Because I didn't want to. I couldn't remember a single time in my life I'd done something so totally wrong, something so completely selfish, just because I *wanted* to. It felt . . . freeing.

And I knew deep down, he'd stop it from happening. I moved slowly, expecting him to push me away any second. But he didn't. And then his mouth was right there, not even an inch in front of mine. I still couldn't bring myself to kiss him. I thought about Alyssa, and Beth, and the fact that he was my choir director, and that I should have hated him for taking my college fund. And God, I couldn't even bear to think of what my dad would say if he knew what was happening right now, right here, in *his* church, of all places.

And then I felt Aaron's hands on my waist, on my skin, and I couldn't stand it anymore. He shouldn't have done that, but he did. And I shouldn't have leaned in closer and kissed him, but I did.

At first, his lips were a hard line beneath mine, and I started to pull away, but then they softened. The kiss was tender and sweet. Then he parted his lips and so did I, and it became something else entirely.

His fingers were under my blouse, trailing the curve of my waist, and he was touching me as if he'd imagined doing all this before. Which I found funny, since I hadn't pictured any of this happening. It might have been the first purely spontaneous thing I'd ever done in my life.

I stepped in closer and opened my mouth a little wider,

ignoring my beating heart and my trembling legs as I kissed him even harder. But then I felt his hands on my shoulders, gently pushing me away.

"I'm sorry," he whispered.

I took two steps back and brought my fingers to my lips, already missing him there.

"I shouldn't have done that," he said, breathing fast. "I don't know what I was thinking, Hannah. I'm sorry. That won't happen again."

My heart sank deep in my chest. I wanted it to happen again. I wished it were *still* happening. But all I could say was "It's okay. Really."

"No, it's not. You don't understand."

I didn't look away. "What don't I understand?"

"I can't. Not here. Not with you."

Everything in my life felt like it was off track. Everything I was so certain was true suddenly wasn't anymore. But those hours with Aaron—shooting video in the quad, editing it in the sound booth, texting late into the night about things that clearly violated the unspoken teacher/student agreement—had all been fun, and they all felt right. Being with him made me feel good in every way, about everything. I couldn't recall the moment I wanted to kiss him, but now I couldn't imagine *not* wanting to.

"Please kiss me again." I was surprised I'd said it but relieved I had.

Neither one of us moved for what felt like a full minute. And then he slowly brushed his fingertip down my back. It gave me shivers everywhere. He leaned in closer.

"Hannah?" There was a hard knock on the sound booth

door. I heard my dad's voice on the other side. "Are you in there?"

Aaron dropped his hand, and I jumped back. He swiveled on the stool, facing the computer and reaching for the mouse, as if he'd been working all along.

"In here." My voice was shaky and my hands were visibly trembling as I walked to the door. There was no way I was going to be able to pull this off. I could feel my heart pounding as I turned the knob.

"Hi." I smiled.

Dad looked at me sideways. "What are you doing up here?"

I gestured toward the computers. "Aaron was showing me all the responses to our video."

Even as the words came out, they sounded ridiculous. There was no way he'd believe that. My face must have been totally flushed, and Aaron kept glancing over his shoulder at us, looking guilty.

"You walked out of chapel. I wanted to be sure you were okay."

"I didn't . . . I was . . ." I stammered, trying to find words that made sense.

"It's okay," Dad said, cutting me off. "I shouldn't have put you on the spot like that. I know the whole thing was traumatic for you. I shouldn't have told everyone. I should have let you take the lead and talk about it when you're ready."

He hugged me. As he did, I looked at Aaron, wondering if we were thinking the same thing.

Dad wouldn't have been proud of either of us if he'd known

what we'd just done . . . if he'd known what we were about to do again if we hadn't been interrupted.

What was I going to say to Alyssa? What was Aaron going to say to Beth?

"I won't talk about it anymore, okay? Not unless you want to." Dad stepped back and kissed my forehead.

"Yeah. Thanks." I kept it to single syllables so he couldn't hear my voice shaking.

"Go," he said, pointing to the door. "You're late. Get to class."

As I walked toward the door, I raised my hand in Aaron's direction. "See you," I said.

"See you," he said.

Emory
Day 284, 153 to go

After Tuesday-night rehearsal, Tyler dropped me off at Luke's house. I climbed out of the car, walked to the top of the steps, and opened the front door. "Hi!" I called as I dropped my backpack on the floor next to a pile of shoes.

I couldn't wait to see Luke in his own room, in his own bed, and out of that horrible hospital gown and back in those old, falling-apart Denver sweats he loved so much.

"Emory?" Mrs. Calletti walked in from the kitchen, rubbing her hands on her SHIITAKE HAPPENS apron and looking surprised to see me.

I inched backward, feeling like I'd shown up to a party on the wrong night.

"Oh . . . Hi. Luke said you had a big rehearsal after school and that you weren't going to be able to join us tonight."

I'd mentioned having a late rehearsal, and Luke said they

weren't having much of a family dinner anyway since he was under strict instructions to stay in bed for the next two days. But he never told me not to come, and I never said I wouldn't be there. I hadn't missed a Calletti Spaghetti since Luke and I first started dating.

"But it's Tuesday."

She smiled at that. "Well, I'm really glad you're here."

I thought she was going to go back to the kitchen, but she stepped in closer. "We got home this morning. I thought being in his own bed would cheer him up, but he's still in a bit of a funk. He's barely eating. He's been watching movies on his laptop all day. I keep trying to talk to him, but he tells me to leave him alone and let him sleep. And that's a lie, because I know he's not sleeping; I don't think he's slept much at all since the accident."

It wasn't really an *accident*, but I couldn't think of anything better to call it either.

"He'll be happy to see you. Go on up. Dinner will be ready in twenty."

She headed back to the kitchen while I started up the stairs.

I usually raced past the family photographs that lined the walls, but that night, I took each step a little more slowly, studying the pictures as I went, lingering a little longer at the ones of Luke in jerseys going back to when he was a little kid. Same full lips and dark curls on a much smaller body, smiling and gripping a lacrosse stick.

I knocked on his door. No one answered, so I cracked it open. "You decent?" I whispered. No response.

When I stepped inside, I saw him. He was sitting on his

bed with his back propped against the pillows, watching something on his laptop. His hair still looked matted, just like it had in the hospital all week. His eyes were bloodshot, and the dark circles underneath were even more pronounced.

When he saw me, he tugged on the earbuds cord and slammed his laptop closed. "What are you doing here?" he asked. He sat up straighter and winced, as if he'd briefly forgotten that it hurt to do that.

I narrowed my eyes at him. "Good to see you, too," I said sarcastically.

"I'm glad to see you, I just . . . I mean . . . I thought you'd skip it tonight." He looked down at his comforter and then back up at me again. "If I knew you were coming, I would have cleaned up a bit. I just got home. I still smell like hospital." His mom told me they got home that morning, but I didn't call him on it.

I sat down on the edge of his bed with one leg tucked under the other. "I don't care." I came in close and kissed him. "It's just me."

"You're not just you." He reached for a chunk of my hair and twisted it around his finger.

"I brought you some things to cheer you up." I reached into my backpack and pulled out a plastic bag.

"Cheap tabloid journalism," I said as I dropped two magazines on his comforter. "So you can catch up on the latest celebrity affairs and whatnot." I reached in again. "Sudoku. That was my mom's idea. I have no idea how you do it, but she says it's easy to figure out and it will keep your mind occupied." I reached in one more time and pulled out a few paperbacks, dropping them next to his hip. "These are a few of my favorites. This one was a really good mystery, and this one," I said, picking up another, "I read in, like, a day. I couldn't put it down."

He opened his mouth to say something, but I held my finger to his lips and raised one eyebrow. "No. Wait. There's more." I tipped the bag upside down and let the Mentos cascade out and land with a soft thud next to him.

He started laughing. "How many rolls did you buy?"

"Thirty-four. For your jersey number." It seemed like a good girlfriend-y thing to do, and I thought he'd appreciate it, but his face fell and I suddenly realized what I'd done. He wouldn't be wearing his jersey for a while. He was probably out for the season. He might not be number thirty-four ever again.

But he let it go. "I love it," he said. He sat up to kiss me but then stopped short, clutching his side. "You're going to have to come here. It still hurts to sit up. And move. And breathe. And pretty much do anything. They say I'll feel better when the staples come out tomorrow."

I moved in closer and kissed him. And when I pulled away, I pointed down at his laptop. "What were you watching when I came in?"

He shook his head. "Nothing."

"So, porn?" I raised an eyebrow.

He started to laugh, but then grabbed his side and winced again. "No," he groaned. "I'm not watching porn. Believe it or not, even with you sitting this close to me, that is the furthest thing from my mind."

I gasped dramatically, as if I was offended. "Who are you and what have you done with my boyfriend?"

He bowed his head. "Trust me, you don't want to know what I'm doing."

"Come on. Show me."

He hesitated, but then he said, "Fine," and carefully scooted over to make room for me. I settled in next to him, sharing the same pillow, and rested my head on his shoulder. He opened his laptop and angled it so we could both see the screen.

There was a picture of a guy in a red-and-white jersey clutching a football. The headline read "Quarterback Dies From Lacerated Spleen." I scrolled down, skimming the story. And then I realized there were dozens of tabs opened in the browser. Careful not to hurt him, I leaned over and began clicking on each one, reading headlines like "High School Lacrosse Player Dies After Collapsing on Field" and "Football Player Dies Hours After Injury on Field."

I'd read enough. I leaned over and shut his laptop. "What are you doing?"

He didn't answer right away. "I can't stop thinking about what happened. I want to, but I can't. That whole night, and then after . . ." He trailed off.

"How is reading about a bunch of athletes who *died* going to help?" I asked, tapping on his laptop. "Seriously, dude, porn would have been better." I laughed at my own joke, but he didn't even crack a smile.

I remembered what Tyler said the day before. "Stop thinking about what happened. It's over. You're safe and healthy and here where you belong. Besides, you can't leave. We have a deal. We shook on it."

"We did?"

"I'm stuck with you until August twentieth." I leaned in closer and kissed him. "We have to go to prom and get our diplomas and you have to take me camping, god help me."

He smiled at me, but it didn't look genuine.

"I'm not belittling what happened to you in any way, but you walked away with eighteen staples in your chest and internal stitches in your spleen. Your family is still here. I'm still here. Your friends are here. You're out for the season, but you'll heal, and you'll play lacrosse again, and this will all be a distant memory. It could have been worse, but it wasn't, right?"

He nodded, but he wouldn't look at me. I tipped my head down, trying to make him meet my eyes so I could get a read on him.

"I think you can spend your time thinking about what could have happened," I continued. "Or you can be here and be happy about it. I'm definitely happy about it."

"Me too," he mumbled.

"Good." I tossed his laptop to the bottom of the bed, out of reach. "No more news. Play video games. Binge-watch a show on Netflix. No death porn. No *actual* porn. Can you do that for me, please?"

He kissed me. "Okay."

I smiled at him. "And . . . maybe go take a quick shower?"

"That bad?"

"Sort of." I crinkled my nose. "Plus, I think it'll make you feel better."

He didn't say anything. He didn't make a move toward the bathroom either.

"What?" I asked.

"I haven't looked at the incision yet."

"At all?"

"I got a glimpse when I changed at the hospital this morning and almost hurled."

"Want me to look first?" I probably sounded a little too excited. "I'm not at all squeamish. I'm actually kind of fascinated by this stuff."

I started to pull the blanket down, but he slapped my hand. "No way."

He was laughing, and it was genuine. It was good to see a glimpse of him again.

"You're right," he said. "A shower will help."

I kissed him. His lips weren't warm and soft like they usually were, and I wished I'd thought to pick up some ChapStick when I was at the store earlier.

"You take a shower and I'll get the spaghetti." I patted his leg. "And while we eat dinner in bed, we're going to start planning that road trip of yours. We'll scour the Internet for the very best camping spots with the fewest bugs between here and Oregon. Doesn't that sound romantic?"

"Extremely."

"Prom. Graduation. Road trip."

"Em?"

"Yeah."

"I love you."

I planted a quick kiss on his lips. "Of course you do."

I went back downstairs feeling like I'd done some good. And like things were already on their way back to normal.

Hannah

Luke was standing on my porch.

I was used to watching him blur by my bedroom window in the dark, and the last time I'd seen him he'd been folded over and lifeless in the front seat of his car. I never expected to see him here.

He was wearing that same varsity jacket he always had on. He looked tired, but better. Clean. A lot healthier than he had that night a week earlier.

"Luke?" I scanned the porch for Emory, but he was alone. "What are you doing here?"

"Hey, Hannah." He jingled his keys nervously and kept looking over his shoulder. "Can I come in?"

I still had no idea what he was doing at my house, but I opened the door wider and he stepped inside. I looked down at my blue-and-green plaid school uniform, wishing I'd changed when I got home.

"Wow! This is so weird," he said as he walked around the house, his gaze moving up and down as we moved from room to room. "Your house is exactly like Emory's but flipped."

"Yeah, all the houses on this block share the same floor plan. They're mirror images."

He was still looking around, taking it all in. "Her living room is over there." He pointed at my kitchen. "And her kitchen is over there," he said, pointing at my living room.

As he said it, something in the living room caught his eye. I followed his line of vision to the giant wooden cross hanging above our fireplace. On the mantel beneath it, I saw my most recent school picture and an old family portrait of the three of us.

Luke walked toward it. "Is that your dad?" he asked.

"Yeah."

He stared at it for a long time, and I was relieved he was no longer looking at me. It gave me time to catch my breath and think of something to say.

"He looks nice," Luke said. "It's been bugging me."

"What has?" I asked.

"That I didn't know what he looked like."

I didn't know what to say to that, so I started babbling. "Do you, um, want something to drink? We have lemonade, water, milk . . ." I realized I sounded like we were on some kind of little kids' playdate, so I added, "Coffee," even though I hated coffee.

"I'm good, thanks." He looked around again. "Can I—?" he asked, pointing at the living-room sofa.

"No, I mean, yes, sit down," I stammered. "Please." I'd never been alone with a guy in my house, let alone one I watched die in my front yard.

He jingled his keys again, caught himself, and went to stuff them into the front pocket of his jeans. When he leaned forward, he grimaced.

He groaned and swore under his breath. "Sorry. They took the staples out this morning, but I'm still sore. I keep moving like that and forgetting how much it hurts."

I sat in one of the armchairs opposite him.

"I didn't expect to be this nervous. It's just that . . ." He gestured toward Emory's house. "She doesn't know I'm here."

"Oh," I said.

"You're probably wondering why I am."

I bit down hard on my lip while he combed his fingers through his hair and stared at the cross above the fireplace. Or maybe he was staring at our family portrait again. I couldn't be sure.

"I didn't remember at first. I assumed Emory was the one who found me the other night. And when I brought it up, she didn't correct me. But I guess that's understandable." He picked a loose thread on his jeans. "But I know now it was you. And your dad. So . . . I guess I just . . . wanted to come by and thank you both."

He looked up at the cross again, and then back at me.

"Actually, that's only part of the reason I came by. I . . . kind of . . . need to talk to someone. I mean, not someone." He tripped over his words. "I need to talk to you . . . about what happened to me that night."

Out of habit, I reached for the tiny silver cross pendant around my neck and held it between my thumb and finger, squeezing it until I felt the sharp points dig into my skin. "What do you need to know?"

"Everything." He sighed. "These last few days have been so strange, and this is going to sound really weird, but for some reason I think you're the only person who will understand."

"Okay . . ."

"I don't know where to start," he whispered.

I thought about the trick Dad always used on me when I had a big thing to tell him. "Start with something easy, like the day of the week."

"Hmm. Okay." He smiled nervously. "It was a Friday," he said, and from there, the words seemed to come easier. He told me about the game, how he got hurt, about the party.

"I honestly don't remember making the decision to drive over here. I guess I was kind of on autopilot." He took a deep breath and locked his eyes on mine. "I was hoping you could fill things in after that."

Every time I thought about that night, I felt sick to my stomach. It was all still there, in vivid detail, hiding in the corners of my mind.

As we sat there together, I filled him in on everything. Standing in the kitchen. Watching his car roll straight into the curb. How I could see him inside, slumped over the steering wheel.

Then he got quiet.

"Can I show you something?" He reached into his pocket, grimacing in pain again as he pulled out his phone. He tipped the screen in my direction.

It was paused on a video of a girl with short hair, dark skin, and a long scar that started at her right ear and ended next to her mouth. Her name was in white block type at the bottom left-hand corner of the screen: *Sienna, 19.*

Luke pressed PLAY.

"Three years ago," she began, "my family and I were driving to a local restaurant. We went there every Sunday night. My dad was driving. My mom was in the front seat. My sister and I were talking about this band we both liked, and my mom turned around to say something about them. And that's the last thing I remember."

I looked at Luke. His eyes were glued to his screen.

"The police told me later that a truck had run a red light and slammed right into our car. It hit the passenger side, killing my mom and sister on impact." She stopped and took a deep breath. "My dad and I survived. I was fine, aside from this," she said, as she traced the length of her scar.

I wanted to reach over and click the PAUSE button. I didn't want to watch. This was horrible.

"I was in a coma for three days. According to the paramedic's report, I was unconscious when they arrived. And I might have been unconscious in the traditional sense, but inside, I was fully present, conscious on a level I'd never experienced before. I was there. I could hear the sirens and the voices as they tried to revive me. If I were to ever hear them again, I'd know those voices in an instant."

Sienna looked off to the side, like she was bringing herself back to that moment. And then leaned in toward the camera.

"According to the paramedic's report, my heart stopped. I

183

was clinically dead for a little over two minutes. And while I was, I got to say good-bye to my mom and my sister."

She pressed her lips together. And then a slow smile spread across her face, making the scar on her right side even more pronounced. "The experience changed everything. I'm happy to be alive, and I know that someday I'll see my mom and sister again. They're waiting for my dad and me."

The video ended.

"Do you think that's crazy?" he asked.

And even though I'd been having doubts of my own lately, I pushed it all from my mind and told him what I knew he needed to hear.

"No. I don't think that's crazy."

It was as if the word *no* gave him the permission he needed to keep going. He reached into his pocket again, this time pulling out a piece of paper. He handed it to me, and as soon as I unfolded it, I recognized the logo on the top from the back of the ambulance.

Dispatched priority 1 to a residence. Upon arrival to scene, found 18-year-old male unconscious in driver's seat of car. No response to questions. No response to painful stimuli. No pulse found. Pupils nonreactive. Skin cold, lung sounds CTA.

Patient was carried to stretcher by EMTx2, leaned back into lower Fowler's position, with feet elevated. Crew began transport. Crew member heard weak groan from patient and began resuscitation with paddles.

Patient revived. Pulse: 80. BP: 60/30. Oral and written
report given and care turned over to hospital staff.

"The doctors said the brain can only handle three minutes
without oxygen, otherwise there's a high likelihood of permanent brain damage. According to everything I've been told, for
about three minutes, I was dead."

My eyes kept going back to that one line in the report: *No
pulse found.* I thought about the girl in the video. "Do you
remember what happened?"

He nodded. "Yeah. Every second."

We were both quiet. Neither one of us seemed to know
what to say next.

"What was it like?" I asked carefully.

He thought about it. "Have you ever woken up from a
dream that seemed so real, and you can close your eyes and
picture being back in it, but when you try to explain it to someone, it never comes out right?"

"Of course."

"It was like that. Only when you wake up from a dream like
that, you know it was a dream. This felt so real. I know I was
someplace else, Hannah. Someplace real."

"What was it like? What did you see?" I needed specifics.
Was there a rotating tunnel? A bright light? People he'd loved
waiting to welcome him to the other side? These were the
kind of details I'd been searching for, the kind of things that
would prove I was right to believe all those things I'd believed
my entire life. I had to know more.

"Have you tried to tell your parents? Your doctors?"

"Sort of. The nurse in the hospital said she's seen a lot of people flatline, and those who wake up always have a story to tell. She said that when the brain can't make sense of something, it automatically fills in the blank with random images.

"My parents took a more science-y approach. My dad said what you see when you die is just the brain losing oxygen and beginning to shut down. It puts pictures together, but none of it is real. But everything that happened that night *was* real. It was as real as the conversation we're having right now." He shook his head slowly. "It's so weird. I've never really thought about what happened when we died. Not until five days ago. And now . . ." He trailed off. "And now, it's all I can think about. I don't know how to stop thinking about it. Something strange happened to me that night and I haven't really been able to explain it to anyone."

He closed his eyes.

"I was here, but I wasn't. I heard your dad's voice. He was muffled, but I could hear him talking. And then everything disappeared. And I didn't feel scared or alone anymore. Like I was ready to go. Just totally at peace with the whole thing. And then I heard you."

"You heard me?"

He nodded.

"You were there twice. The first time, you were muffled, like your dad. But the second time, your voice was crystal clear." He paused and locked his eyes on mine. "Do you remember what you said?"

I pictured that night. I'd sprinted to Emory's house and back again. When I saw the EMTs loading him into the ambulance,

I ran straight through the crowd and into the street. And then I stopped next to the gurney and put my mouth to his ear.

"I said, 'You're not finished here.'" My voice was shaking. "I told you that you couldn't go yet, because you weren't finished here."

He nodded. "Why did you say that?"

I hadn't even thought about what I was going to say before I said it. I thought Luke was dead. I figured Dad had spent all that time trying to get his soul into heaven; the least I could do was tell him not to die in the first place.

"I had meningitis when I was ten," I said. "I had this insanely high fever, and I could barely turn my neck. It was horrible. The pastor at our old church came to see me. I was contagious, so he had to wear a mask over his nose and mouth, but he sat next to me and talked to me for the longest time. I asked him if I was going to die, and you know what he did?"

Luke shook his head.

"He laughed. Right in my face."

"You thought you were dying and he laughed at you? Harsh."

"Right? Anyway, he told me there was a spot in heaven for me, but that I wasn't going to be occupying it for a long time. He told me God had plans for me here, and they were far too big, far too important for me to leave so early."

I pictured our old pastor, perched on the side of my bed, eyes full of conviction. "And then he pulled the mask off his face, smiled down at me, and said, 'Hannah Jacquard, you're not finished here.'"

"And you got better," Luke guessed.

"Actually, no. I got worse. After that, I ended up in the hospital, and then I *really* thought I was about to die. But I kept telling myself those words: *I'm not finished here. I'm not finished here.* The fever finally broke. Dad said that between my faith and all those prayers from all those people, God had no choice but to listen."

Luke smiled.

"Something must have clicked in me when I saw you on the stretcher that night. I didn't think you could hear me. I just said the first thing that popped into my head."

He nodded, like he was taking the whole thing in.

"When the paramedics arrived, they never found my pulse. Then one of them heard me moan, and she started resuscitation efforts. And here I am. But I also wouldn't be if it weren't for you."

My fingers were tingling. My chest felt light.

I saved his life.

"Thank you," he said.

"You're welcome," I said.

"But . . . now I have a problem. I don't know what to do with all this. I can't sleep. I can't eat. Emory wants everything to go back to normal, but I don't know how to do that when all I can think about are those three minutes. And when I try to talk about them, everyone tells me that what happened wasn't real. But I know it was real. And I have to talk about it—I have to remember—otherwise, the feeling is going to fade away, and I can't let that happen."

I stood and moved over to the couch, right next to him. "I think it was real."

He closed his eyes and drew in a deep breath, like I'd said what he needed to hear.

I wanted to tell him about the research I'd been doing. How I'd learned that every religion had a slightly different view on death and the afterlife. I thought he might find it as fascinating as I had.

"Can I come to church with you?" he asked.

"What?" That was the last thing I'd expected him to say.

He seemed as surprised by my reaction as I was by his question.

"I thought you'd be excited. Emory told me you were always trying to get her to go with you."

I wondered how Emory had said it. I had a feeling it wasn't as part of a glowing endorsement of me or my family.

"Of course," I said. "Any time."

"Sunday?"

"This Sunday?"

He nodded.

He was serious. He'd clearly been thinking about this. "Sure. My a cappella group is performing. You can come watch us. It'll be fun." I pointed at the family picture he'd been eyeing earlier. "And my dad will be there. You can meet him. All my friends seem to think he's a pretty easy person to talk to."

Luke turned his head and looked out the living room window at Emory's house. I could tell something was bothering him. "Are there a lot of Foothill kids there?"

"None. They all go to Lakeside. It's closer." I scooted over. "Covenant is two towns away. You won't run into anyone you know. I promise."

"And you won't tell her?"

I almost laughed in his face. "Given that we haven't said a word to each other in over three months, I think you can assume your secret's safe with me." I brought my finger and thumb to my lips and turned an imaginary key.

"Thanks," he said. He tilted his head to one side, considering me. "What happened with you and Emory anyway?"

His question surprised me. "She didn't tell you?"

"Nope. She refuses to."

If he didn't know why we were fighting, that meant she hadn't told him everything that had happened before the fight. And if she hadn't told him, I certainly wasn't about to.

"You should ask Emory." I slid forward onto the edge of the couch cushion and turned to face him. "You should *make* her tell you. It's really important that she does."

He looked completely confused. "Why?"

"Ask her," I said, and I left it at that.

Emory
Day 286, 151 to go

"Sorry. What's my line again?"

Charlotte lifted her copy of *Our Town* and read, "I can't go on—"

"Got it." I waved my hand in her direction, cutting her off. And then I straightened my spine, took a deep breath, and let my eyes fall shut, slowly easing myself back into the character of Emily Webb and her town, Grover's Corners.

I visualized the town. Main Street. The drugstore. The stable and the white fence that surrounded my house. The graveyard.

I opened my eyes and locked them on Tyler. "I can't go on!" I yelled. "It goes so fast. We don't have time to look at one another!" I covered my face and made a sobbing sound, but I knew I didn't sound authentic. Forgetting that line had pulled me out of the moment.

I ran over to Charlotte with panic in my voice and delivered my lines. "I didn't realize. So all that was going on and we never noticed. Take me back—up the hill—to my grave." I stepped forward to the mark. "But first: Wait. One more look." Everything was silent. I glanced to my left, and then my right. I settled my gaze on the audience and said Emily Webb's words with all the passion I could muster.

"Good-bye. Good-bye, world. Good-bye, Grover's Corners . . . Mama and Papa." I gazed around the theater again. "Good-bye to clocks ticking. And Mama's sunflowers. And food and coffee. And new-ironed dresses and hot baths. And sleeping and waking up. Oh, earth, you're too wonderful for anybody to realize you."

Then I walked to my next stage mark. I looked up at Charlotte. "Do any human beings ever realize life while they live it, every, every minute?"

"No," she said matter-of-factly. "The saints and poets, maybe. They do some."

It was silent again as I took one final look around, pressing my lips together as I slowly scanned the stage and the auditorium. "I'm . . ." The line was gone. "I'm . . ."

"Ready to go back," Charlotte whispered.

"I'm ready to go back," I said.

"Okay, stop there," Ms. Martin called out from the front row. The cast let out a collective sigh, and I felt my shoulders relax. Everyone shuffled around as she walked up the steps onto the stage. "Emory, you've got to get those lines down."

"I know," I said. "Sorry. I'm close. I'll get it down."

"This final scene is so important." She was looking at me,

but speaking loud enough for everyone to hear. "This is Emily Webb's famous good-bye monologue. It's a big deal. Every word needs to ring true. Every pause needs to make your audience lean in with open ears and wide eyes, waiting for you to speak again. The entire play hinges on Emily's final words."

"No pressure," Charlotte said as she elbowed me.

Ms. Martin looked at Charlotte. "It is a lot of pressure. Listen, *Our Town* is about the incredible miracle and beauty of life, even the worst moments of it. Emily gets a second chance to see the world, and she appreciates it with fresh eyes and a new perspective. In this scene, she's trying to pass information along to you, to the audience, telling you to wake up every day and take in the world around you as if you'll never see it again."

Ms. Martin snapped her fingers. "I have an idea." She turned to address the cast again. "In this scene, Emily Webb says good-bye to clocks and sunflowers and hot baths. What do you think? Would those be the things you'd choose?"

Tyler shrugged. Charlotte shook her head. Melanie said, "The coffee part was pretty good," and everyone laughed.

"This play is ours. Our town. Seniors, raise your hands."

Nine of us put our hands in the air.

"Emory might have these lines, but she's saying them for all of you. This is your good-bye to this stage. To this school. To this huge chapter in your lives." She paced back and forth across the stage. "Let's make the things Emily Webb says good-bye to uniquely ours, too."

Ms. Martin walked over to a table off to the side of the stage and grabbed a stack of papers. "Think about three things that are important to you. Be specific, like Emily is. Of course, you'd miss your families and friends, but I'm looking for more than that. What would you miss about them? Picture your bedrooms, this campus, your house, your world—think about the little things you would miss here. If you knew you were leaving this earth forever, what would you want to say good-bye to?"

She started ripping up pieces of paper and passing them out to all of us. "Find a spot of your own on the stage and sit down. Write."

Charlotte, Tyler, and I clustered into a circle and everyone else did the same, gathering in various spots, dotting the black-painted stage.

I pictured my room, my books, my laptop, my clothes, but I couldn't think of anything I'd want to say good-bye to. And then I pictured my mom. And Luke. And for some reason I couldn't explain, the view from my bedroom window.

As angry as I was at Hannah, if I were leaving this earth forever, I'd want to say good-bye to her. To the thirty-six steps that separated her window from mine. To seventeen years of memories. I felt the tears prick my eyes, but I bit down hard on my lip to keep them where they belonged as I wrote, *Our patch of grass.*

No one would know what it meant or why it was important, but I did.

The theater was silent for a good ten minutes as we thought and wrote, until a few people started giggling. Ms. Martin took that as her cue and started collecting our paper scraps.

She called me back to the front of the stage.

"Okay, Emory," she said. "Let's do that again."

I stepped to the edge, looking out at the rows and rows of empty seats, preparing to close my eyes and bring myself back to Grover's Corners. But before I could, she pivoted me around by the shoulders, turning my back to the auditorium.

"Do it again, Emory, but stand here this time. Face your fellow cast members. Right now, this is your audience."

I took a long, slow inhale as my eyes fell shut. I blew out a breath. I shook out my hands. And then I opened my eyes.

"Good-bye."

I looked at Tyler. Then at Charlotte.

"Good-bye, world. Good-bye, Foothill High. Good-bye to . . ." Ms. Martin handed me a piece of paper and I read it in place of the actual line. "Songs that make me cry." She handed me the next paper scrap. "And whipped cream. Good-bye to . . . my mom's voice." That one made my breath catch in my throat. I glanced around at my castmates, still seated on the stage and smiling up at me.

"Good-bye to dancing. And the smell after a rainstorm. And chocolate chip cheesecake." I looked at Tyler, knowing that one was his, and he blew me a kiss. "Good-bye to pepperoni pizza. And my favorite books. Good-bye to making out." I laughed as I said it, and so did everyone else. "Good-bye to our Christmas ornaments." I kept going, feeling the weight of all the things my friends and I loved.

When Ms. Martin handed me the last one, I read it to myself first. I had no problem writing it down, but I wasn't sure I was going to be able to get it out without choking up. "Good-bye to this stage and to all the people it let me be."

I glanced around the group, raised my arms to my sides, and delivered Emily Webb's line: "Oh, earth, you're too wonderful for anybody to realize you."

As I walked home from school, I thought about those three things I'd written down on those little slips of paper. The things I'd want to say good-bye to.

I pulled out my phone and typed the word *Grass?*

My finger hovered over the SEND button. But I couldn't bring myself to press it.

Hannah

I went straight to my room, changed into my running clothes, pulled my hair into a ponytail, and sat on the edge of my bed, lacing up my shoes. I rushed through my stretches, eager to get on the path. I had far too much to think about.

On the porch, I started my playlist, stuck in my earbuds, and turned the music up loud. I was just about to run down the stairs when something caught my eye. I looked to my left and saw Emory turning the key in her dead bolt. I moved back toward the door and hid behind a potted plant. I peeked my head out.

She was about to walk inside when she stopped. She turned to look at my house. She stared at my bedroom window for a second. And then she glanced over to where I was hiding.

And then she stepped inside and disappeared.

I missed her more in that moment than I had since the

day we fought. Without giving myself time to think about it, I reached for my phone and opened a new message. I typed the word *Grass?* I was about to press the SEND button, but I stopped.

I pictured Luke, sitting in my living room the day before, asking me not to tell Emory he'd been there or that he was coming to church with me on Sunday. I told him his secret was safe with me. But if I saw her, I wouldn't know how to keep it to myself.

I slipped my phone back in my pocket and took off running in the opposite direction.

Emory
Day 289, 148 to go

I left my room on Sunday morning, eager to get to the coffee-pot. Tyler, Charlotte, and I had rehearsed all night, and then stayed out late at the diner.

I'd barely seen Luke all week. Every time I asked to come over, he said he was in too much pain. When I asked if I could stop by and bring him more books or magazines or Mentos, he said he just needed to sleep. Addison said she'd barely seen him either. She could count on one hand the number of times he'd left his room, and every time she went to check on him, he was in bed with the covers pulled over his chest, his laptop open in front of him, and a pair of big squishy headphones over his ears.

"He's acting super weird," she'd told me on Thursday.

"He'll be okay." I tried to sound reassuring, as if I had a clue what I was talking about. "He'll be back to school on Monday and then everything will be back to normal. You'll see."

And I hoped it was true. I hated how much I missed him. Even worse, I hated how little he seemed to miss me.

"Good morning, sleepyhead," Mom said as I tipped the coffee into my mug. She and D-bag were sitting at the dining room table with her fat wedding notebook splayed open in front of them.

"Hey," I mumbled. "What's up?"

I didn't really want to know. The question just slipped out, and I immediately scolded myself for it. Why couldn't I go to the kitchen, pour my coffee, and go back to my room?

"It's the big cake-tasting day," Mom said. She sounded way too cheery.

"Apparently, it's necessary to go to six different bakeries in a thirty-mile radius so you can find the very best cake," D-bag added. I glared at him while he smiled at my mom and said, "I have no idea how one cake could be that different from another."

She giggled in an octave above her normal speaking voice. "Oh, stop it!" She swatted him with the back of her hand. "It'll be fun. Besides, it's not like I'm taking you to get a root canal. We're eating a bunch of cake."

"Fine. Then six bakeries it is." He ran his fingertip down her nose, and then tapped the end of it twice. "My bride can have anything she wants. If she can't decide, she'll get one cake from each bakery."

It was all I could do to not barf at the way he was referring to her in the third person, when he twisted in his seat and looked at me. "Do you want to come with us, Emory?"

"Oh, that's a great idea!" Mom actually fast-clapped. "We'll make it a family thing."

A what thing? Oh dear god.

"Sorry, I can't. . . ." I forced a smile and made something up. "I'm hanging out with Luke today. In fact, I was just coming out to see if I could borrow the van. He's not allowed to drive yet, not until his internal stitches have healed completely."

Mom and D-bag exchanged a look.

I'd overheard them talking about me a few nights earlier. He was pissed that she didn't ground me for lying about Luke spending the night, and she'd laughed and said she hadn't grounded me since I was thirteen. He told her I might be better behaved if she had. I'd listened closely after that, waiting for Mom to defend me, but she never did.

"What are you two up to today?" she asked.

"Luke's doctor said he needed to get up and start walking around, so I thought I'd take him on an easy hike." I was making it up as I went along, but it wasn't a bad idea. "We'll get some sandwiches, have a picnic."

"That sounds nice."

D-bag didn't say anything. He was studying one of the cake menus like he was committing it to memory.

"The car keys are in my purse," she said. "On the table, next to the front door." As I walked away, I heard them whispering to each other.

I was over in the foyer, reaching for her keys, when I spotted a pile of mail sitting on the table. I froze. It was Sunday. Mail didn't come on Sundays. It must have arrived yesterday. I could see the edge of a white packet sticking out.

"Mom," I said. "Mom! Packet!"

"What?"

I slid it out. I stared at UCLA drama department's return address. I went back to the dining room with the envelope pressed to my chest. "Packet. From UCLA."

She took one look at me and jumped to her feet. "Rejections don't come in packets. Open it!"

"I can't. My hands are shaking too much."

"Want me to open it?"

"No." I laughed. "Okay, here goes."

"It's good news, I can tell." D-bag sounded like he was trying to be excited but he couldn't quite get there.

I ran my finger under the flap, breaking the seal, and pulled out a brightly colored brochure with a letter paper-clipped to the top. I read it to myself.

Dear Emory Kern. It is our pleasure to inform you that you have been accepted . . .

I stopped reading and looked up at Mom. "I'm in."

"You're in." Her whole face came to life.

"I'm in."

Mom pulled me into her arms and squeezed hard, wringing me out like a sponge. "Oh, Emory! I am so proud of you. I knew you'd get in." She pulled away, took my face in her hands, kissed my cheeks, and went right back to hugging me. Then she let go. "Let me see it!" She took the letter from my hands and read it her herself.

"Congratulations." D-bag stepped in close, as if he were going to hug me, but I stepped back, shot him a glare, and shook my head at him. Mom was so busy reading the letter, she didn't notice.

She hugged me again and handed the packet back to me.

"Go! Take the van. Get out of here. I bet you can't wait to show this to Luke."

After the week we'd had, I wondered if he'd even care.

I pulled up at the deli and jumped out of the car. It was a perfect day to be outside. There was a crisp, early spring bite in the air, but it was sunny, with no wind.

Inside, I ordered giant sandwiches, a bag of chips to share, and two bottled waters. I stuffed everything in my backpack along with the picnic blanket I grabbed from the hall closet. I could see the UCLA Drama packet smashed it next to it, and I smiled to myself.

I drove down the streets of Luke's tree-lined neighborhood and turned into his long, narrow driveway. I pulled in next to his mom's BMW, left the engine running, and ran up the steps. I was still trying to catch my breath as I knocked on the front door.

Addison opened it.

"Hi," she said. She looked surprised to see me. "What are you doing here?"

"I'm kidnapping your brother," I said, gesturing toward the van. "I packed a big picnic lunch, and I thought we'd go on an easy hike in the foothills. He seems like he needs cheering up."

"Luke isn't here." Addison had a weird look on her face. "He left early this morning."

"I thought he wasn't supposed to drive?"

"He's not. He talked Mom into it. He said he had to get out

of here for a few hours, that he was going stir-crazy, and Mom caved."

"Where did he go?"

"He didn't say. But I'm pretty sure the only reason my mom let him go was because he said he was spending the day with you."

Hannah

The sanctuary was packed. Alyssa, Logan, Jack, and I were sitting in the front row. When the pastor introduced SonRise, the four of us stepped up onstage and took our spots behind our microphones.

I looked down and saw Aaron at the bottom of the steps, wearing chinos and a gray V-neck sweater. His hair was brushed to one side and he looked all clean-cut and boy-next-door, but I missed the cap. I wondered where it was. Probably up in the sound booth.

The sound booth.

Everything was silent for a moment, until Alyssa counted us down. "Four, three, two, one."

I could barely stand to look at Alyssa. I'd kissed Aaron. Her future husband. I'd kissed him and he'd kissed me. Now he was standing in front of us, moving his hands in time with the music, and all I could think about was how those fingers felt on my back, on my skin. I glanced over at her, smiling out at the crowd, and guilt flooded over me.

The four of us swayed in unison, two times to the right, two to the left, and then back to the right as we sang,

"Bom . . . bom . . . bom . . . bom."

Logan had the first lines.

"How fickle my heart and how woozy my eyes.
I struggle to find any truth in your lies."

I spotted Luke right away, sitting in the second to the last pew on the far-left side of the sanctuary. He was wearing a button-down shirt and his hair looked nice, like he'd tried to make his dark curls behave with a bit of styling gel or something.

He looked at me and waved. I smiled and forced myself to focus on the stained-glass window near the back of the sanctuary, concentrating on the red, blue, and green glass panes so I wouldn't lose my place in the song. When it was my turn, I sang:

"And now my heart stumbles on things I don't know.
My weakness I feel I must finally show."

I tried to connect with people in the audience like Dad taught me to, looking for the ones who seemed to be lost in thought, or those who might have a special need to hear the words I was singing. But my attention kept drifting back to Luke. For some reason, I felt like he needed to hear the words more than anyone else in the room.

All four of us raised our voices at once for the final lines and by then, my eyes were firmly locked on his.

"Awake my soul.

Awake my soul.

You were made to meet your maker."

The congregation burst into applause as the four of us held hands and bowed in unison. Then we tipped our heads back, looked up at the ceiling, and whispered, "Thank you, Jesus," in unison, like we always did. In that moment, while I was still lost in the music, all my questions slipped away and I meant it.

We took our seats and I glanced over my shoulder, trying to look casual as I searched for Luke. I couldn't see him; there were too many people between us.

"All month, we've been talking about the Gospel of John," the pastor said. "The purpose of this gospel, as stated by John himself, was to show that Jesus Christ was the Son of God, and that believers in him might have eternal life."

John 3:16 appeared on the wall behind him in bold letters.

I listened to the sermon closer than usual, trying to hear it from Luke's point of view. It was strange to think about hearing these words for the first time, when I almost took them for granted. They were all I'd ever known. I realized that most of the religions I'd been studying didn't even have a bible with the book of John. The entire New Testament didn't exist for them. None of what our pastor was saying up there was core to their whole belief system the way it was to mine.

All my life, I'd believed that Jesus was God's son. That he walked the earth performing miracles, healing the sick, and feeding the hungry. He spoke about peace and tolerance and forgiveness. And when he was crucified, he rose from the dead to give the rest of us access to a heaven we wouldn't have had otherwise. His life was a gift. His death was a gift to me, and people like me.

I thought back to the day I decided to be saved. I was ten years old. I didn't even remember making the decision to do it that day; I just felt this magnetic pull and I stood, stepping away from my friends in the back pew and into the aisle. As the music played, I took what felt like a million steps until I reached the front of the room.

Our pastor was waiting there for me. When I arrived, he held my hands in his. "Do you understand that you are a sinner?" he asked.

"Yes."

"Are you ready to repent of your sins?"

"Yes."

"Do you invite Jesus to become the Lord of your life, to rule and reign in your heart from this day forward?"

"Yes."

I answered those questions with tears sliding down my cheeks, because I meant them deep in my soul. I believed with everything I had in me. But now I knew that, while two billion Christians believed it, too, three billion deeply religious people didn't. To them, Jesus was a man. An important one, a prophet and a messenger, but not the son of God.

Who was right? Were we? Were they?

I knew one thing for certain: the Jesus I invited into my heart that day wouldn't have wanted us judging one another and fighting about what we believed in.

I wondered how Luke was hearing this sermon. Was it

giving him the answers he was looking for? Was it giving him peace?

Aaron stood with his guitar and took his spot on a stool in the center of the stage and started strumming in the background while our pastor wrapped up his sermon. Then he asked us to stand and sing hymn number 454, "What a Friend We Have in Jesus."

Alyssa leaned into my shoulder. "Logan, Jack, and I are going downtown. Want to come?"

I pictured Luke in the back row, wondering if he was still there or if this whole thing had sent him bolting to the parking lot. He wanted answers, and I wasn't sure he was finding them in the sermon, but I hoped he'd stick around and talk with Dad when it was over. Luke seemed to want certainty when he showed up at my house, and I was in no position to give it to him. But my dad could. He never seemed to have a shortage of certainty.

"I'll meet you there. I have something I have to do right after church." I didn't mention Luke.

Alyssa said, "Okay, cool," and then jumped right into the second verse without looking down at her hymnal.

We bowed our heads for the benediction, and as soon as everyone said, "Amen," the room came to life. People stood and started gathering their things, chatting with one another as they left through the double doors. When the sanctuary was nearly empty, I walked toward Luke.

The hymnal was open on his lap, and he was flipping through the pages, reading the lyrics. I sat down next to him.

"Wow. You, like, *really* sing," Luke said. "You're good."

"Thanks. The four of us have been together since eighth grade. We perform in different churches and festivals and stuff, and we compete against other youth choirs all over the country."

"Singing Mumford and Sons songs?"

"Not just Mumford and Sons. Lumineers. Hardwell. Sia." I stopped there but I could have gone on. "It's kind of our thing. We take popular songs and sing them to Jesus instead."

"Seriously?"

I suddenly realized how lame that sounded. "Um, yeah."

"I just . . . wow. Okay." He changed course. "Do you have a CD or something?"

I laughed. "No. But we have a killer website and a YouTube channel with over six thousand subscribers."

We both looked up at the same time and saw Dad walking down the aisle toward us. He was wearing jeans and a dark blue sweater that made his eyes look even brighter than usual. He held out his hand to Luke. "I can't begin to tell you how happy I am to meet you. And under much better circumstances this time."

"I'm glad to be here." I wasn't sure if he meant in the church or walking the earth in general. Luke bent the edge of the hymnal back and forth and then stuffed it into the wooden rack on the pew.

Dad sat on Luke's other side. I couldn't tell if I was supposed to stay there or leave the two of them alone. I glanced over at my dad for guidance, but he was totally focused on Luke.

"I hope I don't embarrass you by saying this, Luke, but I caught the expression on your face while SonRise was singing."

Luke sat up straighter and wrapped his fingers around the edge of the pew. He fixed his gaze on the floor.

"It sounds like your soul has had a bit of an awakening," Dad said.

Luke nodded.

"That's a good thing, you know?"

"Is it?"

"I think it's a wonderful thing. And it's also kind of a scary thing." Dad angled his body toward him. "Do you want to talk about it?"

Luke didn't say anything for a long time. "I don't know how to," he finally said.

Dad looked at me and tipped his head to the back of the room, and I knew that was my cue to let them talk privately. As quietly as I could, I slid out of the pew and left the sanctuary.

When I got into the foyer, I sat on the bottom step of the staircase that led to the balcony and rested my chin in my hands. I could see the back of Dad's and Luke's heads through the big glass window. The rest of the church was empty and quiet.

"Hannah?" Aaron was on the stairs behind me. "You okay?"

"Yeah. I just needed a quiet place to think for a second."

"Do you want me to leave you alone?"

"No, it's okay."

He sat down on the step behind me. "You sounded great today." I felt his hand brush against my shoulder, and I sucked in a breath. I wanted to turn around and look at him, but I was afraid he'd stop touching me, so instead I carefully leaned back until I felt his knee. I reclined into it, and he took the gesture the way I meant it: as permission to keep going. He moved my hair to one side and then slid his thumb across my skin on the back of my neck. Goose bumps traveled up and down my arms.

"What are we doing here?" I asked.

"Why are you asking me? You're the one sitting on the steps."

I peeked over my shoulder and grinned at him. "That wasn't what I meant."

"I know." He was still brushing his fingers slowly across my skin. "Is it okay?"

I tried to play it cool, even though my body felt like it might melt into the stairs. "Yeah, it's okay."

My eyes were half-closed, my head tilted toward him. "Can I ask you something?" I asked.

"Mm-hmm," he said.

"When did you know you liked me?"

When he laughed, I felt his breath, like a warm puff on my skin. "Seattle."

A month earlier, we'd all been together at the Northern Lights Christian A Cappella Choir competition in Seattle. I spent the weekend listening to Alyssa talk about how she and Aaron had been alone in the hotel elevator together, and how he looked at her during dinner, and how he told her he liked her dress, and how his hotel room was only two doors away from ours.

The only reason I spent that weekend thinking about Aaron was because Alyssa hadn't given me any choice.

But as soon as Aaron said "Seattle," my mind immediately jumped to the flight home.

Alyssa, Jack, and Logan were all together in one row, and Aaron and I were across the aisle from them. I'd been disappointed with my seating assignment; I was hoping to sit next to Alyssa. She knew how much I hated flying. When we hit turbulence, she always knew exactly how to calm me down.

For the first hour, everything was fine, but then things got bumpy. The seat belt sign flicked on and the pilot came over the intercom and asked everyone—including the flight attendants—to take their seats. At one point, the plane dropped hard, and I gasped as I gripped both armrests so hard, my knuckles turned white.

Aaron wrapped his hand around mine. "You okay?"

I shook my head without looking at him.

"Close your eyes," he said, and I did.

"Breathe," he said, and I did.

"Good. Now pretend you're a stick floating down the river." His voice was soft and soothing, and I'd let myself get lost in it. "Let the water take you right around the rocks." I opened my eyes. He was using his hand to show me how the stick moved with the bends and the curves. I closed my eyes again. It was better that way. "We're just the stick and the air pockets are the rocks. We're just going to slide right past them, okay?"

I'd nodded.

"The plane knows exactly how to do this, okay?" As he said it, he uncurled my fingers from around the armrest. He didn't let go of my hand right away.

Aaron squeezed my shoulders, bringing me back to reality. "So, why are you sitting on the steps?" he asked.

I gestured toward the sanctuary. "Waiting for my dad."

Aaron peered over my shoulder. "Who's he with? Is that a friend of yours?"

Was Luke *my* friend? He'd always been Emory's boyfriend. I'd spent time with the two of them in the months before she and I stopped speaking, but that was different. I still barely knew him, but now he was my friend, too.

"Remember that guy who died in front of our house last Friday night?"

"Yeah, of course."

"That's him."

Emory
Day 290, 147 to go

Luke returned to school on Monday.

When I stepped into the cafeteria, I saw him immediately, in his usual spot, at his usual table, surrounded by all the usual people and about twenty others.

He looked better, more like himself. His face wasn't quite as puffy anymore, but I could still see the dark circles under his eyes.

As I walked closer, I could hear the buzz of questions all around him. Everyone wanted to know why he didn't tell anyone he was in pain that night, what it was like to ride in the ambulance, and if it was weird to think that someone else's blood was running through his veins.

By the time I reached his side, he was trying to avoid Dean Foster's questions about the stitches they used to fix the tear in his spleen, and if it had hurt when they took the staples out.

"Hey." I gave him a kiss. "You good here?" I whispered.

Luke barely shook his head, but I felt it against my cheek, and that was all it took for me to step into action. "Excuse us. I need to borrow him for just a minute. Don't worry, fans," I said as I led him away. "I'll bring him right back." I steered him past the tables, through the crowds, and into the hall, and then found a quiet place to hide between two locker banks.

"Thanks," he said. "That was a little overwhelming."

I wrapped my arms around his shoulders, came up on my tiptoes, and kissed him. I waited for him to rest his hands on my hips like he always did, but he left them by his sides.

"How's your first day back?"

"Well, I spent the last hour in the guidance counselor's office. Where, you know, I thought I might get a little bit of guidance or maybe some counseling, but instead he informed me that my scholarship has been put on hold. Which I guess I expected. . . . I just thought I'd hear the news from Coach, not from some guy I've never even met before."

"It's just temporary, though, right?"

"It sounded that way at first. He started off saying they wanted to wait a few weeks to see how I heal, so they know if I'll be able to play next year or not. But then he started talking about my SAT scores and my transcript and . . . well, those are hardly glowing." He stared at his shoes. "There's no way I'll get into Denver or any other D-one schools based on my grades alone. I'm supposed to start making a list of all the schools I might want to apply to instead, just in case Denver pulls my offer. He gave me a long speech about how I've been 'resting on physical skills,' whatever that means, and now I need to focus on my academic record and extracurricular activities for the rest of the year."

"The rest of the year? It's the middle of March."

He let out a hard breath. "Yeah. That's a problem."

Owen Campbell walked by and slapped him on the back. "Dude, glad you're okay."

Luke grimaced as he squeezed my arm. "Thanks, man," he said through clenched teeth. "Me too."

Owen kept walking, oblivious. "See you at practice," he said.

I waited until Owen was out of earshot. "Practice?"

"Coach said he expects me to show up, even if I can't play. Support the team and all. But I can't go. Not today, at least."

"You should go. Get back to normal, you know?"

He rolled his eyes.

"What?"

"I thought you were going to cheer me up, not make me feel worse."

I told myself not to take it personally. The last week had been full of pain and medication and surgeries and hospital beds, and his first day back at school had been full of questions and bad news.

"Fine. If you're skipping lacrosse, I'll skip play rehearsal. We can go to the diner, order apple pie à la mode, sit in our booth and talk."

He looked up at the ceiling. "I just want to go home. I'm exhausted." He pulled my hands off his shoulders.

"Are you sleeping?"

"Not much."

"Are you still staying up all night researching dead athletes?"

He shook his head, but I had a weird feeling he was lying.

He'd been acting strange all weekend. When I asked him where he'd been on Sunday, and why he lied to his parents about spending the day with me, he said he'd taken a drive to the beach to be alone and think. I had a feeling he was lying about that, too.

"Have you thought about talking to someone? Like . . . a therapist?"

"Why would I do that?"

"It might help. It's totally natural to feel depressed after what you went through."

"Depressed?" He chuckled. "What makes you think I'm depressed?"

Because he was acting exactly like Mom used to. Cold. Angry. Avoiding everyone and distancing himself from the things he cared about. The old Luke never would have driven to the beach without me.

"A lot of athletes who've been injured go through this. I've been researching it." I reached for my phone. "I can send you links. It's really common."

He took my phone from my hand, closed the browser, and handed it back to me. "I'm not depressed."

And then he kissed me. I wanted to think it was because he really wanted to, but I felt like he was just doing it to shut me up.

"Okay, you win," he said. "Let's go to the diner. A milk shake actually sounds really good."

"Yeah?"

"Yeah."

"Good," I said. "We'll treat that place like a time machine. The second we walk through that door and sit down in our booth, it's two weeks ago. Nothing bad happened, no one got hurt, and nothing's going to happen."

He opened his mouth to say something, but seemed to change his mind. Then he grinned down at me. "I like the sound of that."

Hannah

It was almost midnight, but I couldn't sleep. All I could think about was Aaron.

Earlier that day, Alyssa and I were cleaning up after practice, carrying the equipment from the stage to the music room, when he came out to help us. Alyssa was flirting with him relentlessly, but he kept looking over at me and giving me that half smile that made my whole face flush. I thought she'd noticed, but when we got in the car, she turned to me and said, "God, could you *feel* that sexual tension between Aaron and me?"

I could, but not between them. Between us. Every time we were together. All day. Even during class, all I could think about was being alone with him in the sound booth, with his hands on my waist and his fingers on the back of my neck and his mouth on mine.

You awake? I typed.

As I stared at the screen, waiting for him to answer, I thought about the excited expression on Alyssa's face in the car that day, and I felt a wave of guilt wash over me. And then a second, much larger wave crashed into me when I thought about the look on Beth's face in that picture I'd only seen once.

I knew this whole thing was wrong. But as soon as my phone screen lit up with a new message, the water calmed and the waves disappeared, and Aaron was there, making my heart beat and my face beam and my toes curl. Making me feel like someone cared about me and I wasn't so completely alone.

Aaron: Yeah. Hi.
Hannah: Hi.
Hannah: I can't sleep.

I thought about the way he sat behind me on the stairs the day before, the way he moved my hair to one side and slid his thumb across my skin.

"What are we doing here?" I'd asked. But he never really answered me.

Hannah: Question for you.

I typed it fast so I wouldn't chicken out.

Aaron: Shoot.
Hannah: You know that thing that happened that you said
              would never happen again?

There was a long delay. Finally, he replied.

Aaron: Yeah.

It took me a long time to gather my nerve. My heart was racing as I stared at the screen. Aaron was waiting. It was too late now. I'd started this and I had to keep going.

Hannah: Are you sure it won't happen again?

He answered right away.

Aaron: No.

I kicked at my covers and squealed into my pillow.

Hannah: Good.
Aaron: See you tomorrow.

Tomorrow. I scrolled back to the top of the screen. I was reading the exchange again when I heard a tap on my bedroom window. I raced to the curtain, pulled it to one side, and looked down. I could see someone standing in the dirt below.

I slid the window open and stuck my head outside. "Emory?"

"No. It's Luke."

"Luke?" I asked sharply. "What are you doing here?"

He stepped into the sliver of light coming from the streetlamp. "I have to talk to you." He pointed toward my front door, and then stepped out from between the bushes and disappeared around the corner.

I zipped up my sweatshirt and tiptoed down the hall.

"Hi." He was wearing his Foothill High jacket, rubbing his

hands together to warm them. "I would have texted you, but I don't have your number."

I gave the street a paranoid glance. "Where did you park?"

"Under the streetlamp. Where I always do." He gestured toward my kitchen window.

I felt a surge of adrenaline rush though me. I was sneaking a guy into my room in the middle of the night, and it was kind of exciting, breaking the rules like that. I'd been watching Luke sneak into Emory's house for months, wondering what that would be like.

I looked over my shoulder to be sure my parents hadn't heard us, and then brought my finger to my lips. "Shh . . . Follow me." We padded down the hall and slipped into my bedroom. "What are you doing here?" I asked again.

"I snuck out. I had to show you something." He sat on the edge of my bed and whipped his phone from his pocket. "I've been doing research on NDEs." I must have looked confused, because he added, "Near-death experiences. Check it out." He angled the phone toward me. "There are millions of people like me. Their stories are all over the Internet, all these people who died and came back."

He opened his Notes app and pushed his phone into my hands. I scrolled through a long list of names along with what they saw when they died: *Bright light. Open field. Tunnel and light. Jesus. Fire. Childhood puppy. Grandmother.*

He grinned as he elbowed me. "I'm bummed about that one. I didn't see *my* grandma, and I was totally her favorite."

He was in a good mood. Better than he was the last two times I'd seen him.

"What are all these links?"

"Their videos." He combed his fingers through his hair like he was trying to find the right words. "They've all recorded their stories, right, but none of them match what happened to me. I keep looking for one that explains it, you know?"

I stared at him. "Why is that so important to you?"

He sighed. "It just is. I tried to tell Emory again last night, but every time I try to talk to her, she looks at me like I'm nuts. She doesn't want to hear any of this, you know? She doesn't want to think about me dying, and she doesn't want *me* to think about me dying, and she seems to believe that if I don't talk about it, eventually I'll forget the whole thing and—"

"Everything will go back to normal," I said, finishing his sentence.

He nodded. "Exactly. But . . . that's the thing. I don't want to forget what happened. I don't want to go back to normal. And I don't want to be the person I was. It was like your dad said the other day: My soul woke up. And now I'm different. I know more. I feel more." He stood and started pacing the room.

"After I left the church yesterday, I couldn't stand the idea of going back to my house, so I drove right past my exit, and before I knew it I was getting on PCH. I just kept driving, and soon I was at the ocean.

"I sat there for the longest time, thinking about my conversation with your dad, and I started to realize that I've been spending all my time watching videos and trying to figure out what happened to me through these strangers' stories, but it isn't working. I need to tell *my* story. I'm afraid if I don't, I'll forget all the little details, you know?" He pressed his fingertips into his temples. "I don't want to forget."

His words made me think about something I stumbled on while I was doing my research the night before. "The soul has been given its own ears to hear things the mind does not understand," I said.

He nodded. "Nice. Is that a Bible quote or something?"

"No. Actually it's Rumi."

"Rumi?"

"He's a Muslim poet."

"Oh."

"Look," I said. "I barely knew you before. I have no connection to the old Luke, so that person you were doesn't matter to me. Tell me what you saw."

"I can't."

"Sure, you can."

He looked around, taking in the things on my walls. He looked at the cross that hung next to my door, and the shelving unit filled with books and framed photos of me and my friends.

"Not here," he said. "Not now. But trust me, if I could tell anyone, it would be you."

That made me smile. And it gave me an idea.

"I run almost every day," I said. "I take the same route, and I always end my run at this one spot at the top of a hill. There's this big boulder, and I love to climb to the top and just sit there . . . thinking and watching the world below. Do you have a place like that?"

"Do I have a pet rock?" he said sarcastically. "Um, no." And then he got serious. "I drive. I turn up my music as loud as it can go and I drive until I find a place where I can stop, like I did yesterday."

It was a good answer, but it wasn't really what I had in mind. "You need a room or something. A place that makes you feel safe. Someplace quiet and peaceful where you can be alone."

He thought about it. "Actually, I liked being in your church. That room felt like that to me. For the first time in a week, my thoughts didn't feel overwhelming and terrifying."

It was perfect. The church would be quiet.

"What if we made a video? Not to post or anything . . . Just for you." He was listening, so I went on. "You said you were afraid you'd forget. If you have it recorded, when the experience starts to fade, you can watch it and remember all those little details. And you could show it to Emory. That way, you could tell her without really telling her."

He thought about it for a few moments.

"I can help. Our choir director has a professional video camera. He could shoot it for you." Luke looked panicked, so I backpedaled. "Or, you could just drive somewhere quiet, prop up your phone on the dashboard, and make it all by yourself. You don't need me there."

But I kind of wished he needed me there.

"When?" he asked.

"Whenever you're ready. No rush."

Luke thought about it for a long time. I was sure he was going to pass.

"Meet you around the corner under the streetlight at the same time tomorrow," he said.

Emory
Day 1

Luke and I met on a Friday night during the last week of our junior year.

He and his friends stopped by the diner. My friends and I had already been there for hours. He kept looking over at our table, and when I pointed it out, Charlotte dared me to go over and talk to him.

I'd never been one to pass on a dare, so I jumped up from my seat in the corner of the booth and onto the table, stepping over french fry baskets, coffee cups, and half-eaten cheesecake, while the waitress shot me dirty looks from a few tables away. I landed on the floor with a thud and walked straight over to him. I asked if he wanted to join us, and he stood and let me take his hand like I already knew him. I led him back to our booth. Everyone made room so he could squeeze in next to me.

"I'm Luke Calletti," he said. I already knew that.

"Emory Kern."

We shook hands. He had dark curly hair, piercing green eyes, and full lips. When he spoke, I watched them, wondering what it would be like to kiss them. He was cute. Really cute. "What school do you go to?" he asked.

"Yours," I said, still staring at his mouth.

"Then why don't I know you?"

I shrugged as if I didn't know the answer, but I did: Same school. Different worlds.

After an hour or so, his friends left to go to a party, but he stayed with me. And we kept talking. Then my friends left to go home, but I stayed with him. And we kept talking. And soon, it was just the two of us, sitting alone in the booth, picking at the last piece of apple pie and sipping black coffee while his phone buzzed and chirped on the table.

"I see you have that app that sends nonstop alerts so you'll look super popular to girls you're trying to impress," I said.

He grinned. "My friends are wondering where I am." He silenced the phone and flipped it upside down on the table, hiding the screen.

"You should go to your party."

"Only if you'll come with me."

"I'm not really into parties. But I'll take a ride home if it's on the way."

We left the diner together and walked to the Foothill High student lot.

"That's mine," he said, pointing at a lonely red Jetta parked in the back by the tennis courts.

It was only three blocks to my house, but we talked the

whole way, and when Luke pulled into my driveway, I wasn't ready to say good-bye.

"Do you want to come in?" I asked. "My mom's working late tonight."

"And your dad?"

"Lives in Chicago."

He followed me inside. We sat next to each other on the living room couch, innocently at first, but then he leaned in to kiss me, and that was all it took. We sank deeper into the couch while I stole glances at the door, prepared to push him off me and leap back into my spot the second I heard Mom's key working the dead bolt. But I lost myself in his mouth on mine and his hands on my skin, and before I knew it, I was asking him if he had a condom. I silently scolded myself for being so impulsive, but then I decided I didn't care. In that moment, I wanted him and he wanted me, and I didn't feel like stopping, so I didn't.

Afterward, when I kissed him goodnight on the porch, he pulled away and looked at me. And then he smiled and said, "I think I'm in big trouble, Emory Kern."

It made me laugh. I came up on my tiptoes, wrapped my arms around his neck, and looked him right in the eye. "You are in so much trouble."

He raised his eyebrows. "This is going to be fun."

"The time of your life, I'm guessing."

I pushed my body against his and kissed him harder. It felt like we'd known each other for months, even though we didn't really know each other at all. I pulled away and looked up at him. "Hey, I just want you to know that . . . I've never done anything like that. I've had one boyfriend. We were together for about six months. Until tonight, I've never slept with anyone but him." A nervous laugh escaped my lips. I wasn't sure why I was telling him that. It wasn't really his business. And it shouldn't have mattered. It's not like a guy would have justified a one-night stand that way. But for some reason, I kept talking. "I'm impulsive, but I'm not usually *that* impulsive. I just . . . really like you."

He kissed me again. "You don't owe me an explanation. I really like you, too." We kissed under the porch light for a long time. I was afraid if we kept going, I might suggest sneaking him into my room for the night and letting him hide in my closet. Mom had been so distracted with her new boyfriend and her catering business, she probably wouldn't have even noticed he was there.

But then his phone buzzed and he checked the screen. "My mom," he said. "I'm late." He kissed my forehead. "She can't sleep until I get home, so I'd better put her out of her misery."

I melted. As if he could be more adorable.

"Hey, I have an idea," he said. "Want to have one of those cheesy eighties movie summer romances?"

I laughed. "Yes, I do."

"Good." He gave me a peck on the cheek. "I'll pick you up tomorrow. We'll be a total cliché and go to the beach."

Hannah

I couldn't remember the last time I'd been at the church so late at night. Everything looked different. Quiet. Peaceful. I wrapped my fingers around the back of the last pew and squeezed hard. I still loved this room, but it didn't feel like it used to. It didn't make me feel special, or touched, or inspired. I wasn't awestruck, and for a moment, that filled me with sadness. I didn't want this room to feel like any other room.

We started down the aisle toward the stage, and when Luke and I were halfway there, the side door opened. Aaron stepped onto the stage holding a bunch of recording gear in his hands.

He set everything down on the brown mahogany bench and met us at the bottom of the steps. The two of them shook hands, and Aaron waved toward the stage. "I grabbed a bunch of stuff. Boom mics, lav mics—" He gestured toward all the equipment. "But this is your show, you just tell me what you feel most comfortable with."

"I'm not sure I feel comfortable with any of this," Luke said as he let out a nervous laugh. "I guess we should just get started before I lose my nerve, and I'll figure it out as I go along."

Aaron reached for the lav mic. "Let's start with this." He pinned it to Luke's T-shirt, snaked the cord around his waist, and clipped the battery pack to his jeans. "How's that?"

"Good," Luke said. "Thanks."

Aaron started setting up the tripod.

"Where do you want to sit?" I asked Luke.

His gaze traveled around the room like he was taking it all in, from the narrow, stained-glass windows evenly spaced along the walls, to the huge metal cross that hung over the baptistry. Then he walked to the edge of the stage, sat down on the top step, brought his elbows to his knees, and rested his head in his hands.

"You don't have to do this, okay?" It was true, but still, I couldn't help but wonder if I'd made a mistake bringing him here, calling Aaron, and making it a bigger deal than it needed to be.

"Actually"—he looked up and scanned the room—"I think I like it right here."

"On the step?" I asked, and Luke nodded.

I turned around to look at Aaron, motioning to the video recorder, silently showing him where to set it up. "Perfect. Then I'll be right back. I'm just going to go turn on the stage lights."

"No," Luke said decisively. "I like it this way." When Aaron explained that the camera wouldn't be able to see him very well, Luke said, "That's kind of the whole idea."

Aaron quietly set up the tripod, off to the side, so Luke was in profile, and then he called me over. He stepped to one side so I could see the screen.

I wondered if Aaron was jealous. I secretly hoped he was.

Luke's face was in shadow. I could make out his features, but unless you knew who he was, you probably wouldn't be able to identify him. It was perfect. That was the way he wanted it. I peeked over the top of the camera. "Do you want to check it out first?" I asked him.

"Nope," he said plainly. "I trust you."

Aaron asked him to test the mic, and when Luke said, "Testing, testing," I could hear his voice shake.

"Okay," Aaron said as he pressed the record button. "We're rolling, but no rush. And I'll be editing this, so don't worry about how it sounds. I'll cut out any pauses, or anything you don't like, so take your time."

The room was so silent, I could hear myself breathe.

Luke looked right into the camera. "Hi. My name is Luke."

I moved to the side so I could watch the real Luke and not the one on the tiny screen.

"To be honest, I'm not really sure why I'm doing this." He shifted in place and looked up at me. "I feel like an idiot, Hannah."

"You're thinking about it way too much. Pretend you're alone. It's just you and the camera."

Luke pointed to the first pew, where I sat every Monday

233

morning next to Alyssa, Jack, and Logan. "Maybe it would be easier if I could see you."

"Oh, okay." I crossed the room and sat a few feet away, in front of him but out of the camera's shot. He leaned back, resting his forearms against the stage, already looking a little more comfortable. He took a deep breath and blew it out hard.

"Hi," he repeated. "My name is Luke. And, well, I died eleven days ago." He laughed a little as he said it. "I was dead for three minutes. Three minutes probably doesn't seem like a long time, but it is. Go ahead, set the timer on your phone for three minutes, and don't do anything. Just sit there. I've done that myself about a hundred times since . . ." He trailed off. And then he shot me a questioning look.

"It's good. I promise," I said. "Keep going."

"Maybe you could ask me something?"

There were hundreds of questions swirling around in my mind, but I wanted to start with something small, something easy, to help him build up to what exactly happened in those three minutes. "What's the last thing you remember?"

"I was at a party. I left and got into my car, and as soon as I sat down behind the wheel, I felt this horrible pain in my left side, like I was being stabbed, but I kept driving. When I got to that stop sign by your house, I finally lifted my shirt and looked down. My whole left side was purple. In the dark, it almost looked black. And I felt like I was going to faint, so I punched the gas. All I could think about was getting across the street so I could park."

I thought back to that night. How his car rolled to a stop, like no one was driving it. "What happened next?"

"I reached for my phone on the passenger seat, but it slid to the floor when I hit the gas. When I tried to reach for it again, I threw up. And then . . . I guess I passed out."

I wrapped my hand around my cross pendant and squeezed until it hurt.

"I heard your voice. And then your dad's voice. And then everything was gone."

I rested my elbows on my knees and leaned in closer. I couldn't take my eyes off him.

"Suddenly, I was in this stark white room, only it wasn't a room. There were no walls. But I was standing on something solid, and I was up to my knees in this warm blue water." He smiled at the memory. "It wasn't just warm, it was like a bathtub. And it wasn't just blue, it was more like the color of sapphires. And it glistened. It was thick, like honey, but it wasn't sticky or anything. My legs were heavy, but I could move, and when I did, the water kind of molded to my skin, like it was wrapping itself around my legs. It sounds weird but it felt . . . comforting. Safe.

"I stood there and the water started rising and rising, first past my knees, and then past my waist, and up to my chest. I wasn't afraid when it got to my chin; I somehow knew that I'd be able to breathe even when it covered my mouth and nose.

"And when it finally did, I opened my mouth and drank it in, and I could feel it slide down my throat and move into my stomach and out of my fingertips and down to my toes. And I felt . . . like . . . pure love. Love for my family, and everyone I'd ever known . . ." He rested his hand on his chest. "It was indescribable. It was as if my whole body was filled with pure love. I've never felt so much love before." He'd drifted off somewhere else as he said it, and I assumed he was reliving that feeling. I didn't expect to envy him, but I kind of did. I wanted to feel "pure love." I wanted to experience something like that . . . something so overwhelming and indescribable and profound that there would no longer be any room left for all my questions and doubts.

Then Luke shook his head, bringing himself back to the room, and glanced over at me. He rolled his eyes. "See why I didn't want to tell you this?"

I had goose bumps up and down my arms. "This is amazing. Keep talking."

"I didn't fight it. I didn't want to. I closed my eyes and stretched my arms to my sides and let the water lift me off the ground. I floated around and laughed, because it was all so incredible. Just . . . perfect." He smiled again.

"Could you see the surface?" I asked.

"Yeah. But I wasn't trying to reach it. I was just floating and drinking in the water, and feeling it move though my body. It was so peaceful." He closed his eyes, like he was bringing himself back there. "I felt like I floated that way for hours. And then I heard your voice." He opened his eyes again and locked them on mine. "It wasn't muffled by the water or anything. It came through so clearly."

"You're not finished here," I said.

He nodded. "And I instantly knew what you meant. I thought, 'She's right, I'm not.' And that was it. It was like someone pulled the plug on a bathtub. The water went rushing out to all sides, spilling over the edges of the room without walls, and I was thrown to the surface, gasping for breath. And just like that"—he snapped his fingers—"I was in the back of the ambulance. I heard the EMT yell, 'I've got him!'"

I smiled.

Luke didn't.

"I was so sad." He rubbed his forehead. "I didn't even feel pain, I just felt . . . so empty. And lonely. God, the sadness was so intense. I wanted to get back to that room, back to the water."

I'd been hovering on the edge of tears, and his words sent me over. "I'm so sorry," I murmured, even though apologizing for him being alive didn't make any sense.

"The water was the first thing I remembered when I woke up after surgery, and I felt that sadness all over again. Over the next few days, I started to piece everything together."

He was quiet. I wondered if I was supposed to ask another question.

"What is your life like now?" I asked.

"I can't sleep. I can't eat. Those three minutes are haunting me. I just want to bring myself back there—not because I want to die again or anything—I just need to feel that feeling again, you know?"

I nodded.

He shook out his hands and shifted in place. I thought he was finished. But then he looked at me and said, "Ask me something else."

I didn't skip a beat. I knew exactly what to ask. I'd been wanting to ask it ever since that day he showed up on my front doorstep. "Do you think you saw heaven?"

He locked his eyes on mine again. "When I was a little kid, I was terrified of dying. I hated all those apocalypse-type movies and books, where huge numbers of the population have been wiped out; basically, anything that had to do with death. I'd have nightmares for months." He paused. And then he stared right into the camera. "I don't know if I saw heaven. But I believe my soul was on its way somewhere else. Someplace good. I'm happy to be alive, but someday, I know I'm going to be in that water again. I'm not ready to die or anything, but I'm not afraid of it anymore."

I stood and walked over to him. I sat next to him on the top step and wrapped my arms around him. He hugged me back. "Thank you," he said.

"You're welcome."

I felt how much he needed me. I couldn't remember the last time anyone needed me like that.

And in that moment, I realized this was how Dad felt all the time. People needed him like this every day. It helped me understand his drive and his passion in a way I never had before. I could see why it was addictive.

"See?" I pulled away and smiled at him. "I told you."

"What?"

"You are nowhere *near* finished yet."

We drove home in silence. I didn't know what to say and I figured he was all talked out, so I just stared out the window, watching the neighborhood blur by.

Luke pulled up to the stoplight a few blocks later and let his forehead fall against the steering wheel. He let out a big breath, like he'd been holding it in for miles. Or maybe eleven days.

"Feel better?" I asked and he nodded. "Good," I said as I rested my hand on his back.

The light turned green and he pulled into the intersection.

"Thanks for asking the questions. That helped a lot. But . . . I guess I can't show Emory the video now."

"I'll make sure Aaron edits me out."

We drove a few more blocks. "Why won't you tell me what happened with you two?"

I couldn't give him the details, so I left it vague. "I just said something I shouldn't have said. And she said something she shouldn't have said. You know how those fights go? The words slip out and as soon as they do, you wish you could go back in time, just for thirty seconds, and undo the whole thing. But you can't."

I paused. "Anyway, Emory's words got stuck in my head. They wouldn't go away. I started questioning everything I'd always known, and for a little while, I hated her for that. In less than a minute, with just a few words, she'd taken this huge part of my life away. I found myself listening to Dad's sermons differently. I would go to my praying rock and sit there for hours, trying to feel something." I rested my palm on my chest. "A presence. A voice. Anything. But over the past few weeks, I've started seeing the whole thing differently."

Everything.

What happened to Luke eleven days ago, and even what happened back in the church twenty minutes earlier.

"Like what?" he asked.

I tucked one leg under the other and turned toward him. "Two weeks ago, I would have told you, in no uncertain terms, that you got a three-minute glimpse of heaven. I would have told you that there *is* an afterlife, no question, and that you saw it. I wouldn't have known this, of course, but I would have believed it with such certainty that it became one and the same. I would have told you that the thick blue water was washing you clean from the inside out. I would have told you that if you ever wanted to float in it again, there was only one choice: to ask Jesus into your life as your Lord and savior. To ask for forgiveness of your sins and choose to be born again. That's what I'm *supposed* to tell you right now."

He smiled at me. "But?"

"But I can't. I'm totally fascinated by what you saw, but I have no idea what it was."

"Thanks a lot. That's not very helpful." He raised an eyebrow. I could tell from the look on his face he was joking.

I played along. "And here you thought I was a sure thing."

"Daughter of a preacher man . . ."

"Looking for answers," I said, finishing his sentence.

Luke pulled up under the streetlight next to my house. He put the car in park, but he didn't kill the engine. I started to get out of the car, then I stopped and turned to him. "My dad is convinced that there's some big reason I was the one who found you that night. That it was part of 'God's plan.'" I put it in air quotes. "But I know you were sneaking into Emory's room. You always park right here. I got up to get a glass of water and saw you."

"Do you think there was a reason you found me? That it was all part of some bigger force at work?" Luke asked.

I thought about it. "I'm not sure. But then again, I'm not sure of anything these days."

He was quiet again, staring out the windshield, like he was contemplating something. "Don't edit your voice out of the video. I want Emory to hear it."

"Really? Why?" I asked.

He shook his head. "Who knows? Maybe it did happen for a reason. Maybe I'm supposed to be your glue."

Emory

Day 292, 145 to go

In the cafeteria, Charlotte and I paid for our lunches and went our separate ways. "See you in ten," I said.

I turned toward Luke's table. It was lively. Much louder than usual, with everyone laughing and talking over one another and fighting for airtime.

I slid in next to him.

"Hey, Em." He wrapped his hand around my leg and leaned in to kiss me. It was a school kiss. A nice kiss. A real kiss.

"You're in a good mood today," I said.

"Yes, I am."

"What's up? Did you hear from the Denver coach?"

"Nope, not yet." He took a big bite of his sandwich and washed it down with his soda.

"You're feeling better?"

He took another bite. "Understatement," he mumbled with

242

a mouth full of food. "God, I'm starving. And this tastes delicious. When did our cafeteria food get so good?"

I still hadn't unwrapped my ham and cheese, but I felt confident it was going to taste the same as it did the day before, and the day before that.

Luke finished his sandwich, wadded the wrapper into a ball. He took another big draw on his straw, and he kept going until the sound made it clear he'd hit nothing but ice. Then he turned to Dominic. "Dude, are you going to eat those chips?" Dominic shook his head and tossed the bag to Luke.

"I slept like a rock last night," Luke said as he ripped the chip bag open. "My mom had to wake me up this morning, and I swear, if she hadn't, I think I would have slept the entire day." He devoured the chips in a matter of seconds, and I handed him my water. He took three big gulps.

"Sorry, I can't stop eating," he said with a laugh.

I laughed along. "No, it's good. Keep going. At some point, you could slow down and actually taste the food," I joked. "But—"

He cut me off. "That's the thing. I'm tasting every bite. It's like my taste buds are on overload." He took another drink of water. "Even this water tastes delicious."

"Maybe it's one of your meds," I said, still smiling. I didn't care about the reason; I was just glad to see him back.

"Maybe." He downed the rest of my water.

He reached into the pocket of his hoodie and pulled out a roll of Mentos. The wrapper caught my eye. I thought about the one pinned to my bulletin board. The one with the map he'd drawn.

I turned to face him, straddling the bench, and threw one leg over his. And then I took his face in my hands and kissed him. He tasted like cold cuts and Doritos and peppermint, all mixed together, but I didn't care. He was back.

"What was that for?" he asked.

"What are you doing Saturday night?"

"Hmm. Saturday . . ." He looked out of the corner of his eye, as if he were mentally walking through his jam-packed calendar, and I giggled because I already knew he had nowhere to go. "No plans," he said. "Why?"

"Good. We have a date."

"We do?"

"Yep."

"What are we doing?" he asked.

"I'm not telling you. It's a surprise."

He rested his forehead against mine. "I like surprises."

"I know you do." I kissed him one more time before I stood and grabbed my sandwich. "I've got to get to the theater. Pick me up for the game tonight?"

"I'll be there at six." I got up and started to leave, but he grabbed my hand. "Em? Can I ask a stupid favor?"

"Of course."

"Will you wear my jersey tonight? I know it's dumb, but seeing you in it makes me feel like the guy I was two weeks ago."

I wrapped my arms around him from behind. "I was planning to," I whispered in his ear.

"Thanks." He pulled me in closer and kissed me harder. That time, it wasn't a school kiss. It wasn't even close. It left me wishing we could disappear and spend the rest of the day alone together, just talking and laughing and kissing like we used to. God, I'd missed kissing him.

I left the cafeteria and headed for the theater, feeling like my feet weren't even touching the ground. Luke was back. I was back. We were Luke and Emory again, and everything was going to be fine.

Hannah

After SonRise practice ended, I walked up to the sound booth and knocked on the door. Aaron opened it so quickly, I wondered if he'd run from the other side of the room. "There you are. Just in time. Come look."

He sat on his stool and reached for the mouse. "I lightened the whole thing up a bit. I thought Luke would want to keep it kind of dark, and I couldn't do too much more without it getting grainy, but I adjusted a few things so you can see him a little better."

Luke was still in shadow, and the whole thing had the same mysterious look to it, but now I could make out the hint of a smile on his face. It was clearer, but it was still dark, the way Luke wanted it. "It's perfect."

Aaron pressed PLAY. "Hi. My name is Luke. To be honest, I'm not really sure why I'm doing this."

Aaron and I sat in silence, watching Luke talk about the thick blue water, the room without walls, and the overwhelming sense of love he felt. And then he snapped his fingers and explained how it ended—how my words ended it—and I felt my heart break for him. Luke's expression changed. He choked up. Then we heard my voice. "Do you think you saw heaven?"

He talked about fearing death, and how he believed his soul was safe and on its way to another place. And then, with his eyes fixed right on the camera, he said, "I know I'm going to be in that water again. I'm not ready to die or anything, but I'm not afraid of it anymore."

The tape went black.

"It's amazing," I said.

"It really is. He's articulate and charming," Aaron said. "He draws you in, even before he gets to the part about the water. He's so . . . real."

I knew what Aaron was saying. The video was raw and emotional, unfiltered and powerful, thought-provoking and life-affirming. It made me want to cry and turn cartwheels, both at the same time.

"He reminded me of the kids we picked for the testimonial video, you know? Sincere and earnest without being cheesy," Aaron said. "Actually, I had an idea."

I looked at him out of the corner of my eye. "What?"

"What if you asked Luke to speak at Admissions Night? He could give his testimonial live."

I let out a laugh. "You're joking, right? There's no way he'd do that. He doesn't even go to school here. And besides, he's not going to say yes." I paused. "He's only told us what happened to him. No one else can see this."

Aaron shifted in place. "About that . . . Your dad came up here a few hours ago. I went to open the door and didn't think to hide what I was doing. He walked straight to the computer, thinking I was working on one of the videos for the campaign, and he saw Luke's face. I didn't have any choice but to play it for him."

That meant Dad had heard me asking the questions. He knew I'd snuck out of my room in the middle of the night. I wrung out my hands, already dreading the ride home. "He must have been furious."

"Not at all. He loved it."

I stopped fidgeting. "He did?"

"He was happy to see you talking to Luke about what happened to him. And he didn't say anything, but I think he was also a little bit happy to see his sanctuary in the background."

I pictured Dad sitting in front of the monitor a few hours earlier, watching Luke onstage, speaking so honestly about what he'd been through, and suddenly, everything became clearer. "It was Dad's idea to ask Luke to speak at Admissions Night, wasn't it?"

"How did you know that?"

I locked my eyes on his. "I know my dad."

Aaron looked impressed. "Luke is this good-looking, nice, clean-cut kid who wasn't a believer before, but died and came back changed. He believes something important happened to him."

"He doesn't know what happened to him," I corrected.

"Maybe not, but he's starting to realize he's part of something bigger. Don't you think he's supposed to pass it on?"

"Not if he doesn't want to."

I thought back to the conversation Luke and I had after we shot the video. He didn't necessarily believe he went to heaven. Or maybe he did, and I was the one who told him he might not have. I wasn't sure. But either way, he was still figuring this whole thing out. I couldn't put him on a stage in front of hundreds of applicants and their parents and make him talk.

"Luke experienced something intense that night," Aaron said. "He's trying to figure out what it all means. And talking about it with you, and to a camera . . . it seems to be helping a little, don't you think?"

I had to admit, Aaron was right about that. Luke had seemed like a totally different person when we drove home from the church the night before, like a weight had been lifted from his shoulders. And he'd been texting me all day, telling me how everything tasted better, and colors were more vivid, and his sense of smell seemed to be heightened. He said he hadn't researched NDEs at all when he got home. He fell asleep right away and didn't wake up until his alarm went off in the morning. He hadn't slept for three hours in a row since the accident.

"He'll say no," I said. Aaron didn't respond. He just sat there, watching me, waiting for me to continue. "I'll ask him, but I want to do it in person."

I needed Luke to see my face and to know he wasn't under any pressure to say yes.

I pulled out my phone and started a new text to him. I typed, *Video's done. It's incredible. Come by tonight?* I pressed

SEND and dropped the phone on the table next to the keyboard. It buzzed right away.

Luke: Can't tonight. Tomorrow?

Hannah: Sure

Luke: Meet you at the corner

"He's coming over tomorrow night," I told Aaron.

"Oh . . . good. When?"

"Midnight, I guess. He'll wait until our parents all go to bed. He has to sneak out. He's not allowed to drive."

Aaron picked up the mouse and started clicking around, closing windows, dragging files into folders. He wouldn't look at me. I thought about our text exchange a few nights earlier, remembering the way we flirted, talking about the thing that wasn't supposed to happen again but might happen again.

"I have no right to be jealous," he said under his breath.

"No, you don't." He was the one with the girlfriend. He was the one breaking all the rules. "But are you?"

Aaron turned around. He looked at me like he had something to say, but he wasn't sure he should say it. "You two on the stage . . . when he hugged you."

"He needed a friend."

"It looked like more than that."

"It wasn't." I shook my head slowly. "He's Emory's boyfriend. I'm trying to help him."

He sighed. "Look, I realize I have no right to ask this, but I have to know." He twirled a mic cord around his finger. "Did he try to kiss you after you two left here?"

He was jealous. He was *definitely* jealous. Like he'd said, he had no right to be, but I kind of liked that he was.

"No."

"Did you want him to?"

I looked right at him. "No. Not at all."

"Are you sure?"

"I told you. I want *you* to kiss me. I've spent the last week wanting you to kiss me again."

He traced my jawline with his finger and brushed his thumb over my lips. And then he leaned in closer and brought his mouth to mine. His lips were soft and warm, and when he parted them, I did the same. I knew I should have asked him about Beth, but I didn't want to know. I knew I should have stopped him, but I didn't.

"What are you grinning about?" he asked between kisses.

"This," I said. "You." And that made him kiss me even harder.

Emory
Day 293, 144 to go

"Finally!" Mom came barreling around the corner, holding a big box in her arms. "I've been waiting for you all afternoon. Where have you been?"

"Where else? The play is one week from tomorrow. I was running lines at the diner with Charlotte and Tyler." I knew she'd been lost in her own little world lately, but it was almost as if she'd entirely forgotten what was happening in mine. But I wasn't about to let it get to me. I'd just done the whole third act off book, and I was finally beginning to feel like I didn't suck after all. "I've gotta say, I'm on fire."

"Of course you are," Mom said. "I told you you'd get your lines down. You always do."

I tried to remember when she'd told me that, but I was coming up blank. I didn't let that get to me either. Instead I gestured toward the box and changed the subject. "What are you all giddy about?"

"Invitations are here!"

Good feeling, gone. That glow I'd been happily basking in was instantly replaced by an uncomfortable knot deep in my gut. Mom stepped behind me, using the box to push me through the entryway and into the kitchen. "Come on," she sang. "Let's look."

Her giant three-ring bound wedding planner was on the table, open to the guest list. She set the box down next to it, disappeared into the kitchen, and came back with a knife.

"Drumroll, please . . ."

I thought she was kidding, but then she pointed at the table and widened her eyes. I drummed my fingers against the edge of the table while she slid the knife across the seam, splitting the packing tape in two. Then she peeled the top back and took out a smaller white box wrapped in shiny gold ribbon.

"Oh, it's so beautiful."

"It's the box, Mom."

"I know . . ." She tugged at the ribbon, and it fell to the table. Then she opened the lid and grabbed the invitation on top. She handed it to me. The paper was soft and a pretty shade of light green, and I stared at it while she picked up another invitation and read aloud:

"Jennifer Fitzsimmons and David Mendozzi request the honor of your presence at their wedding."

She stopped reading and held her arm in front of my face. "I've got chills!"

I didn't have chills. I had a lump in my throat the size of Canada. But I shot her a fake grin, and she went back to ogling the invitation.

"Oh, I love embossed type." She brushed her fingertip over the raised lettering. "Isn't this elegant?"

I didn't reply. I just dug through the box. "How many did you order?"

"Sixty. The guest list has ninety-two people, most of them couples, but I wanted to get a few extra in case I decide to add anyone."

I reached for her binder and scanned the list. Ninety-two names. Ninety-two people who were going to show up at a hillside ceremony, dance in an enormous tent under tiny white lights, and eat and drink thousands of dollars' worth of food and wine. I figured D-bag's friends would make up the majority of the wedding list, but a lot of the names were familiar. Friends from her catering circle. High school friends. Couples she and Dad used to have over for dinner, and families we used to visit and go on vacations with.

They might all come to her wedding, but not a single one of them could have been bothered to call or text when Mom wouldn't get out of bed for nearly a year. I would have given anything for just one of these ninety-two people to show up on our doorstep back then.

"You're inviting the Jacquards?" I asked.

"Of course I am. We've known them all your life." She unwrapped the cellophane and started stacking the invitations and envelopes in two neat piles. "And you're going to have to figure out how to be in the same room with Hannah by then, because I'm not about to let this ridiculous fight of yours ruin my big day."

"It's not ridiculous," I muttered.

I checked the list. At least Luke and his family would be there, too. I could always hide out with the four of them.

I peered into the box and pointed at a small cellophane-wrapped bundle tied with a bright blue bow. "What's that?"

Mom reached for it, tugged at the ribbon, and slid the covering away. "Oh, Emory. Look. It's our Save the Date card."

The background was a black-and-white image of Mom and David at the beach, him down on one knee, presenting her with a ring, and her covering her mouth, looking completely shocked. A local photographer staged the whole thing. In real life, D-bag proposed to her one night at our house. When I went out one Saturday night, she wasn't wearing a ring, and when I came home, she was.

"We should start addressing these this weekend. *The Knot* says you should send out Save the Date cards six to eight months in advance, so I'm already way behind."

This weekend.

And after that, there would be no taking it back.

Hannah

I should have been sick of Luke's video by that point—I'd already lost count of how many times I'd seen it—but watching it next to him made me feel like I was seeing it for the first time.

On-screen, Luke stared into the camera and said, "Someday, I know I'm going to be in that water again. I'm not ready to die or anything, but I'm not afraid of it anymore."

The screen went dark and the car was silent.

"What do you think?" I asked.

He made a face. "It's good, I guess. It's just weird watching myself talk about what happened like that. I sound so . . . clearheaded. I don't feel that way most of the time."

"You were being totally honest."

"Yeah." He slid his finger across the glass, rewinding the video back to the beginning. "I'm not sure I could do that again, but . . ."

"You're glad you did it?" I asked, finishing his sentence.

He smiled at me. "I'm glad I did it."

As he pressed PLAY, watching it a second time, I thought about what Aaron said. I looked at Luke's face. He seemed relieved. Happy. Happier than I'd ever seen him.

"I'm supposed to ask you a question," I said when the video ended. I had to say it fast before I chickened out. "We have this big admissions event coming up. It's basically the way we get kids to apply to Covenant. SonRise is singing. The dance team is performing. And a few people are sharing short testimonials."

He shot me a look. "If you're going where I think you're going with this, no way."

"Why not? It's the exact same room, only with, like, two hundred more people in it." I thought a joke might lighten things up, but he didn't even crack a smile.

"No way," he repeated.

"I'm kidding. I figured that's what you'd say. My dad needs another speaker, and I guess he happened to walk into the sound booth while Aaron was editing this and he got all excited. He thought—"

Luke cut me off. "Wait. Your dad saw this?"

I steeled myself, preparing to hear him lay into me for being so careless. "It was an accident. I'm sorry."

I waited, still expecting him to be angry or embarrassed, but he didn't seem to mind. "I don't care. It's your dad. He was there when it happened, so . . ." His sentence hung in the air, unfinished. "Is your dad the one who wants me to speak at your admissions thing?"

"Yeah."

"Why?"

I was surprised he'd ask, but he genuinely didn't seem to understand why anyone would care. "He was moved by the video, and he thinks other people will be, too. You're relatable, you know? You're just a normal, average guy who had this extraordinary thing happen to him. And there's something about you. When you talk, you make people want to listen."

Luke tapped his fingers on the steering wheel, taking it all in. I didn't want to push him, but I couldn't help but think that Aaron had been right about what he'd said in the sound booth.

"It seems like talking about what happened is helping you. You're sleeping. You're eating. That day you showed up on my doorstep, you looked battered and broken. But now you look like I remember you. Like the Luke before all this happened."

Luke stared out the window for almost a full minute. "I honestly don't know who I am anymore."

I had no idea how to respond to that, so I sat there quietly, waiting for him to break the silence again.

"I can't say no to your dad. I owe him."

I shook my head. "You don't owe him anything. Really. Do this because you want to, not because you feel obligated to my dad or me or anyone else. Do it because talking about what happened to you is helping you to get it out of your head."

"When is it?" he finally asked.

"Next Friday. At seven o'clock."

Luke thought about it some more. And then he said, "I have a lacrosse game." I thought that was the end of it, but then he shook his head hard. "But what the hell. I can't play anyway. And I can't stand to watch my team and hear them down on the field, talking about their college plans, while I sit on the bench and cheer like an idiot. Tell your dad I'll do it."

I had to ask. "Are you sure?"

His mouth twisted up on one side. "It'll be fun."

Emory
Day 295, 142 to go

I'd recruited Tyler, Charlotte, and Addison to help me with my big date.

As soon as rehearsal ended on Saturday, Tyler drove us to Charlotte's house and we hauled a plastic box with the word CAMPING written on the side from the garage to the backyard. We dropped everything on the grass.

Tyler opened the box and started rummaging through it, while Charlotte untied a string on the long, narrow bag and let the blue-and-orange tent spill out.

"So first, you unroll it and lay it flat, like this," Charlotte said, demonstrating. "And then you just feed these bendy poles through these little pockets. See, the whole thing pops up as you go. Once all the poles are threaded through, you tuck them into the grommets and stake it down with these—although it's not like it'll be windy or anything, you really don't need to do that part."

"Wait, go back. What are grommets?" She showed me the little holes with the colorful reinforced stitching that lined the edges of the tent. "That's a good word. I like that. Grommet." I said it a few more times.

"Weirdo," she said, handing me a thin, bendable pole. "Here, you take that side, I'll take this one."

"Okay, so when you're actually camping, what do you do after you put up the tent?" I asked.

"Get in and get naked," Tyler said.

"Can't," I said, still working on the tent. "His doctor hasn't cleared him. I've seen the post-op instructions, and it's all very clear. Three weeks, no sooner. Besides," I added, "he won't let me see his scar."

"You haven't seen it?" Charlotte finished her side of the tent. I was still struggling to get mine past the halfway point.

"He says it's disgusting. And maybe it is, but I really don't care." I finally got the pole over the top of the tent. I started onto the other side.

Tyler returned to the camping box. "Well, if you're not having sex, you might as well have these," he said as he pulled two long metal sticks from the box and held them in the air.

"What on earth are those for?" I asked.

"S'mores," Charlotte said.

"Oh." I pictured the fire pit on Luke's patio. His parents always sat out there after Calletti Spaghetti with their feet propped up on the edge and wineglasses in their hands. "Yeah, we definitely need s'mores. Add those to the pile." The grocery store was our next stop anyway. I added graham crackers, chocolate, and marshmallows to my mental list.

"And if you get bored, you can duel." Tyler tossed one of the metal sticks to Charlotte, and the two of them danced around the lawn, pretending to fight.

I finished my side of the tent. As I then stood back, admiring my work, my phone buzzed in my pocket. I took it out and read the screen.

Addison: Coast is clear!

"Guys." I waved my phone in the air, and Tyler and Charlotte stopped dueling. "We're on."

We took everything apart and loaded it in the back of Tyler's car.

My feet were kicked up on the edge of the fire pit, and I was pretending to read a book when Luke opened the sliding glass door and stepped outside.

"What's going on?"

"Surprise." I stood and gestured toward the bag of marshmallows, the box of graham crackers, and the giant chocolate bars. And then I pointed at the blue-and-orange tent I'd pitched on his lawn. Those tiny strands of twinkle lights made it glow from the inside out.

"You said you wanted to turn me into a camper, remember?"

I came up on my tiptoes and kissed him. And then I took his arm, leading him to the grass. I could hear the music playing as I unzipped the tent and crawled inside.

"Where did you get all this?" he asked as he climbed in next to me and collapsed onto the pile of pillows.

"The tent and the sleeping bags are Charlotte's. Addison let me borrow the lights."

"Addison helped you with this?"

"Mm-hmm."

I reached into my pocket and pulled out his hand-drawn map. I handed it to him and he held it up to the light. "You drew that two weeks ago. Can you believe that? It seems like it was months ago."

He turned it over in his hands. "Yeah, it does."

"Well, I thought we'd better get planning. Prom. Graduation. Road trip."

"I like the sound of that," he said, looking up at me.

"Good." I sat up, folded my legs underneath me, and started pulling books from the stack. "I went to the library. Check it out. We have *Northern California Camping*." I held it in the air. Then I reached for another one. "*Beach Sleeps: A California Camping Guide*."

Luke smiled. "Sleeping is good."

"And *California Coast Camping*."

"Nice. A for alliteration," he joked.

"And my personal favorite." I held it up. "*Curious George Goes Camping*. I'd figured I'd better start with the basics."

We spent the next hour going through the books, plotting our trip, stopping to kiss, and breaking for s'mores. I wasn't sure if it made him feel better, but it gave me what I needed: time alone with him and something to look forward to. He already seemed more like himself.

We were cuddled up on the patio sofa in front of the fire pit, when he kissed the top of my head and said, "There's something I want to show you." He reached into his jeans pocket and pulled out his phone. "But I'm afraid you're going to be mad."

"What is it?"

"Promise you won't be mad."

The last thing I wanted to do was get in a fight with him. "I won't be mad."

"It's about that night I got hurt." He said it like he was dreading my reaction, and I sighed. I didn't want to talk about that again. I was trying to move on to camping and s'mores and good things that had nothing at all to do with almost losing him.

"Look," he said, shaking his head. "I know what you're thinking. You want me to stop dwelling on what happened. And trust me, I want that, too. But I can't. I'd love to turn off my brain and make this whole thing go away, but it's not that easy." He got quiet. And then he handed me his phone. I looked at him out of the corner of my eye, and he gestured toward it with his chin. "Play it."

I hit the button, and Luke appeared in the frame. The room around him was dark and his face was in shadow, but I could tell it was him.

"Hi. My name is Luke. To be honest, I'm not really sure why I'm doing this." He looked off to one side and then back at the camera. "I died eleven days ago." He said it casually, like it was no big deal. "I was dead for three minutes. Three minutes probably doesn't seem like a long time, but it is."

I sat up straight and held the phone in both hands. I never took my eyes off the screen. Luke kept talking, then he suddenly stopped. "Ask me something," he said.

And then I heard a girl's voice. "What's the last thing you remember?"

I'd know that voice anywhere.

In the video, Luke kept talking. The party. Driving to my house. Blacking out behind the wheel. I tried to listen to what he was saying, but I couldn't get past hearing Hannah's voice.

Luke talked about the thick, warm water and the room without walls and how he heard Hannah say, "You're not finished yet," and suddenly, the water was gone and he was back. He said he didn't want to be there. He talked about not being afraid of dying. And then the screen went black.

I stared at him. "Why didn't you tell me any of this?"

"I didn't know how to."

"But you knew how to tell Hannah?"

He was quiet. "I can't explain it, Emory. I feel like I can talk to her. Maybe it's because she was the one who found me that night."

"So, if I'd been the one to find you, would you have told me instead?" I waited for him to answer, but he didn't have to; his face said it all.

"When did you make this video?"

"Last Tuesday?"

I replayed the details of the day in my mind. We'd spent lunch together. He'd sat in the back of the theater after school and watched my *Our Town* rehearsal, and then we went back to his house for Calletti Spaghetti and everything felt so totally normal, like it had before. I stuck around for a long time afterward. We talked. We kissed. He seemed a little distracted, but not distant. Addison drove me home. I wanted him to sneak out later, climb our ladder, and hang out with me longer, but I knew he wasn't allowed to drive, so I didn't even ask. But he'd snuck out and driven over to my house that night anyway. Not to see me—to see Hannah.

"It felt good to talk about it. I know you want to forget the whole thing and move on, but I need to remember. You have no idea what life has been like in my head. This huge thing happened to me two weeks ago, and I swear, it's like that *Groundhog Day* movie, repeating over and over again, all day long. But talking about it helped. I felt better yesterday. Last night, I slept for twelve hours! I haven't slept like that since I got hurt."

I wanted to be happy for him. I wanted to be understanding. I wanted to let the whole thing with Hannah go, but I couldn't. It was impossible to wrap my head around it. He'd talked to her about everything. He hadn't talked to me about any of it.

"There's more," he said.

I didn't want to hear any more. "What?"

"Her dad wants me to speak at some admissions thing next week."

I knew all about their Admissions Night. Hannah and her parents had begged me to go freshman year. And sophomore year. They'd trot out their best students and make high school feel like a day at a theme park.

266

"You don't even go to school there."

He had a strange look on his face, as if he'd been wondering the same thing. "I guess he thinks people will connect with my story anyway, you know? I'm a normal guy and this, like, miracle happened to me."

"Is that what happened?" I rolled my eyes. "He's using you, Luke."

I *got* it. Completely. Luke was perfect. He was charming. Articulate. Handsome. An all-American boy talking openly about his life-altering experience, how he didn't believe in heaven, and now he did, or at least he thought he might.

"It's not like that. And so what if he is? He and Hannah saved my life. I have no idea why speaking at his school thing will help, but he seems to think it will. And I kind of owe him one, don't you think?"

I didn't think he owed Pastor J a thing, but I couldn't figure out how to tell Luke that without sounding like I was jealous. And I could tell he needed my support on this.

I picked at some lint on my jeans. "Can I come?"

He nodded. "I was hoping you would."

That made me feel a bit better. "When is it?"

"Friday."

"Next Friday?"

"Yeah."

"That's opening night of *Our Town*."

"Oh. It is?"

Oh? I wanted to punch him.

"But the play is on Saturday night, too, right?" he asked. "I can do both."

It felt like he'd punched *me* instead. He'd miss opening night? For this?

"I've been working on *Our Town* for five months. You've known Hannah and her family for, like, two seconds."

I stood up and walked away. I heard him call my name, but I didn't stop. I marched across the lawn, unzipped the tent, and gathered the map and my books.

I couldn't believe this was happening. And it wasn't only about the fact that he'd confided in Hannah. As much as it hurt, I could see why he would. It was the other thing. The thing I couldn't tell him. The thing Hannah knew and no one else on the planet did.

"Emory!" he yelled. I could hear him struggling to get up.

I grabbed my things and marched back to him. "Did she tell you what our fight was about? What started it? Did she tell you?"

He shook his head. "No. She keeps telling me to ask you."

I pressed my books against my chest.

He stood, taking slow, cautious steps in my direction. He took the books, set them on the couch, and then gripped my arms with both hands. "Tell me. Please. What was your fight about? Talk to me."

I wanted to. I honestly did. But telling him would be like lighting the fuse on the first stick in a room full of dynamite. It would be unstoppable, and it wouldn't end well.

"Why should I talk to you when you couldn't talk to me?" I asked as I jerked my arms out of his grasp.

That shut him up. I left the books where they were and headed for the sliding glass door. As soon as I was inside the empty house, I reached for my phone and called Tyler.

He picked up after the third ring. "Speak."

"Can you come get me?"

"Be right there," he said.

I walked through the living room, past the wall of photos of the Callettis, out the front door, and down the driveway. I rounded the corner and waited on the other side of the tall hedges that lined Luke's property, out of sight from the house. As I stood in the dark, I thought about Hannah and the ten minutes it took for her to come get me that night. Ten minutes. Those ten short minutes had changed everything.

When Tyler finally pulled up, I got inside and fastened my seat belt. "Everyone's at the diner," he said. "Want to go there?"

I nodded.

Tyler and I drove in silence for the next two blocks. Eventually, he broke it.

"What one question would you ask a time traveler about the future?"

I thought about it longer than Tyler normally would have allowed, but there were too many questions swirling around in my mind to pick just one. And every one of them had to do with my future with Luke. I ignored all of them and took it in the direction I knew Tyler intended.

"Are we living on other planets?" I said. I let my head fall to one side.

"Does McDonald's still make the Shamrock Shake?" Tyler asked.

It felt good to laugh.

Hannah

Alyssa was waiting for me at my locker at lunch on Monday. "Hey, you."

"Hi." I dialed my combination and started unpacking my books.

I hadn't told Alyssa about Luke. If I told her about the video, she'd want to see it. If I told her about his testimonial, she'd want to listen to him rehearse.

"Did you hear? Aaron canceled SonRise practice today."

"He did?" It was unlike him, but it wasn't like we really needed to work on the two songs we were singing at Admissions Night anyway. And if the sanctuary was going to be empty right after school, Luke could come by even earlier.

As I was shutting my locker, my phone chirped.

Dad: Need to see you in my office.

"That's weird." I showed Alyssa the screen. "Come with me. I'm sure it will just take a sec." We changed course, heading for the office instead of the cafeteria.

I opened the glass door. Dad's assistant was on the phone, but she covered the mouthpiece and said, "Go in. He's expecting you."

"What's up?" I asked as I flung the door open. And then my stomach dropped. Aaron was sitting in one of the chairs on the other side of his desk, facing Dad. They both looked upset.

No.

He knows about Aaron and me.

How can he know about Aaron and me?

"Have a seat," Dad said. "Alyssa, would you excuse us, please?"

This is bad. This is very, very bad.

Alyssa backed out of his office and closed the door behind her.

Aaron is going to lose his job. Because of me.

"What's going on?"

They looked at each other. My heart was beating so hard I could feel the steady thump in the back of my throat.

"We need to tell you something," Dad said. "We were planning to tell you and Luke later today, but now it can't wait."

Luke? What did he have to do with it?

"What's going on?"

I was waiting for my dad to reply, but Aaron jumped in instead. "I've been sending all our promotional videos to the local pastors so they could help us promote Admissions Night."

I raised an eyebrow. "I know. And?"

"A couple of them have been really helpful and especially vocal. Like the pastor at Lakeside."

Lakeside Christian Church was a few towns away from us and easily three, maybe four times bigger than we were. They televised their Sunday services, streamed sermons on their website, and had a huge following on YouTube. Dad had never told me which churches invested in the school, but I'd always assumed Lakeside was one of them.

Aaron looked at Dad. Dad looked at me.

"What's going on?" I asked.

"I sent him Luke's video. I told him it wasn't part of the campaign . . . that I was only sending it because I thought he would find it powerful and inspiring."

My stomach dropped. "You didn't . . ."

"I told him to," Dad quickly added.

I looked at my dad, and then back at Aaron, trying to decide which one of them to scream at first. Instead I asked a stupid question. "When?"

"On Saturday," Aaron said. I could tell by the look on his face that he had more to say. "He posted it online."

"He what?" I dug my fingernails into the leather chair and stared at him, trying not to scream.

"I'm sorry," Aaron said. "I'm so sorry."

I looked at Dad, waiting for him to parrot Aaron's words, but he didn't. "Come see this," he said as he curled his finger toward him. I stood and walked around to his side of the desk. Luke's video was open on his monitor.

Dad pressed PLAY.

"Hi. My name is Luke . . ."

Dad pointed to the lower left-hand corner and I saw a heart next to the number 5,438. As I was watching, it climbed to 5,439. 5,440. 5,441.

I couldn't speak. I couldn't move. I wanted to yell, and I wanted to storm out of the room, and I wanted to drive straight to Foothill High and find Luke so I could tell him what they had done. But my feet seemed to be rooted to the floor; my mouth no longer seemed capable of forming words.

"I'm sure he thought he was doing Covenant a favor by posting it," Dad said. "There's a link to the website and details about Luke speaking at Admissions Night."

There was something about the way he said it, as if the fact that it was serving a purpose made it somehow okay. I narrowed my eyes on him. "Why hasn't it been deleted yet?"

Dad folded his arms across his chest. "Because it's working. More than a hundred people have downloaded applications since yesterday," he said. "The phone has been ringing off the hook. We've been getting RSVPs to Admissions Night all afternoon."

I looked back and forth at the two of them. "You're kidding me right now. You shared Luke's video without his permission and you're talking about applications?"

The numbers on Dad's screen climbed higher:

5,459

5,467

5,475

"Luke *trusted* me. I trusted *you*, Aaron. And you both . . ." I couldn't finish my sentence.

"It was an accident," Aaron said.

I covered my mouth. "I don't believe you," I said. It might have been a mistake initially, but neither one of them had done anything to stop it or fix it. Dad still hadn't even apologized for his role in the whole thing.

"You have to see something," Dad said. He closed the video and opened an email.

The message was addressed to Luke. The writer identified herself as a forty-two-year-old woman with stage four bone cancer and three kids, two sons and a daughter, all in high school. She'd seen Luke's video, and she had to write to thank him, because his words had given her and her whole family hope—not that she would survive, because they knew that was impossible—but that she would be going to a good place. She called his message a gift from God, an answered prayer.

"I'm not saying what we did was okay," Dad said. "It wasn't okay. Not at all. But we have messages like this one from people all over the country. They've been coming in all day." Dad tapped his finger against the monitor. "Luke might not think he's ready to talk and share his story, but look at him, Hannah. Look." He paused. I listened to Luke's words. I watched his facial expressions. He looked confident and strong. A lot stronger than he'd looked either time he'd come to my house. "Luke is helping all these people. He's healing them. And he's healing himself at the same time. Even if he doesn't know it yet."

"And we're getting messages from pastors all over the country, too," Aaron added. "They all want Luke to come speak at their churches and give presentations at their schools."

I wasn't following any of this. "What does that have to do with Covenant? Luke's not even a student here."

"It doesn't matter. You know what they say—'A rising tide lifts all boats.'" Dad stood and walked over to me. "Enrollment is down at schools like Covenant because people don't think their kids need faith-based schools and youth groups and Sunday services. But that's exactly what kids need. We need them to believe again. We need them to feel invested in something bigger than themselves. This isn't a problem that affects our school, it's a problem that affects our country. People need faith."

"And Luke is going to fix that?"

"Not alone, but he's a fantastic start."

"Pastor J." Aaron looked up from his phone and cleared his throat. "I just got an email from another news outlet."

I felt the color drain from my cheeks. "A news outlet?"

Luke was going to flip. He was going to hate me.

I turned to leave. I had no idea where I was going to go, but I had to get out of that office so I could text Luke and tell him what happened. I wasn't about to let him hear it from them. And I couldn't stand there a second longer. But Aaron was standing in the doorway, blocking my path.

I glared at him. "Move."

"I will," he said, "but first, let me say one thing."

I crossed my arms.

"Luke's last name isn't anywhere," Aaron said. "I've checked. No one has any idea who he is, and we're not going to tell them. He doesn't have to speak publicly unless he wants to, okay? This is totally up to him."

I wasn't sure my dad agreed with that, but I didn't turn around to see his expression.

"How could you do this to him?" I asked.

"It wasn't just for Luke. It was for you, too." Aaron looked over his shoulder at my dad, and then turned back to me. "I know about Boston."

I thought back to that day Dad and I sat in the parking lot after that painfully silent ride to school, when he begged me not to be angry with him for what he'd done. "I'm going to do whatever it takes to make this right, okay? Do you trust me?"

I told him I did.

"I'm so sorry," Aaron said. "I had no idea."

I hated what the two of them had done to Luke. It was even worse that they'd convinced themselves that it was okay, because of me.

I looked straight into Aaron's eyes. "Move. Now."

Emory
Day 297, 140 to go

At lunch on Monday, I found Luke waiting for me outside the theater doors.

"I won't do it, Emory. Is that what you want me to say?"

He'd been texting me since I left his house on Saturday night, begging me to talk to him. He texted me on Sunday morning, and when I didn't reply he came over. I made Mom kick him out.

I pushed past him and started dialing my combination. "No, that's not what I want you to say. I don't want you to come to my play because I made you feel guilty about it." I shoved my books inside and slammed the door. "I can't believe you're doing this."

"I already said yes. I don't have a choice."

"Of course you do. You're making your choice. Right now. No one is forcing you to do this, Luke."

"I can't tell Pastor J no."

It sounded so familiar. All my life, I'd been listening to Hannah tell me how she couldn't say no to her dad.

"You want to know why Hannah and I are fighting? Because of this. She never stands up to her dad, especially when it counts most. I don't get it. He's just a guy. If you don't want to speak at their Admissions Night, just tell him that. Tell him you don't want to do it."

Luke fixed his gaze on his shoes.

And I knew.

"It's not about Pastor J, is it?"

He shook his head.

"You want to do it, don't you?"

He shifted his weight from one leg to the other. He wouldn't look at me.

"Yeah. I think I do." He combed his fingers through his hair and finally met my gaze. "I don't expect you to understand this, Emory."

"Good. Because I don't."

"Hey, Luke!" We both turned around and found Courtney Schneider standing behind us, surrounded by all her friends. She shoved her phone at him. "Is this you?"

His voice filled the air. "Hi. My name is Luke. To be honest, I'm not really sure why I'm doing this."

The color drained from his face, and despite that fact that I'd been yelling at him seconds earlier, I threaded my arm through his.

"Where did you get this?" he asked.

"Someone posted the link on Twitter."

"Twitter?" Luke asked.

"I just had to tell you how amazing this was." She rested her hand on her chest and stared at Luke with her big brown doe eyes. "I . . . we . . ." She glanced around at her friends, and they all shot him sympathetic smiles, like he needed their pity or something. "No one had any idea what you'd been through. That was just . . . wow." She hugged him. "I'm glad you're okay. If you ever want to talk . . ." She trailed off.

She didn't glance at me once. It was as if I'd become invisible.

When Courtney walked away, Luke turned to me. He looked like he was going to be sick. "I don't . . ."

My whole body was on fire and my mind was racing. I was beyond furious, ready to fight for him.

"You were right," Luke said. "I shouldn't have trusted her."

I couldn't believe Hannah would do that to him, and yet somehow, against all proof otherwise, I wasn't entirely sure she had.

Luke dug his fingertips into his scalp and walked in small circles. Then he stepped back and kicked a bottom locker so hard that he made a dent in the door.

I pulled him away. "Stop! You're going to rip your internal stitches."

He twisted away from me, but then he stepped forward again and pulled me into his arms. I could feel him breathing hard and fast, and I wrapped my arms around his neck and held him as tight as I could. I kissed his neck and told him it would be okay, that we'd figure out what happened together.

"Do you have your keys on you?" I asked, sliding my hand into his front pocket where he always kept them. I answered my own question when I pulled them out and spun them around my finger. "Let's go. I'm driving."

Hannah

I barreled out of the office and ran straight into Luke. Emory was right behind him. He didn't say a word, he just stared at me, looking disheveled and betrayed.

"I didn't do this," I said. "I swear."

Luke didn't speak. I wished he would. Or that Emory would. Their collective silence was worse than anything they could have said.

"You have to believe me. I just found out."

His expression softened. I probably should have felt relieved, but I still couldn't get past the guilt. Even if I hadn't shared the video, it was my fault it existed it in the first place. The whole thing was my fault.

"She's telling the truth." Dad rested his hand on my shoulder, but I pulled away from him. "Come in. I'll explain everything."

Dad leaned on his desk and Aaron sat in the leather chair. Luke and Emory sat next to each other on the couch, but I was too pumped with adrenaline to sit. I stayed in the back of the room, leaning against the wall with my arms folded across my chest, trying not to scream.

Luke was fuming. "Why have a bunch of people at my school—people I barely know—seen a video I made and didn't share with anyone?" He inhaled sharply. I could hear his voice shaking.

"It's my fault," Aaron said. "I thought your video was incredible. I shared it with a local pastor I trusted, but I guess I wasn't clear enough that it wasn't supposed to be public. I never told him to share it, I promise." He held up one hand. "And then it was out there and . . . I never thought it would go this far this fast."

"I made this for myself!" He slammed his hand on the desk. "It was for *me!*"

No one said anything. It was all I could do to stand silently at the back of the room. I wanted to grab Luke's hand and pull him away from Dad and Aaron and the horrible thing they'd done, not only to protect him, but also to show Emory that I was no longer my dad's sheep. That I'd changed. But maybe I hadn't, because I stood frozen in place anyway, unsure how to make the first move.

"I told you I would come speak at your admissions thing as a favor," Luke said. "I figured I owed you one. Was this your plan all along?"

I glanced over at Emory, but she wouldn't look at me. She was too busy glaring at my dad.

"No," Dad said in a calm, even voice. "I swear."

I stared at him. There was something about the look on his face that made me wonder if he was telling Luke everything.

"That video wasn't yours, Dad." My voice was quiet and tentative, but I was relieved to have found it. "It wasn't Aaron's or mine either. It was Luke's." I spoke a little louder. "You had no right to share it. That was *Luke's* story. It was *his* decision to share it."

"I know," Dad whispered. "I'm sorry. I truly am." He curled his finger toward his chest. "But look . . . you need to see something."

Dad stood from his chair, swiveling it around so Luke could take it. He pointed at his computer monitor. "Open any one of these emails. They've been coming in since yesterday. They're all for you."

Luke started reading. When he finished one message, he closed it and opened another one. And then another one.

"I knew your experience would resonate with people and I was right. We've been getting calls all day from pastors around the country. They're all asking me about you."

I watched Dad, pacing excitedly, and suddenly, this whole thing made sense. Pastors were calling him. They wanted something *he* had for a change. He felt important, I could see it in his eyes. It wasn't just about Admissions Night. Because of Luke, Dad mattered to them again.

"Everyone wants to meet you," he continued. "They want to hear what you have to say."

"Me?" Luke yelled, pressing his fingertips into his temples.

"Why? I said everything on that video. I don't have anything else to say!"

"Oh, I doubt that," Dad said. "Look, I'm sorry your friends at school saw it. I really am. But since people know anyway, maybe you just . . . make the most of it." Dad made it sound like it was no big deal. "There are a few local TV channels that want to talk to you."

I glanced over at Emory and watched her, watching my dad. And suddenly, I was hearing this whole conversation through her ears instead of mine. Dad didn't sound like he was in this for Luke. He sounded like a shepherd, leading a stray member of his flock where he needed him to go.

"I think it could do some good," Dad continued.

"Some good?" I blurted out. "For who? Not for Luke."

"Yes, for Luke," Dad said to me. "And also for all those people who wrote to us, and the thousands of people who clicked 'like' on his video, and everyone else who hasn't heard him yet." He turned back to Luke. "You could do the interviews here on campus if you want to."

Dad probably thought that would be enough to keep me quiet, but I wasn't finished. "Where, Dad?" I asked with a huff. "In front of the Covenant Christian School sign? Maybe he could shout out the details of Admissions Night at the end."

My dad opened his mouth to say something, but I didn't give him time to speak. I turned to Luke. "Don't do this."

His gaze was fixed on my dad. I tried to figure out what he was thinking.

Dad kept going. "There's also an invitation for you to appear live on one of the local LA morning shows on Thursday. They'd cover all your expenses and put you up in a hotel the night before. You'd miss a day of school, of course, but I'd be happy to call your parents and chat with them about everything . . . if you want me to."

Luke stood and paced the room. "This is totally insane. I don't get any of this. Why do the TV stations care? Why would they want to talk to *me*?"

"You're inspiring. You're genuine. You're a star athlete, but also a totally normal kid who experienced something extraordinary. What happened to you gives people hope."

"Hope for what?" Luke asked.

"Everything."

Emory had been uncharacteristically silent, sitting next to Luke with her arms crossed, glaring at Dad and me. She finally spoke up. "You're not actually considering this, are you, Luke?"

Luke reached for the doorknob, but that didn't stop my dad. "I completely understand," he called out. "I don't blame you for leaving. I wouldn't be surprised if you left this room and never spoke to any of us ever again."

Luke didn't turn around, but he rested his hand on the door frame. He was listening.

Dad continued. "You're under no obligation to do anything for any of us, but if there's a part of you that enjoyed telling your story on camera the other night . . . if you felt better when it was over, like a weight had been lifted . . . if there's even a tiny part of you that thinks telling your story to more people would make a difference in your life, and in theirs, you owe it to yourself to consider this."

"Luke." Emory took his face in her hands, forcing him to look at her. "This isn't you. This isn't what you need."

He pulled her hands away. "How do you know what I need?"

Emory reeled back like he'd slapped her.

Luke looked back at Dad. "It's only a couple interviews?"

Dad looked like he was holding back a smile. "A few here on campus tomorrow, plus a short trip to LA on Wednesday night. You'll be on *Good Day LA* early Thursday morning, and back home before lunch."

Luke pressed his lips together. "And that's it?"

"That's it."

Luke crossed his arms. The room was completely silent. And then he turned to me.

"I need Hannah there, too."

Emory's jaw dropped open. She started to say something but changed her mind.

She stood and stormed out of the room instead.

I ran after her, calling her name, but she wouldn't stop.

"I have nothing to say to you," she said.

She turned down the hall, quickening her steps. I finally caught up to her when she got to the faculty lot.

"Please," I said, grabbing her arm. "You have to believe me, none of this was supposed to happen. I'm so sorry." She pushed me to one side and kept walking toward Luke's car. "I swear. I had nothing to do with this. Luke and I made the video for him . . . for *you*. Luke made it so he could tell you his story. All I did was help him tell it."

She jerked her arm away and kept walking.

"I think about that day all the time," I yelled. "I think about it constantly. At night, when I can't sleep, all I do is replay that conversation in my head. All those things my dad said. How I didn't defend you. And I didn't help you. But I still want to help you. You need me—"

Emory stopped cold and turned around. "He practically said it was my fault. And you agreed with him."

"I didn't mean . . . You took it the wrong way. . . ." I panicked. It was happening again. I didn't have time to think about what I wanted to say, and none of my words were coming out right. I was making this whole thing worse, and I didn't think that was even remotely possible.

"I don't need your help," she said.

"Please." I reached out for her but she stepped backward. "You have to tell Luke."

"No," she said, shaking her head slowly. "I don't. And if you tell him, that will be it, Hannah. I'll never be able to forgive you for that. Our friendship will be over forever."

She turned around and walked to the car. She got in, turned the key in the ignition, and backed out of the parking space. And then she rolled down the window. "Tell Luke to text me when he's ready to go."

Emory
Day 299, 138 to go

By Wednesday, Luke's video was everywhere. Everyone at school was talking about it. And everyone had one question for me: Who was that girl in the background who hugged him at the end?

I called Hannah a friend of ours and left it at that.

Day 300, 137 to go

On Thursday morning, I sat on the living room couch, turned on the TV, and flipped to channel 106. Mom handed me a mug of black coffee and settled in next to me with one of her own.

The *Good Day LA* theme music came on. The two anchors took turns reading the relevant news, and then they flashed on Luke and Hannah, back in the greenroom, smiling and waving.

They cut to commercial. When the show returned, the two of them were sitting next to each other on a tan couch.

Luke looked nice, dressed in dark gray jeans and a bright blue button-down shirt that showed off his eyes. His hair looked especially good. His loose curls had the perfect amount of definition, and I wondered if someone had styled it with product or something before the show.

And then there was Hannah. She looked so prim and proper in a flowy white dress with tiny gray dots all over it, like she and Luke color coordinated on purpose. Her scoop-neck collar dipped just low enough to reveal the cross necklace she always wore.

She settled in on the couch and talked about seeing him pull up in front of the window that night. "I happened to be up getting water."

She talked about watching his car swerve before it came to a stop against the curb. "He was right under my streetlight. I ran out there as fast as I could. He wasn't moving or breathing, and I could tell he was hurt, so I ran inside to call nine-one-one and get my parents."

Then Luke talked about floating in the water. "And then, out of nowhere, I heard Hannah's voice. She said something I'll never forget." And then, as if they'd rehearsed this, she looked right into the camera and said, "I told him, 'You're not finished here.'"

The talk-show hosts sighed into their respective microphones at the exact same time, and that triggered a collective sigh from the audience. Luke shot Hannah a smile.

I pretended to stick my finger down my throat.

When the noise died down, Luke said, "When I got home from the hospital, I felt lost. And just . . . really sad. I didn't feel like I could talk to anyone about what happened to me, because they didn't really want to hear it. Everyone wanted everything to go back to normal."

By "everyone," Luke meant me.

I thought about the night I'd gone to his house for Calletti Spaghetti after, when I sat in his bed and he showed me articles about athletes who had died from their injuries. I told him to stop. And when he first returned to school, we stood in the hallway and I convinced him to go to the diner with me. "We'll treat that place like a time machine," I'd said. "The second we walk through that door and sit down in our booth, it's two weeks ago. Nothing bad happened, no one got hurt, and nothing's going to happen." Even that first morning in the hospital, when the nurse said he almost died, and Luke whispered, "I did." I'd heard him. But I never asked him what he meant by that.

If I'd let him talk, would he have told me everything he'd told Hannah?

I'd spent the last few weeks blaming those ten minutes for the friendship that sprang up between the two of them, but maybe I was the one to blame after all.

"I couldn't sleep," Luke continued. "I was so afraid to fall asleep. I was certain if I did, I wouldn't wake up. And then Hannah suggested making the video, and as soon as I did, it was like a weight was lifted off my shoulders. That video wasn't supposed to be for anyone but me, but now I'm glad it got out. It's helping me to talk about it."

He looked so certain. So convinced he'd done the right

thing by telling Hannah. Telling the world. And it felt like a knife twisting in my heart.

Every so often, Hannah looked over at Luke, and damn, the camera guy loved it when she did that. He'd start with a close-up of her face, then pan to Luke's, and then pull back when the two of them smiled at each other like lovestruck kids.

"Well, you two certainly make a cute couple," one of the hosts said.

"They do, don't they?" the other one added.

Luke laughed. "It's not like that," he said. He looked at Hannah and smiled. "We're just friends. Really good friends."

But when the camera panned back to Hannah, her cheeks were bright red, and I wasn't sure she felt the same way.

She recovered quickly. "Yes, we are."

She smiled at him.

And he smiled back at her with this look in his eyes that told me why he'd confided in her and not me.

She'd listened to him.

Hannah

There was a knock on my hotel-room door. I opened it and found Luke standing there holding up a bag of gummy bears, a Snickers bar, a Twix, and two bottles of Coke. "I robbed the minibar. Want to get wasted with me?"

"Please." I opened the door wider, giving him room to step inside.

After our appearance on *Good Day LA*, *Mornings on Six* wanted us, too. I thought Luke would refuse when Dad asked him if he wanted to stay another night, but he actually seemed a little excited about it.

He flopped down on the bed next to me and dropped the bag of gummy bears between us.

"Who are those for?" I asked.

"Both of us."

That reminded me of Emory. Whenever we'd have a sleepover, she'd bring the microwave popcorn and I'd bring the gummy bears. One time, I dared her to eat a handful of both at the same time. "That's kind of tasty," she said as she chewed. Then she started laughing hard and got up to spit it all into the trash can. "Kidding. Ugh. That's disgusting."

I ripped open the bag of gummy bears while Luke held the two candy bars out in his open hands. He balanced his hands like a scale. "I'm thinking you're a Twix girl."

"Aw, how did you know that?" I popped a bear into my mouth.

"Oh, it's all part of being a 'cute couple.' I'm required to know these things." He handed me the Twix. "Lucky guess."

I picked up another gummy bear and chucked it at Luke's head. "Too bad I don't think of you that way."

"Oh, but clearly you *would* think of me that way if you weren't already thinking about someone *else* that way." Luke raised his eyebrows at me.

I felt my face get hot, just like it had on camera earlier. "No, I'm not."

When the hosts called us a couple, all I could think about was Aaron and that day he'd told me he was jealous of Luke. And then we'd kissed. We'd kissed for the longest time that day, and no one interrupted us. Thinking about it made me blush.

Luke laughed. "You're a terrible liar. Come on. Who is he?"

"No one." I tried keep a straight face, but he was making it really hard when he kept smiling at me like that.

I couldn't do it. No one knew about Aaron. I wasn't even sure why I'd reacted that way onstage earlier. I hadn't talked to him since that day in Dad's office, even though he kept texting me, apologizing and begging me to reply. I'd deleted each one the second it arrived.

"Tell me."

I played with a loose string on the comforter, twisting it around my finger. "He's this guy."

"Excellent start. And?"

"And . . . he's this guy I hated. But then I got to know him, and I started to like him. But then he blew it, and now I . . ." I started to say *hate* again, but I trailed off. *Hate* was too strong a word. I didn't hate Aaron, I just didn't want to hear anything he had to say. Not yet.

"Classic rom-com material. I like it. Go on."

I flopped backward onto the bed and kicked my feet up to the ceiling. "I never should have liked him in the first place."

"Ooh . . . taboo, too. Now we're talking. Why can't you like him?"

"I can't like him for so many reasons, I don't even know where to begin."

"Pick one," Luke said as he stretched out next to me. He unwrapped his Snickers bar, propped himself up on an elbow, and took a big bite.

"Fine. He works at the church."

"Which is also your school."

"Yeah."

"So, hot janitor?"

I laughed. "No."

I could practically see the puzzle pieces clicking together in his mind as he chewed. "A teacher?"

"Sort of." I squeezed my eyelids shut while I waited for him to figure it out.

"Have I met him?" He asked the question in a way that made me think he already knew the answer.

"Maybe." I tried not to react, but I must have failed, because Luke reached over and punched me lightly on the arm.

"No wonder you wanted Aaron to shoot the video. This is all making sense now."

I was still blushing as I told Luke about working with Aaron on the testimonial videos for Admissions Night. I told him how the two of us had talked one day, and then started texting each other late at night. "And one day, right after your accident, the two of us were alone in the sound booth and I kind of kissed him."

My hands felt clammy and the room felt even warmer.

"And?"

"And he kissed me back."

"And?"

"And then my dad knocked on the door, and things got super awkward. Aaron apologized to me in a text that night. He said he felt horrible for letting it happen, but I didn't. I wanted it to happen again. And then when we were editing your video, we . . . kind of . . . kissed again."

Luke was grinning at me. I reached over and smacked him on the arm that time. "Stop looking at me like that."

"Like what?" he asked, still smiling.

I chucked another gummy bear at his head, but he buried his face in the comforter and it flew over him and hit the wall instead.

"Okay. But I still don't understand why you can't like him. Aside from the fact that he's a lying sack of shit and you're way too good for him."

I'd listed all the reasons I couldn't like Aaron in my head, but for the first time, I said them out loud. Too old for me. Practically a teacher. Works for my dad. Alyssa called dibs. Has a girlfriend/almost fiancée.

As I rattled them off, they didn't feel as important as I'd built them up to be. Until I got to the last one.

Beth.

He was still with her. He'd never said a word about breaking up with her. I had no idea if he was planning to. I couldn't imagine he'd told her about us.

Everything had happened so fast, and it wasn't like Aaron and I were planning a future together or anything, but he had a girlfriend. A serious girlfriend. My stomach twisted into a tight knot.

What was I doing?

"Have you talked to him since we left town?"

I shook my head. "I don't want to talk to him. Not yet."

"Emory won't talk to me either."

I couldn't really blame her. I hadn't wanted to come to LA with him—that made it seem like Dad and Aaron had been right. Like they'd won. And I knew the second I climbed into the passenger seat of his car, I'd make things between Emory and me even worse than they already were. But Luke begged me not to make him go on TV alone, and after a lot of convincing, I'd reluctantly agreed. I figured I'd gotten him into this mess in the first place; I should probably stick with him until it was over.

And I couldn't wait until it was over.

"I miss her," Luke said out of nowhere.

"You'll be home tomorrow."

"No. I mean, I *miss her* miss her. I miss the way we used to be before the accident." He stared down at the pattern on the comforter. "I got my life back that night. But I lost Emory. I never meant for that to happen."

I remembered the card I found in his car after he'd been whisked away in the ambulance and I thought he was dead. He'd listed all the things he loved about her. Seeing her onstage. Seeing her in his jersey. The way she looked at him like he was the most important person in the room.

"Have you told her everything you just told me?"

He shook his head.

I grabbed his phone off the nightstand and handed it to him. "Go. Right now."

"Right now?"

"Right this second."

He was smiling to himself, like he was already plotting his words.

"Now who's the glue?" he said as he typed.

I smiled, remembering that night in his car, when Luke told me to keep my voice in his video so Emory would hear it. I didn't think the glue analogy had the same meaning, since I was the one who broke them in the first place, but I wasn't about to tell him that.

Emory

Day 300, 137 to go

"If you could do something dangerous knowing there wasn't any risk, what would you do?" Tyler pulled up to the red light at the intersection a few blocks from my house and turned to Charlotte and me.

"Free-climb the face of Half Dome," Charlotte said.

"Jump out of an airplane," I said.

"Swim with great white sharks," Tyler said. "If you had a hundred dollars to give away, would you give it all to one person or ten dollars to ten people?" he asked.

"Ten dollars to ten people," Charlotte said.

"Five dollars to twenty people," I said.

"A hundred to one," Tyler said. Without skipping a beat, he asked, "Favorite Muppet?"

"Kermit," Charlotte said.

"The Swedish Chef," I said.

"Yoda," Tyler said. "The original one, not the CGI one."

"Ha! Sing!" I sat up straight and pointed at him. "Yoda's not a Muppet."

Tyler looked over at me. "Sure he is. He has legs. Look it up!"

"He's still a puppet." I slammed my hand on the dash, laughing. "Oh, you're so singing."

"Hey, easy on the Prius."

We'd been playing all night at the diner with the rest of the cast. By that point, we might have been a little punchy.

I reached for my phone and did a quick search.

"Yes! Right here. 'It is a popular misconception that Yoda is a Muppet,'" I read as Tyler pulled up to a stoplight. I twisted the screen so he could see the article. "You're wrong!"

"So?" he asked.

"So, sing," I said.

"Sing," Charlotte echoed from the backseat. I lifted my fist in the air toward her and she gave it a bump.

Tyler sighed. "Fine," he said as he pulled into the intersection.

Just as I leaned down to stuff my phone into my backpack, a message appeared on the screen.

Luke: There are five things you need to know

In the background, I could hear Tyler rapping something from *Hamilton*, but I was only half listening. I was too busy reading the texts as they rolled in.

Luke:	1. Hannah and I are just friends.
Luke:	2. I'm a complete asshole.
Luke:	3. I am so sorry for everything.
Luke:	4. I should have told you, not her.
Luke:	I don't know why I didn't tell you.
Luke:	See #2.
Luke:	5. I miss you so much.
Luke:	I feel horrible about opening night.
Luke:	I'll make it up to you, I promise.
Luke:	Okay, I guess that was eight things.
Luke:	Are you there? Please answer me.
Luke:	Em?

I tucked the phone under my leg.

Tyler finished his penalty song and jumped right back into the game. "Which celebrity do people say you resemble?" he asked as he took a left on my street.

"Charlize Theron," Charlotte said.

"Emma Stone," I said.

"Chris Pratt," Tyler said.

I laughed. "Yeah, you wish."

I waited for him to ask another question, but he didn't speak. And then he finally said, "Your turn, Emory."

I looked at him. "For what?"

"No commentary. Sing, Kern."

"Oh, look. We're here." Tyler stopped in front of my house. I tried to open the door, but every time I did, he'd hit the master switch and lock it again. "Stop it!"

"I'm not letting you out of the car until you sing," he said.

I looked to Charlotte to back me up, but I could tell by her expression that she wasn't on my side. "Come on," she said. "Tyler did it."

"Fine." I leaned on the console, right in his personal space. And then I sang the first song that popped into my head. *"Five hundred twenty-five thousand, six hundred minutes. Five hundred twenty-five thousand moments so dear."* It sounded off-key and horrible, but Tyler clearly didn't care. *"Five hundred twenty-five thousand, six hundred minutes. How do you measure, measure a year?"*

"Can I go now?" I asked.

Charlotte leaned in between the seats. *"In daylights, in sunsets, in midnights, in cups of coffee."* She was even more off-key than I was.

"In inches, in miles, in laughter, in strife," Tyler sang. He actually sounded good.

"Five hundred twenty-five thousand, six hundred minutes," the two of them sang together. I just stared at them. *"How do you measure a year in the life?"*

The lyrics reminded me of the 300 days of Luke-isms I'd captured so far, and the 137 blank spaces I still had left to fill. If Luke wasn't ready to stop counting, I wasn't either.

I took the next line. This time, I belted it out. *"Measure in . . . love . . ."*

Luke answered on the first ring.

"Em?" He sounded surprised.

"Hi."

"Hi. Wait. Hold on." I could hear him shuffling around. A door opened, and then closed. "I'm heading back to my room." I wanted to ask where he was, but I bit my tongue. "Okay, I'm alone now."

I assumed that meant he'd been with Hannah.

"I got your texts," I said.

He sighed. "I meant it. I'm sorry. I'm just so sorry."

I bit down hard on my lip. "I'm sorry, too." We were both quiet for a long time. "I saw you today. You were good."

"Thanks."

I thought back to what he'd said during the interview. I remembered how his words had caused something to shift in me. It was the moment I realized I was no longer angry at Hannah for being there for him, and angry at myself because I hadn't been.

"You said you felt like you couldn't talk to anyone. That everyone wanted you to go back to normal. Clearly, you were talking about me, and I just wanted you to know that I'm so sorry I made you feel that way." My voice hitched.

"It's okay, Em."

"No," I whispered. "It's not okay." He was quiet, so I kept going. "Will you talk to me now? Please? I'll listen, I promise."

And then I stayed silent. He didn't say anything for a long time, and I fought the urge to speak. I waited and waited.

"I'm obsessed with death," he finally said. "Death. Near-death experiences. Everything that has to do with death." I heard him pull in a breath. "You keep asking me what I'm doing alone in my room all the time . . . I'm watching videos of all these other people who have experienced death." Once he started talking, he couldn't seem to stop. I tried not to breathe too loudly for fear of interrupting him. "There are thousands of stories out there, and I swear, I think I've watched every one of them. In that week after the accident, I barely slept at all. I stayed up all night, reading articles, watching videos, and listening to all these supposed 'experts' talk about life after death, desperately trying to figure out what happened to me. That's why I made the video with Hannah. And it helped. Talking about it, even to a camera, helped. It didn't wipe it out completely, but that night, I slept, and I had normal dreams, and I didn't wake up thinking that I was dying all over again like I had every other night. And since then, it's been gradually getting better. I'm not afraid to go to sleep, not like I was at first."

"That's why you said yes to Admissions Night."

"Yeah."

"That's why you're doing these interviews."

"I think it's the only thing keeping me sane right now."

I resisted the urge to tell him I thought he might have PTSD, and that was totally okay and understandable, and that I'd help him find someone he could talk to—a real doctor, not Hannah's dad. "And talking about it helps."

"For some reason, it does."

He made it sound like I was supposed to run screaming once he admitted everything, but none of it changed how I felt about him. Not even a little bit.

"I've lost count of how many times I've watched the video you made," I said. "I taped every interview you've done this week, and I've watched each one, multiple times. And I can tell you one thing I'm certain about: I'm as in love with that guy as I was with Foothill High's star midfielder. Nothing's changed."

I could tell he was smiling, even though I couldn't see his face.

"It is called a midfielder, right?" I asked.

"Yeah." He laughed under his breath.

"Good."

"I should have told you sooner," he said.

"I should have let you."

Hannah

It was still dark when I stepped out of the hotel doors, and downtown Los Angeles was unusually quiet and still. I pulled one foot to my hip and stretched, and then switched legs to loosen up the other one. I shook out my hands, rocked my head from side to side, and then I took off running.

My music was loud in my ears, and I synchronized my footsteps in time with the beat. It felt good to race past unfamiliar buildings and turn down new streets. I had no idea where I was going, and I didn't care. I was happy to be outside and alone, feeling my soles on the cement, pumping my arms, widening my stride.

I hadn't quite hit the three-mile mark when I spotted a small park. I took a sharp left and followed the path around the baseball diamond and swings, looking for a rock that could substitute for the one back home. I didn't see one.

I circled around toward a tall wooden slide near the park entrance. When I reached it, I stood there, staring up, feeling the sweat on the back of my neck. It looked peaceful at the top, so I climbed the ladder and looked around. I was alone and I felt safe, hidden by the wooden slats, so I sat and folded my legs in front of me.

I killed the music, took out my earbuds, and set the timer on my phone for ten minutes. I tucked my chin to my chest. I closed my eyes and let the sounds of chirping birds and passing cars drift in and out of my mind.

Luke was all buzzy when I found him in the lobby an hour later.

"I take it you and Emory talked?" I asked.

"Until three in the morning." He blew out a breath full of nervous energy and gestured toward the café. "Let's get a coffee while we wait for the cab."

I laughed. "You do *not* need one."

"Whatever." He walked off, talking as he went, and I followed him, trying to keep up with his words and his steps. "We talked about everything. What happened to me. What I've been dealing with. She asked me questions and let me babble, and . . . I told her things I hadn't told anyone. Things I hadn't really even admitted to myself."

"That's great," I said. It made me a little sad to think there were things he hadn't told me, but I knew deep down that was unfair.

"I can't wait to do this interview, get home, and get back to real life."

I wasn't exactly sure what real life looked like anymore. I hadn't spoken to Aaron in two days. I was keeping my responses to Alyssa's messages as short as possible. I was only responding to my dad when he texted me about logistics. And I had no idea what my mom thought of any of this, because I was avoiding her phone calls completely.

"She's upset about me missing the play tonight," Luke said. "She's upset that you're missing it, too."

Maybe I wasn't supposed to see that as good news, but I did. After all we'd been through, I didn't think she'd care if I was there or not. The fact that she did gave me hope.

Luke stepped up to the counter. He studied the chalkboard menu on the back wall but kept talking to me. "And she's upset that David's going to be there. God, she hates that guy. I don't get it. He's always been nice to me."

My stomach dropped. Luke didn't understand why she hated him so much, but I did. I understood completely. I pictured Emory standing onstage in her costume, peering out into the first row and seeing him sitting there.

"Want anything?" Luke asked, pointing up at the menu.

I think I shook my head. I must have, because I heard Luke's voice, ordering a coffee and a bagel. Just the mention of food made my stomach turn.

She had to perform in front of him. I had no idea how she was going to do that. And then I realized she'd been performing in front of him, and in front of her mom, every second of every day since last December. She'd been performing as she and her mom shopped for dresses and planned seating assignments and decided on flower arrangements and addressed invitations. She had to be prepared to perform every morning as she walked to the kitchen, just in case he'd spent the night. She acted her way through every meal with him. I had no idea how she'd done it. But she had.

It had to stop.

I had to make it stop.

I was the only one who could do it.

"Hannah?" Luke was staring at me, holding his coffee and a small bag. "Hey. You okay?"

I wasn't okay. I was far from okay.

"You have to go to her play tonight," I blurted out without thinking.

"Yeah." Luke looked at me sideways. "I was thinking the same thing."

My stomach twisted into an even tighter knot.

If you tell him, that will be it, Hannah. I'll never be able to forgive you for that. Our friendship will be over forever.

"I have to tell you something." I felt like my mind had separated from my body, like I was no longer fully present in that café. I wished I hadn't said those words. I wanted to take them back. But deep down, I knew I was doing the right thing.

Luke steered me over to a nearby table and we sat, facing each other.

"What's going on?"

My hands were shaking and my chin was trembling and I had no idea how I was going to get through the next few minutes. I hadn't planned any of this.

"Emory has been there for every major event in my life. She's literally in the photograph of me taking my very first steps, out on the grass that separates our houses." I wasn't thinking about the words before I said them. I just opened my mouth and let the thoughts tumble out the way they wanted to. "She was at my baptism and every big SonRise competition and when I took my driver's test. When my grandmother died, Emory didn't leave my side for, like, a week solid. She brought me candy and crawled in bed with me to watch movies in the middle of the day, and let me cry until I didn't have any tears left."

Luke's eyebrows pinched together, like he was trying to figure out where I was going with all this, but he didn't stop me.

"The two of us drifted apart a little bit once we started going to different high schools," I continued. "We drifted apart a little bit more when she started dating you, because she was so into you. But we were still *us*. Can you even imagine what that's like, growing up with someone, having them be part of almost every single memory?"

"Um, yeah. I'm a twin."

I'd forgotten that for a moment. "Emory's the closest thing I can think of to having a twin sister. We're different." Picturing all the ways we were different made me smile to myself. "We couldn't be more different, but that has never mattered."

Luke nodded. "Why are you telling me all this, Hannah?"

Sweat was beading up on my forehead and under my arms. I shifted in place, wondering how I was ever going to get through this.

I'll never be able to forgive you for that.

"I've been keeping a secret for her." I had no idea how I was going to get this out.

"Tell me," Luke said.

Our friendship will be over forever.

"I can't." I brought my hand to my stomach. I felt like I was going to throw up.

"You have to."

I scanned the café to be sure no one else was within earshot. And then I rested my elbows on the table and leaned in closer. Luke mirrored me, closing the distance between us.

Keeping my voice low, I told him the whole story, starting from the moment I came home from church that day and found Emory waiting in my bedroom, looking pale and disheveled, scared and in shock. I told him how I'd gone looking for my mom but found my dad instead. I told him what Dad said about Emory. And what I'd said back. And what I didn't say that day, and what I didn't do.

Luke reeled back, eyes wide and full of anger. "When did this happen?"

I spat the word out like it was toxic. "December."

"You've known this for more than three months?" he asked, and I nodded slowly. "And you kept it to yourself?"

"She begged me to."

"What the fuck does that matter?" he yelled as he slammed his hand on the table. Everyone behind the café counter turned to look at us. Luke didn't notice. Or maybe he just didn't care.

"I'm sorry."

He covered his mouth and stared past me.

And then he reached into his back pocket for his phone

and began typing on the screen. I reached across the table and grabbed it from his hands. "You can't tell her you know . . . Not before she goes onstage tonight. You can't do that to her."

His eyes narrowed at me. "You want me to go all day without telling her I know? No way."

"I've gone three months without telling anyone."

Luke laughed under his breath. "Try not to sound so proud of yourself."

"I'm not." My voice caught on the last word. I opened my mouth to tell him how horrible I felt and hard it had been, but the words sounded lame, even in my head. I wasn't proud. I was ashamed of what I'd done. The expression on Luke's face told me I was right to be.

My phone chirped and I reached for it, hands shaking as I checked the screen. "We have to go. It's a ten-minute walk to the studio."

Luke stood. "I'll see you there," he said. He tossed his uneaten bagel and his full coffee cup into the nearest trash can and stormed out through the hotel doors and onto the street.

I didn't try to catch up to him.

Luke must have given the front-desk person his name, because by the time I arrived at the studio, our escort was already there, waiting to take us to makeup.

We sat next to each other in silence while someone named April fixed my hair and put powder on my face. I'd been holding back tears since the café, and now, as hard as I fought them back, I couldn't keep them from streaming down my cheeks. April squeezed my shoulders and bent down low. "Are you okay, sweetie?" she whispered as she handed me a tissue. "You have to stop crying or I can't do your makeup."

I didn't care. It didn't matter. I couldn't stop.

"You're on in three minutes," a voice behind me said.

Luke didn't skip a beat. "I'll do it alone."

He got up and left the room, and I didn't see him again until he appeared on the monitor, sitting on the couch next to an interviewer with black hair named Adam.

The two of them took their seats: Adam on a chair and Luke on the couch, facing him. Luke didn't even glance over at the empty spot next to him where I should have been sitting.

Luke gestured with his hands more than he usually did, but aside from that, he told his story exactly the same way he had over the last few days. Right until Adam asked him the final question: "So, Luke," he said, leaning in closer to him. "Tell me. Do you believe in heaven now?"

And then he went rogue.

Luke laughed. "Hell, I don't know," he said. "Who knows anything. You don't know. I don't know. I'm just happy to be alive. I've always been kind of a live-for-the-moment guy, but I'm even more so now. The world looks different. Colors are brighter and food tastes better and the air smells cleaner, even in LA." He was talking faster now, like he'd finished that coffee, chased it with a chocolate bar, and washed it all down with a Red Bull. "I'm in love with this amazing girl named Emory, and we only have four more months together before we go off to separate colleges, so I'm going to get back home tonight and wake up tomorrow and enjoy every second I have with her. If anything, this experience has taught me to soak up every second of every day, because we never know when it will be over. I'm not afraid of what happens next. I honestly don't care. I'm just damn glad to be here."

Adam held up his hand and Luke high-fived him.

The ride home was brutal. Luke barely said a word. When he pulled up in front of Covenant, he put the car in park, but he didn't even bother to look at me. He kept his gaze fixed on the windshield. "Tell your dad I'm not coming tonight," he said. "I've done enough to help him."

Emory
Day 301, 136 to go

Once I was in my costume, with my makeup on, standing at my stage mark under the lights, I felt like a whole new person. I *was* a whole new person. I was Emily Webb, and I was killing it.

When the curtain came up for Act Two, the spotlight shone on Charlotte. She stood confidently in the center of the stage and delivered her lines.

"George and Emily are going to show you the conversation they had when they first knew that—as the saying goes—they were meant for one another. But before they do, I want you to try and remember what it was like to have been very young. And particularly the days when you were first in love; when you were like a person sleepwalking. You're just a little bit crazy. Will you remember that, please?"

When the stage lights dimmed at the beginning of the show and I could see out into the audience, I spotted Mom in

313

the aisle seat in the first row, waving wildly at me. D-bag was next to her, staring down at his program. Mr. and Mrs. Calletti were sitting next to him, and Addison was on their other side. And then I spotted Luke and did a double take.

I stared at him, hardly able to believe he was sitting there. He'd come after all. He'd picked me over them.

"Hi," I mouthed.

"Hi," he mouthed back.

The stage went dark and the spotlights came up, shining warm and bright on Tyler and me, and I went back to work.

"Emily, why are you mad at me?" Tyler asked.

"I'm not mad at you," I said.

"You've been treating me so funny lately."

The lines came easily, and my feet seemed to carry themselves to the stage marks without me even having to think about it. By the time we reached the final scene, I was pumped and ready.

Someone handed me a tissue so I could dab the sweat from my face. Someone else handed me my water bottle, and I drained it in one gulp. I was taking slow, even breaths through my nose, when Ms. Martin grabbed my hands and knelt next to me.

"This is it. Remember, you're saying good-bye to the things that matter most to you in this world. You're telling this roomful of people to think about the things that matter most to *them.* Close your eyes." I did. "Picture the three things you wrote down that day. What did you want to say good-bye to?"

I thought about Hannah and my patch of grass. And the sound of my mom's voice. And this stage.

"Ready?" she asked. I handed her my empty glass as I nodded. "Go."

She stepped away and the curtain rose.

I stared across the stage at the mourners gathered together at the graveyard, and when I heard my cue, I stood and walked slowly to my stage mark.

"Good-bye." I crinkled my forehead, preparing to produce fake tears. "Good-bye, world. Good-bye, Grover's Corners . . . Mama and Papa. Good-bye to clocks ticking . . . and Mama's sunflowers. And food and coffee. And new-ironed dresses and hot baths . . . and sleeping and waking up."

As I said the words, everything came rushing over me like a wave. And I suddenly understood the whole play. Tyler had tried to tell me that day on the platform, but I didn't *get* it, not really. Now I did.

I didn't need to know what happened when our time on earth came to an end. I just wanted to be here, soaking it in, squeezing every drop out of my life. Appreciating little things, like chocolate chip cheesecake and Christmas ornaments and patches of grass and best friends. Sleeping and waking up.

I let my eyes fall shut, and I felt the warmth of the spotlight on my face.

A tear slid down my cheek. I hadn't faked it.

I opened my eyes and looked out into the audience. "Oh, earth, you are too wonderful for anybody to realize you."

I felt another tear, and another one, but I didn't wipe them away. And then I locked my eyes on Luke and said my final line, just for him. "Do any human beings ever realize life while they live it every, *every* minute?"

Hannah

Inside the sanctuary, everything was the managed chaos I expected to find. Dad was up onstage, dispensing jobs in that calm way of his, and the room was full of people at work, placing printed programs on seats, draping the offering table at the front of the room, and setting up the refreshments. The crew was testing the lights and the projection system.

Alyssa, Logan, and Jack were together onstage, mic-ing one another up with the lavaliers.

"How's that?" Alyssa asked as she looked up in the sound booth. Aaron must have replied in her ear, because she gave him a big smile and a thumbs-up. Then she saw me. She came barreling down the steps and threw her arms around my shoulders. "I'm so glad you're home. Come back to the music room, we need a quick rehearsal."

"I have to talk to my dad first." I threaded my arm through

hers and pulled her along for protection and moral support. Dad saw me coming and met me halfway.

"Luke isn't going to be here tonight," I said.

I'm not sure how Dad would have taken the news if we'd been alone, but since there were so many people around, hanging on his every word, he took it in stride.

"Well, that's okay. That gives us about five minutes to fill in the program, but we can figure something out," he said cheerfully as he scanned the room. Logan and Jack were right behind me, and Alyssa was at my side. Seeing the four of us together like that must have given him the idea he needed.

"Let's do a second SonRise song. You can start us off and wrap up the night."

I wasn't sure how I was going to get through one song, let alone two. I didn't want to be there. I wanted to be in the front row at Foothill High School watching *Our Town*, rooting on Emory. I didn't want to be anywhere else, and I certainly didn't want to be in Dad's sanctuary any longer than I had to be. If it wasn't for SonRise I would have blown the whole thing off.

Dad snapped his fingers. "How about 'Dare You.' That's one of my favorites. And that last line is so perfect: 'I dare you to be here now.' That's the kind of message we want to close with anyway."

"It's perfect," Jack said.

"We'll sing it without percussion," Logan added. "Just straight-up harmony, like we did at Northern Lights."

"Fine," I said as I walked away. I didn't care what we sang. I didn't care about BU or attendance at Admissions Night. I didn't even care what Dad and Aaron had done to Luke. I just couldn't wait for the night to be over so I could get back to my room, stand in my window, and wait for Emory to come home.

By 7:00, every seat in the room was taken and there were people lined up along the back wall. I expected some of them to leave when Dad announced that Luke couldn't be there in person, but no one did.

SonRise took the stage and kicked everything off with "Brighter Than Sunshine," like we'd planned. I was working overtime to meet eyes with people in the crowd, not only because I knew that was part of my job, but also because it kept me from having to look at Aaron. When we were finished, we took our seats to the side of the stage and watched the next performances.

Dad talked about the school, introduced the drama and dance groups, talked about the music program, and introduced the band. We were nearing the end of the program and everything was going off without a hitch. Dad was passionate and charming and funny. He connected with the kids in the room like he always did.

He introduced SonRise, and the four of us took our spots at the center of the stage.

Dad once told me our music was just as important as his sermons, and we should always choose them the same way. "Think about the people you're performing for," he'd said. "You know the lyrics backward and forward, but the people in the audience are hearing it sung this way for the first time, and they're hanging on your every word. Think about what people in the congregation need to hear."

Now we smiled out at the audience, meeting eyes with a few people, trying to make a link before we even began. Aaron stood at the bottom of the stairs, arms extended, ready to direct us.

Under her breath, Alyssa said, "Four, three, two, one . . ."

Logan kicked us off:

"We're a million lonely people, all together on this needle in the sky, afraid of heights."

Alyssa had the next verse, and I had the one after that. And then Jack took the first lines of the chorus, with all of us harmonizing with him.

"I dare you to love, I dare you to cry.

"I dare you to feel, I dare you to be here now."

Dad had picked this song because he thought it would make people feel connected to us and to this room, to give them that sense of inclusiveness that made our school so special. But as I sang the words, I didn't hear them the same way he had.

This song had nothing to do with being in a room that made you feel like you belonged. It was more personal than that. It had to do with being brave and taking chances, falling and failing, and feeling everything—love and sadness and pain and joy—simply because it was all part of the human experience. It all felt very Zen. Like meditation, it was all about being present in the moment and appreciating everything about it, the good, the bad, the *everything*. It was about finding your own truth and letting everyone else find theirs. It was about being in the world without hating and judging, just *being* and letting everyone else *be*, too.

And as I listened to Logan sing the lines, *"Let your heart be your religion, let it break you out of this prison you became,"* I felt the lyrics deep in my soul, as if he were talking directly to me.

I remembered the words Emory said to me that day three months ago, about blindly following my faith and never asking questions. And I thought about what Luke said that morning on TV, about living in the moment and soaking up every second.

When we reached the last line, we sang it in four-part harmony.

"I dare you to be here now."

The three of them let their heads fall backward, looking up at the sky. But I rested my hand on my chest, and let my head fall forward instead. Dare accepted, I thought.

Emory
Day 301, 136 to go

Ms. Martin stuck her head in the dressing room to tell me there was someone asking for me at the backstage door. I hadn't even had time to change out of my costume.

I opened the door and found Luke standing there. He was wearing the same gray button-down shirt and black chinos he'd been wearing when I saw him on TV that morning. I threw my arms around his shoulders. "You came."

Everyone was still bustling around backstage, but it was quiet on the other side of the door. I stepped into the hallway where we could be alone.

"I couldn't miss this." He kissed me. "You were incredible up there."

I fluffed out my frilly white dress. "Hardly my style, I know. I tried to get Ms. Martin to let me alter it a bit, but you know . . . 1901." I smiled.

Luke smiled back.

"You skipped it," I said.

"Yeah." He locked his eyes on me, and I could tell there was something else he wanted to say.

"Why?" I asked.

He shook his head and bit hard on his lip. I could tell he was angry about something, but it didn't feel like he was angry at me. More like he was angry *for* me. I stared at him, but he didn't answer my question. And then he didn't have to. I already knew the answer.

"She told you."

My heart started racing and my chest felt heavy. The hallway walls seemed to be closing in on me.

"Em. Why didn't you tell me?"

I wanted to punch something, but I pulled myself together instead. "Because it's no big deal. It happened. It's over."

"It is a big deal," he whispered. "It's a really big deal."

I piled my hair on top of my head for something to do with my hands. I knew it. I knew she'd cave. I knew I should have done more to keep the two of them apart.

"Hannah had no right to tell you."

I didn't want to have this conversation. Not here. Not now. Not ever.

"I didn't give her much of a choice," he said. "I knew something wasn't right when we hung up last night, and when I mentioned it to Hannah, her face gave it away. Don't be mad at her."

"Don't be mad?" My hands balled into fists by my sides as I stepped away from him. "How can you say that?"

322

"She's trying to help and so am I." He took a step forward. I took a step back. "Emory, you have to tell your mom."

He took another step forward. I backed away from him faster that time.

"See," I said, shaking my head. "That's the whole reason I never told you. Because I knew you'd say that, and you don't understand. I *can't* tell her. Not ever."

I turned the doorknob, eager to get back inside, but it had locked behind me. I panicked, feeling like I had two choices: fight or flight. I picked flight.

I took off running down the hall, out the theater door, and into the parking lot, weaving around lines of cars leaving after the show. I caught a glimpse of my white patent leather shoe, and I realized how ridiculous I must have looked, tearing through campus in my Emily Webb costume. But I didn't care. I picked up the pace, running past the tennis courts and the swimming pool, until I was near the classrooms, away from the cars and the crowds.

"Emory!" Luke was right on my heels. "Please. Stop and talk to me."

I reached the restrooms and pulled hard on the door, hoping it was unlocked, but it wasn't. Luke caught up to me.

I folded my arms across my chest. "I am not going to talk to you about this."

"You're going to ignore the whole thing and pretend it never happened?"

"Yes." I leaned against the lockers. "It's what I've been doing for months. Until tonight, it's worked perfectly fine."

"Emory . . ." Luke wouldn't let up. "Tell me what happened."

"You know what happened!" I yelled.

"I know Hannah's version. I want to hear yours."

I stared at him. I was only three blocks from home. I could take off running and be there before he could get in his car and catch up to me. If I wanted it to, this whole conversation, this whole night, could end right now. But I didn't want to run away. I wanted to tell him. I needed someone other than Hannah to hear me say it. I pressed my back against the cold metal locker bank.

"I don't know where to start," I whispered.

The ground felt like it was wavering under my feet. I tried to steady my breathing like I did onstage when I got nervous, but I couldn't stop my chin from trembling.

Luke rested one hip against the lockers, facing me. "Start with something easy. What day of the week was it?" he asked.

He got that from Hannah. That was how she always got me to tell her my secrets.

"It was a Sunday morning." I heard the words come out of my mouth, but it didn't sound like my voice. I closed my eyes and pictured my bedroom. Opening the door. Stepping into the hallway.

"The football game was blaring." I twisted my dress around my finger for something to do with my hands. "I walked into the kitchen and went straight for the coffeepot. D-bag was standing at the stove making breakfast, and I asked him where my mom was. He told me she just left for the gym. He said he would have gone with her, but he had more important things to do . . . and then he pointed at the TV with the spatula."

I sucked in a breath, but my chest felt so tight, like it had shrunk and there was no longer enough room for air.

"There was a pile of mail on the kitchen table. Charlotte and I had both applied to Tisch for early acceptance. She had just received her early acceptance letter, so I'd been checking the mail every day, hoping to get one, too. I picked up the stack and started thumbing through it. And . . . and . . ." I stammered. "I didn't hear him come up behind me."

The memory made me squeeze my eyelids tighter.

I remembered the way he put his palms on the kitchen table on either side of my hips and pressed his chest against my back.

"He leaned into me and I felt his breath on the back of my neck. He kissed me here." I pointed to a spot behind my right ear. "And then he slid his hands over my chest and said, 'You shouldn't walk around wearing stuff like this. You know I can't control myself. . . . I can't be responsible for what I'll do to you.'"

I looked up at Luke. "He said I walked around like that on purpose, just to tease him." I shook my head. "I started to tell him that was total bullshit, but I didn't." I forced out a breath. "I didn't say anything."

Luke looked furious. I'd never seen him so angry.

"He had me trapped against the kitchen table. I couldn't move. Or, I don't know, maybe I could have moved. I've played it over in my head a million times, but . . . I . . . I didn't move. I didn't even *try* to move."

Luke took my hands in his. "You didn't do anything wrong," he said.

I shook my head because it wasn't true. I should have moved that day. It was the easiest thing in the world to do, and instead I'd stood there, frozen. I'd always pictured myself as someone who'd throw elbows and punches and knees, but I hadn't. I'd stood there.

"I didn't *get* it," I continued. "I was wearing a tank top and sport shorts. It was what I'd *slept* in. You'd been there the night before. You snuck out my window, and when you left, I changed into something I probably picked up off the floor before I crawled into bed. My shirt was probably kind of sheer . . . I honestly didn't think about it." I felt a tear slide down my cheek, and then another one followed. I brushed them away quickly. "He was my mom's boyfriend. He was going to be my stepdad. I liked him. I was happy for them."

Luke kissed my forehead and it made me feel safe. Safe enough to keep talking.

"David was still behind me with his hands on the table, and I could feel him pressed against me. It's funny . . . I remember staring at his watch, like I needed to focus on something while I figured out what to do," I continued. "But then he lifted his hands away, and the watch suddenly disappeared, and I was so relieved, because I thought that was the end of it. But before I could move, he wrapped his arm around my waist and pulled me into him. I stepped backward and lost my balance, and sort of fell into him, and I guess he thought I'd meant to do it because—" My voice was shaking so hard, I wasn't sure I'd be able to finish the sentence. "He started kissing my neck, and I felt his hand on my stomach, pulling me into him again, and I felt his fingers between my legs and—"

"Stop." Luke squeezed his eyes shut, like he could stop the progression of events that way.

"It's okay," I said. "That was it. I twisted away from him, and he let go. He didn't fight me." I wrapped a chunk of hair around my finger. "That's the part I've played back in my head over and over again. He let me go."

I tried to hold back the tears, but I couldn't. They were hot and fat and streaming down my face, and I couldn't control them, as hard as I tried.

"I don't know why I didn't walk away earlier. I stayed there. I let him—"

Luke took my face in his hands. "No. You didn't 'let him.' You didn't do anything wrong, okay? Not by what you were wearing. Not because it took you a few minutes to figure out what was happening. He did this. You did *nothing* wrong. Okay?"

I nodded. I couldn't stop those damn tears from falling. And for some reason, I couldn't stop talking.

"I started backing down the hall, never taking my eyes off him. I was waiting for him to come after me, or say something, but he didn't. I went into my room, locked my door, and sat on my floor for the longest time, trying to figure out what to do. And how to tell Mom. And then I realized, I couldn't tell her. Not ever.

"I had to get out of there, and all I wanted to do was talk to Hannah, but she was still at church, so I used our ladder to climb out my bedroom window, and I ran across the grass. I snuck into her house using the hide-a-key her mom always keeps under the planter by the back door."

I thought back to that morning. I spent the first fifteen minutes walking around their house, checking every door and window to be sure they were locked. I went into Hannah's room

327

and shoved her desk chair under the doorknob, just in case. And then I stood to the side of her window, peeking between the curtains, watching my house, feeling for the first time in my life that it didn't belong to me anymore. I'd never felt unsafe in that house. Not once. Of all the things D-bag stole from me that day, that might have been the one that hurt the most.

"When Hannah finally got home, I told her what he did, and she freaked out, like I expected she would. She said she was going to get her mom, and I tried to stop her, but deep down, I kind of wanted her to." I paused to take a breath. "But then I heard her dad's voice in the hallway instead. Hannah's always been so close to her dad—she tells him everything—so I don't know, maybe she thought the two of them were interchangeable, but they weren't to me. I hid in her closet. I heard everything . . ." I trailed off.

Luke hugged me tight.

"She didn't defend me," I said into his neck.

"She should have."

We didn't say anything after that. I was all talked out, so we both stood there, staring at the lockers. After a while, we walked to his Jetta.

He opened the passenger door and closed it behind me, and I let my head fall against the window. The glass was cold against my cheek.

I closed my eyes as the car started up, and we backed out of the lot. I didn't know where we were going. I didn't care.

My phone chirped and I checked the screen. "My mom keeps texting me."

"Tell her you're not coming home tonight," Luke said matter-of-factly.

We wound up his hill, through the trees, past the lights, and pulled up next to his mom's car. Inside, the house was dark and quiet.

"Where is everyone?" I asked as we climbed the stairs.

"They're at dinner with your mom and . . . him." It made me grin. I liked that he refused to say D-bag's name, like he was Voldemort or something.

Luke opened his bedroom door and closed it behind us. And then he went straight to his dresser. He took out a pair of sweats and one of his lacrosse sweatshirts, and handed them to me. I felt a lot more comfortable once I was out of my costume.

He walked over to his bed and pulled back the covers, motioning for me to climb inside. When I did, he pulled the comforter up to my chin, walked around to the other side of the bed, and climbed in next to me, still wearing his clothes. I curled up in the crook of his arm, rested my head on his shoulder, and tucked my legs between his.

We were quiet for a long time. My eyelids felt heavy and my whole body was weak. I was exhausted from all the drama of the night, onstage and otherwise.

"Can I ask you something?"

"Mm-hmm," I mumbled.

"Why did you go to Hannah's house that day? Why didn't

you call me? Or Tyler, or Charlotte? Any of us would have been there in ten minutes or less. Why Hannah?"

"I needed to get out of there. Her house was closest."

Luke kissed the top of my head. "I don't believe you."

I propped myself up on my elbow, preparing to argue with him, but then I stopped. I felt my chest tighten and a huge lump form in my throat. I hadn't admitted it to anyone, especially not myself, but I knew exactly why I went over there that morning.

"I act without thinking. I always have. But Hannah never does. She thinks everything through, sometimes to a fault. I'm impulsive, but she's thoughtful. She's wise. She always used to say I made her brave, but she makes me smart."

He smoothed my hair off my head.

"We used to joke about this yin/yang thing we have, but it's true. We complement each other in ways people don't understand. She's always totally honest with me. She doesn't let me get away with stuff, and that can be annoying sometimes, but it's good, you know? Because she challenges me. She makes me want to be a better person. And she knows about all my flaws, and she loves me, not in spite of them, but because of them. And I love her the same way."

Luke twisted my hair around his finger and never took his eyes off me.

"I didn't come to you that day because Hannah was the one I needed. I knew she'd tell me what to do. She'd make it all okay. Deep down, I was still wondering if I'd done something wrong, and I knew she'd tell me I hadn't. She'd get mad for me and protect me . . ."

". . . but she didn't," Luke said, finishing my sentence.

I rested my head on his chest and closed my eyes.

"I didn't know what to do after that. I felt insecure and . . . broken for a little while there, and I didn't want you to see me that way. I'm supposed to be the fun one, right? I'm supposed to surprise you. I never want to show you my flaws, but I don't mind showing them to Hannah. She's seen every single one. And she loves me no matter what."

"I love you no matter what."

"Not like she does." I shook my head slowly. "No one loves me like she does."

That was the last thing I remembered before I fell into a deep sleep.

Hannah

After Dad led everyone in the final prayer, I was supposed to walk back into the audience and work the room like I had every other year, proudly introducing myself as Pastor J's daughter, chatting with parents and prospective students, talking up Covenant. That's what Aaron and the rest of SonRise were doing. But I didn't have it in me. I was still all buzzy from the performance and I just needed to be alone, away from it all, where I could concentrate on what really mattered: Emory.

I made my escape through the door off the stage and hid in the music-department storage room. It was dark, and there were no chairs, so I sat on the floor and leaned back against the metal shelving unit.

I'd only been there a minute or so when I heard a soft knock on the door. I assumed it was Alyssa, so I yelled, "Come in."

My heart started racing when I looked up and realized it

was Aaron. I wasn't ready to see him. Or talk to him. Or hear his apologies and explanations. Or think about what he'd done to Luke. And to me. I already had too many thoughts in my head and I didn't want to make room for any more.

"Why are you sitting in the dark?" he asked as the door closed behind him with a soft click.

"I'm thinking."

"Do you want me to turn the light on?"

"No." I knew where the switch was. If I wanted the light on, I would have turned it on. I was mad at him all over again. "What do you want, Aaron?"

Saying his name made butterflies start to come to life in my stomach, so I rested my hand there and pictured all of them getting caught up in a bug zapper.

He crossed the room. He took my hands in his. I tried not to notice how nice they felt wrapped around mine. "Can we talk?"

I pulled my hands from his grip. "Not right now. I have more important things on my mind."

He didn't reach for them again. "More important than us?"

I laughed in his face. "Yes, Aaron. A lot more important than *us*." Emory was more important than anyone.

He stepped backward, giving me space. "Okay . . . I get it. I'll leave you alone. I just wanted to tell you how sorry I am. It's all I've been able to think about, and I'm just . . . so, *so* sorry for what I did. I betrayed your trust. And Luke's trust. What I did was . . . inexcusable."

He paused, and I wondered if he was waiting for me to jump in and tell him I forgave him and that it was okay. I didn't.

He continued. "After your dad told me about your college

fund, I didn't feel like I had any other choice. I knew Luke's video would draw attention to us and get kids in the door, and I knew once we got them here and they saw your dad in action, we'd get all the applications we needed."

That wasn't what he'd told me earlier. It wasn't what he'd told Luke.

"So you sent the video out on purpose? You asked someone to upload it and make it public."

Aaron dropped his chin to his chest. I took that as a yes.

"Our methods were wrong," he said, locking his eyes on me. "But they worked. We had a waiting list before anyone even walked in that door tonight. We're solid. You'll go to BU in the fall, like you're supposed to. And I've got a stack of applications from kids who want to audition for SonRise, so Jack, Logan, and I can keep this going after you and Alyssa are gone."

It was good news, but hearing him say it made me reach for my stomach again. It wasn't the butterflies that time; those were long gone. Now I just felt empty. This wasn't the way I wanted it to happen.

"Have you apologized to Luke?" I asked.

He shook his head. "Not yet, but I will. I promise." And then he stepped in closer and started to reach for my hands again. "I just need you to forgive me. Please. I miss you."

As I looked at him, I realized I couldn't say it back. I'd thought about him. A lot. But I hadn't missed him.

Suddenly, all I could think about was that card Luke wrote to Emory. And how he'd talked about her in the hotel room the night before. How he'd put himself out there on TV that morning, completely going against my dad so everyone would know how he felt about her. Luke never would have done what Aaron did to me. And it hit me like a slap. Luke never would have done to Emory what Aaron was doing to Beth.

It looked like he was about to lean in to kiss me, but I didn't give him a chance. I put both hands on his shoulders and pushed him as hard as I could. "What about your girlfriend, Aaron? Have you apologized to her?"

He combed his fingers through his hair. It was quiet for a long time.

"Look," he finally said. "You once asked me if I loved her, and I was honest with you. I do. I've loved her for a long time. But we're not like this." He gestured back and forth in the empty space between us. "I don't think about her *all* the time, the way I think about you. I don't want her the way I want you. I didn't care that things were kind of lukewarm between Beth and me, but now that I understand how this is *supposed* to feel, I can't pretend it doesn't matter. It matters. A lot. And now I can't go backward. I can't settle for less than this."

Emory and Luke. That's what I wanted. That's what I deserved. It was a high bar, and I didn't want to settle either.

My phone chirped. I pulled it from my pocket and checked the screen.

Mom: We're ready to go. Where are you?

"I have to go." I pushed past him, moving for the door.

"Can I call you later?"

I didn't even turn around. "I don't know," I said as I reached for the door handle.

Nothing mattered to me but getting home so I could see if Emory was there. And if she was, I wouldn't even text her first; I'd just sprint across the grass and slap my hand against the side of her house until she opened her window and let me in so we could talk. Aaron's apologies didn't matter. All I cared about was getting to her. And after I did—if she understood and accepted my apology—I'd never let her go again.

Dad tried to talk to me on the way home, but I told him I wasn't ready. He apologized at least four times. He told me how impressive I was during all the interviews. Repeatedly. Until Mom finally rested her hand on his shoulder, silently telling him to give it a rest.

After he pulled into the garage and cut the engine, I went straight to my room without saying another word. My whole body was heavy and my mind was spent, but I couldn't go to sleep until I saw Emory.

I watched at the window. At midnight, her mom and D-bag finally came home. But Emory never did.

I typed at least ten messages to her, but I never sent them. I forced myself not to. But somewhere around 1:00 a.m., I finally caved and sent one to Luke.

Hannah: Is she okay?

"Please reply," I begged as I pressed SEND. "Please."

A few minutes later, my phone chirped.

Luke: She's here.
Hannah: She knows everything?
Luke: Yeah.
Hannah: And she's okay?
Luke: She will be.

I thought back to how stupid I'd been in the car on the way home from LA. I sat there in silence for over an hour, beating myself up for what had happened, when I should have been using that time to strategize with Luke. How could I have been so selfish when Emory needed us?

Hannah: There are so many things I need to say to you, but I'll save them for later. For now please tell Emory I love her.
Hannah: And that I'm so sorry.
Hannah: I let her down and I'll never forgive myself for what happened that day.
Hannah: And I know she hates me for telling you what happened, but I'm not sorry about that part. I'm glad I did.

There was a long pause, but then those three dots appeared on the screen and I could tell he was typing.

Luke: Now you sound like her best friend.

Emory
Day 302, 135 to go

The next morning, I woke up surprised to find myself in Luke's clothes and in his bed. The sun was peeking through the opening in his curtain. I could tell it was early.

I turned over on the pillow. He was still sleeping, so I dozed a little longer, too. When I opened my eyes again, he was starting to stir. He blinked, and when he saw me, he gave me a sleepy smile.

"Good morning." He ran his thumb along my cheek.

"I've been waiting forever to hear you say that."

"This isn't quite what we had in mind, is it?"

"Not so much."

He kissed me, and I didn't want it to end, because I knew that when it did I'd have to get out of his bed and go back to a world I didn't want to face.

"My mom knows you're here. I told her last night. I didn't

tell her why, or what happened, but she knows you need to be here. And she understands. But I think you should talk to her."

I squeezed my eyes shut. I wasn't ready for this. Not yet.

"Think about it, please." He kissed me softly, and then whispered, "Stay here. I'll be right back."

When he got up, I could see he was still wearing his clothes from the night before. He climbed out of the sheets, crossed the room, and opened his desk drawer. He pulled out a bright blue envelope and handed it to me.

"I wrote this the night I got hurt. I keep trying to give it to you, but . . . I can never seem to find the right time." He climbed back in bed and slid his arm under my neck, while I worked the flap on the envelope.

I opened it and read it to myself. I smiled at the line, *I love the way you play with your hair when you're nervous* and I melted when I read *and the way you look at me like I'm the most important person in the room.* I laughed a little at his *P.S. Sorry. I know that's a bit long for Day 280. Feel free to paraphrase.*

"I loved all these things about you," he said. "Before the accident, I pictured giving you this card, and hearing you tell me all the things you loved about *me*. But after the accident, everything changed. I couldn't imagine what you'd say."

"Luke . . ."

"Last night, you said you didn't want me to see your flaws . . . your broken places. Well, I didn't want to let you see mine either. My mind is a mess. My whole stomach is one huge, disgusting scar. I have horrible nightmares. I wake up constantly, sweating and shaking and feeling like I'm dying all over again. I'm different. And I know you want it to be tempo-rary, but it's not. What happened to me changed me."

"It's okay," I said.

"How is it okay?" He closed his eyes tightly. "I don't know who I am anymore."

"You're still you."

He wrapped his arms around me, and I buried my face in his neck as I intertwined my legs with his. We held each other like that for a long time. When he brought his mouth to mine, neither one of us closed our eyes. I felt like I could see through him, all the way down to his soul, and I loved what I saw.

"I missed you," he said, and then we kissed again, and I closed my eyes and paid attention to the little things—his taste on my tongue, and his hands in my hair, and his breath rising and falling with mine—and all I could think about was how much I loved him. The old Luke. The new Luke. I didn't care.

I slowly climbed on top of him, carefully straddling his hips. I checked to be sure I wasn't hurting him. He assured me I wasn't. I pulled my sweatshirt over my head and felt his hands slide around my waist. I started unbuttoning his shirt.

I could see his scar, starting right after the fourth but-ton, just below his rib cage, and I kissed it. And then I undid another button, and kissed him again. I kept going, and when I reached the last button, I let his shirt fall open. I planted a soft kiss on his scar, and traveled back up again, kissing him all the way to his chin.

"I love kissing you," I said. "I love the way you make me laugh without even trying. I love when you call me Em. I love the way you taste like peppermint all the time. I love wearing your jersey. I love talking to you, super close, like this." That made him laugh. "I love the way your brain works. I love that what happened to you that night mattered to you, and that you want to talk about it, and figure it out, and tell other people, because it might give them hope in something they can't see." I brought my mouth to his. "I love you more right now than I did two weeks ago, and that's really saying something."

I unbuttoned his jeans, slid them over his hips, and tossed them on the floor. He helped me out of my sweats and added them to the pile next to his bed. I unhooked my bra and dropped it on the floor, and we were both giggling as we struggled with his socks and our underwear, getting all tangled up in the sheets as we tried to get rid of everything.

Finally, we slid back inside the warm covers, the sun streaming through the window, skin to skin, with nothing in between us. I wanted him so much I could barely stand it, but I forced myself to slow down, because I didn't want to forget this morning, just like I didn't want to forget any of the nights we'd had together. He rolled over slightly, reaching in between the mattress and the box spring for a condom, while I slid my hands over his skin, loving the way his body felt under my fingertips.

He wrapped his hand around the back of my neck, pulling me closer. I brushed my lips against his neck, and his cheek, and his lips, and I felt his fingertips slide down my spine and rest on my hips. We moved together for a long time, kissing and touching and teasing each other, until neither one of us could stand it a second longer. And when he was inside me, I told him I loved him again, even though I'd already said it

341

too many times to count, and I thought I might choke on the words, because I meant them in a way that made my heart ache. I couldn't stand the idea of us not being *us* someday. But we were here now. Alone in his room. Waking up together. Exposing all our secrets and flaws to each other.

I closed my eyes and lost myself in him, pretending we would be that way forever.

Afterward, I had no idea what to type. I had far too many choices. So I kept it simple.

Day 302: "Good morning."

Hannah

I stayed in bed all day Saturday, dozing and binge-watching movies on my laptop.

Every so often, I'd get up and look out the window. David's car was there, but then it was gone. Emory's mom's catering van was there, but at some point, it disappeared, too.

I still hadn't seen any sign of Emory.

A little after 2:00, I finally saw Luke's Jetta pull into her driveway. I watched them kiss good-bye, and then Emory got out and Luke drove off. She worked her key in the front door, stepped inside, and closed it behind her.

I waited.

And waited.

I waited until I couldn't stand it a second longer, and then I reached for my phone.

I started to type the word, but it popped up on my screen before I had a chance to.

Emory: GRASS?

Her shade snapped up and she was standing there, looking at me.

I held my hand up and waved.

She waved back.

As I walked down my hallway, I pictured her walking down hers at the exact same pace.

I stepped off our back porch, and she stepped off hers at the same time.

My legs were trembling and my heart was beating so fast, but it felt good. Without saying a word, we walked to the center of the grass and threw our arms around each other. I squeezed her as tightly as I could, and she held on for the longest time, like she didn't want to let me go.

"If I could go back to that day, I would have done everything differently."

Emory blew out a breath. "Me too."

"I should have defended you to my dad."

"I shouldn't have called you a fucking sheep."

I squeezed her harder. "Turns out I was a fucking sheep."

"You're not." She took a step backward and her hands found mine. We interlaced our fingers together. "You believe in something big and important, and you believe it with your whole heart. I love that about you. I've always loved that about you."

I rolled my eyes. "I'm not sure what I believe anymore."

I told her how the words she said to me that day got me thinking, first in a way I wasn't sure how to handle, and later, in a way that had changed my life. I told her how I was finally feeling good about questioning my faith, when Luke came along and made me question everything all over again.

"And now?" she asked.

I pressed my lips together and thought about it. I remembered the song we'd sung at Admissions Night, and the dare I'd accepted. "Now I'm just . . . here."

She smiled. "I'm glad."

"Me too." I smiled back at her, and the sight of her almost made me break down in tears. For a while there, I hadn't been sure I'd ever be this close to her again. And now that we were, I had to say the thing I'd wanted most to tell her for the last three months.

"Hey," I said.

"Yeah."

"It wasn't your fault. You know that, don't you?" Emory's eyebrows pinched together, like she wasn't sure of the answer, so I said it again. "It wasn't in any way your fault. And I never thought it was. I didn't defend you to my dad, and I should have, but that was about my dad and me. It wasn't about you. Still, I should have stood up for you that day. I'll never be able to tell you how sorry I am about that. And . . . about everything that happened afterward." I swallowed hard. "I'm so sorry."

"It's okay."

We were quiet for a long time. And then she spoke. "What am I going to do, Hannah?"

I pulled away and looked at her. "What do you want to do?"

"Move to London." She chewed on her bottom lip while she thought about her real answer. "Seriously, you should see her, Hannah. Her business is doing great. And she's so excited about this wedding. It's all she talks about. And UCLA isn't London, but I'm moving out in a few months anyway."

"But she deserves to know."

She nodded. "So . . . say I tell her. And she dumps him. And then she stops cooking and stops seeing her therapist and conveniently forgets to take her meds and stops working out. And we're back where we were, only this time, I'm over an hour away and I can't take care of her like I did before."

"Or?" I asked.

Emory reached for a blade of grass. "Or . . . I tell her. And none of that happens. She defends him. Or he lies to her and she believes him. Or she believes me, but marries him anyway."

"You're leaving out the most likely scenario," I said. "You tell her. She believes you. She calls off the wedding and she's heartbroken for weeks, maybe even months. But she gets back on her feet. She returns to her clients and the work she loves."

She plucked another blade of grass, and then blurted out, "D-bag is going to New York on Tuesday. I was thinking that would be a good time to tell her."

"Do you want me to be there?" I asked.

She shook her head. "Just be thirty-six steps away, would you?"

Emory
Day 305, 132 to go

When I got home from school on Tuesday, I logged on to WeekdayGourmet.com and scanned Mom's recipes. The dishes were all familiar. Kid-Friendly Stuffed Peppers. Simple Smothered Pork Chops. Weekday Coq Au Vin. They reminded me of the nights Dad and I would tie each other's apron strings and help her chop vegetables while we waited for delicious scents to start filling the house. She was always proud of her Chicken Parmesan, and Dad and I always agreed it was our favorite.

I was glad to find her recipe on the website, and I followed the directions exactly. I flipped the chicken in the skillet and waited for the pieces to brown, and then I transferred them to the baking pan and sprinkled them with her cheese mixture.

When I heard the door open and close, my stomach dropped.

"You're making dinner?"

"Chicken Parmesan. Your recipe."

"But you always have dinner at Luke's house on Tuesdays. Everything okay with you two?"

"Yeah, we're great," I said.

She kissed me on the cheek. And then she took a deep breath in. "It smells amazing in here. I'm going to enjoy every bite and not even think about the calorie count of that dish. And if I can't fit into my wedding dress at my next fitting, I'm blaming you."

My heart started racing. I ignored it.

"David's out of town?" I asked. I said my line, exactly the way I'd rehearsed it, and I'd hit the tone perfectly.

I'd decided it would be easiest to think of this whole exchange with Mom as a play, complete with stage marks and a rehearsed script. So when I got home from school, I walked from the kitchen to the table and back again, picturing invisible Xs on the carpet as I spoke the words aloud, listening to the way they sounded. I crafted and re-crafted my words carefully.

It was a good exercise. It helped me distance myself from the fact that this conversation was happening in real life, and that when it was over, Mom and I would never be the same.

"He's in New York until Friday," she called out as she grabbed a bottle of wine from the rack and reached into the drawer for the corkscrew. She worked the bottle while I put the finishing touches on the chicken and started rinsing the spinach. She leaned against the counter and swirled her wine in the glass. "Hey, while you're cooking, let's go over the list."

"Can we not?"

"Oh, it'll only take a minute. You've been so busy with the play and distracted by all that's been going on with Luke. But from here on out it's all about proms and weddings. Nothing but happy things. Sound good?"

It sounded great. I wished it was going to happen that way.

She left the room and returned with her giant binder. She set it on the counter, popped open the three rings, and removed the top sheet.

"Okay, so according to *The Knot* we're in good shape. Invitations are out and we've got my last two dress fittings scheduled. Your dress is being altered." She kept going through the list, reading aloud, checking boxes while I tried to block out her voice. "The caterer has been paid, the cake is ordered. Oh, and, Emory . . . I forgot to tell you! You know how David keeps saying the music is a surprise?"

Hearing her say his name made the spatula start shaking in my hands.

"Well . . . I think I know what he's up to." She leaned against the counter. "This band played at his company Christmas party last year, and we danced *all* night. He keeps reminding me of that night, telling me how much he loved that band."

Stay calm. Stick to the script.

"I'm thinking maybe he pulled some strings to get them to play at the wedding. . . ."

"Yeah, maybe."

"I bet he's paying them a fortune." She took a sip of her wine and then let out a sigh. "He's the sweetest man."

My hands were clammy, and I could feel the sweat beading

up on my forehead. I couldn't take it. I couldn't hear her say one more word about D-bag or the wedding reception or bands or invitations.

"No, he's not," I whispered, but she didn't hear me.

"What?" she asked.

"No, he's not!" I yelled. I tossed the spatula into the skillet and sauce went flying everywhere, splattering all over the counters and onto the wall.

Mom set her glass down and brought her hands to her hips. "What do you mean by that?"

I couldn't say anything. I couldn't remember the first word in my script. I sat there, frozen and frustrated, trying to remember where I was supposed to start. Mom was staring at me, looking confused and maybe even a little bit irritated, and I was staring back at her, begging her to read my mind so I didn't have to speak the words aloud.

Slowly, her expression changed, and I swear, I saw a trace of panic in her eyes, as if she already knew. "Are you okay?" she asked cautiously.

I nodded. "I'm fine."

It was true. I was fine. I'd always been fine. The thing with David was weird and awkward and *over*. I. Was. Fine. Why was I even having this conversation with her?

But Mom wasn't letting it go. She stepped in closer, gripping my arms, making me keep talking to her.

I remembered the first line of my script. It was totally out of context, but I was relieved to have discovered it, so I blurted it out. "I was looking at the mail."

"The mail? What are you talking about?"

"You were at the gym. The game was on TV and I was looking at the mail. I didn't even hear him come up behind me." I was barely one minute into this thing and I was already way off. I had no idea what I was saying or what I was going to say next. The words just started spilling out of my mouth.

"He's your boyfriend. I thought of him as your boyfriend. And my future stepdad. And I never thought he saw me as anything but your daughter."

Mom's face went pale. "What did he do?"

I wanted to pull away from her grasp and race out the door. Hannah promised she'd be home. Luke was only a text away.

"What did he do, Emory?" she repeated, gripping my arm even harder.

I pointed to the kitchen table. "It was last year . . . right before Christmas. You weren't home. He came up behind me . . . and he pressed me against the table and he . . . he . . ." My voice was shaking too hard to finish my sentence.

I forced myself to stop and breathe, like I did when I got nervous on stage. "He told me I should know better than to dress that way around him. He told me he couldn't be responsible for what he'd do to me."

Mom covered her mouth as thick tears welled up in her eyes and started spilling down her cheeks.

"He tried to kiss me. And he—"

"Did he touch you?" Mom cut me off. Her voice was shaking now, too. I was glad she asked so I didn't have to say it first.

"Yeah."

"Where?"

"Where do you think?"

She walked toward the other side of the kitchen, clutching her head, and then returned to me. "What happened then?"

"Nothing. I went to my room and that was the end of it. He didn't follow me. He hasn't done anything since. It's no big deal."

"No big deal?" Mascara was streaming down Mom's face.

"Seriously. I wasn't even going to tell you. It happened, and I'm fine, and it's over." I wrapped my hands around her arms. "You're so happy now and I don't want you to be sad again. . . ." All the color drained from her face, and I wished I hadn't said anything. "Forget it, Mom. Please."

She took off for the bathroom. I could hear her throwing up, flushing the toilet, running the water.

She was gone for a long time, and when she finally came back to the kitchen, her eyes were puffy and red, and her hair was pulled back in a clip. She looked horrible, and I felt even worse.

"I'm sorry I'm not handling this very well," she said.

"You're handling it fine. Look, I didn't even want to tell you, but I figured you should know. And now you do. So this can all be over. I'll move out when school starts in August, and you can move into David's loft like you planned, and we can just forget this ever happened, okay? We'll never talk about it again. I thought you should know, that's all."

Mom pulled me into her, and I inhaled that scent that was so uniquely her and always made me feel safe. When she pulled away, she took my face in her hands. "I love you more than anything in this world. You know that, right?"

I nodded.

"More than anything in this world." She repeated it for emphasis.

She stood there for a long time, like she was trying to figure out what to say next. Her bottom lip started trembling and she bit down on it hard.

"I'm glad you told me."

I nodded again.

"You did the right thing."

"Did I?" I asked, because it sure didn't feel like it.

"You did," she said, but she looked like she was barely holding it together. "I need to be alone. Is that okay with you?"

I didn't know what else to do, so I nodded again.

And Mom went into her room and shut the door.

Hannah

I was out on the back deck, sitting on the top step. I'd been there for at least a half hour. It made me feel closer to Emory. But it had been too quiet on her side of the grass, and I was starting to wonder if she'd changed her mind about telling her mom.

I heard the screen door open and close behind me. I didn't move.

"Hey. What are you doing out here?" Dad asked.

"Thinking."

"About what?" He sat next to me.

"Everything," I said. "Mostly you."

"Funny," Dad said. "I've been inside praying. Mostly about you."

I looked at him. "About me? Why?" I didn't need his prayers. Emory did. Of course, he had no way of knowing that.

He turned sideways and leaned back against the post, bending one knee, facing me.

"Well," he began, "I was praying for guidance. Praying for God to give me the right words to say to you. Praying that you'd hear them, and understand, and maybe even forgive me for what I did. And I was praying that you'd find the words you needed to say to me, too. And that you'd know how important it is to say them, whatever they are."

I smiled up at him. "That's a lot of stuff for one prayer."

He smiled back. "I like to be efficient. You know, knock it all out at once." He punched the air with his fist.

Even after everything he'd done, a big part of me was struggling to stay angry at him. I didn't want to be mad anymore. I still loved him fiercely, despite how clear his flaws had become.

"I have a lot to say to you," he said.

"I have a lot to say to you, too."

"Can I start?" he asked, and I nodded, grateful for the extra time to pull my thoughts together.

He shifted in place and looked around, like he needed a little extra time to collect himself.

"I made a mistake," he said with a big exhale. "Actually, I made a bunch of mistakes, starting with your college fund. I blew it. And then I tried to fix it. I thought I was doing it for you." He paused and looked around again, like he was searching the yard, hoping to find the words he needed in the trees and flower beds. "I don't know what it is, Hannah. When it comes to you, I don't always see the big picture. I get singularly focused on making things right for you, regardless of the consequences."

It reminded me of what Emory had said that day we fought. "You have a blind spot when it comes to your dad." It hadn't occurred to me that he also had something of a blind spot when it came to me.

"I was trying to make you happy," he continued. "But I kept making it worse. And then, I didn't know how to unravel all the knots I'd made along the way. It was wrong of me to share Luke's video. I told myself I was helping him, helping you, and helping the school, all at the same time. But that wasn't fair to him. . . . He didn't want any of this."

"No, he didn't." I thought back to that day in the living room, when Luke stood in front of the fireplace studying our family portrait. "I think he just wanted to know you. For what it's worth, I think he still does."

Dad let his head fall back against the post and closed his eyes, like he was taking it all in. "I owe him an apology. And I owe you one, too." He opened his eyes and locked them on mine. "I'm so sorry."

I bit down hard on my lip. "It's okay."

Dad didn't look away. "I know you have more to say to me than that."

I did. I had a lot more to say. But I wasn't sure where to start. I could have told him how I'd been more devastated about the college fund than I ever let on. Or I could have told him how he let me down in ways I never thought he could when he betrayed my trust and shared Luke's video. Or I could have told him how I'd been questioning everything I'd ever believed, and how for the last couple weeks, I'd been meditating a lot but hadn't prayed once.

I could have started with any of those things. But none of them were more important than the one that kicked everything off. Dad had said that he'd made a bunch of mistakes, starting with my college fund, but that wasn't where it all began. He didn't even know about the first mistake he'd made.

"I need to tell you why Emory and I got in our fight." I pointed at her house and Dad turned his head. "She's over there right now, telling her mom."

"Telling her *what*?" He was clearly confused. "What does Emory have to do with any of this?"

"Everything," I said. My heart was racing and my hands felt clammy. I took a deep breath and let it out slowly. "Remember that day I told you she was in my room and needed to talk to you? But when we got there, she was gone."

"I remember."

"Well, she wasn't gone. She was hiding in my closet. She heard everything we said."

He looked even more confused. "That was months ago. I don't think you ever told me what she wanted to talk to me about. What did we say?"

I wrung my hands and stared out at the garden. "I started to tell you that she was upset about a guy. But you cut me off. You started talking about how Emory had changed over the years. That our friendship might not be in my best interest anymore."

"And she heard me?" He cringed, like he remembered saying the words, but they sounded even worse when he heard them coming back at him. "You know I didn't mean that."

I nodded. I knew. But it didn't matter. Whether he meant it

or not, that wasn't really the point. "That wasn't what upset her."
I felt sick as I remembered the two of us sitting on the edge
of my bed in my room, talking about Emory like she wasn't
there when she was behind a thin closet door the entire time.
"I agreed with you. I didn't defend her. And then after you left
and she opened the closet door, I made it even worse. I told
her maybe you were right—that maybe we shouldn't be friends
anymore."

Dad nodded slowly, like he could see the puzzle pieces of
our fight fitting together, clicking into place, creating a picture
of the last few months that explained everything.

But he still didn't know the worst part.

And the worst part was so much worse.

I sat up straighter, steeling myself for what I had to say
next. "Dad," I said. But that was as far as I got. My heart was
pounding and my legs were trembling and my chin was quiver-
ing and I hadn't even said anything yet.

"What?"

Spit it out, I told myself.

"She didn't come to our house that day because she was
upset about a guy. I mean . . . she did . . . but it was . . ." I
stammered, trying so hard to get his name to come out of my
mouth, but I couldn't do it. "It wasn't just *any* guy."

Dad looked at me sideways. He hadn't looked especially
concerned about what I was trying to tell him, but he did now.
"It was David." I threw his name into the air like it was toxic.
And then I squeezed my eyes closed, as if that would help block
out the vision of what he had done to Emory that day. "He . . .
He trapped her. He wouldn't let her go." Tears were streaming

down my cheeks and I had to fight to get a breath. "And when she got away she ran away from him. And she ran . . . here." My voice broke on the last word, but I felt an overwhelming sense of relief to have it all out.

I cried harder. I expected to feel a supportive hand on my back, but when I looked up, Dad was just staring at me, eyes wide, mouth open, fingertips pressed into his temples. And then he stood and walked down the steps, out to the lawn, like he needed to get far away from me and what I'd just said. He stopped when he reached the back fence, and then he stood there under the tree, staring down into the dirt.

I followed him. "She came to me for help," I said between sobs. "And I didn't help her." I hated admitting it out loud. It sounded worse than it felt. I sat there for what felt like a full minute, drawing air deep into my lungs and trying to pull myself together. "You just said that when it comes to me, you don't always see the big picture. Well, I tend to do the same with you. I follow your lead instinctively. I don't even realize I'm doing it. When you have an opinion about something, I let myself lose sight of what *I* think, what *I* know is best. I take your opinions on as if they're my own. What happened to Emory that day was the most important thing, and instead, I got all wrapped up in your opinion of her. And that's not your fault, it's mine."

He wouldn't look at me.

"I'm sor—" I began, but he turned around and started yelling before I could finish.

"Why didn't you tell me what happened to her? You needed to tell me that!"

"Emory changed her mind. She made me promise I wouldn't tell you and Mom."

"That's not a promise you can keep, Hannah. That wasn't a detail you could leave out!"

"I know. I made a mistake. But you did too, Dad. You knew Emory needed to talk to you, and you got all bent out of shape because I happened to mention it was about a guy!" Now I was in his face, yelling right back at him. "You're so quick to judge her. What if it had been Alyssa? Would you have said that? Or *thought* that? If anyone at school had said they needed to talk to you, you would have dropped everything and been there, and listened, and helped. If Emory had come to the church, would it have been different? If she'd met you on your terms, on your *turf*, like Luke did that first time, would you have taken her seriously? Or would you still have dismissed her because she'd 'changed' and our friendship might not be in my 'best interest'?"

I watched my words sink in. Dad didn't seem to know what to do once they did. His eyes had been fixed on mine, but he finally broke the connection when he turned his back to me. He began pacing the lawn, combing his fingers through his hair, looking up at the sky.

I kept talking. "I didn't know what to do, so I did nothing. And because of me, my best friend has had to live in that house for months, looking over her shoulder, keeping her bedroom door locked, and the whole time, helping her mom plan her *wedding.*"

Then I heard a click. Dad must have heard it, too, because our heads both snapped in the direction of Emory's house.

The door opened, and she stepped outside and walked to the edge of the deck. She gripped the railing, and I could see her shoulders heaving. Then she looked up and saw Dad and me.

She wiped her nose with the back of her hand and took off running down the stairs, heading straight for us. I moved to meet her halfway and she threw her arms around me, hugging me hard and crying even harder.

Now I felt Dad's hand on my shoulder. And then I heard his voice. "I'm sorry, Emory," he whispered. I could tell by the way his voice was shaking that he was crying, too. "I'm sorry for what I said. And for not talking to you that day. I'm so sorry." Emory squeezed me harder, and I knew that meant Dad had said what she needed to hear.

After a long time, she loosened her hold on me. She took a sharp inhale and wiped her face dry with her shirtsleeve.

"Is your mom okay?" Dad asked.

Emory nodded. "She wants to be alone."

"Do you?" he asked.

She shook her head.

"Good," he whispered. "Come inside. Tell us what you need us to do."

He wrapped his arm around her and led her toward our house.

Emory

Day 306, 131 to go

When I woke up, the sun was streaming through Mom's bedroom window. I blinked a few times and looked over at her. She was still asleep.

"Mom," I said. When she didn't move, I sat up and gave her a shake. "It's time to get up. You have to go to work."

I shook her again.

"Mom. Time for work."

That time, she rolled over, facing me. She fluffed up her pillow but didn't open her eyes. "It's okay," she slurred. "I canceled all my clients today."

I watched her settle back into her pillow, and I wanted to yank it out from underneath her head. There was no way this was going to happen again. Instead I stroked her hair gently and said, "Please, Mom. You have to get up and go to work."

Then I started telling her all the things her therapist used to tell me to say when she slipped into a funk. "You love your job. You're good at your job. Cooking for your clients makes you happy."

That time she opened her eyes and looked at me. "I know all that, Emory."

"Do you need me to call Dr. Wilson?"

"No. I'm okay, I promise. I just need the day to get my thoughts together, okay? Please."

She seemed lucid, so I climbed out of her bed, showered, and got ready for school. I texted Hannah with an update, and she said her mom would find an excuse to come over and check on her.

During school, I called her cell phone three times: once after first period, once after third, and again at lunch. She never answered.

As I stared at the phone, willing her to pick up, I felt caught between two conflicting emotions: anger and fear. I was mad with her for making this all about her, checking out on me like that when I needed her most. And at the same time, I was terrified that she'd disappear into her shell like she had before, and that it might be months or years before I saw her again. It all felt horribly familiar.

At lunch, I didn't have the energy for Luke's friends, so I took my sandwich to go and followed Charlotte to the theater. Tyler was already there.

Our Town was over and the backdrops and stage props had been cleared away, and for the first time in as long as I could remember, the theater was completely quiet during lunch. The three of us didn't seem to know what to do with ourselves. No lines to rehearse. No marks to memorize. No one there but the three of us.

We sat on the edge of the stage, our feet dangling over the side, looking out into the empty auditorium at the rows and rows of red crushed velvet–covered chairs.

"How much are we going to miss this room?" Tyler asked.

I took it to mean the room and the people in it. Based on our answers, we all did.

"Every day," Charlotte said.

"Constantly," I added.

"I can't even think about it," Tyler said.

Hannah

I missed my rock.

As soon as I got home from school on Wednesday, I went straight to my room, changed into my running clothes, pulled my hair into a ponytail, and sat on the edge of my bed, lacing up my running shoes.

My music was loud as I turned onto the sidewalk and ran to the intersection. The light was already green, so I ran across the street and headed straight up Foothill Drive. When it hit the trail, I focused on that wooden sign and pressed toward it.

At the top, I turned right and kept going, following the bends and curves of the narrow path until I reached my boulder three miles later. I slowed to a walk and shook out my arms, cooling off and catching my breath.

It was quiet up there. I crossed my legs, breathed in deeply, and I let my eyes fall shut. I just listened.

I could hear the birds chirping from their nests in the nearby trees, and the faraway whoosh of the traffic at the bottom of the hill. I could smell the flowers blooming below me and the sharp tinge of new grass. I could feel the crisp, early April air, and as I breathed it in, I pictured it traveling into my body and all the way through me—down to my toes and into my fingertips and through every strand of hair on my head. I sat there like that for a long time.

I was getting better at meditating. I'd see the thoughts pass through my mind, recognize them, and let them drift right out again. Each time, it felt a little less like work. It took less effort to find stillness and hold it.

I wasn't sure how much time went by—ten minutes, twenty, thirty—it didn't matter. I was lost in my own peaceful little world, when my phone buzzed.

I opened my eyes and read the message.

Luke: I miss you.

I smiled at the screen as I typed.

Hannah: I miss you, too.
Luke: Can we talk?
Hannah: Anytime.
Luke: How's now?
Luke: I'm sitting here with Emory. We have a plan for
          tomorrow, but we need your help to pull it off.
          You in?

My body didn't seem to know whether to smile or cry. I was doing both as I typed my reply.

Hannah: Where are you?
Luke: Diner

I stood and started down the rock. When I landed at the bottom, I typed, *On my way.*

Emory

Day 308, 129 to go

On Friday after school, Luke and I went straight to my house and found Mom out of bed, buzzing around. She said she'd been to the gym, and when I asked her about work, she said her catering clients were all lined up for the following week.

She'd cleaned the house, top to bottom. Key pieces of the last year of our lives seemed to be missing, or at least hidden. Her wedding binder wasn't on the dining-room table like it usually was. There was no sign of the box we'd been using to keep the extra invitations and all the RSVP cards that had been arriving. The photo of her and David on the day he fake-proposed had been removed from the mantel. She wasn't wearing her engagement ring.

"I'm glad you're both here. I could use your help with a few things." She was all business. "I've got two storage boxes full of David's things in my bedroom, and another box I need help putting up in the rafters in the garage."

"Luke isn't allowed to carry anything yet. The internal stitches are still healing."

"I can carry some things," Luke said with a fake pout.

"Nope," Mom said. "Have a seat. We've got it."

"Fine," Luke said as he collapsed on the couch. "I'll just be here. Feeling useless." He pulled out his phone to keep himself busy.

All day, I'd been dreading walking through the front door, but seeing Mom up and around had me feeling better already. I followed her to her room, and together, we carried everything out to the garage. I didn't ask her what was in the boxes bound for the rafters, but I had a feeling I knew.

"I take it you talked to him?" I asked her as I set up the ladder.

She handed me the box. "No. I wanted to do it in person. He's coming straight from the airport, and he should be here in an hour. You and Luke need to leave, okay?"

No. Luke and I had already talked it through. "We'll stay in my room, out of sight."

"Why?" she asked.

"I don't think you should be alone when you tell him."

She let out a huff. "Oh, don't be so melodramatic. He'll come over, I'll tell him the wedding is off and why. I'll tell him he's damn lucky I'm not pressing charges. And then I'll give him his things and walk him out to his car." She steadied the ladder as I climbed back down. "And then, after he's gone, I'll have a complete breakdown—which I've scheduled to begin tonight and end on Sunday, so please don't freak out—and when it's over, that will be the end of it. I will move on. I will be fine."

"I still think I should be here," I said as my feet hit the floor.

She brought her hands to her hips. "I don't want you here. I don't want you to see him tonight. I don't want you to see him ever again."

She seemed so calm and clearheaded. But I remembered those times I'd seen her back down to him in a way that wasn't at all like her, and I couldn't help but think there was a small part of her that was afraid of him.

"Are you sure?" I asked.

"Positive." She took my hands in hers. "Are you sure you don't want me to press charges?"

I'd thought about it. A lot. I didn't need to press charges to make myself feel better about what happened; I just wanted him out of our lives.

"I think losing you is punishment enough." I smiled at her. "And I'm fine. Really."

"Okay. Then go. Get out of here before he shows up."

I agreed, but it was a lie. I'd be in my room the entire time, because that was part of my plan with Luke and Hannah. I had to be there to protect her, just in case she needed me. And I had to hear what he said when she told him.

She hugged me. "I'll text you when he's gone and you and Luke can come back here and watch a movie or something." She pulled away and looked me in the eyes. "But you don't have to. It's a Friday night. Go have fun. I'll be fine."

When she went to the kitchen, I disappeared into my bedroom. Working quickly so she wouldn't get suspicious, I reached deep into the back of my closet and pulled out the metal stepladder. I carried it over to the window, lowered it into the dirt below, and returned to the living room.

"All set?" Luke whispered, and I gave him a thumbs-up.

We told her good-bye and left through the front door. We climbed into his car, and he backed out and drove around the corner, parking under the streetlamp in front of Hannah's kitchen window. We checked to be sure the coast was clear, and then we snuck around the corner and darted up her front steps.

Hannah was already there, waiting for us, watching through the crack in the doorway. She opened it wider so we could come inside.

We followed her into the living room. Pastor J was standing at the window, peering through the side of the white linen curtain. When he heard my voice, he looked over his shoulder and smiled at me.

I smiled back.

"How did it go?" Hannah's mom asked.

"Fine, I guess. He's on his way." I figured I shouldn't call him D-bag in front of Hannah's parents, but I wasn't about to call him David, either.

Pastor J waved me over to the window so I could watch by his side.

"Are you okay?" he asked, and I nodded, trying to ignore how clammy my hands felt and the giant knot deep in the pit of my stomach.

I'd lost count of how many times Hannah's dad had apologized to me over the last two days. And now he was trying to make up for it by saying all the right things, like I'd always been part of their family and I always would be.

Hannah's mom gave me a supportive pat on the back. "I wish you'd let us all go over there with you. We could confront him together. Your mom wouldn't be alone."

It was true, but I knew that wasn't the way Mom wanted it. She wanted to confront him by herself. And I was happy to let her, as long as she had backup.

"She's got this." I was about to say more, but instead I said, "He's here."

The adrenaline kicked in as soon as I saw David's car pull into the driveway. We all gathered in front of the window, watching as he got out, took a duffel bag from the trunk, and walked to the front door. He was carrying his bag in a way that made his arm look huge and powerful, even from that distance.

He didn't knock, he just opened the front door and disappeared inside my house.

That was our cue.

Luke was already at the edge of Hannah's living room, waiting for me. The two of us left through the back door, ran across the grass, climbed the stepladder, and slipped inside my bedroom.

I opened the door a crack, and the two of us poked our heads into the hallway, listening.

I could hear Mom's voice, but I couldn't make out what she was saying. She and David went back and forth a few times, but everything was muffled. And then I heard him, loud and clear. "She's a liar, Jennifer."

I steeled myself, waiting for her to respond. Luke gripped my arm, and I turned to look at him. His face was red, his eyebrows pinched together, and I think if he had been standing anywhere near D-bag, he would have punched him. I loved him for that.

"You're actually trying to tell me she made this up?" Mom was yelling now, too. "Come on, David. She would never do that."

I wanted to hug her.

"Of course she would! Emory has never liked me. She's lying to you, and you're falling for it. That girl has you wrapped around her little finger and you don't even see it!"

I shook my head. He was making this up as he went. I never had any reason to manipulate my mom. Why would I?

It was way too quiet for far too long.

"Get out," Mom said calmly. "Get your things and get out of my house."

"You're siding with her?"

"Of course I'm siding with her."

"Jennifer, please. Listen to me."

"Get out. Now."

"I'm not leaving."

I felt Luke start to push past me, and I turned around and looked at him, silently begging him to stay put. I pointed at his side, reminding him about his stitches.

His injury was the only reason I'd let him convince me to

get Hannah's family involved in the first place. I wasn't about to let him step in.

"She misunderstood," David said, changing tack. "When she gets home we can all sit and talk about it. I'll explain. I'll apologize." He caught himself, or maybe Mom shot him a look, because he edited his words in real time. "I'll apologize, even though I didn't do *anything* wrong."

He sounded convincing, even from where I stood. I couldn't see his face, but Mom could, and I had no idea what she was thinking. She didn't speak for the longest time.

"Come on. You don't really think I could do something like that, do you?"

"Don't touch me." Her voice was trembling.

"Jennifer."

"Stop it!" Mom yelled. "Get your hands off me."

That was all I needed to hear. I pressed the SEND button.

And then I took off running through the hallway and into the living room. David was in Mom's face, and he had a tight grip on both her arms.

I grabbed a chunk of his shirt and pulled as hard as I could. "Let go of her!" I yelled, and he spun around, looking shocked to see me there.

He put his hands in the air, like I was a cop and he was proving he wasn't carrying a weapon. I backed away from him, but he walked toward me. "This was a big misunderstanding. I didn't mean to upset you." He reached out to grab my wrist, but I took another big step back. "You misunderstood, that's all."

Then Luke was right in next to me.

I could see the panic in David's eyes. Not that Luke was much of a threat in his condition—at the moment, David was stronger than both of us put together—but the two-against-one thing suddenly seemed to click.

But it wasn't supposed to be two against one. It was supposed to be six against one. I was sure Hannah and her parents would be there any second, but time seemed to be moving in painfully slow motion.

Mom stepped up behind him. "Leave," she said. Her voice sounded steady. Strong. Brave. "I'm not going to tell you again."

He didn't even turn around to look at her. His eyes were fixed on mine, narrowed into slits, glaring at me like I was the evil one.

"Leave," she said again. That time, she sounded different. Even fiercer.

He looked like he was about to do as he was told, but then he realized I was blocking the most direct path to the front door. I didn't even have time to register the look on his face, I just felt him push me out of his way with both hands.

I stumbled backward. I tried to find my footing, but my body had too much momentum. I was off-balance. I put out my hands to try to break my fall, but it didn't help. And when I landed, I landed hard, right on the corner of the coffee table.

I tried to stand, but my left leg was throbbing, and as soon as I put pressure on it, it gave out. I was back on the floor and within seconds, David was crouched down next to me.

"I'm sorry," he said. He was right in my face, wrapping his hand around my arm to help me stand, muttering more apologies.

I slapped his arm away. I didn't want him anywhere near me, sorry or not.

Suddenly, I looked up and saw Pastor J hovering behind him. "Don't touch her," he said.

David turned around, shocked to hear the sound of another voice in the room, and scrambled to his feet. I scooted backward, away from him and the coffee table and everyone else, until I felt the wall. I used it to help me stand.

David looked stunned as he scanned the room, taking all of us in. Mrs. J was now next to my mom with a protective arm around her shoulder. Pastor J was inches away from him, his hands balled into fists and his jaw tight, like he was ready for whatever came next. Luke was next to me, helping me balance. And Hannah was standing in the entryway, holding her phone to her ear and rattling off my home address to what was clearly a 911 operator.

My mom pointed toward the door. "Right now, it's a restraining order, but only because that's what Emory wants. But if you're still here when the police arrive, I'll press charges. For *everything*."

He looked at my mom. At first, I thought he was going to walk toward her. Mrs. J must have thought the same thing, because she stepped right in front of her and threw her arms out to her sides, like he'd have to get through her first.

He turned and walked toward Hannah instead, and she moved to one side and let him pass. I heard the door open and close again. We were all silent as we listened to his car start with a hum, and then drive away.

Mom was next to me in a matter of seconds. She wrapped her arms around me, telling me she loved me and promising me I'd never see David again.

"You were a badass," I said as I pulled away. I could tell by the way she was smiling that this wasn't like the time with Dad. This time, she was going to be okay.

"So were you," she said as she kissed my forehead.

Hannah

I'd managed to avoid Aaron for an entire week. It wasn't hard. Now that SonRise practices were over, I didn't have any reason to go to the sanctuary outside Monday Chapel. And as much as I'd missed sneaking up to the sound booth after school, I'd found a place all my own to spend my time while I waited for Dad: in the Grove, at the table nestled in the trees, where I could study or meditate or just *be*. I liked it there. It made me feel especially alone, in a good way.

On Friday, Alyssa had to make up a test after school, but she promised to drive me home afterward. I was sitting at a picnic table, working on an essay for English class, when I looked up and found Aaron standing there.

"Hi," he said. He looked cute. He was wearing jeans, flip-flops, and a plain white T-shirt. He had his baseball cap on as usual. "Can I talk to you for a second?"

I knew I couldn't avoid this discussion forever. "Sure," I said, tipping my chin toward the spot across from me. He sat.

I'd expected to be mad when I saw him again, but I wasn't. Not anymore.

"Your dad told me I could find you here. I know you're studying, and I don't want to bother you or anything." He shifted nervously. "I just wanted to tell you something. Actually, a few things."

I closed my notebook and set my pen down.

"First, I'm sorry."

I wasn't sure why he was saying it. He'd already apologized to me. And to Luke.

"There's no reason to apologize again."

He shook his head. "Not for that. For . . . the rest of it. For kissing you. For kissing you while I was with Beth. I shouldn't have done that. And . . ." He tipped his head back, eyes fixed on the sky, like it pained him to look at me. "Because you're a student. And that was just so stupid of me."

"I kissed you first," I said plainly.

"Maybe." He rested his elbow on the table and covered his face with his hand. "But still, I'm sorry. I shouldn't have let it happen."

I wanted to tell him that I didn't regret any of it, but I had a feeling he did, so I kept that part to myself. "It's okay."

He leaned in closer, like he was telling me a secret. "I also wanted to tell you that I broke up with Beth this week."

I hadn't expected that. "You did?"

"I couldn't stay with her once I figured out . . ." He paused, trying to decide how to finish his sentence. "That she wasn't what I was looking for."

I think he expected me to feel bad for him, but I didn't. I felt bad for her. "Is she okay?" I asked.

"Beth?" he asked. When I nodded, he said, "Yeah. It was harder on both of us than I expected it to be, but . . . she's tough. She'll be okay."

He didn't seem to know what to say after that. He looked around at the trees, at the ground, at the table. He finally looked at me. "I also just wanted to tell you that . . . I really liked talking to you, Hannah. And I . . ." He trailed off and started tapping his fingers on the table nervously. I didn't make him finish his sentence.

"I liked talking to you, too."

"Good. So we can keep talking? As friends?" He smiled at me and held out his hand.

I shook it as I smiled back. "Yeah. Friends."

Deep in my heart, I wanted to be more and it hurt my feelings that he didn't want that, too. But my heart wasn't in control anymore; my brain had a firm grip on the wheel.

I stood and started gathering my things. "I'd better go. I told Alyssa that I'd meet her in the parking lot."

My instinct was to hug him, but that seemed weird given everything that had happened between us. And if I was being honest, I was a little afraid of what I'd do if I let myself get that close to him. My heart could have easily grabbed the wheel, shoved my brain to the backseat, and taken over.

"Get out of that man cave of yours," I said over my shoulder as I walked away. "Make some more friends. Like, ones who aren't moving to the East Coast in a few months."

Alyssa was waiting by her car when I arrived.

"Where have you been?" She bounced on her toes, and I could tell she was excited about something. "I've been dying here!"

I checked the time on my phone. "Relax, I'm, like, two minutes late."

"Whatever!" She bounced in place again. "I have news!"

How had she already heard that Aaron broke up with Beth? I kind of assumed he was telling me first, but apparently not.

"Man, word travels fast around here," I said.

Alyssa shot me a look. "What are you talking about?"

Maybe she hadn't heard.

"Nothing," I said. "What's your news?"

She shook her shoulders back and forth. "Kevin Anderson just asked me to prom."

"He did? I didn't even know you two knew each other."

"We don't really. But I ran into him in the hall the other day, and I told him how much I loved what he had to say in his testimonial. He seemed to appreciate the compliment, and we got to talking, and . . . I guess I made an impression."

"Of course you did."

She laughed as she opened the car door. I got in next to her. She turned the key in the ignition, backed out of the parking space, and drove away, down the narrow road, lined with roses and lavender bushes.

She cranked up the music and I rolled down the window. I stuck my head outside and closed my eyes, inhaling the scent of flowers and feeling the warm breeze on my face.

I'd planned to tell her about Aaron and me on the way home. But under the circumstances, I'd changed my mind. I didn't think she needed to know.

Maybe someday I'd tell her. For now, it seemed fitting that Aaron and I were the only ones at the school who knew what happened in that sound booth.

Emory
Day 315

Mom was asleep. I crossed the room and sat on the edge of her bed. "I'm home."

She was five days past the end of her scheduled breakdown, but I still spotted a few tissues on her comforter. And the TV was blaring, tuned to some cheesy romance channel. I lifted the remote and turned it off.

"Mom," I said, and she opened one eye. "Here, have some water."

She sat up. "Thanks." She took a few sips and then set it on her nightstand. She settled back into her pillow. "How was the game?"

"Good. We won."

She reached up and took the sleeve of my altered jersey-dress between her thumb and forefinger and studied my face. "Charlotte did a great job on your hair. You look beautiful."

Before I could say anything, she moved her hand to my knee. "Your leg still looks horrible."

"It's okay. It doesn't hurt anymore." Over the last week, the bruise had turned black, then purple, and finally yellowish green. I was hoping it would have faded away completely by now, so Mom and I could enjoy the fact that we had a restraining order in place and all traces of D-bag were gone from our lives. But the bruise lingered, a constant reminder that he still existed.

"Hey," I said. "Luke's here. Is that okay?"

Mom nodded. "Yeah. That's okay."

It was part of our new pact. No more secrets. No more sneaking around.

"He got word from Denver today. He's going as planned."

"Oh, really? That's great!" And then she saw the look on my face. "That's great, right?"

I forced a smile. "Yeah. Actually it is."

She rested her hand on my lower back. "You okay?"

I was. And I wasn't. It was like being hot and cold at the same time, and it didn't make any sense. "What can I do? It's the way it's supposed to end."

"Love sucks, doesn't it?" she asked.

"Yes." I sighed. "And no."

"Exactly." She sounded impressed, like I'd said something wise beyond my years. She patted my hand. As I smiled down at her, I could tell she was fighting to keep her eyes open.

I pulled the covers under her chin and kissed her forehead. "Get some sleep. We'll go to a movie tomorrow. And not a romance. I'm taking you to see something with zombies or pirates or total world destruction."

"Sounds perfect," she said. Her eyes fell shut. "I love you."

"I love you, Mom." I closed her bedroom door behind me and walked down the hallway to mine.

Inside, Luke was sitting on the edge of my bed. He'd taken off his Foothill Falcons jacket and draped it over my chair.

I turned the lock, crossed the room, and stepped in between his legs. "Hey, you." I rested my forearms on his shoulders and twisted his curls around my fingers. I leaned in closer to kiss him, but something was off. He wasn't kissing me back, not like he normally would have. "What's wrong?" I asked.

"This is weird. I can't do it with your mom in the next room."

"She's always in the next room."

"Yeah, but . . . now she knows I'm here."

"So?" I leaned down and kissed him again, and this time he let go. His mouth was warm, and his lips were soft, and for the millionth time, I thought about how much I loved kissing him. Now that everything was settling into a new normal, I decided that was the new plan: to spend the next one hundred and twenty-two days kissing as much as humanly possible.

I hooked my thumbs under his T-shirt and started to lift it over his head, but he grabbed the hem and pulled it down again.

"It's okay," I whispered. "She's already asleep again, I promise."

He wrapped his arms around my waist and rested his forehead on my stomach. "It's not that. I . . . I have to talk to you about something."

"Okay." I let my fingertip skate over the back of his neck. "What's up?"

He scooted all the way onto my mattress and sat with his back pressed against the wall. I crawled up on the bed and joined him. And then the room got too quiet.

Finally, he spoke. "I've been to see Hannah's dad. Twice this week."

"You did?" I couldn't help but feel a little betrayed. We'd spent the entire week together, often talking at length about other people he could go to for help, and he hadn't mentioned Pastor J once. "I thought you were going to talk to a therapist?"

Last Tuesday, during Calletti Spaghetti, he'd finally told his parents about his insomnia, and how he'd spent those hours he should have been sleeping watching YouTube videos and researching near-death experiences. His doctor referred him to someone he thought could help.

"I am. My mom made an appointment for me next week. And I know you don't completely understand this, but I need to talk to Pastor J, too. He helps me wrap my head around this whole thing. Talking to him makes me feel better about what happened."

I wanted to say I *did* understand, but I didn't. Not completely.

"Earlier this week, I asked Pastor J to send me all the emails he received about my video. I started answering them. They're still coming in, and I'm not sure I'll ever be able to reply to all of them, but it's a start. I'm sleeping better. My appetite is back. And when I close my eyes, images in my head aren't quite so vivid, you know?" He tapped his finger to his temple. "It's not so noisy in there anymore."

I reached for his hand and interlaced his fingers with mine. He kept talking.

"I don't know what I'm looking for, Em. I don't know if I'll ever figure out what happened to me or if it matters. And I don't know if I'll ever be the same again, but I know I need to keep talking about it, because it keeps me sane."

"That's okay. Talk to him. Talk to a therapist, too. Talk to me. It's all good, okay?" He didn't reply, and I could tell there was more he needed to say. "What?" I asked, even though I wasn't sure I wanted to know.

He rocked his head back and forth. "I've decided to go away for the summer."

I sat up, twisting to face him. "Where?"

"Guatemala. On the mission trip with Hannah's mom."

I stared at him as his words sank in, but I had no clue how to respond. He'd caught me completely off guard.

"They need someone to run the program full-time, and I said I would do it. I'll be working with kids, just like you and Hannah did. And I'll help rebuild homes, fix up libraries, and churches. I'll be part of a community that needs me."

But I need you, I wanted to say.

"I've thought about this a lot. I've talked to my parents. And I've decided I have to go. I don't need to be at Denver until August twentieth, and in the meantime, I've got to do something to distract me from . . . everything."

He got quiet after that. For a moment, I thought he might ask me to come with him.

If he had, I wasn't sure how I would have answered. I wanted to spend my summer with Luke, but I didn't want to spend it in a foreign country on a three-month mission trip. I wanted to drive along the coast in his Jetta, stopping to camp, hiking to hot springs, playing Skee-Ball, sleeping under the stars, and waking up with the sun. I no longer cared about the bugs. I wanted to spend my summer alone with Luke, like we'd planned.

But he didn't ask.

"Are you breaking up with me?"

He shook his head. "We'll still have the rest of the year. Prom, graduation—"

"But no road trip." I glanced over at my bulletin board where I had pinned the Mentos wrapper with his hand-drawn map.

That clock in my head started speeding up, the minute hand moving around the dial faster and faster.

"Please tell me that some small part of you understands this?" he asked.

I wanted to, for his sake. And a small part of me did understand. I'd seen Luke on those newscasts and morning shows, talking about what happened to him in a way that I'm sure moved total strangers to tears. He was good up there. And apparently, he needed it, too. I wished he didn't. I wished I were enough.

"Part of me understands," I said. "But every part of me hates this."

He wrapped his arm around my shoulder and pulled me into him. I let my forehead fall against his chest. "Every part of me hates this, too."

We sat like that for a long time, neither one of us wanting to be the first to let go.

I thought back to the day we met at the diner three hundred and fifteen days earlier, and I tried to picture every day from that first one on in order, but it was impossible. I wished

I'd saved more than his words. I wished I'd somehow mentally captured every second we'd had together and filed it away for safekeeping so I could pull them up for the rest of my life, every time I needed one. I thought back to that night I almost broke up with him, when he told me I was ridiculous; that this was worth the pain of it ending and that he'd never regret a second we'd spent together.

He took my face in his hands and rested his forehead against mine, and I could tell he had something to say but he didn't know quite how to say it. I made it easier on him.

"I have to let you go, don't I?" I wasn't talking about the mission trip. Even though he wasn't leaving for another forty-nine days, I had to let him go now, not in June. I couldn't count down the days to the end of us anymore, not if he no longer saw them the way I did, as precious and worth holding on to.

Still, I thought he'd try to talk me out of it like he had that night he drew me the map.

"Yeah." He practically choked on the word. It was clear from the look on his face that he wasn't talking about the mission trip either.

And then he leaned in closer and kissed me, but it felt like an act of desperation, like he was doing it to shut both of us up. And I was glad he did, because the words we'd already said hurt way too much as it was.

My throat felt tight, and it was all I could do to hold back the tears.

The kiss went on, but eventually, it changed. It became softer. Sweeter. And it felt like good-bye.

Luke rested his forehead on mine again. "I can't imagine what my senior year would have been like without you," he said.

His words felt like good-bye, too.

I pretended they didn't.

"I can," I said, forcing a smile. "It would have been boring. You would have hated every second."

He kissed me again. "No question in my mind."

I waited until he left to fall apart.

I was still in Luke's jersey. I ran my fingertip over the number thirty-four, remembering how I didn't want to wear it at first. Now I didn't want to take it off. I hugged my knees to my chest. And then I turned on the playlist he made me and sat there in the dark, ugly-crying for hours, until I'd demolished an entire box of Kleenex, my pillow was soaked through, my throat was dry and sore, and my eyelids were so puffy I could barely see through the slits.

But I wasn't done. I opened my Notes app and scrolled down, reading every single thing I'd captured over the last three hundred and fifteen days. I read all the words he said to me at least four times, crying all over again.

Somewhere around 4:00 a.m., when I was so exhausted I could no longer keep my eyes open, and my body was so empty, I couldn't manufacture a tear if I'd wanted to, I took a deep breath and held it in as long as I could. And then I let it out.

And I told myself I was done.

I went back to my Notes app, scrolled down to Day 315, and added a new entry.

> "I can't imagine what my senior year would have been like without you."

It was a good last line. I wasn't sure he'd be able to top it. I deleted all the empty lines and left it at that.

Hannah

On Saturday morning, I pulled my shades open. I was about to open my window, too, but I stopped cold. Emory was sitting cross-legged on the grass, smack in the middle of our houses.

She held up her hand and waved. And then she curled her finger toward her chest and patted the empty space in front of her.

It was warmer than it had been in a while, so I went straight for the back door without grabbing a sweatshirt. I didn't even put my shoes on. I stepped off the back porch and let the grass tickle my feet.

I sat down next to her. And I knew right away.

"He told you about the mission trip?" I asked.

Emory nodded. "How long have you known?"

"Just since last night. My mom told me he was considering it, but it didn't sound like a done deal or anything."

She sucked in a breath. "Well, it is now."

"Are you okay?"

She plucked a blade of grass and wrapped it around her pinky finger. "No. I'm . . ." She paused, searching for the right word, and settled on, "Heartbroken."

I hugged her. When she hugged me back, she squeezed me a lot harder than usual.

Then she pulled away and reached into her pocket. She handed me a slip of paper.

"Why are you giving me a Mentos wrapper?"

"Turn it over."

On the other side, there was a hand-drawn map of the California coastline, starting in Orange County and ending in San Francisco.

"Luke drew this one night. It was our summer plan." She rested her chin on my shoulder and began pointing at each of the dots. "We were going to camp in Santa Barbara, Santa Cruz, and Big Sur. We planned to make our way up the coast, stopping along the way whenever we felt like it, until we reached San Francisco. We figured our road trip would take two weeks, maybe more, and if we weren't done, we could keep going up to Oregon or Washington."

She pointed at the Mentos wrapper. "Anyway, I was stress-cleaning my room this morning, and I had this crazy thought. Luke made other plans for the summer, but this," she said, tapping the map with her fingertip. "This was *my* plan. This is what kept me going when I was worried about my mom, or missing you, or watching Luke struggle with what happened to him. I was holding on to this. And I might have to let Luke go, but I'm not ready to give this up, too. I still need this trip."

"You should go."

"I know, right?" She smiled at me. "And you should come with me."

I laughed in her face. "That's ridiculous! I can't go to San Francisco."

"Why not? What's keeping you here?"

Nothing, I realized. There was nothing keeping me there. Aaron and I were over. Alyssa was spending the summer at a music program in New York. Mom would be on the mission trips off and on, and Dad would be at the church every day, like he always was.

"Look," Emory continued. "You're leaving for Boston and I'm going to LA. We've spent our whole lives thirty-six steps away, and in a few months, we're going to live two thousand nine hundred and eighty-four miles away."

"You know the exact number?"

"I googled it."

"I don't know—" I began, but she cut me off.

"Look, I need to get away from here. I need to breathe in ocean air and feel sand between my toes. Don't you?"

I didn't say anything.

"We'll make an epic playlist. We'll blast it and sing at the top of our lungs, and it won't matter that I can't carry a tune to save my life, because you'll be the only one who can hear me. We'll drive winding roads, and stick our arms out the windows and flap them like wings."

I was warming to the idea. When Emory grinned, her eyes

twinkled, and I could tell from the look on her face that she knew she was getting to me.

"Okay, so . . . a couple thoughts," I said.

"Hit me."

"We don't have camping gear."

Emory made a check mark in the air with her finger. "Charlotte said I could borrow her family's stuff. They don't need it."

"We don't have a car."

She got this funny look on her face. "Luke wants us to take the Jetta."

"You told him about this already?" I asked.

"Yep."

"And he offered his car, just like that?"

"He said he wouldn't be needing it. He practically insisted." She crinkled her nose. "He said something about being our glue."

My face lit up.

Emory was waiting for an answer.

"When?" I asked.

"Right after graduation. The day after or two days later, I don't care, you decide." She knew she had me right where she wanted me. She leaned in close to my ear. "Don't think about it, Hannah. Just say yes."

I wanted to sleep on it, or at least go for a run and ponder it from the top of my rock, but instead, I acted on impulse.

"Yes," I blurted.

"Yes? Like, yes-yes?" Emory came up on her knees and

threw her arms around my neck, practically choking me with her hug. "You won't regret this, I promise."

But she didn't have to tell me that. I already knew I wouldn't.

"How many steps did you say there were between our windows?" I asked.

She looked offended, like this was information I should have committed to memory. "Thirty-six."

"That was over two years ago." I lifted my foot and wiggled it in the air. "We've grown."

Emory jumped up, grinning as she offered her hand to help me stand. We walked to my house and slid in between the rosebush and the flowering shrub, and I pressed my back against the siding as I looped my arm through hers.

We stepped forward in unison. And then we each tapped our heels to our toes and stepped forward again. We counted aloud.

"Nineteen. Twenty. Twenty-one."

And then Emory stumbled and fell to one side, so we walked back to my house and started over. The next time, we took slower, more careful steps. We wobbled a few times, but we didn't lose count.

"Twenty-three. Twenty-four. Twenty-five."

But Emory tickled me in the side and I lost my balance, and we had to start again.

When we took off the third time with our arms interlocked, we were laughing so hard we were almost crying.

We did better. As we neared Emory's window, we were so

focused on our objective, we didn't say a word. I was counting in my head.

Thirty. Thirty-one. Thirty-two.

She tightened her grip on my arm and yelled, "Thirty-three."

We took one more step, and at the exact same time, we each slapped our palms against her house.

"Thirty-four," we yelled in unison.

I felt a smile tugging at the corners of my mouth.

All my life, I'd believed that everything happened for a reason. That it was all part of God's plan. A puzzle He'd created, made up of tragedies and joys and everything in between, each event clicking into place exactly the way it was supposed to.

I didn't think I believed that anymore. Each choice, good and bad, branched out and created a new path, and on and on, piecing itself together along the way, with no real vision for how it would all come together in the end. God wasn't in control. None of us were really in control either.

But then I thought about Luke pulling up in front of my house that night, and me getting a glass of water exactly as he did. I thought about him saying that maybe it *had* happened for a reason.

"That's weird," Emory said, crinkling her nose. "Luke's jersey number is thirty-four. Isn't that weird?"

"Yeah," I said. "Weird."

Maybe it was totally random.

Maybe it was meant to be.

I'd never know.

Author's Note

While this is a work of fiction, both Hannah's and Emory's stories are deeply personal ones.

Like Hannah, when I was young, I went on a similar quest to better understand my faith. I wanted to ask myself big questions, learn as much as I could about religions that were different from my own, and discover what I believed in context with everything I'd been taught growing up. The experience opened my mind and changed me forever. It felt like an important one to share when I began writing this novel in 2014. Today, in an environment more focused on dividing us because of who we are and what we believe than uniting us as human beings, it feels even more important.

While some of the details of Emory's assault were fictionalized, the words she hears are the same ones that were said to me when I was a young woman, word for word, by an older man in power who I trusted completely. Those words were incredibly difficult to write, not only because they forced me to relive a moment that terrified me, but also because they're so painfully indicative of the larger problem that has since (thankfully) come to light through the #metoo movement. "I can't be responsible for what I'll do to you," he said. In other words, this is happening, there's nothing you can do about it, and it's your fault, not mine. I haven't forgotten those words in over twenty-five years, and it took me that long to find the courage to tell this story. To all the people who have lived with this secret, and to those who still do, you're not alone. You did nothing wrong. We see you. We believe you. #metoo

Acknowledgments

I am grateful to the five brilliant, patient, and supportive women who believed in this story from the very beginning and helped me figure out how to get it out of my head and onto the page: Emily Meehan, Hannah Allaman, Julie Rosenberg, Caryn Wiseman, and Lorin Oberweger. This novel simply wouldn't exist without them. Huge thanks to everyone at Hyperion, especially Holly Nagel, Cassie McGinty, Seale Ballenger, and Dina Sherman. Special gratitude to Marci Senders and Sabeena Karnik for the absolutely stunning work of art that graces this cover.

Four inspiring people allowed me to weave pieces of their personal stories into the pages of this one. I'm forever grateful to:

My two dads, who both had near-death experiences they can recount with absolute clarity and were forever changed by them, but in very different ways. James Stone and Bill Ireland, thank you for sharing every detail with me. It was an honor to hear you tell your stories and I'll never forget them.

And my two moms, both deeply spiritual women, each drawn to different faiths, yet always open-minded and respectful of everyone's chosen path. Susan Cline Harper and Rebecca Stone, thank you for always putting love above everything else.

This is a story about friends who truly get each other; I'm lucky I got to marry a friend like that. Mike, there are so many lines in this book that are just for you. I know you'll smile when you find them.

TAMARA IRELAND STONE writes young adult and middle grade novels. Her *New York Times* best seller, *Every Last Word*, won the Cybils Young Adult Fiction Award, the Georgia Peach Book Award, and was a YALSA Teens' Top Ten pick. She is also the author of *Time Between Us*, which has been published in over twenty countries; its sequel, *Time After Time*; and *Click'd*, the first book in her new middle grade series.

Before she began writing fiction full-time, Tamara spent twenty years in the technology industry. She cofounded a woman-owned marketing strategy and communications firm where she worked with small startups as well as some of the world's largest software companies. When she's not writing, she enjoys skiing, seeing live music, watching movies, and spending time with her husband and two children. She lives in the San Francisco Bay Area. Visit her at TamaraIrelandStone.com.